Home

Harlan Coben

W F HOWES LTD

This large print edition published in 2017 by
W F Howes Ltd
Unit 5, St George's House, Rearsby Business Park,
Gaddesby Lane, Rearsby, Leicester LE7 4YH

1 3 5 7 9 10 8 6 4 2

First published in the United Kingdom in 2016
by Century

A CIP catalogue record for this book is available
from the British Library

ISBN 978 1 51006 526 0

Typeset by Palimpsest Book Production Limited,
Falkirk, Stirlingshire

Printed and bound by
T J International in the UK
Printforce Nederland b.v. in the Netherlands
Ligare in Australia

Home

To Mike and George and midlife bromances

CHAPTER 1

The boy who has been missing for ten years steps into the light.

I am not one for hysterics or even feeling much of what might be labeled astonishment. I have seen much in my forty-plus years. I have nearly been killed – and I have killed. I have seen depravity that most would find difficult, if not downright inconceivable, to comprehend – and some would argue that I have administered the same. I have learned over the years to control my emotions and, more important, my reactions during stressful, volatile situations. I may strike quickly and violently, but I do nothing without a certain level of deliberation and purpose.

These qualities, if you will, have saved me and those who matter to me time and time again.

Yet I confess that when I first see the boy – well, he is a teenager now, isn't he? – I can feel my pulse race. A thrumming sound echoes in my ears. Without conscious thought, my hands form two fists.

Ten years – and now fifty yards, no more, separate me from the missing boy.

Patrick Moore – that is the boy's name – leans against the graffiti-littered concrete support of the underpass. His shoulders are hunched. His eyes dart about before settling on the cracked pavement in front of him. His hair is closely cropped, what we used to call a crew cut. Two other teenage boys also mill about the underpass. One smokes a cigarette with so much gusto I fear the cigarette has offended him. The other wears a studded dog collar and mesh shirt, proclaiming his current profession in the most obvious of uniforms.

Above, the cars roar past, oblivious to what is below them. We are in King's Cross, most of which has been 'rejuvenated' over the past two decades with museums and libraries and the Eurostar and even a plaque for Platform 9¾, where Harry Potter boarded the train for Hogwarts. Much of the so-called undesirable element have fled these dangerous in-person transactions for the relative safety of online commerce – much less need for the risky drive-by sex trade, yet another positive by-product of the Internet – but if you go to the other side of the literal and figurative tracks, away from those shiny new towers, there are still places where the sleaze element survives in a concentrated form.

That is where I found the missing boy.

Part of me – the rash part I keep at bay – wants to sprint across the street and grab the boy. He would now be, if this is indeed Patrick and not a look-alike or mistake on my part, sixteen years old. From this distance, that looks about right to me. Ten years ago – you can do the math and calculate how young he'd been – in the über-affluent community of Alpine, Patrick had been on what they insist on calling a 'playdate' with my cousin's son Rhys.

That, of course, is my dilemma.

If I grab Patrick now, just run across the street and snatch him, what will become of Rhys? I have one of the missing boys in sight, but I have come to rescue both. So that means taking care. No sudden moves. I must be patient. Whatever happened ten years ago, whatever cruel twist of mankind (I don't believe so much in fate being cruel when the culprit is usually our fellow human beings) took this boy from the opulence of his stone mansion to this filthy toilet of an underpass, I worry now that if I make the wrong move, one or both boys might disappear again, this time forever.

I will have to wait for Rhys. I will wait for Rhys and then I will grab both boys and bring them home.

Two questions have probably crossed your mind.

The first: How can I be so confident that once the boys are in sight, I will be able to grab them both? Suppose, you may wonder, the boys have been brainwashed and resist. Suppose their kidnappers or whoever holds the keys to their freedom are many and violent and determined.

To that I reply: Don't worry about it.

The second question, which is far more pressing in my mind: What if Rhys does not show up?

I am not much of a 'crossing that bridge when we get there' sort of fellow, so I hatch a backup plan, which involves staking out this area and then following Patrick at a discreet distance. I am planning exactly how that might work when something goes wrong.

The trade is picking up. Life is about categorization. This street urinal is no different. One underpass caters to heterosexual men seeking female companionship. This underpass is the busiest. Old-fashioned values, I suppose. You can talk all you want about genders and preferences and kinks, but the majority of the sexually frustrated are still heterosexual men not getting enough. Old-school. Girls with dead eyes take their spots against the concrete barriers, cars drive by, girls drive off, other girls take their places. It is almost like watching a soda-dispenser machine at a petrol station.

In the second underpass, there is a small contingency of transgender or cross-dressing women of various alterations and stages, and then, at the tail end, where Patrick is now standing, is the young gay trade.

I watch as a man in a melon-hued shirt struts toward Patrick.

What, I had wondered when Patrick first appeared, would I do if a client chose to engage Patrick's services? At first blush, it would seem that it would be best that I intercede immediately. That would appear to be the most humane act on my part, but again, I can not lose sight of my goal: bringing *both* boys home. The truth is, Patrick and Rhys have been gone for a decade. They have been through God knows what, and while I don't relish the idea of allowing either to suffer through even one more abuse, I had already added up the pros and cons and made my decision. There is no use in lingering on that point anymore.

But Melon Shirt is not a client.

I know that immediately. Clients do not strut with such confidence. They don't keep their heads up high. They do not smirk. They do not wear bright melon shirts. Clients who are desperate enough to come here to satisfy their urges feel shame or fear discovery or, most likely, both.

Melon Shirt, on the other hand, has the walk and bearing and crackle of someone who is comfortable and dangerous. You can, if you are attuned to it, sense such things. You can feel it in your lizard brain, a primitive, inner warning trill that you cannot quite explain. Modern man, more afraid of embarrassment sometimes than safety, often ignores it at his own peril.

Melon Shirt glances behind him. Two other men are on the scene now, working Melon's flanks. They are both very large, decked out in camouflage fatigues, and wear what we used to call wifebeaters over shiny pectorals. The other boys working the underpass – the smoker and the one with the stud collar – run off at the sight of Melon Shirt, leaving Patrick alone with the three newcomers.

Oh, this is not good.

Patrick still has his eyes down, his quasi-shaved head gleaming. He is not aware of the approaching men until Melon Shirt is nearly on top of him. I move closer. In all likelihood, Patrick has been on the streets for some time. I think about that for a moment, about what his life must have been like, snatched from the comforting bubble of American suburbia and dumped into . . . well, who knows what?

But in all that time, Patrick might have developed certain skills. He might be able to talk his way out of this situation. The situation might not be as dire as it appears. I need to wait and see.

Melon Shirt gets right up in Patrick's face. He says something to him. I can't hear what. Then, without additional preamble, he rears back his fist and slams it like a sledgehammer into Patrick's solar plexus.

Patrick collapses to the ground, gasping for air.

The two camouflaged bodybuilders start to close in. I move fast now.

'Gentlemen,' I call out.

Melon Shirt and both Camouflages spin at the sound of my voice. At first, their expressions are those of Neanderthal men hearing a strange noise for the first time. Then they take me in, narrowing their eyes. I can see the smiles come to their lips. I am not a physically imposing figure. I am above-average height and on the slight side, you'd say, with blond-heading-toward-gray hair, a skin tone that runs from porcelain in the warmth to ruddy in the cold, and features that some might consider delicate in, I hope, a handsome way.

Today I'm wearing a light-blue Savile Row hand-tailored suit, Lilly Pulitzer tie, Hermès pocket square in the breast pocket, and Bedfordshire bespoke shoes custom made by G.J. Cleverley's lead craftsman on Old Bond Street.

I am quite the dandy, aren't I?

As I saunter toward the three thugs, wishing I had an umbrella to twirl for maximum effect, I can feel their confidence growing. I like that. Normally I carry a handgun, often two, but in England, the laws are very strict about such things. I'm not worried. The beauty of the strict British laws means that it is highly unlikely that my three adversaries are carrying either. My eyes do a quick three-body scan for locations where one might conceal a gun. My thugs favor extraordinarily tight attire, more suitable for preening than weapon concealment.

They might be carrying knives – they probably are – but there are no guns.

Knives do not worry me much.

Patrick – if it is indeed Patrick – is still on the ground gasping for air as I make my arrival. I stop, spread my arms, and offer them my most winning smile. The three thugs stare at me as though I am a museum piece that they can't comprehend.

Melon Shirt takes one step toward me. 'Who the fuck are you?'

I am still smiling. 'You should leave now.'

Melon Shirt looks at Camouflage One on my right. Then he looks at Camouflage Two to my left. I look in both directions too and then back at Melon Shirt.

When I wink at him, his eyebrows jump high.

'We should cut him up,' Camouflage One says. 'Cut him into little pieces.'

I feign being startled and turn toward him. 'Oh my, I didn't see you there.'

'What?'

'In those camouflage pants. You really blend in. By the way, they are very fetching on you.'

'Are you some kind of wiseguy?'

'I'm many kinds of wiseguy.'

All the smiles, including mine, grow.

They start toward me. I can try to talk my way out of this, perhaps offer them money to leave us be, but I don't think that will work, for three reasons. One, these thugs will want all my money and my watch and whatever else they can find upon my person. Money offers will not help. Two, they all have the scent of blood – easy, weak blood – and they like that scent. And three, most important, I like the scent of blood too.

It has been too long.

I try not to smile as they start to make their approach. Melon Shirt takes out a large bowie knife. That pleases me. I don't have many moral qualms about hurting those whom I recognize as evil. But it is nice to know that for those who require such self-rationalizations to find me 'likable,' I could claim that the thugs were the first to draw a weapon and thus I was acting strictly in self-defense.

Still, I give them one last out.

I look Melon Shirt straight in the eye and say, 'You should leave now.'

Both overmuscled Camouflages laugh at that, but Melon Shirt's smile starts to fade. He knows. I can see it. He looked in my eyes and he knows.

The rest happens in seconds.

Camouflage One comes right up to me, getting in my personal space. He is a large man. I am face-to-face with his waxed and toned pectorals. He smiles down at me as though I am a tasty treat he might devour in one bite.

There is no reason to delay the inevitable.

I slash his throat with the razor I'd kept hidden in my hand.

Blood sprays at me in a near perfect arc. Damn. This will require another visit to Savile Row.

'Terence!'

It's Camouflage Two. There is a resemblance, and, now sliding toward him, I wonder whether they are brothers. The thug's grief stuns him enough to make disposing of him very easy, though I don't think it would have helped much had he been better prepared.

I am good with a straight razor.

Camouflage Two perishes in the same manner as dear Terence, his possible brother.

That leaves Melon Shirt, their beloved leader, who has probably attained that rank by being somewhat more brutish and cunning than his fallen comrades. Wisely, Melon Shirt has already started to make his move while I was dispensing with Camouflage Two. Using my peripheral vision, I can see the glint of his bowie blade heading toward me from above.

That is a mistake on his part.

You don't strike a foe from above like that. It's too easy to defend. Your adversary can buy time by ducking or raising a forearm for the purpose of deflection. If you shoot someone with a gun, you are trained to aim for the middle mass so that if your aim is slightly askew, you can still hit something. You prepare for the likelihood of error. With a knife, the same is true. Make the distance of your stab as short as possible. Aim for the middle so that if your adversary moves, you can still wound him.

Melon Shirt didn't do that.

I duck and use my right forearm to, as noted above, deflect the blow. Then, with my knees bent, I spin and use the razor across his abdomen. I don't wait to see his reaction. I move up and finish him in the same manner as I had the other two.

As I said, it is over in seconds.

The cracked pavement is a crimson mess and getting messier. I give myself a second, no more, to relish the high. You would too, if you didn't pretend otherwise.

I turn toward Patrick.

But he is gone.

I look left, then right. There he is, nearly out of sight. I hurry after him, but I can see very quickly it will be useless. He is heading toward King's Cross station, one of London's busiest. He will be in the station – be in the public eye – before I can reach him. I am covered in blood. I might be good at what I do, but despite the fact that King's Cross station is indeed where Harry Potter headed off for Hogwarts, I do not possess an invisibility cloak.

I stop, look back, consider the situation, come to a conclusion.

I have messed up.

It's time to make myself scarce. I am not worried about any CCTV recording what I have done. There is a reason the undesirable element choose spots like this. It stands apart from all prying eyes, even the digital and electronic ones.

Still. I've blown it. After all these years, after all the fruitless searches, one lead has finally come my way, and if I lose that lead . . .

I need help.

I hurry away and press the 1 on my speed dial. I haven't pressed the 1 for nearly a year.

He answers on the third ring. 'Hello?'

Hearing his voice again, even though I had steeled for it, sends me reeling for a moment. The

11

number is blocked, so he has no idea who has called him.

I say, 'Don't you mean "articulate"?'

There is a gasp. 'Win? My God, where have you been—?'

'I saw him,' I say.

'Who?'

'Think.'

The briefest of pauses. 'Wait, both of them?'

'Just Patrick.' 'Wow.'

I frown. Wow? 'Myron?'

'Yes?'

'Catch the next plane to London. I need your help.'

CHAPTER 2

Two minutes before Win called, Myron Bolitar lay sprawled naked in bed with a knee-knockingly gorgeous woman at his side. They both stared up at the fancy wainscoting on the ceiling, gulping in breaths, lost in the aftermath of the bliss that comes only from, uh, bliss.

'Yowza,' Terese said.

'I know, right?'

'That was . . .'

'I know, right?'

Myron had a way with postcoital banter.

Terese swung her legs out of bed, rose, and moved toward the window. Myron watched. He liked the way she moved naked, panther-like, all coiled and toned and confident. The apartment was perched above Central Park on the West Side. Terese looked out the window toward the lake and Bow Bridge. If you've ever seen a New York City movie where a couple in love runs across a foot-bridge, you've seen Bow Bridge.

'God, what a view,' Terese said.

'I was just thinking the same thing.'

'Are you ogling my ass?'

'I prefer to think of it as watching. Guarding.'

'In a protective manner, then?'

'It would be unprofessional of me to look away.'

'Well, we wouldn't want you to appear unprofessional.'

'Thank you.'

Then, with her back still toward him, his fiancée said, 'Myron?'

'Yes, my love.'

'I'm happy.'

'Me too.'

'That's scary.'

'Terrifying,' Myron agreed. 'Come back to bed.'

'Really?'

'Yep.'

'Don't make promises you can't keep.'

'Oh, I can keep them,' Myron said. Then: 'Is there a place around here that delivers oysters and vitamin E?'

She turned, gave him her best smile, and ka-boom, his heart exploded into a million pieces. Terese Collins was back. After all the years of separations and anguish and instability, they were finally going to get married. It felt incredible. It felt wonderful. It felt fragile.

And that was when the phone rang.

They both stopped as though they sensed it. When things are going this well, you sort of hold your breath because you want it to last. You don't want to stop or even slow down time as

14

much as you just want to stay safe in your little bubble.

That phone ring, to keep with this piss-poor metaphor, was a bubble burster.

Myron checked the caller ID but the number was blocked. They were in the Dakota building in Manhattan. When Win had disappeared a year ago, he had put the place in Myron's name. For most of that year, Myron had chosen to stay in his childhood home in nearby Livingston, New Jersey, trying his best to raise his teenage nephew, Mickey. But now his brother, Mickey's father, was back, and so Myron had given them the house and come back to the city.

The phone rang a second time. Terese turned to the side, as though the sound had slapped her across the cheek. He could see the scar from the bullet wound on her neck. The old feeling, the need to protect, started to rise in him.

For a moment, Myron debated letting it go to voicemail, but then Terese closed her eyes and nodded, just once. Not answering, they both knew, would only delay the inevitable.

Myron picked up on the third ring. 'Hello?'

There was an odd hesitation and some static and then the voice he hadn't heard in so long came through: 'Don't you mean "articulate"?'

Myron had tried to brace himself, but he still gasped. 'Win? My God, where have you been—?'

'I saw him.'

'Who?'

'Think.'

Myron had wondered, but he hadn't dared voice it. 'Wait, both of them?'

'Just Patrick.'

'Wow.'

'Myron?'

'Yes?'

'Catch the next plane to London. I need your help.'

Myron looked at Terese. The shatter was back in her eyes. That shatter had always been there, since they first ran off together years ago, but he hadn't noticed it since her return. He reached out his hand toward her. She took it.

'Life's a little complicated right now,' Myron said.

'Terese has returned,' Win said.

Not a question. He knew.

'Yes.'

'And you're finally getting married.'

Again not a question.

'Yes.'

'Did you buy her a ring?'

'Yes.'

'From Norman on Forty-Seventh Street?'

'Of course.'

'More than two carats?'

'Win . . .'

'I'm happy for you both.'

'Thank you.'

'But you can't get married,' Win said, 'without your best man.'

'I already asked my brother.'

'He'll step aside. The flight leaves from Teterboro. The car is waiting.'

Win hung up.

Terese looked at him. 'You have to go.'

He wasn't sure if it was a question or a statement.

'Win doesn't make casual requests,' Myron said.

'No,' she agreed. 'He doesn't.'

'It won't take long. I'll be back and we will get married. I promise.'

Terese sat on the bed. 'Can you tell me what it's about?'

'How much could you hear?'

'Just bits and pieces.' Then: 'Is the ring more than two carats?'

'It is.'

'Good. So tell me.'

'Do you remember the Alpine kidnappings ten years back?'

Terese nodded. 'Sure. We reported on it.'

She had worked for years as an anchorwoman on one of those all-news channels.

'One of the kidnapped boys, Rhys Baldwin, is related to Win.'

'You never told me that.'

Myron shrugged. 'I didn't really have much to do with it. By the time we got involved, the case was pretty cold. Still, it's always been on my back burner.'

'But not Win's.'

'Nothing is ever on Win's back burner.'
'So he has a new lead?'
'More than that. He says he saw Patrick Moore.'
'So why doesn't he call the police?'
'I don't know.'
'But you didn't ask.'
'I trust his judgment.'
'And he needs your help.'
'Yes.'
Terese nodded. 'Then you better get packed.'
'You're okay?'
'He was right.'
'About?'
She rose. 'We can't get married without your best man.'

Win had sent a black limo. It was waiting under the Dakota's archway. The limo took him out to Teterboro Airport in northern New Jersey, which was about half an hour away. Win's plane, a Boeing Business Jet, was waiting on the tarmac. There was no security, no check-in, no ticket. The limousine dropped him off by the steps. The flight attendant, a lovely young Asian woman, greeted Myron in an old-fashioned fitted uniform, complete with puffy blouse and pillbox hat.
  'Nice to see you, Mr Bolitar.'
  'You too, Mee.'
In case you didn't get the memo: Win was rich.
Win's real name was Windsor Horne Lockwood III, as in Lock-Horne Investments and Securities

18

and the Lock-Horne Building on Park Avenue. His family was old money, the kind of money that got off the *Mayflower* with a pink polo shirt and desirable tee time.

Myron ducked his six-four frame through the plane's door. There were leather seats, wood trim, a couch, plush green carpeting, zebra-striped wallpaper – the plane had been owned by a rapper, and Win decided not to refurbish it because it made him feel 'phat' – a wide-screen television, a sofa bed, and a queen-sized bed in the back bedroom.

Myron was alone on the plane, which made him feel self-conscious, but he'd get over it. He took a seat and buckled up. The plane began moving toward the runway. Mee did her safety demonstration. She kept the pillbox hat on. Win, Myron knew, liked that hat.

Two minutes later, they were up in the air.

Mee came over and said, 'Is there anything I can get you?'

'Have you seen him?' Myron asked. 'Where has he been?'

'I'm not allowed to answer that,' Mee replied.

'Why not?'

'Win told me to make you comfortable. We have your customary beverage on board.'

She was carrying a Yoo-hoo chocolate drink.

'Yeah, I'm off those,' Myron said.

'Really?'

'Yes.'

'That's sad. How about a cognac?'

'I'm good right now. What can you tell me, Mee?'

Me, Mee. Myron wondered whether that was her real name. Win had liked the name. He would take her to the back of the plane and make intentionally cringe-worthy double-entendre puns like 'I need a little Mee time' or 'I enjoy having carnal knowledge alone with Mee' or 'I like the pillbox hat. It suits Mee.'

Win.

'What can you tell me?' Myron asked again.

Mee said, 'The weather forecast in London calls for intermittent rain.'

'Gee, that's a shock. I mean, what can you tell me about Win?'

'Good question,' she said. 'What can you tell Mee' – she pointed to herself – 'about Win?'

'Don't start with that.'

She gave him a smile. 'There's a live feed of the Knicks game, if you'd like to watch.'

'I don't watch basketball anymore.'

Mee gave him a look of sympathy that almost made him want to turn away. 'I saw your sports documentary on ESPN,' she said.

'That's not why,' Myron said.

She nodded, not believing him.

'If the game holds no interest for you,' Mee said, 'there's a video for you to watch.'

'What kind of video?'

'Win instructed me to tell you to watch it.'

'This isn't, uh . . .'

Win liked to film his, uh, carnal trysts and play them back while meditating.

Mee shook her head. 'He keeps those for his own private viewing, Mr Bolitar. You know that. It's part of the waiver we sign.'

'Waiver?' Myron held up a hand before she could reply. 'Never mind, I don't want to know.'

'Here's the remote control.' Mee handed it to him. 'Are you sure there isn't anything I can get you at this time?'

'I'm good, thanks.'

Myron spun toward the mounted television and switched it on. He half expected Win to be on the screen with some *Mission: Impossible*–type message, but no, it was one of those true-crime shows you see on cable television. The subject was, of course, the kidnappings, a look back now that the boys had been missing ten years.

Myron settled back and watched. It was a good refresher. In simple terms, here was the gist:

Ten years ago, six-year-old Patrick Moore was on a playdate at the estate of his classmate Rhys Baldwin in the 'tony' – they always used that word in the media – suburb of Alpine, New Jersey, not far from the isle of Manhattan. How tony? The median home price in Alpine last quarter was over four million dollars.

The two boys were left in the care of Vada Linna, an eighteen-year-old au pair from Finland. When Patrick's mother, Nancy Moore, came to pick up her son, no one answered the door. This was not

21

a huge cause for concern to her. Nancy Moore figured that young Vada had taken the boys for an outing or ice cream or something along those lines.

Two hours later, Nancy Moore returned and knocked on the front door again. There was still no answer. Still only mildly concerned, Nancy called Rhys's mother, Brooke. Brooke called Vada's mobile phone, but it went immediately to voicemail.

Brooke Lockwood Baldwin, Win's first cousin, rushed home at this juncture. She unlocked the door to the house. The two women called out. At first there was no answer. Then they heard a noise coming from the finished basement, which was an expansive playroom for the young children.

That was where they found Vada Linna tied to a chair and gagged. The young au pair had kicked over a lamp to get their attention. She was scared but otherwise unharmed.

But the two boys, Patrick and Rhys, were nowhere to be found.

According to Vada, she had been fixing the boys a snack in the kitchen when two armed men stormed in through the sliding glass door. They wore ski masks and black turtlenecks.

They dragged Vada to the basement and tied her up.

Nancy and Brooke immediately called the police. Both fathers, Hunter Moore, a physician, and Chick Baldwin, a hedge fund manager, were summoned from their places of work. For several hours, there was nothing – no contact, no clues, no leads. Then a ransom request via an anonymous email came to Chick Baldwin's work account. The note began by warning them not to contact the authorities if they wanted to see their children alive.

Too late for that.

The note demanded that the families get two million dollars ready – 'one million per child' – and that further instructions would be forth-coming. They gathered the money and waited. Three agonizing days passed before the kidnappers wrote again, directing Chick Baldwin and only Chick Baldwin to drive alone to Overpeck Park and leave the money in a specific spot by the boat launches.

Chick Baldwin did as they asked.

The FBI, of course, had full surveillance on the park, all entrances and exits covered. They had also put a GPS in the bag, though a decade ago, that technology was slightly more rudimentary than it would be today.

Up until this point, the authorities had done a good job of keeping the abductions a secret. No media found out. At the urging of the FBI, no friends or family members, including Win, were contacted. Even the other Baldwin and Moore children were kept in the dark.

Chick Baldwin dropped off the money and drove away. An hour passed. Then two. During hour three, someone picked up the bag, but that ended up being a Good Samaritan jogger who planned to bring it to lost and found.

No one else picked up the ransom money.

The families gathered around Chick Baldwin's computer and waited for another email. In the meantime, the FBI pursued a few theories. First, they took a hard look at Vada Linna, the young au pair, but there was nothing there. She had been in the country only two months and barely spoke English. She had only one friend. They scoured her emails, her texts, her online history, and came up with nothing suspicious.

The FBI also looked at the four parents. The only one who gave them serious pause was Rhys's father, Chick Baldwin. The ransom emails had come to Chick, but more than that, Chick was something of an unsavory character. There were two cases of insider trading and several lawsuits involving embezzlement. Some claimed that he ran a Ponzi scheme. Clients – some of whom were powerful – were upset.

But upset enough to do something like this?

So they waited for word from the kidnappers. Another day passed. Then two. Then three, four. Not a word. A week went by.

Then a month. A year.

Ten years.

And nothing. No sign of either boy.

Until now.

Myron sat back as the credits rolled. Mee sauntered over and looked down at him.

'I think I'll have that cognac now,' he said.

'Right away.'

When she came back, Myron said, 'Sit down, Mee.'

'I don't think so.'

'When was the last time you saw Win?'

'I am paid to be discreet.'

Myron bit back the wisecrack. 'There were rumors,' he said. 'About Win, I mean. I was worried.'

She tilted her head. 'Don't you trust him?'

'With my life.'

'So respect his privacy.'

'I've been doing that for the last year.'

'Then what's a few more hours?'

She was right, of course.

'You miss him,' Mee said.

'Of course.'

'He loves you, you know.'

Myron said nothing.

'You should try to get some sleep.'

She was right about that too. He closed his eyes, but he knew sleep wouldn't come. A close friend had recently convinced Myron to take up Transcendental Meditation, and while he wasn't sure he completely bought into it, the simplicity and ease made it perfect for those moments when sleep eluded him. He set his Meditation Timer app – yes, he had one on his phone – for twenty minutes, closed his eyes, and started to sink down.

People think meditation clears the mind. That's

nonsense. You can't clear the mind. The harder you try *not* to think about something, the more you will think about it. You need to allow the thoughts in if you really want to relax. You learn to observe them and not judge or react. So that was what Myron did now.

He thought about seeing Win again, about Esperanza and Big Cyndi, about his mother and father down in Florida. He thought about his brother, Brad, and his nephew, Mickey, and about the changes in their lives. He thought about Terese finally being back in his life, about their impending marriage, about starting a life with her, about the sudden, tangible possibility of happiness.

He thought about how shockingly fragile it all felt.

Eventually, the plane landed, slowed, taxied. When it came to a complete stop, Mee pulled the handle and opened the door. She gave him a wide smile. 'Good luck, Myron.'

'Same to you, Mee.'

'Tell Win I say hello.'

CHAPTER 3

The Bentley was waiting for him on the tarmac. As Myron started down the steps, the back door opened. Win came out.

Myron hurried his step, feeling his eyes brim with tears. When he was ten feet away from his friend, he stopped, blinked, smiled.

'Myron.'

'Win.'

Win sighed. 'You're going to want to make this a moment, aren't you?'

'What's life without them?'

Win nodded. Myron stepped forward. The two men hugged fiercely, hanging on as though the other were a life preserver.

Still holding on, Myron said, 'I have a million questions.'

'And I'm not going to answer them.' They both let go. 'We need to concentrate on Rhys and Patrick.'

'Of course.'

Win gestured for Myron to get in the back. Myron did so, sliding across to make room for Win. The Bentley was a black stretch. The privacy window to the driver was up. There were only two seats, lots of legroom, a stocked bar. Most stretches have more seating. Win didn't see the need.

'A drink?' Win asked.

'No, thanks.'

The car started to move. Mee was by the plane door. Win lowered his window and waved. She waved back. There was a wistful look on Win's face. Myron just stared at his friend, his best friend since their freshman year at Duke University, afraid that if he looked away, Win might vanish again.

Win said, 'She has a top-quality derriere, don't you think?'

'Uh-huh. Win?'

'Yes.'

'Have you been in London the whole time?'

Still looking out the window, Win said, 'No.'

'Where, then?'

'Many places.'

'There were rumors.'

'Yes.'

'They said you'd become a recluse.'

'I know.'

'Not true?'

'No, Myron, not true. I created those rumors.'

'Why?'

'Later. Right now we need to concentrate on Patrick and Rhys.'

'You said you saw Patrick.'

'I believe so, yes.'

'Believe so?'

'Patrick was six when he disappeared,' Win said. 'He would be sixteen now.'

'So there was no way you could get an exact ID on him.'

'Correct.'

'So you spotted someone you believed was Patrick.'

'Correct again.'

'And then?'

'And then I lost him.'

Myron sat back.

'This surprises you,' Win said.

'It does.'

'You're thinking, "That's not like you."'

'I am indeed.'

Win nodded. 'I miscalculated.' Then he added: 'There was collateral damage.'

That was never a good thing with Win.

'How much?'

'Perhaps we should press the rewind button first.' Win reached into his suit pocket and pulled out a piece of paper. 'Read this.'

Win handed him what looked to be a printed email. It was addressed to Win's personal email account. Myron had sent the account half a dozen messages over the past year. He had never gotten a reply. The sender was listed as anon5939413. It read:

You are looking for Rhys Baldwin and Patrick Moore. For most of the last ten

29

years, they have been together, but not always. They've been separated at least three times. They are back together now.

They are free to go but might not with you. They aren't who you think they are anymore. They aren't who their families remember either. You may not like what you find. Here is where they are. Forget the reward money. I will one day ask for a favor.

Neither one of them remembers much of their life before. Be patient with them.

Myron felt a chill scramble down his spine. 'I assume you tried to figure out where the email came from?'

Win nodded.

'And I assume you got nothing.'

'VPN,' Win said. 'No way to track down where or from whom it originated.'

Myron read it again. 'That last paragraph.'

'Yes, I know.'

'There is something about it.'

'An air of authenticity,' Win said.

'Which is why you took it seriously.'

'Yes,' Win said.

'And this address they list?' Myron asked.

'It's a rather small yet sordid area in London. An underpass where all sorts of illicit trade takes place. I canvassed the spot.'

'Okay.'

'Someone who strongly resembles those age-progression images of Patrick showed up.'

'When?'

'About an hour before I called you.'

'Did you hear him talk?'

'Pardon?'

'Did he speak? I'm trying to get a better handle on his ID. Maybe his accent was American.'

'I didn't hear him speak,' Win said. 'We also don't know. He could have been here, on these streets, for his entire life.'

Silence.

Then Myron repeated, 'His entire life.'

'I know,' Win said. 'No reason to dwell on it.'

'So you saw Patrick. Then what?'

'I waited.'

Myron nodded. 'You were hoping Rhys would show.'

'Yes.'

'And then?'

'Three men who appeared to be unhappy with Patrick assaulted him.'

'And you stopped them?'

For the first time a small smile played with Win's lips. 'It's what I do.'

It was indeed.

'And all three?' Myron asked.

Win smiled, shrugged.

Myron closed his eyes.

'These men were the worst sort of thugs,' Win said. 'They will not be mourned.'

'It was self-defense?'

'Yes, fine, let's go with that. Are we really going to second-guess my methods right now, Myron?'

He was right.

'So then what happened?'

'Whilst I was preoccupied with said thugs, Patrick fled. The last time I saw him, he was heading into King's Cross station. Not long after that, I called you for help.'

Myron sat back. They were approaching Westminster Bridge and the river Thames. The London Eye, basically a gigantic Ferris wheel that moved at what could generously be dubbed a glacial pace, shimmered in the afternoon sunlight. Myron had gone on it once years ago. It had bored him silly.

'You understand,' Win said, 'how pressing this is.'

Myron nodded. 'They'll make the boys disappear.'

'Precisely. Move them out of the country, or if they feel threatened with exposure . . .'

Win didn't have to finish the thought.

'Have you told the parents?'

'No.'

'Not even Brooke?'

'No,' Win said. 'I saw no reason to give her false hope.'

They were driving north. Myron looked out the window. 'They've been gone since they were six years old, Win.'

He said nothing.

'Everyone thought that they were long dead.'

'I know.'

'Except you.'

'Oh, I thought they were dead.'

'But you kept looking.'

Win steepled his fingers. It was a familiar gesture, one that brought Myron back to younger days. 'Last time I saw Brooke, we opened some very expensive wine. We sat out on a deck and looked out over the ocean. For a while, she was the Brooke I grew up with. Some people are conduits for misery. Brooke is the opposite. She brings joy. Always has. You know the cliché that some people light up a room?'

'Sure.'

'Brooke could do that from a distance. You could just think about her and be happier. You want to shield a person like that. And when you see someone like that in such pain, you want – nay, need – to relieve it.'

Win bounced his fingertips together. 'So there we were, drinking wine and staring out at the ocean. Most people use alcohol to anesthetize the kind of pain Brooke faced. But with Brooke, the opposite was happening. The alcohol made the facade fall away. The smile she still forced up was gone. She confessed something to me that night.'

He stopped. Myron waited.

'For a long time, Brooke fantasized about Rhys's homecoming. Every time the phone rang, she felt the jangle in her blood. She hoped it would be

Rhys telling her he was okay. She would see him in crowded streets. She would dream about rescuing him, about seeing him, about their tearful reunion. She would constantly replay that day in her head, staying home instead of going out, taking Rhys and Patrick with her instead of leaving them with that au pair – altering something, anything, to make it not have happened. It stays with you, Brooke told me. A permanent companion. You may run a few steps ahead, but that day is always there, tapping you on the shoulder, pulling at your sleeve.'

Myron sat very still.

'I knew all this, of course. It isn't revelatory that parents suffer. Brooke still looks wonderful. She's a strong woman. But things have changed.'

'What do you mean, "changed"?'

'It has to end.'

'What do you mean?'

'That was Brooke's confession. When the phone rings, do you know what she hopes?'

Myron shook his head.

'That it's the police. That they've finally found Rhys's body. Do you understand what I'm saying? The not knowing – the hope – has become more painful than death. And that just makes the tragedy all the more obscene. It is horrible enough that you make a mother suffer like this. But this, she told me – wishing, no matter what, that it would just end – was even worse.'

They sat in silence for a few moments.

Then Win said, 'Hey, how about those Knicks?'

'Funny.'

'You need to be loose.'

'Where are we going?'

'Back to King's Cross.'

'Where you can't really show your face.'

'I'm extraordinarily handsome. People remember me.'

'Ergo needing my help.'

'Glad my absence hasn't dulled your sharp investigative tools.'

'So tell me everything,' Myron said. 'Let's make a plan.'

CHAPTER 4

When they drove past the train station, Myron read the sign and said, 'King's Cross. Isn't that from *Harry Potter*?'

'It is.'

Myron took another look. 'Cleaner than I expected.'

'Gentrification,' Win said. 'But you never really get rid of the dirt. You just sweep it into dark corners.'

'And you know where those dark corners are?'

'I was told in the email.' The Bentley came to a stop. 'We can't get any closer without the risk of being seen. Take this.'

Win handed him a smartphone.

'I have a phone,' Myron said.

'Not like this one. It's a complete monitoring system. I can follow you via GPS. I can listen in on any conversations via microphones. I can see what you see via the camera.'

'The key word,' Myron said, 'is "via."'

'Hilarious. Speaking of a key word, we will need a distress signal if you get into trouble.'

'How about "help"?'

Win looked at him blankly. 'I. Missed. Your. Humor.'

'Remember when we first started out?' Myron couldn't help but smile. 'I would call you on the old cell phones and you would listen in.'

'I remember.'

'We thought we were so high tech.'

'We were,' Win said.

'Articulate,' Myron said.

'Pardon?'

'If I'm in trouble, I'll say "articulate."'

Myron headed out past the station. He realized that he was whistling a show tune – 'Ring of Keys' from *Fun Home* – as he walked. That might strike some as odd. This situation was, after all, horrible and dangerous and deadly serious, but he'd be lying to himself if he said it wasn't also a thrill to be working with Win again. Most of the time, it was Myron who kicked off their often foolhardy rescue missions. In fact, come to think of it, it had always been Myron. Win had been the voice of caution, the sidekick dragged along, joining in more for the fun of it than for any form of justice.

At least, that was Win's claim.

'You,' Win would tell him, 'have a hero complex. You think you can make the world better. You are Don Quixote tilting at windmills.'

'And you?'

'I'm eye candy for the ladies.'

Win.

It was still daylight, but only the naïve believe

37

this sort of trade goes on solely under the blanket of darkness. Still, as Myron arrived at the lookout spot Win had used yesterday, he looked down and saw that this would not be easy.

The police were here.

In the spot where Win had seen probably-Patrick, there were two uniformed officers and two what looked to be lab technicians. The splattered blood, even from up here, still looked wet on the pavement. There was also a lot of it. It looked as if someone had dropped cans of paint from a great height.

The bodies were nowhere to be seen. Nor, naturally, were any streetwalkers – they knew enough to stay away from scenes like this. A dead end, Myron thought. Time for a new plan.

He turned to head back to where the Bentley had dropped him off when something caught his eye. Myron stopped. There, in the 'dark corner,' as Win had put it, at the end of Railway Street, he spotted what had to be a streetwalker.

She was dressed in Seventies American Hooker – fishnet stockings, high boots (those two looks seemed to be a contradiction), a skirt that covered up as much of her as, say, a belt would, and a purple top so tight it could have been sausage casing.

Myron started toward her. When he got closer, the woman turned to him. Myron gave her a little wave.

'Looking for company?' she asked him.

38

'Uh, no. Not really.'

'You don't really get how this works, do you?'

'I guess not, sorry.'

'Let's try again: Looking for a little company?'

'You bet I am.'

The woman smiled. Myron expected something horrific in the dental category, but she had a full mouth of nice, even white teeth. He guessed her age at around fifty, but it could have been a hard forty. She was big and shapely and sloppy and spilling out everywhere, and the smile made it all kind of work.

'You're an American,' she said.

'Yes.'

'Lots of my clients are American.'

'Doesn't look like you have much competition.'

'Not anymore, no. See, the girls stay off the streets nowadays. Do everything with a computer or an app.'

'But you don't.'

'Nah, it ain't me, you know what I mean? So cold, everyone on Tinder or Ohlala or whatever. Shame really. What happened to human contact? What happened to the personal touch?'

'Uh-huh,' Myron said, because he wasn't sure what else to say.

'Me, I like the streets. So my business model is to be something of a throwback, you know what I mean? I appeal to people's – What do you call it?' She thought about it for a second and then snapped her fingers. 'Nostalgia! Right? I mean, people are on holiday. They visit King's Cross to see a hooker, not fiddle with their iPhone. You know what I mean?'

'Uh-huh.'

'They want the full experience. This street, these clothes, the way I act, what I say – see, I'm what they call niche marketing.'

'Good to fill a need.'

'I used to be in porn.'

She waited.

'Oh, you probably don't recognize me. I was only in three films back when – Well, a girl has to keep some of her secrets. My most famous role was Third Wench in a scene with that famous Italian guy, Rocky or Rocco something. But for years I was a top-notch fluffer. You know what that is, don't you? A fluffer?'

'I think I do.'

'Most of the guys, truth is, with all the cameras and lights and all the people watching, well, it wasn't easy on them to stay, you know, hard. So that was what the fluffers provided. Offstage. Oh, it was great work. I did it for years, knew all the tricks, I can tell you.'

'I'm sure you can.'

'But then Viagra came along and, well, a pill was a lot cheaper than a girl. Shame really. We fluffers are extinct now. Like dinosaurs or VHS tapes. So here I am, back out working on the streets. Not that I'm complaining, am I right?'

'As rain.'

'Speaking of which, you're on the clock.'

'That's fine.'

'Some girls sell their bodies. Not me. I sell my time. Like a consultant or barrister. What you do with that time – and as I say, the clock is ticking – is up to you. So what are you looking for, handsome?'

'Um, a young man.'

That made the smile flee. 'Go on.'

'He's a teenager.'

'Nah.' She made a swatting motion with her hand. 'You're no short eyes.'

'No what?'

'Short eyes. A pedo. You're not going to tell me you're a pedo, are you?'

'Oh no. I'm not. I'm just looking for him. I mean him no harm.'

She put her hands on her hips and looked at him for a long moment. 'Why do I believe you?'

Myron forced up his most winning smile. 'My smile.'

'No, but you do have a trusting face. That smile is bloody slimy.'

'It's supposed to be winning.'

'It's not.'

'I'm just trying to help him,' Myron said. 'He's in real danger.'

'What makes you think I can help?'

'He was here yesterday. Working.'

'Ah.'

'What?'

41

'Yesterday.'

'Yes.'

'So are you the one who killed those cockwombles?'

'No.'

'Too bad,' she said. 'I would have thrown you a freebie for that.'

'This kid. He's in real danger.'

'So you said.' She hesitated. Myron took out his wallet. She waved him off. 'I don't want your money. I mean, I do. But not for that.'

She seemed unsure what to do.

Myron pointed to himself. 'Trusting face, remember?'

'None of the boys'll be back here for a bit. Not with the coppers around. They'll go to their other spot.'

'And where is that?'

'Hampstead Heath. They usually hang near the west end of Merton Lane.'

CHAPTER 5

'Hampstead Heath,' Win said when Myron was back in the car. 'Historic.'

'How so?'

'Keats walked its lanes. Kingsley Amis, John Constable, Alfred Tennyson, Ian Fleming – they all had residences there. But that's not why it's best known.'

'Oh?'

'Do you remember when George Michael was arrested for having sex in a public bathroom?'

'Sure. It was here?'

'Hampstead Heath, indeed. This has been a gay cruising spot forever, but from my understanding, there is very little prostitution. It has always been more about cottaging.'

'Cottaging?'

'God, you're naïve. Cottaging. Anonymous sex between men in bushes, public toilets, like that. Cash rarely changes hands. Still, young hustlers could try to ply their trade here, perhaps locate a potential sugar daddy or network for clients. I would suggest heading into the park and veering left toward the public toilets. Continue down the lane past the ponds. That seems to be the apropos area.'

'You're pretty knowledgeable on the subject.'

'I'm knowledgeable on all subjects.'

That was true.

'I also use this new thing called Google.' Win held up his smartphone. 'You should try it sometime. Do you need to take these?'

Win handed Myron the age-progression photographs of both Patrick and Rhys. He also described with startling detail what the maybe-Patrick he'd seen yesterday looked like, and what he was wearing.

Myron stared at the faces. 'How old would Patrick and Rhys be now?'

'Both would be sixteen. Coincidentally – or maybe not – sixteen is the age of consent in Great Britain.'

Myron snapped photos of the photos before handing them back to Win. He reached for the door handle and stopped.

'We're missing something here, Win.'

'Probably.'

'You feel it too?'

'I do.'

'Are we being set up?'

'Could be,' Win said, steepling his fingers again. 'But the only way to find out for certain is to proceed.'

The car was idling at the corner of Merton and Millfield Lane.

'All set?'

'Onward,' Myron said and slipped out of the car.

Hampstead Heath was lush and green and beautiful. Myron took the stroll, but there was no sign of Patrick or Rhys. There were men, lots of them, from eighteen (or younger, he supposed) to eighty, mostly in unremarkable garb, but what had Myron expected? Myron saw nothing sexual going on, but that was because, he assumed, there was a public toilet and bushes deep off the paths.

Fifteen minutes into the walk, Myron put the phone to his ear.

'Nothing,' he said.

'Anyone hit on you?'

'No.'

'Ouch.'

'I know,' Myron said. 'Do you think these pants make me look fat?'

'We still joke,' Win said.

'What?'

'We believe in complete equality and get angry at anyone who displays the slightest bit of prejudice,' Win said.

'Yet we still joke,' Myron finished for him.

'Indeed.'

That was when Myron spotted something that gave him pause.

'Hold up a second,' Myron said.

'I'm listening.'

'When you described the, uh, scene yesterday, you mentioned two other guys working the street.'

'Correct.'

'You said one had a shaved head and wore a dog collar.'

'Correct again.'

Myron moved the phone so that the camera was pointing at the young leather-clad man near the pond.

'Well?'

'That is he,' Win said.

Myron put the phone back in his pocket and crossed the path. Dog Collar had his hands jammed into his pants pockets as though he was searching for something that had pissed him off. His shoulders were hunched. He had a tattoo on his neck – Myron couldn't tell what it was – and he was pulling on his cigarette as though he meant to finish it with one inhale.

'Hey,' Myron said, wanting to get his attention, but also afraid that anything too loud might startle the . . . boy? Man? Guy? Kid?

Dog Collar spun toward Myron, trying his best to look tough. There is a certain cringe behind false bravado. Myron saw that here. It usually derives from a person who, one, has been beaten too many times, hence the cringe, and, two, has discovered the hard way that showing weakness makes the beatings even worse, hence the false bravado. The damage – and there was a lot of it here – came off the boy in waves.

'Gotta light?' he asked.

Myron was going to answer that he didn't smoke

or carry a lighter, but maybe asking for a light was some sort of code, so he stepped closer.

'Can we talk for a second?' Myron asked.

Dog Collar's eyes darted like a bird moving from branch to branch. 'I know a place.'

Myron didn't reply. He wondered about the boy's life, about where it had started, about the path it had traveled, about when it started to go wrong. Was this a slow descent, a childhood steeped in abuse maybe, something like that? Was this boy a runaway? Did he have a mother or father? Was he beaten or bored or on drugs? Had the downward spiral been gradual, or had hitting bottom been more sudden – a snap, a scream, one hard, clean blow?

'Well?' the kid said.

Myron took in this skinny kid with his pale, reed-thin arms, a nose that had been busted more than once, the piercings in his ears, the guyliner, that damn dog collar, and he thought about Patrick and Rhys, two boys who had grown up in the lap of luxury and been snatched away.

Did they now look like this boy?

'Yeah,' Myron said, trying not to sound too deflated, 'I'm ready.'

'Follow me.'

Dog Collar headed up the ridge toward the path between the two ponds. Myron wasn't sure if he should keep up and walk side by side with the boy – Myron was guessing his age to be between eighteen and twenty, and that was young enough to still be called a boy – or if he should stay behind him. Dog Collar kept hurrying ahead, so Myron settled for walking behind him.

There had been no request for money yet. That troubled Myron a bit. He kept an eye on his surroundings. They were heading farther up, toward the thicker bushes. There were fewer men around now. Myron turned his attention to Dog Collar. When they walked past a guy wearing camouflage pants, Myron saw a small, almost indiscernible nod pass between the two men.

Uh-oh.

Myron wanted to give Win a little bit of a warning.

'Who's that?' Myron asked.

'Huh?'

'That guy you just nodded at. The guy with the camouflage pants.'

'Don't know what you're talking about.' Then he added, 'You're an American.'

'Yes.'

The kid circled behind a bush. They were completely out of sight now. Myron spotted a used condom on the ground.

'So what are you into?' the kid asked.

'Conversation.'

'What?'

Myron was a big guy, six four, a former collegiate basketball star. He had weighed 215 in his playing days. He was up ten pounds since then. He positioned his body so that Dog Collar couldn't just run off. Myron didn't know if he would use force to stop him, but he didn't want to make it easy either.

'You were there yesterday,' Myron said.

'Huh?'

'When that . . . that incident took place. You saw it.'

'What are you . . . Wait, are you a copper?'

'No.'

'So why would an American . . .?' His voice faded away and his eyes widened. 'Oh, look, I ain't seen nothing.'

Myron wondered whether Win had spoken and if Dog Collar was putting it together like this: An American kills three people – and another American finds the witness.

'I don't care about that,' Myron said. 'I'm looking for the boy who was there. He ran off.'

Dog Collar looked skeptical.

'Look, I'm not here to harm you or anyone else.'

He tried to show Dog Collar his most trust-worthy face, but unlike the throwback street hooker, this kid had probably never seen one. People were either abusers or marks in his world.

'Pull down your trousers,' Dog Collar said.

'What?'

'That's what we're here for, right?'

'No, listen, I'll pay you. I'll pay you a lot.'

That made him pause. 'For?'

'Do you know the boy who ran off?'

'And if I do?'

'I'll pay you five hundred pounds if you bring me to him.'

The eyes started darting again. 'Five hundred?'

'Yes.'

'You have that much on you?'

Uh-oh. But in for a penny, in for a . . .

'Yeah, I do.'

'So you probably have more.'

As though on cue, two guys came around the bush. One was the man in camouflage pants Myron had noticed earlier. The other guy was a big brawler type with a tourniquet-tight black T-shirt, a Cro-Magnon forehead, and arms as big as ham hocks.

The brawler was chewing tobacco like a cow with a cud and playing to type; he was actually cracking his knuckles.

'You're going to give us all your money,' Camouflage Pants said, 'or Dex here is gonna give you a pounding – and then we'll just take it.'

Myron looked at Dex. 'Are you really cracking your knuckles?'

'What?'

'I mean, I get it. You're a tough guy. But cracking your knuckles? It's over the top.'

That confused Dex. He frowned. Myron knew the type. Bar fighter. Takes on smaller guys. Never did battle with anyone who had any kind of skill.

Dex moved into Myron's space. 'You some kind of smart-ass?'

'How many kinds are there?'

'Oh man, oh man, oh man.' Dex actually rubbed his hands together. 'I'm going to so enjoy this.'

'Don't kill him, Dex.'

Dex smiled with tiny pointy teeth like an ocean predator circling a guppy. There was no reason to wait. Myron made his fingers into a spear, cupped his hand slightly, and, leading with the fingers, he struck Dex straight in the throat. The blow landed like a dart.

Dex's hands both went to his neck, leaving him completely exposed. Myron wasn't in the mood to do any serious damage here. He quickly swept the guy's leg, knocking him to the ground. He turned his attention to Camouflage Pants, but he was having none of it. Maybe it was watching his muscle get taken down so easily. Maybe it was the knowledge of what had happened to his haute couture brethren yesterday at the hands of Win. He ran.

So did Dog Collar.

Damn.

Myron was fast, but as he turned, he felt the old injury tighten his knee joint. Between the plane and the car, he'd probably spent too much time sitting. Should have stretched it more during his walk.

Meanwhile the kid moved like a jackrabbit. He had, Myron surmised, been forced to run a lot, and while Myron might normally sympathize, there was no way he was going to let this lead slip away.

He couldn't let Dog Collar get too far ahead of him.

If he got too far ahead – if he found people and civilization – Dog Collar would be safe from whatever Myron wanted to, well, do to him. He might also call out for help. These areas had a way of policing their own.

But then again, would a thief trying to roll a guy in a park like this want to draw attention to himself?

It might not matter. Myron was on the path now too, but the kid already had a substantial lead, and that lead seemed to be widening. If Myron lost him, it would be yet another missed opportunity. The ties to what Win had seen yesterday – the ties to Patrick and Rhys – were tenuous at best. If this kid got away, it could be game over.

Dog Collar veered around the street lamp and out of sight. Damn. No chance, Myron thought. No chance of catching up.

And then Dog Collar went flying.

His legs were up in the air, his body horizontal to the ground. Someone had done the simplest thing in the world.

Someone had stuck out his foot and tripped him. Win.

Dog Collar was splayed on his belly. Myron made the turn. Win barely glanced his way before disappearing into the shadows. Myron hurried over and straddled Dog Collar. He spun him onto his back. Dog Collar covered his face and waited for the blows.

The kid's voice was pitiful. 'Please . . .'

'I'm not going to hurt you,' Myron said. 'Just calm down. It's going to be all right.'

It took another few seconds before he lowered his hands away from his face. There were tears in his eyes now.

'I promise,' Myron said, 'I'm not going to hurt you. Okay?'

The boy nodded through the tears, but you could see he didn't believe a word of it. Myron risked rolling off him. He helped him sit up.

'Let's try this again,' Myron said. 'Do you know the boy who ran away yesterday, the one they were fighting over?'

'The other American,' Dog Collar said. 'He your friend?'

'Does it matter?'

'He killed all three of them, like he was taking a stroll. Just sliced them up without a care.'

Myron tried another avenue. 'Did you know those guys?'

'Course. Terence, Matt, and Peter. Used to beat the shit out of me, all three of them. If I had a pound in my pocket, they wanted me to give them two.' He looked up at Myron. 'If you had something to do with it, well, I'd shake your hand.'

'I didn't,' Myron said.

'You just want the boy they was hassling.'

'Yes.'

'Why?'

'It's a long story. He's in need of rescue.'

Dog Collar frowned.

'Do you know him, yes or no?'

'Yeah,' Dog Collar said. 'Course I know him.'

'Can you take me to him?'

Some wariness came back to the kid's eyes. 'You still got the five hundred pounds?'

'I do.'

'Give it to me now.'

'How do I know you won't run again?'

'Because I saw what your friend did. You'll kill me if I run.'

Myron wanted to tell him that wasn't so, but it probably wouldn't hurt to keep him scared. Dog Collar stuck out his palm. Myron gave him the five hundred pounds. The kid jammed the money into his shoe.

'You won't tell anyone you gave it to me?'

'No.'

'Come on, then. I'll take you to him.'

CHAPTER 6

Myron tried to chat up the kid as they hopped on a train at Gospel Oak. For the first part of the ride, the kid jammed in earphones and turned up the volume so loudly Myron could clearly hear the misogynistic lyrics through the kid's ear canal.

Myron wondered whether the phone's signal could still reach Win. When they changed lines at Highbury and Islington, the kid turned off the music and said, 'What's your name?'

'Myron. What's yours?'

'Myron what?'

'Myron Bolitar.'

'You're pretty good with your fists. Took care of Dex like he was wet tissue.'

Myron wasn't sure what to say to that, so he said, 'Thanks.'

'Where in the States you from?'

Curious question. 'New Jersey.'

'You're a big bloke. You play rugby?'

'No. I . . . I played basketball in school. How about you?'

The kid made a scoffing sound. 'School. Right. Where did you go to school?'

'A university called Duke,' Myron said. 'What's your name?'

'Don't worry about it.'

'How come you're working the streets?' Myron asked.

The kid tried looking tough, but as with most kids, it came out as more sullen than threatening. 'What's it to you?'

'I don't mean it as an insult or anything. I just hear most of the, uh, business is online nowadays. It's on Grindr and Scruff and apps like that.'

The kid lowered his head. 'It's punishment.'

'What's punishment?'

'The streets.'

'For what?'

The train stopped. 'We get off here,' the kid said, rising. 'Come on.'

The street outside the station was crowded and noisy. They headed down Brixton Road, past a Sainsbury's store, and ducked into a shop front called AdventureLand.

The cacophony of sounds, none pleasant except perhaps in a nostalgic way, was the first thing to assault the senses. There was the crash of bowling pins, the digital ding-ding of arcade scoring, the harsh buzzing of missed shots, the mechanical whoop-whoop-whoop of made free throws. There were the artificial noises of virtual planes being struck down and monsters dying under heavily armed assault. There were neon lights and Day-Glo colors. There were Skee-Ball machines and Pac-Man and air hockey and shoot-'em-ups and race-car simulators and those claw cranes trying to snag generic stuffed animals from within a glass cage. There were bumper cars and Ping-Pong and pool tables and a karaoke bar.

There were a lot of teenage boys.

Myron's eyes swept the room. There were two rent-a-cops by the door. They couldn't have looked more bored without some sort of neurosurgery. He didn't pay them much attention. What Myron did notice, almost immediately, were the several men milling about trying to fit in – no, trying to *blend* in.

They wore camouflage pants.

The kid with the dog collar weaved through the crowd toward an area called Laser Maze, which looked like one of those scenes in *Mission: Impossible* where someone tries to move without crossing one of the beams and setting off an alarm. There was a door marked EMERGENCY EXIT behind it. The kid moved over to it and looked up at a surveillance camera. Myron joined him. The kid gestured for Myron to look up into the lens. Myron did so, smiling widely and giving the camera a little wave.

'How do I look?' he asked the kid. 'My hair's a mess, right?'

The kid just turned away.

The door opened. They walked through it. The

door closed. Two more camouflage-pants-clad men were there. Myron pointed at the pants.

'Was there, like, a really big sale on those?'

No one found this amusing.

'You got a weapon on you?'

'Just my winning smile.'

Myron demonstrated. Neither man appeared particularly impressed.

'Empty your pockets. Wallet, keys, phone.'

Myron did so. They even had one of those bowls where you empty your keys and change before heading through airport security. One of the men took out a metal wand and ran it over Myron. That wasn't good enough. He started to pat down Myron with a little too much gusto.

'Oh God, that feels good,' Myron said. 'A little left.'

That made the man stop.

'Okay, second door on the right.'

'Can I have my stuff back?'

'When you come out.'

Myron looked at Dog Collar. Dog Collar kept his eyes on the floor.

'Why do I have a feeling I'm not going to find what I'm looking for behind that door?'

This door too was locked. There was yet another security camera above it. The kid looked up at it. He gestured for Myron to do the same. Myron did it, but this time there was no winning smile. Show them.

There was a clanging noise. The door, made of

reinforced steel, swung open. The kid went inside first. Myron followed.

The first word that came to mind: 'high tech.' Or was that two words? AdventureLand was kind of a dump, with arcade games that had seen better days. This room was sleek and modern. There had to be a dozen, probably more, high-end monitors and screens on the walls, on desks, everywhere. Myron counted four men. None wore camouflage pants.

Standing in the middle of the room was a heavyset Indian man with a shaved head. He wore headphones and held a game controller. They were all playing a military-style shooter video game. While everyone around him frantically attacked their controllers, the heavyset man seemed relaxed, almost casual.

'Shh, give us a second, will you? Those damn Italians think they have us beat.'

The heavyset Indian turned his back to them. All eyes were on the center screen on the far wall. It was a leaderboard in some sort of game, Myron guessed. First place listed ROMAVSLAZIO. Second place was FATGANDHI47. Third place was HUNGSTALLION12. Uh-huh, dream on, gamer boy. Other teams on the leaderboard included UNECHANCEDETROP, GIRTH-VADER (probably a friend of HUNGSTALLION12), and MOMMY'S-BASEMENT (honesty – finally, a self-aware gamer).

The heavyset Indian raised his hand slowly, like a conductor about to begin. He looked over at a thin black man by the keyboard.

'Now!' the heavyset Indian said, lowering his arm.

The thin black man clicked a key.

For a moment, nothing happened. Then the leaderboard changed so that the top name read FATGANDHI47.

The men in the room cheered and high-fived one another. That transitioned to backslaps and hugs. Myron and Dog Collar just stood there until the celebrations slowly wound down. The other three men got back behind their computer terminals. Myron could see the reflections from the screens on their glasses. The big monitor in the middle, the one that had been tracking the leaders, turned to black. As it did, the heavyset Indian turned to Myron.

'Welcome.'

Myron glanced at Dog Collar. The kid looked petrified.

Calling the Indian heavyset was being politically correct. He was rotund, with slabs and slabs of skin and a belly like he'd swallowed a bowling ball. His T-shirt couldn't quite reach his waist and hung out almost like a skirt. His neck fat flowed directly into a smoothly shaved head, so that it looked like one trapezoidal entity. He had a small mustache, wire-rimmed glasses, and a smile that one might mistake for gentle.

'Welcome, Myron Bolitar, to our humble offices.'

'Nice to be here,' Myron said, 'Fat Gandhi.'

This pleased him. 'Ah yes, yes. You saw the leaderboard?'

'I did.'

He spread his arms, his triceps flapping in the no-breeze. 'Does the name not fit?'

'Like a well-tailored sock,' Myron said, even though he had no idea what that meant.

Fat Gandhi turned his gaze toward Dog Collar. The kid withered to the point where Myron felt the need to step in front of him.

'Aren't you going to ask how I know your name?' Fat Gandhi asked.

'The kid asked for it on the subway,' Myron said. 'He also asked me where I was from and where I went to school. I guess you must have been listening in.'

'We were indeed.'

Fat Gandhi offered up another beatific grin, but now – and maybe this was just his imagination – Myron could see the decay behind it.

'Do you think only you can use your phone as a listening device?'

Myron said nothing.

Fat Gandhi snapped his fingers. A map appeared on the big screen. There were blinking blue dots all over it. 'All of my employees carry such phones. We can use them as listening devices, as GPSs, to page. We can keep track of all our employees at all times.' He pointed at the blue dots on the screen. 'When we get a match on one of our apps – let us say one of our clients has a desire for a malnourished white male with a studded dog collar . . .'

The kid started to shake.

'. . . we know where such an employee is and can arrange a meeting at any time. We can also listen in if we wish. We can discover if there is any danger. Or' – and now the smile looked positively predatory – 'we can see if we are being cheated.'

The kid reached into his shoe, pulled out the five hundred pounds, and held it out toward Fat Gandhi. Fat Gandhi didn't take it. The kid put the money on one of the desks. Then he actually slid behind Myron. Myron let him.

Fat Gandhi turned toward the map. He spread his hands again. The other men in the room kept their heads down and typed.

'This is our nerve center.'

Nerve center, Myron thought. This guy should be petting a hairless cat. He sounded like a Bond villain.

He looked over his shoulder at Myron. 'Do you know why I don't fear telling you all this?'

'Is it my trusting face? That's come in handy tonight.'

'No.' He spun back toward Myron. 'It's because there is nothing you could really do. You've noticed the security. Sure, the authorities could eventually get in, maybe whoever is on the other end of your smartphone even. By the way, one of my men is driving around with your phone. Just to make it all the more fun, no?'

'Sounds like big laughs.'

'But here is the thing, Myron. May I call you Myron?'

'Sure. Should I call you Fat?'

'Ha-ha. I like you, Myron Bolitar.'

'Great.'

'Myron, you may have noticed that we have no hard drives in here. Everything – all of the information on our clients, our employees, our dealings – is kept in a cloud. So if someone comes in, we press a button, and voilà' – Fat Gandhi snapped his fingers – 'there is nothing to be found.'

'Clever.'

'I tell you this not to boast.'

'Oh?'

'I want you to understand with whom you are dealing before we do business. Just as it is my responsibility to know who I am dealing with.'

He snapped his fingers again.

When the screen came back on, Myron almost groaned out loud.

'Once we heard your name, it didn't take long to learn much more.' Fat Gandhi pointed to the screen. Someone had paused the video on the title:

THE COLLISION: THE MYRON BOLITAR STORY

'We've been watching your documentary, Myron. It's very moving.'

If you were a sports fan of a certain age, you knew the 'legend' of Myron Bolitar, former first-round draft pick of the Boston Celtics. If you were not, or if you were younger or foreign like these guys, well, thanks to a recent sports documentary on ESPN called *The Collision* going viral, you still knew more than you should.

Fat Gandhi snapped his fingers again, and the video started playing.

'Yeah,' Myron said, 'I've already seen it.'

'Oh, come, come. Don't be so modest.'

The documentary started off optimistically enough: tinkling music, bright sunshine, cheers from the crowd. Somehow they had gotten clips of Myron playing AAU ball as a sixth grader. Then it moved on. Myron Bolitar had been a high school basketball superstar from Livingston, New Jersey. During his years at Duke University, his legend grew. He was a consensus All-American, a two-time NCAA champion, and even College Player of the Year.

The tinkling music swelled.

When the Boston Celtics picked him in the first round of the NBA draft, Myron's dreams, it seemed, had all come true.

And then, as the documentary voice-over of doom intoned, 'Tragedy struck . . .'

Sudden stop on the tinkling music. Cue something more ominous.

'Tragedy struck' in the third quarter of Myron's very first preseason game, the first – and last – time he would don the green Celtics uniform number 34. The Celtics were playing the Washington Bullets. Up until that point, Myron's debut had lived up to the hype. He had eighteen points. He was fitting in, clicking on all cylinders, lost in the sweet, sweaty bliss he found only on a basketball court, and then . . .

The *Collision* filmmakers must have shown the 'horrific' replay two dozen times from a variety of angles. They showed it at regular speed. They showed it in slow motion. They showed it from Myron's vantage point, from above, from courtside. Didn't matter. The result was always the same.

Rookie Myron Bolitar had his head turned when Big Burt Wesson, a journeyman power forward, blindsided him. Myron's knee twisted in a way neither God nor anatomy ever intended. Even from a distance you could actually hear a nauseating sound like a wet snap.

Bye-bye, career.

'Watching this,' Fat Gandhi said with an exaggerated pout, 'made us sad.' He looked around. 'Didn't it, lads?'

Everyone, even Dog Collar, quickly mimicked the pout. They all then stared at Myron.

'Yeah, I'm over it.'

'Are you?'

'Man plans and God laughs,' Myron said.

Fat Gandhi smiled. 'I like that one. Is that an American expression?'

'Yiddish.'

'Ah. In Hindi, we say knowledge is bigger than debate. You see? So first, we learned your name.

Then we watched your documentary, we broke into your email—'

'You what?'

'There was nothing very interesting, but we haven't finished. We also checked your phone records. Your mobile phone received a call from an untraceable number whilst in New York City fewer than twenty-four hours ago. The call originated from London.' He put out his hands, palms up. 'And now you are here. With us.'

'Thorough,' Myron said.

'We try to be.'

'So you know why I'm here.'

'We do.'

'And?'

'I assume you are working for the boy's family?'

'Does it matter?'

'Not really. We do rescues, of course. It is all a matter of profit, to tell you the truth. I learned this from the great Eshan, who had a religion – you'd call it a cult – outside Varanasi in India. He was a wonderful man. He spoke of peace and harmony and charity. He was so charismatic. Teenagers flocked to him and gave his temple all their earthly possessions. They lived in tents on well-guarded barren land. Sometimes the parents wanted their child back. The great Eshan would accommodate. He wouldn't ask too much – never be too greedy, he would say – but if he could receive from the parents more than he could make from having their child work or beg or recruit, he would take the money. I am no different. If one of my workers makes the most contribution working sex, that is what he or she does. If the worker is best suited for robbery, as our friend Garth attempted with you, that is where we place him.'

Man, this guy liked to talk.

'How much?'

'One hundred thousand pounds cash for each boy.'

Myron did not reply.

'This amount is nonnegotiable.'

'I'm not negotiating.'

'Wonderful. How long will it take you to raise this sum?'

'You can have it immediately,' Myron said. 'Where are the boys?'

'Come, come. You don't have that kind of cash on you.'

'I can get it within an hour.'

Fat Gandhi smiled. 'I should have asked for more.'

'Never be too greedy. Like the great Eshan said.'

'Are you familiar with Bitcoin?'

'Not really.'

'Doesn't matter. Our transaction will be via cybercurrency.'

'I don't know what that is either.'

'Get the cash. You'll be instructed what to do.'

'When?'

'Tomorrow,' Fat Gandhi said. 'I will call you and set it up.'

'Sooner is better.'

'Yes, I understand. But you should also understand, Myron. If you try to circumvent our arrangement in any manner, I will kill the boys and they will never be found. I will kill them slowly and painfully and there will not be an ash left. Do I make myself clear?'

An ash? 'You do,' Myron said.

'Then you can go.'

'One thing.'

Fat Gandhi waited.

'How do I know this isn't a scam?'

'You question my word?'

Myron shrugged. 'I'm just asking.'

'Perhaps it is a scam,' Fat Gandhi said. 'Perhaps you shouldn't bother coming back tomorrow.'

'I'm not trying to play chicken here. You' – Myron pointed at him – 'you are smart enough to get that.'

Fat Gandhi stroked his chin and nodded.

Psychos, Myron knew, fall for flattery almost every time.

'I just think,' Myron continued, 'for that kind of money, a little evidence would be nice. How do I know you have the boys?'

Fat Gandhi raised his hand again and snapped his fingers.

The documentary disappeared from the screen.

For a moment, there was only black. Myron thought that maybe they had shut off the television.

But no, that wasn't it. Fat Gandhi moved toward a keyboard and slowly started tapping the brightness button. The screen started to light up now. Myron could see a room with concrete walls.

And there, in the center of the room, was Patrick.

His eyes were black. His lip was swollen and bloody.

'He's being held off-site,' Fat Gandhi said.

Myron tried to keep his voice steady. 'What did you do to him?'

Fat Gandhi snapped his fingers again. The screen went dark.

Myron stared at the blackness. 'What about the other boy?'

'I think that's enough. It is time for you to leave.'

Myron met his eye. 'We have a deal now.'

'We do.'

'So I don't want anyone touching either one of them. I want your word.'

'And you won't get it,' Fat Gandhi said. 'I'll contact you tomorrow. Now please get out of my office.'

CHAPTER 7

Last time they were in London, Win had put them in his favorite suite, the Davies, at Claridge's Hotel on Brook Street. That trip had ended poorly for all of them. This time, maybe to change it up a bit, Win chose the more boutiquey Covent Garden Hotel on Monmouth Street near Seven Dials. When Myron got to his room, he used a throwaway phone Win had given him to call Terese.

'You okay?' she asked.

'I'm fine.'

'I don't like this.'

'I know.'

'There's been too much of this in our past.'

'I agree.'

'We wanted to put this all behind us.'

'We did. We do.'

'I don't do the wait-and-worry wife well.'

'Nice alliteration. The two *D*'s and then all those *W*'s.'

'Years of being a top-rated news anchor,' Terese said. 'Not that I like to brag.'

'Alliteration is only one of your many skills.'

70

'You can't help yourself, can you?'

'Love me for all my faults.'

'What else is there? Okay, so fill me in. And please don't make the obvious double-entendre joke using my "fill me in" opening.'

'Opening?'

'I love you, you know.'

'I love you too,' Myron said.

And then he told her everything.

When he was done, Terese said, 'He likes being called Fat Gandhi?'

'Loves.'

'It's like you and Win live in an old Humphrey Bogart film.'

'I'm too young to get that reference.'

'You wish. So you'll be doing the ransom drop?'

'Yes.'

Silence.

'I've been thinking,' Myron said.

'Uh-huh.'

'About the families, I mean. The parents, mostly.'

'You mean Patrick's and Rhys's.'

'Yes.'

Silence.

'And,' she said, 'you want my expert opinion on the matter.'

Terese had lost a child many years ago. It had nearly destroyed her.

'I shouldn't have brought it up.'

'Wrong response,' she said. 'If you tiptoe around it, it's much worse.'

'I want to start a family with you.'

'I want that too.'

'So how do we do it?' Myron asked. 'When you love something that much. How do you live with the fear that they can be hurt or killed at any time?'

'I could tell you that that's life,' Terese said.

'You could.'

'Or I could point out, what choice do you have?'

'I hear a "but" coming,' Myron said.

'You do. But I think there's another answer, one that took me a long time to understand.'

'And that is?'

'We block,' Terese said.

Myron waited. Nothing. 'That's it?'

'You expected something deeper?'

'Maybe.'

'We block,' she said, 'or we would never be able to get out of bed.'

'I love you,' he said again.

'I love you too. And so if I lose you, I will experience crippling pain. You get that, right?'

'I do.'

'If you want to experience love, then you have to be ready for pain. One doesn't come without the other. If I didn't love you, I wouldn't have to worry about losing you. If you want laughter, expect tears.'

'Makes sense,' Myron said. Then: 'You know what?'

'Tell me.'

'You're worth it.'

'That's the point.'

Myron heard the key in the door. Win stepped into the room. Myron said his good-byes and hung up the phone.

'How is she?' Win asked.

'Concerned.'

'Let's hit a pub, shall we? I'm famished.'

They started down toward Seven Dials. *Matilda the Musical* was playing at the Cambridge Theatre.

'I always wanted to see that,' Myron said.

'Pardon?'

'*Matilda*.'

'Now doesn't seem the time.'

'I was joking.'

'Yes, I know. Your humor is your defense mechanism. It's a very engaging personality quirk.' Win started to cross the street. 'And the show is eh.'

'Wait, you saw it?'

Win kept walking.

'You saw a musical without me?'

'Here we are.'

'You hate musicals. I even had to drag you to see *Rent*.'

Win didn't reply. Seven Dials was, per the name, seven roads converging clocklike, producing seven corners around a circle. There was a sundial column maybe three stories high in the middle of the circle. One corner housed the Cambridge Theatre. A small pub called the Crown was wedged on another. That was where Win entered now.

The Crown was old-school, complete with a polished bar and dark wood paneling and, despite having about three feet of throwing space, a dartboard. The place was cozy and cramped and packed with standing patrons. Win caught the barman's eye. The bartender nodded, bodies parted, space cleared, and suddenly there were two stools open. Two pints of Fuller's London Pride awaited them on beer coasters.

Win sat on one stool, Myron on the other. Win raised his stein. 'Cheers, mate.'

They clinked mugs. Two minutes later, the barman threw down two orders of fish and chips. The smell made Myron's stomach rumble with joy.

'I thought this place didn't serve food,' Myron noted.

'It doesn't.'

'You're a beautiful man, Win.'

'Yes. Yes, I am.'

They enjoyed the dinner and drinks. Whatever else Win had to say could wait. Somewhere along the way, they finished the fish and chips and ordered a second round. There was a rugby match on the television. Myron didn't know much about rugby, but he still watched the screen.

'So our friend Fat Gandhi,' Win said. 'He saw your documentary on ESPN?'

'Yes.' Myron turned toward him. 'Have you seen it?'

'Of course.'

Dumb question.

'I'm curious, though,' Win said, 'about your reaction.'

Myron shrugged into his beer mug. 'I thought it was accurate enough.'

'You gave them an interview.'

'Yep.'

'You never did that before. Talked about the injury.'

'True.'

'You wouldn't even watch replays of what happened.'

'True.'

It had been too overwhelming to watch. Normal, right? Your dream, your life goal, everything you ever wanted – it's there, in your grasp at the age of twenty-two, and snap, lights out, buh-bye, it's over, *nada mas*.

'I didn't see the point,' Myron said.

'And now?'

Myron took a deep swill of the ale. 'They kept saying that this injury "defined" me.'

'At one point, it did.'

'Exactly. At one point. But not anymore. Now I could finally watch Burt Wesson slam into me, and I felt little more than a ping. The stupid narrator. He kept saying the injury' – Myron made quote marks with his fingers – ' "destroyed my life." But now I know it was just a fork in the road. All those guys I started out with, all those superstars who made it and had successful NBA careers – they're all retired now. The light went out for them too.'

'But in the meantime,' Win said, 'they scored boatloads of chicks.'

'Well, yes, there's that.'

'And the light didn't snap off for them. It dimmed.'

'Slowly,' Myron said.

'Yes.'

'Maybe that makes it harder.'

'How so?'

'You rip off the bandage all at once versus slowly peeling it away.'

Win took a sip of his beer. 'Fair point.'

'I could also add the cliché about being thrown into the deep end. The suddenness forced me to act. It made me go to law school. It made me become a sports agent.'

'It didn't "make" you,' Win said.

'No?'

'You were always a competitive – nay, overly ambitious – son of a bitch.'

Myron smiled at that and raised his mug. 'Cheers, mate.'

Win again clinked his glass, cleared his throat, and said, '*Der mentsh trakht un got lakht.*'

'Wow,' Myron said.

'I taught myself the Yiddish,' said the blond-haired, blue-eyed Anglo-Saxon. 'It does wonders when I hit on Jewish chicks.'

Der mentsh trakht un got lakht. Translation: Man plans and God laughs.

Man, it was good to be back with Win.

They both went quiet for a moment. They were both thinking the same thing.

'Maybe the injury isn't such a big deal anymore,' Myron said, 'because I know there are a lot of worse things in life.'

Win nodded. 'Patrick and Rhys.'

'What do you know about cybercurrency?'

'Ransoms are sometimes paid with it, but with all the recent antilaundering laws now, it is extraordinarily difficult. My expert says that you have to buy the currency, put it in some kind of online wallet, and then transfer it to them. It's part of the dark web.'

'Do you understand what that means?'

'I told you. I'm an expert in nearly anything.'

Myron waited.

'But no, I don't have a clue.'

'We may be getting old.'

Win's phone buzzed. He checked it. 'I'm getting information on our friend Fat Gandhi from a constable friend.'

'And?'

'His real name is Chris Alan Weeks.'

'For real?'

'Age twenty-nine. The authorities know about him, but according to this, he mostly works on the dark web.'

'That term again.'

'He dabbles in prostitution, sexual slavery, robbery, blackmail . . .'

'Dabbles?'

'My term, not theirs. And . . . ah, no surprise. He's into computer hacking. His syndicate operates several online money scams.'

'You mean like a Nigerian prince wants to give you all his money?'

'A tad more sophisticated, I'm afraid. Fat Gandhi – I prefer his nom de plume if you don't mind.'

'I don't.'

'Fat Gandhi is good with computers. He matriculated and graduated from Oxford. As we both know, law enforcement hates referring to criminals as "geniuses" or "masterminds" – but our cherubic friend seems pretty close to being both. Hmm.'

'What?'

'Fat Gandhi also has a reputation for being – and this is their phraseology – "creatively violent."'

Win stopped and smiled.

'He sounds a bit like you,' Myron said.

'Ergo my smile.'

'Is he into kidnapping?'

'Human trafficking is slavery for the purposes of sexual exploitation. By definition, that's kidnapping.' Win held up a hand before Myron could interrupt. 'But if you mean grabbing wealthy children for the purpose of making them sexual slaves, no, there is no indication he does that. Plus, Fat Gandhi would have been nineteen when the kidnappings occurred. By all accounts he was studying at Oxford at that time.'

'So any theories about how Patrick and Rhys ended up with him?'

Win shrugged. 'Several. The original kidnapper sold them off. The boys could have changed hands dozens of times over the past ten years. He may not be their first predator.'

'Ugh.'

'Yes, ugh. It could be that Patrick and Rhys were somehow runaways living on the streets. A parasite like Fat Gandhi gets them that way too. Offers them work. Helps them get strung out and thus hooked on drugs, so that they have to earn. There are a dozen ways it could have gone down.'

'None of them good,' Myron said.

'None that I can think of, no. But as we've learned, people, especially the young, are resilient. Right now, we concentrate on rescuing them.'

Myron stared in his beer. 'You saw Patrick on the street.'

'Yes.'

'If he had that kind of freedom—'

'Why didn't he call home?' Win finished for him. 'You know the answer. Stockholm syndrome, fear, he could have been watched, or perhaps he doesn't remember his old life. He was six when he was taken.'

Myron nodded. 'What else?'

'I have people casing the arcade.'

'For?'

Win didn't answer. 'One of my people will follow Fat Gandhi when he leaves. The money will be arriving in approximately ten minutes. Our rooms are adjoining. When he calls you, we move. Other than that . . .'

'We wait.'

The call came in at four A.M.

Myron scrambled out of sleep and reached for the phone. Win appeared in the doorway, still dressed. He nodded for Myron to answer and held his duplicate phone to his ear.

'Good morning, Mr Bolitar.'

It was Fat Gandhi. He had done this on purpose, the four A.M. call. Myron understood. He was trying to catch Myron off guard, in the middle of a sleep cycle. He hoped to find Myron disoriented and just slightly off his game. Classic move.

'Hey,' Myron said.

'Do you have the money?'

'I do.'

'Lovely. Please go to the NatWest Bank on Fulham Palace Road.'

'Now?'

'As soon as possible, yes.'

'It's four in the morning.'

'I am aware. There is an employee named Denise Nussbaum, who will be standing by the door. Go to her. She will help you open an account and make the proper deposit.'

'I'm not following.'

'You will, if you listen. Go where I tell you. Denise Nussbaum will give you wiring instructions.'

'You expect me to wire the money to you before I get the boys?'

'No. I expect you to do what I say. The boys will show up once the account is open. When you see them, you will complete the wire transfer to our cybercurrency account. Then you get the boys.'

Myron looked over at Win. Win nodded at him.

'Okay,' Myron said.

'What, Mr Bolitar, you prefer the old-fashioned way? Did you think I would make you use various red telephone boxes and jump on the Underground and perhaps drop the ransom off in a hollow tree?' Fat Gandhi chuckled. 'You watch too much television, my friend.'

Oh boy. 'Are we done?'

'Not so fast, Mr Bolitar. I have a few more, shall we say, requests.'

Myron waited.

'Bring no weaponry of any kind.'

'Okay.'

'You come alone. You will be followed and watched. We realize that you have some sort of backup in this country. Other people working with you. If we see any of them within smelling distance of this transaction, there will be consequences.'

'Now who's the one watching too much television?'

Fat Gandhi liked that one. 'You don't want to cross me, mate.'

'I won't,' Myron said.

'Good.'

'But one thing.'

'Yes?'

'I know you're scary and all,' Myron said. 'But so are we.'

Myron waited for a reply, but the phone went dead. Myron and Win exchanged a glance.

'Did he hang up?' Win asked.

'Yes.'

'Rude.'

CHAPTER 8

They sat in the back of the stretch Bentley. Win had put the money in a rather elegant leather suitcase. Myron read the label.

'A Swaine Adeney Brigg bag for a ransom drop?'

'I had nothing cheaper on hand.'

'Do you know Fulham Palace Road?' Myron asked.

'Not well.'

'So where should we drop me off so we won't be seen?'

'Behind Claridge's Hotel.'

'That's near this bank?'

'No. It's approximately a twenty- to twenty-five-minute ride.'

'I'm not following.'

'I switched out your phone last night.'

'Right, I know.'

'When your rotund friend from the arcade temporarily confiscated said phone, he put a tracking chip into it.'

'For real?'

'Yes.'

'So he's been keeping tabs on my location.'

'Well, not yours, of course. I had one of my men bring the phone to Claridge's. He checked into the hotel under the alias of Myron Bolitar.'

'Did my alias stay in the Davies Suite?'

'No.'

'My alias is used to luxury.'

'Finished?'

'Just about. So Fat Gandhi thinks I'm at Claridge's?'

'Yes. You'll go in through the side employee entrance. My man will give you back your phone. He will also place two listening devices on your person.'

'Two?'

'Depending on where you go, they may search you again. They probably won't find both.'

Myron understood. When Win put tracking devices on cars, he always put one under the bumper – where it could easily be found – and one in a more difficult space to find.

'Use the same safe word,' Win said.

'Articulate.'

'Yes, very nice that you remember.' Win turned and looked at Myron full on. 'Use it even if you do not believe it will do any good.'

'Huh?'

'We've spent the evening with eyes on the arcade,' Win said. 'Your chum Fat Gandhi has not left. No one matching either Patrick's or Rhys's description has entered.'

'Theories?'

'He may be holding them in the arcade. We've seen signs of' – Win paused, tapped his lip with his finger – 'signs of life coming from the basement.'

'Like there's someone down there?'

'Like there's more than one someone down there.'

'You using a thermal scanner?'

'We are, but the basement walls are thick. Still . . .'

'What?'

Win shook it off. The car stopped.

'My man is directly inside on the left. Go in, get your phone, get wired up, catch a taxi to that address on Fulham Palace Road.'

Myron did as Win asked. He had brief flashbacks to his last time in the hotel, to the death and destruction and mayhem that followed, but he pushed them away. Myron didn't recognize the man who helped him. The man went about his tasks in silence. First, he put a listening device on Myron's chest under his shirt.

'Yikes, that's cold,' Myron said.

Nothing.

The man put the second device inside Myron's shoe. Myron headed out the front door. A uniformed doorman complete with top hat said, 'May I help you, sir?'

Gripping the money bag a touch too tightly, Myron did his subtle scan, searching for someone suspicious who might be watching him. There was no one out on the streets yet – no guy leaning against a wall pretending to read a paper or stopping to tie his shoelaces or anything like that.

The only thing maybe worth noting: a gray car with tinted windows down the block on his left.

'Taxi, please.'

The doorman blew a whistle, even though a black Hackney carriage was a car's length from where Myron stood. He made a big production of opening the door for Myron. Myron fumbled for some change, didn't have any, gave the doorman a hopeless shrug. The doorman seemed unimpressed. Myron slid into the back, digging the legroom, and gave the driver the bank's address on Fulham Palace Road.

After three blocks it was clear to Myron that the gray car was following him. Myron knew the line was open between him and Win so that Win could hear everything. But there was no reason to play games with that yet. Myron picked up the phone and put it to his ear.

'You there?'

'I am.'

'There's a gray car following me,' Myron said.

'Make?'

'I don't know. I'm not good with cars. You know that.'

'Describe, please.'

'The logo looks like an aggressive lion standing.'

'Gray Peugeot. It's French. You love the French.'

'Indeed I do.'

Despite its being five A.M., Fulham Palace Road

still had plenty of traffic. The taxi dropped Myron off in front of the NatWest Bank. It was, of course, closed. Myron paid the driver and stepped out. The taxi drove off. Myron stood in front of the bank, holding the bag of cash. The bills were 'marked' – that is, Win knew the serial numbers on them – but Fat Gandhi had not asked for unmarked bills. Or was that another movie trope? Who checked the serial numbers of bills when you spent money?

After a full minute of standing like a dope, Myron's cell phone rang. The number was blocked, but it had to be Fat Gandhi. Myron picked it up, put on a bad fake British accent, and intoned in his best Alfred the butler, 'Wayne Manor. I'll summon him, sir.'

'A Batman reference,' Fat Gandhi said with a chortle. 'Who was your favorite? Christian Bale, right?'

'There is only one Batman, and his name is Adam West.'

'Who?'

Today's youth.

'Do you see the gray car with the tinted windows?' Fat Gandhi asked him.

'The Peugeot,' Myron said, showing off his new car knowledge.

'Yes. Get in.'

'What about Denise Nussbaum at the bank?'

Fat Gandhi hung up.

The car pulled up. The thin black guy from the

arcade's back room opened up the back door and said, 'Let's go, mate.'

Myron checked the car. One driver. One thin guy.

'Where are the two boys?'

'I'm taking you to them.'

Thin Guy slid over, making room for Myron. Myron hesitated but got in. Next to him, the thin black guy was on a laptop. 'Give me your phone,' he said.

'No.'

'It won't do you any good anyway.' He smiled widely. 'I got your cell jammed.'

'Pardon?'

He smiled at Myron. 'This here laptop? I'm using it to scramble your signal. So like yesterday, when you had all that data going back and forth between you and whoever was listening? Well, he can't hear you anymore. Oh, and if you put any kind of wire or listening device on yourself? Same thing.'

'Just so I'm clear,' Myron said, 'your laptop is cutting off all signals?'

The guy's grin grew. 'Exactly.'

Myron nodded. Then he slid open the car window, snatched the laptop from the skinny guy's hands, and tossed it out the window.

'Hey! What the—?' He looked out the back window to where his smashed laptop lay, guts split open. 'Are you for real? Do you know how much that cost?'

'A billion pounds?'

88

'This ain't funny, mate.'

'I'm sure it's not. Now, enough games. Call Fat Gandhi.'

The kid looked as though he might cry. 'Ah, you didn't have to do that,' he said in a high-pitched whine. 'I was just doing what I was told.'

'Now do what I'm telling you. Call Fat Gandhi. Tell him I got the money. I want the boys.'

His shoulders dropped. 'You know how much that laptop cost me?'

'I don't care. If you piss me off again, I'm going to throw you out that window. Now, call him.'

'No need to call.' He pointed toward the front windshield. 'We're here. Couldn't you have just been patient?'

Myron looked out the window. That same arcade was up the block.

The Peugeot cruised to a stop. Myron got out without bothering to apologize. Two guys in camouflage pants opened the door. The skinny kid followed, pleading his case. 'The bastard threw my bleeding laptop out the window!'

It felt as though someone had pulled the plug on the entire arcade, which, for all Myron knew, was exactly what had happened. No sounds, no lights, no movement. The entire arcade, so bursting with furious light and color a few hours ago, seemed shades of gray now. With all the machines off, their shadowy outlines felt odd, menacing, grotesque. There was an almost postapocalyptic feel to the whole place.

'Let's go,' Pants One said to Myron.

'Where?'

'Back room.'

Myron didn't like this. 'The place is deserted. We can make the exchange out here.'

'That's not how it works,' Pants Two said.

'Then I think I'll leave.'

'Then I think' – Pants One crossed his arms and tried to flex his biceps – 'the two of us will beat the hell out of you and take the money anyway.'

Myron's grip on the bag tightened. He could take them both out, no problem – he was actually rehearsing his first strike in his head – but then what? For better or worse, he had to play it out. So he followed the same path he'd taken the last time he was here, when Dog Collar was with him, and stopped at the exit door.

There was the surveillance camera by the door again. Myron looked up, gave it a bright smile and cheery thumbs-up. Mr Confident. Rule 14 of ransom drops: Never let the bad guys see you worried. The door opened. The Camouflage Pants Guys emptied Myron's pockets. The wand found the listening device on his chest.

They were about to take the device off him when Fat Gandhi opened the door to the back room, stuck his head out, and said, 'No weapons?'

'None.'

'It's fine, then; let him keep the rest.'

Myron didn't know if that was a good thing or not.

He entered that same room with all the computers and flat-screens. The skinny black kid was already back at his station. 'He broke my bleeding laptop!' he cried out, pointing at Myron. 'Just threw out it out the window like it was last week's rubbish.'

Fat Gandhi was resplendent in what looked to be a yellow zoot suit. 'The cash is in that bag?'

'It isn't in my underwear,' Myron said.

Fat Gandhi frowned at the joke, which was fair.

'There is someone listening on the other end of your phone,' Fat Gandhi said.

Myron didn't bother denying or agreeing.

'There is only one entrance into this lair,' Fat Gandhi said. 'Do you understand?'

'Did you just call this a lair?'

'We have cameras everywhere. Derek and Jimmy, raise your hands.'

Two guys staring at their monitors raised their hands.

'Derek and Jimmy are watching the surveillance cameras. If someone tries to get in, we will see them. The two doors you entered to arrive here are steel reinforced, but you probably know that already. In short, there is no way anyone could get into this room in time to save you, even if they were fast and heavily armed.'

No fear. Show no fear. 'Yeah, okay, cool. Can we move this along now? You said something about cybercurrency.'

'No.'

'No, you didn't say—'

'It makes no sense, Mr Bolitar. You'd have to get the Bitcoin or more fashionable assorted cybercurrency in the first place. Then I would have to give you a long public key address, which is basically the equivalent of a unique bank account. You would then transfer the money via a network, and, poof, gone. That was how I originally planned to make the exchange.'

'But not anymore?'

'No, not anymore. See, it works fine for small amounts, but something this big, well, it would be tracked. Cybercurrency is too public nowadays. You want to know the truth?' He leaned in as though to whisper something conspiratorial. 'I think cybercurrency has turned into a giant sting operation so law enforcement can gather intel on the black market. So I started thinking. Why do Somali pirates always demand cash?'

He looked at Myron as though he expected an answer. Myron figured that if he didn't reply, maybe the guy would stop talking.

'Because cash is easiest, simplest, and best.'

Fat Gandhi reached out for the bag.

'Hold up,' Myron said, 'we had a deal.'

'You don't trust my word?'

'This is how it will go,' Myron said, trying to take some semblance of control. 'The two boys leave here. They go outside. Once they are outside, I give you the money.'

'Go where outside?'

'You said you knew someone was listening to us.'

'Go on.'

'He knows where I am. So he'll pull up in a car. The boys go in the car, I give you the money, then I leave.'

Fat Gandhi made a tsk-tsk noise. 'That won't work.'

'Why not?'

'Because I told you something of an untruth.'

Myron said nothing.

'Your friend is not listening to you. All devices, including our own cell phones, are jammed right now. That is how this room is designed. Just to be completely safe. Our advanced Wi-Fi is working, but it's password protected. You're not on it, I'm afraid. So whatever devices you may have hidden in whatever crevices are completely useless.'

The fingers typing on the keyboards seemed to slow down a bit.

'Doesn't matter,' Myron said.

'Say again?'

'I smashed your friend's laptop.'

Thin Guy: 'Cost me a fortune! The bastard—'

'Quiet, Lester.' Fat Gandhi turned back toward Myron. 'So?'

'So the phone wasn't jammed when I arrived. My people know I'm here. They'll be waiting outside. You send the two boys out; they'll pick them up. Easy, right?'

Myron gave them all Smile 19: The 'We're All Friends Here' deluxe.

Fat Gandhi stuck his hand out. 'Give me the bag, please.'

'Give me the kids.'

He waved his chubby hand, his bracelet tight on his wrist, and the big flat-screen on the wall lit up.

'Happy?'

It was the cell again. The two boys were seated on the floor, their knees up, their heads down.

'Where are they?'

Fat Gandhi's smile felt like a dozen snakes running down your back.

'I'll show you. Wait here, please.'

Fat Gandhi pressed a code into the door's keypad, making sure that Myron couldn't see him. He stepped out of the room. Two more camouflaged guys stepped in as he left.

Hmm, why?

The room grew quiet. The typing came to a stop. Myron tried to read their faces.

Something wasn't right.

Two minutes later, Myron heard Fat Gandhi's voice say, 'Mr Bolitar?'

He was on the big flat-screen now.

In the cell with the two boys.

Win had gotten it right. They were being held right here in the arcade.

'Bring them out,' Myron said.

Fat Gandhi just smiled into the camera. 'Derek?'

One of the guys said, 'I'm here.'

'Any movements on the surveillance cameras?' Fat Gandhi asked.

'None.'

Fat Gandhi waved his finger. 'No cavalry on their way to rescue you, Mr Bolitar.'

Uh-oh.

'Rescue me from what?'

'You killed three of my men.'

The temperature in the room changed, not in a good way. Everyone started moving slowly.

'I didn't have anything to do with that.'

'Please, Mr Bolitar. Lying is beneath you.'

Pants One took out a large knife. So did Pants Two.

'Do you see my dilemma, Mr Bolitar? It would have been one thing if you and your partners had approached me in a respectful manner.'

A third guy rose from behind his computer. He also had a knife.

Myron tried to work it through. *Grab Pants One's knife, then go after the guy on the right . . .*

'You could have come to us. Like businessmen. You could have asked for a fair exchange. An arrangement. We could have worked with you . . .'

No, that wouldn't work. Too much distance between them. And the door is locked . . .

'But you didn't do that, Mr Bolitar. Instead you slaughtered three of my men.'

Derek took a knife out. Jimmy too.

Then the skinny kid produced a machete.

Six guys, all armed, in a small room.

'How can I let you just walk out of here after

95

that? How would it look? How could my men ever trust me to take care of them?'

Maybe duck down, throw a back kick . . . but no. Have to get the machete first. But he's farther away. Too many of them, the space too tight.

'I would stay in the room and observe the outcome, but in this suit? It's new and rather lovely.'

There was no chance. They started coming closer.

'Articulate!' Myron shouted.

Everyone stopped for a second. Myron dropped to the floor and braced himself.

That was when the wall exploded.

The sound was deafening. The wall gave way as though the Incredible Hulk had burst through from the street. The others were caught off guard, Myron not so much. He knew that Win would come up with something. He had figured that Win would find a way past the cameras. He hadn't. He said he had cased the place last night. He had found the exterior wall to this room. He had probably placed a strong listening device on it, so he would know when to make a move.

Had he used some sort of dynamite or rocket-propelled grenade?

Myron didn't know.

Shock and awe, baby. Win's forte.

The guys in the room didn't know what hit them. But they would.

Myron moved fast. From his position on the

floor, he snaked his leg out and took one of the guys down. It was Pants Two. Myron grabbed the man's knife hand. Pants Two, running on pure survival instinct, held on tight. That was okay. Myron counted on that. He had no intention of trying to wrestle the knife away. Instead, holding the man by the wrist, Myron jerked his hand upward.

The blade, still being gripped by the guy's hand, lodged into Pants Two's throat.

Blood spurted. And the hand dropped away.

The knife made a noise like a wet, sucking pop as Myron pulled it free. The rest was pandemonium. The dust from the collapsed wall made it difficult to see. Myron could hear coughing and shouts. The commotion must have gotten the attention of the guy standing guard in the corridor.

When he opened the door, Myron was on him. He landed a punch straight to the nose, driving the man back into the corridor. Myron stayed on him. He didn't want to kill anyone else if he didn't have to. He threw another punch. The guy staggered back against the wall. Myron grabbed him by the throat and placed the tip of the bloody knife right up against the guy's eye.

'Please!'

'How do I get to the basement?'

'The door on the left. Code 8787.'

Myron punched the guy in the stomach, let him slide to the floor, and ran. He found the door, hit the code, pushed it open.

The first thing that hit him, almost knocking him back, was the stench.

There are few things that cause déjà vu like powerful odors. Something like that was happening here. Myron was traveling back to his basketball days, to the stink of a locker room after a game, the wheeled laundry carts loaded up with the sweat-filled socks, shirts, and athletic supporters of adolescents. The smell had been awful, but after a game or practice, when it was something as pure as previously clean boys playing basketball, there had been an underlying sweetness that made the smell, if not pleasant, tolerable.

That wasn't the case here.

It was dirt filled and rancid and bad.

When Myron looked down from the top of the stairs, he couldn't believe what he saw.

Twenty, maybe thirty teenagers were scampering like rats when you hit them with a flashlight beam.

What the . . .?

The basement looked like a bad refugee camp. There were cots and blankets and sleeping bags. No time to worry about that. As Myron started down the stairs, he saw the cell.

Empty.

He reached the bottom and turned to his right. The kids clambered toward that corner like something out of a zombie film – like they were climbing over one another and feeding on something stuck there. Myron started toward it. Kids got in his way. Myron pushed them aside. They were boys mostly, but there were a few girls sprinkled in too. They all looked at him with hollow, lost eyes, still pushing forward.

'Where is Fat Gandhi? Where are the boys he had in that cell?'

No one answered. They kept pushing and shoving toward that corner. Was there a door there or . . .

A hole?

The kids were disappearing into some kind of hole in the concrete.

Myron picked up his pace now, even if it meant being rougher than he wanted with these kids. One of them started screaming and clawing at Myron's face. Myron knocked him away. He moved like a linebacker now, lowering his shoulder, throwing body blows, until he got to the hole.

Another kid started to climb into it.

It was a tunnel.

Myron grabbed the kid from behind. Other kids pushed in, trying to get to the opening. Myron held firm. He pulled the kid so that his face was right up against his.

'Is that where Fat Gandhi went? Did he take two boys with him?'

'We're all supposed to go,' the boy said with a nod. 'Otherwise the coppers will find us.'

They were pushing in again. Myron had two choices. Move to the side or . . .

He dived into the hole and landed on the cold, damp floor. When he stood up, his head whacked concrete. He saw stars for a moment. The tunnel's ceiling was low. Shorter guys could probably run. Myron was not so lucky.

Other kids started flowing in behind him.

Have to move, Myron thought.

'Patrick!' he screamed. 'Rhys!'

For a moment, he could hear only the scraping sounds of kids escaping through this dark tunnel. And then he heard someone scream: 'Help!'

Myron felt his pulse race. The scream might have been short and only a word, but Myron knew one thing for certain.

The accent was American.

He tried to pick up his pace. There were boys already crowded into the tunnel, blocking his progress. Girls too. He swam past them.

'Patrick! Rhys!'

Lots of echoes. But no one returned his call.

The tunnel's height and thickness were inconsistent, constantly changing. It twisted and turned in unexpected ways. The walls were black and old and wet. The few dim lights made the place feel more ghostly.

There were teenagers on either side of him, behind him, in front of him. Some rushed forward; some fell behind.

Myron grabbed one harder than he meant to and pulled him up to his face: 'Where does this tunnel lead?'

'Lots of places.'

Myron let him go. *Lots of places. Terrific.*

He reached a fork and stopped. Some kids went left, others right.

'Patrick! Rhys!'

Silence. And then a voice that sounded American: 'Help!'

To the right.

Myron hurried after the voice, trying to move faster, trying so hard to keep a pace and yet not whack his head on the ceiling. The stench was starting to make him gag. He kept moving. He wondered how long these tunnels had been here – centuries maybe – the whole place feeling suddenly like something out of Dickens, when he saw two boys up ahead.

And a fat man in a yellow zoot suit.

Fat Gandhi turned toward him. He took out a knife.

'No!' Myron shouted.

There were still more teenagers in front of them. Myron sprinted as hard as he could toward the boys, lowering his head, pumping his legs.

Fat Gandhi raised the knife.

Myron kept moving. But he could see he was too far away.

The knife came down. Myron heard a scream.

A boy collapsed to the ground.

'No!'

Myron dove toward the fallen body. The zoot suit started to run away. Myron didn't care. More teens were starting to push on through. Myron crawled on top of the stabbed boy.

Where was the other boy?

There. Myron reached out and grabbed his ankle. He held on. Other teens scrambled over him. Myron kept his grip on the ankle. He stayed on top of the stabbed boy, using his own body as a shield. He found the stab wound and tried to stem the flow with his forearm.

Someone's foot landed on Myron's wrist. His grip on the other boy's ankle was starting to loosen.

'Hang on,' he shouted.

But the ankle was being pulled away.

Myron gritted his teeth. How much longer could he keep this up?

Myron held on, even as the boy tried to pull away, even as a kick landed hard on his face, even as the second kick landed. And then, on the next kick, his grip slipped.

The boy was swept away in the river of other teenagers.

Gone.

'No!'

Myron kept low, making his body a protective shell for the injured boy. He pressed his forearm down hard on the wound.

You aren't dying. You hear me? We didn't come all this way for you . . .

When the current of teenagers passed over him, Myron quickly ripped off his shirt and applied pressure to the wound. He finally looked down at the boy.

And recognized his face.

'Hang in there, Patrick,' Myron said. 'I'm taking you home.'

CHAPTER 9

Three days passed.

The police asked Myron a lot of questions. He gave a lot of half answers and also, as a bar-licensed attorney, he called upon attorney-client privilege, known in the United Kingdom as legal professional privilege, so as not to name Win. Yes, he had flown over at the request of a client on the Lock-Horne jet. No, he couldn't say a word about having spoken to or seeing his client. Yes, he delivered money in the hopes of securing the release of Patrick Moore and Rhys Baldwin. No, he had no idea what happened to the wall. No, Myron said, he had no idea who stabbed a twenty-six-year-old man with a long rap sheet of trouble named Scott Taylor in the throat, killing him. No, he didn't know anything about three men killed near King's Cross station days before. He was, after all, in New York City at that time.

No sign of Fat Gandhi. No sign of Rhys.

There was only so long the cops could hold him. They had no evidence of any serious wrongdoing. Someone (Win) had sent a young lawyer named Mark Wells to represent Myron. Wells helped.

So they reluctantly cut Myron loose. Now it was noon and he was back at the Crown pub cooling his heels on the same stool. Win came in and took the stool next to him. The barman dropped down two ales.

'Mr Lockwood,' he said. 'It's been months. Wonderful to see you again.'

'And you too, Nigel.'

Myron looked at the barman, then at Win, then arched an eyebrow to indicate a question.

'I just flew in from the United States today when I heard the news,' Win said.

The barman stared at Myron. Myron stared at the barman, then at Win, and then said, 'Ah.'

The barman moved away.

'Won't customs have you entering the country before today?'

Win smiled.

'Of course not,' Myron said. 'By the way, thanks for sending that lawyer, Wells.'

'Solicitor.'

'What?'

'In Great Britain, you call him a solicitor. In America, you call him a lawyer.'

'In Great Britain, I call you anal. In the United States, I call you an assh—'

'Yes, quite, I see your point. Speaking of solicitors, mine is currently with the police. He will explain that it was indeed I who retained your services and that you, as my other solicitor, were protecting my interests.'

Myron said, 'I did tell them attorney-client privilege.'

'So I will back that up. We will also turn over the anonymous email sent to me that started this. Perhaps Scotland Yard will have better luck tracking down the sender than I did.'

'You think?'

'No chance. I was feigning modesty.'

'It doesn't wear well on you,' Myron said. 'So how did you do it?'

'I told you that we cased the arcade. But not just inside.'

Myron nodded. 'So you figured out where that safe room was.'

'Yes. Then we hooked up a Fox MJ listening device. If you press it to any wall, you can hear everything. We waited until you called out the safe word.'

'And then?'

'It was an RPG-29.'

'Very subtle.'

'My forte.'

'Thank you,' Myron said.

Win pretended not to hear.

'So how's Patrick?' Myron asked. 'The cops wouldn't tell me anything. I saw in the papers that his parents flew over, but no one will even confirm if it's him.'

'Wait.'

'What?'

'We will soon get some additional information on all that from a better source.'

'Who?'

Win shook him off. 'You may be wondering why the police didn't question you more about the throat stabbing.'

'Not really,' Myron said.

'No?'

'In the confusion, no one saw it. I figured that you probably took the knife with you, so they had nothing to tie me to it.'

'Not exactly. For one thing, the police have confiscated your clothing.'

'I liked those pants.'

'Yes, they were very slimming. But they'll test the blood on them. It will be a match with the victim's, of course.'

Myron finally gave in and took a sip. 'Will that be a problem?'

'I don't think so. Do you remember your black friend with the machete?'

'Black friend?'

'Oh yes, let's be politically correct right this very moment. Is he Anglo-African? I must consult the handbook.'

'My bad. What about him?'

'His name is Lester Connor.'

'Okay.'

'When the police arrived on the scene, Lester was unconscious and – surprise, surprise – had the bloody knife in his hand. Naturally he said the knife had been planted.'

'Naturally.'

'But you could say that you saw Lester stab Scott Taylor in the throat.'

'I could indeed.'

'But?'

'But I won't,' Myron said.

'Because?'

'Because it wouldn't be true.'

'Mr Connor tried to kill you.'

'Yeah, but to be fair, I broke his laptop.'

'False equivalency,' Win said.

'Better than false testimony.'

'Touché.'

'If they ask, I'll say that someone stabbed the guy and he fell on me. In the confusion, I didn't see who or even notice.'

'That should play,' Win said.

'Are there any leads on Rhys?'

'Remember what I said about a better source,' Win said.

'What about him?'

'What about *her*?' Win shook his head. 'God, Myron, you're such a sexist. And here she is now.'

Win looked toward the door. Myron did the same and immediately recognized the woman who'd entered. It was Brooke Baldwin, Win's cousin and, more to the point, mother of the still-missing Rhys.

Myron hadn't seen Brooke in, what, five years, he surmised.

A barstool appeared between Myron and Win. They both scooched over to make room. Brooke walked over without hesitation, grabbed the beer that Nigel had already put out for her, and started guzzling. Half was gone when she put it down. Nigel gave a nod of approval.

'Needed that,' Brooke said.

Myron had met too many parents/spouses/loved ones of missing people. Most appeared frail and drained, which seemed both obvious and right. With Brooke, it was more the opposite. She was tanned, defiant, healthy, with a coiled energy, as though she had just finished her morning laps in some Olympic-sized pool or gone a few rounds with a boxing trainer. Her petite frame was thick with ropy muscles. The word that first came to mind when you saw this wealthy suburban soccer mom who had taken one of life's cruelest body blows: fierce.

Brooke Lockwood Baldwin might have been raised in stone mansions and elite prep schools, but she fit in in a pub like this. She could probably challenge you to a game of darts or sweep the glasses off the bar and kick your ass in arm wrestling.

Brooke turned to Myron and, without so much as a hello, said, 'Tell me exactly what happened.'

He did. He told her everything from his arrival in London through the police questioning. She gazed at him steadily with bright green eyes.

When he finished, Brooke said, 'So you had Rhys by the ankle.'

'I think so, yeah.'

Her voice was softer now. 'You touched him.'
The words hung in the air for a long moment.
'I'm sorry,' Myron said. 'I tried to hang on.'
'I'm not blaming you. Did you see his face?'
'No.'
'So we don't know for certain it was Rhys.'
'I can't say for sure, no,' Myron said.
Brooke looked at Win. Win said nothing. She turned back to Myron.
'On the other hand, we have no reason to believe it isn't my son, do we?'
Win spoke for the first time. 'Depends.'
'On?'
'Do we know for certain the other boy is Patrick?'
'Yes,' Brooke said. 'At least, Nancy says he's Patrick.'
'She's sure?' Myron asked.
'That's what she and Hunter say. They're divorced now, you know. Hunter and Nancy. They broke up not long after.'
She didn't say after what. She didn't have to.
'We all flew over together. The four of us. Back together again. I don't remember the last time we even talked to each other. We're still neighbors. We should have moved out, I guess, but . . . she always blamed me. Nancy, I mean.'
'Seems unfair,' Myron said.
'Myron?'
'Yes?'
'Don't patronize me, okay?'

'Not my intent.'

'The boys were at my house. It was my au pair. I should have been home watching them. If the roles were reversed . . . Whatever; it was a long time ago.'

Win asked, 'Is there any independent confirmation that the boy is Patrick?'

'Like what?'

'Like DNA.'

'I mentioned that. I guess they'll do it eventually, but right now there is some sort of legal mumbo jumbo. Patrick – I mean, assuming it's Patrick – is a minor, so they need to get permission from his parents.'

Win nodded. 'And yet there is no concrete proof Nancy and Hunter are the boy's parents.'

'Irony, right?'

'So what has Patrick said?' Myron asked. 'Where have they been? Who took them?'

Brooke picked up the mug, looked at the contents for a second, then downed them. Myron and Win watched and waited.

'Patrick hasn't said anything yet.'

Silence for a moment.

'He's that wounded?'

'Apparently. It's not like they let me see him. Only family allowed in the hospital room.'

'How serious are the injuries?'

'Nancy says he'll survive, but he's been pretty much out of it. Talk about irony. For ten years, we don't have a clue about Rhys. Not a peep. Now suddenly there is someone who can give me answers, and I can't even talk to him.'

Brooke closed her eyes and rubbed them with a thumb and forefinger. Myron reached out to touch her shoulder. Win stopped him with a shake of his head.

'Anyway,' she said as her eyes opened, 'we are holding a press conference this afternoon. As you know, the media has gotten some of the story. Now it's time to release the rest.'

'It's been three days,' Myron said. 'Why the wait?'

Brooke stood and turned so she could lean her back on the bar. 'So, day one, two detectives or whatever they call them from Scotland Yard sit Chick and me down. "We have a dilemma," they say. If we go to the press and splash Rhys's age-progression photograph all over the place, there are, the detectives explained, two things that might happen. One' – Brooke raised her index finger – 'we mount pressure and find Rhys. Two' – the middle finger joined the index – 'we mount pressure and whoever is holding him kills him and dumps the body.'

'They told you that?' Myron said.

'Just that way. They advised us to give them a little time and see if they could dig up any leads quietly.'

'I assume they haven't.'

'Correct. Rhys, it seems, has vanished without a trace. Again.'

Again.

And again her eyes closed. And again Myron reached his hand out. And again Win stopped him with a shake of his head. Win wasn't being cold. He just didn't want her to fall apart yet. Myron got it.

'So the investigators,' Win said, 'they changed their suggestion?'

'No,' Brooke said, 'I did. I decided. My choice. We go public. Will that help find my son or kill him? Don't know. Nice, right?'

'It's the right move,' Win said. 'It's the only move.'

'You think so?'

'I do.'

Myron saw Brooke's two fists tighten. Her face started to redden, and when it did, Brooke suddenly looked like her cousin Win, or at least you could see the family resemblance. When Brooke spoke again, there was an edge in her voice.

'So now you think I should have a say in what happens to my son?'

Win did not reply.

'You received an anonymous email,' Brooke said.

'Yes.'

'You showed up and ended up killing three guys.'

'Louder,' Win said. 'I think the gentlemen in the corner didn't hear you.'

But Brooke was having none of it. 'Why didn't you tell me about the email?'

'It was anonymous. I figured that it would go nowhere.'

'Bullshit,' Brooke said. 'You found it credible enough to check it out.'

'Yes.'

'So why didn't you tell me, Win?'

No reply.

'Because you thought I'd fall apart? Because you didn't want to get my hopes up?'

Silence.

'Win?'

He turned and faced her full on. 'Yes,' he said. 'That's why.'

'That wasn't your decision to make.'

He spread his hands. 'Yet make it I did.'

'What, you think I couldn't take it? You think you were sparing me additional pain?'

'Something like that.'

'You know nothing about my pain.' Brooke leaned in closer. 'How dare you? How dare you decide that for me?'

She stared at him hard. Win said nothing.

'Win?'

'You're right,' he said. 'I should have told you.'

'Not good enough.'

'It's going to have to be, Brooke.'

'No, sorry, you don't get off that easily. Maybe if you told me about the email, I would have flown over. Maybe I could have helped in some way. Maybe – no, definitely – things would have gone differently.'

Win said nothing.

'Instead,' Brooke said, pointing out the window

of the pub, 'my boy is still out there. Alone. You messed up, Win. You messed up big-time.'

'Let's slow down a second,' Myron said. 'We don't know if that would have changed—'

Brooke snapped her gaze toward Myron, cutting him off. 'Is Rhys here, Myron?'

Now it was Myron who said nothing.

'Bottom line: Is he here?' She turned back to her cousin. 'We had our first real lead in ten years. In ten horrible, miserable years. And now . . .'

'Brooke?'

It was Win.

'I get it,' he said. 'You're angry.'

'Man, you're perceptive.'

'But more than that, you're trying to motivate me,' Win said. 'There is no need. You know that too.'

Their eyes met. If someone passed a hand between those eyes, it would probably have been chopped off via laser.

Her phone rang.

'Find him, Win.'

'I will.'

They both blinked. Brooke took out her phone and put it to her ear. 'Hello?' She hung up a few seconds later. 'That was the police.'

'What did they want?'

'It's Patrick. He's awake.'

CHAPTER 10

Win didn't come with them to the hospital. For now, he felt that it would be best to keep his distance from anything involving law enforcement. They considered having Myron stay away too – the cops had been less than thrilled with Myron's explanation for the violence at AdventureLand – but in the end, they decided that he should be nearby in case he was somehow needed.

Brooke stayed busy on her phone during the taxi ride. She called her husband, Chick, and told him to meet her at the hospital. She made more calls and grew more agitated.

'What's wrong?' Myron asked.

'They are saying we can't see Patrick yet.'

'Who?'

'The police.'

Myron thought about that. 'Is it their decision?'

'What do you mean?'

'I mean, who decides that you can't see him? Is it up to the police? Can't the parents overrule them?'

'I still don't know if Nancy and Hunter have legal standing.'

'I assume you have their numbers?'

'Only Nancy's.'

'Try it.'

She did. No answer. She sent a text. No reply.

When they pulled up to the front of the hospital, Chick was smoking and pacing. Chick threw the cigarette down hard on the pavement and made a production out of stamping it out. He opened the taxi door with a scowl on his face. Brooke got out. Myron followed.

Chick's scowl grew when he saw Myron.

'You're Win's friend. The basketball player. What are you doing here?'

Win didn't like Chick, which told Myron all he needed to know about him.

Chick looked at Brooke. 'What's he doing here?'

'He was the one who rescued Patrick.'

Chick turned the scowl back toward Myron. 'You were there?'

'Yes.'

'So how come you didn't save my kid?'

My kid, Myron noted. Not ours.

'He tried, Chick,' Brooke said.

'What, he can't answer for himself?'

'I tried, Chick.'

Chick stepped toward him. The scowl was still there. Myron started to wonder whether it was indeed a scowl or just his default expression. 'You being a wiseass with me? Huh?'

Myron didn't step back. He didn't make a fist, but man, he wanted to. Despite the rushed call from his wife, Chick wore a shiny silk suit with a tie so perfectly knotted it looked fake. His shoes had an almost supernatural shine, like they were somehow more than new, and his hair was black with just the right amount of gray, slicked back and a little too long. His skin had the waxy glow of a recent facial or some sort of high-end cosmetics, and the word 'manscaped' was encompassed in every move Chick made.

Brooke said, 'We don't have time for this.'

Chick did that thing where you look the person in one eye, then the other, then back to the first. Myron just stood there and let him. You don't judge a guy by his appearance. Win was the walking, talking embodiment of that. The guy was also hurting. You could see that too. He might be a vainglorious asshat, but his son had been snatched away from him ten years ago. You could see that in Chick's face somehow, despite all he tried to do to cover it up.

So part of Myron felt sorry for the man.

And part of Myron remembered that Win didn't like him.

'I tried my best,' Myron said to him. 'He got away. I'm sorry about that.'

Chick hesitated and then nodded. 'I'm sorry too. This has been . . .'

'Don't worry about it.'

Brooke's voice was gentle. 'Chick?'

Chick gave Myron's arm an apologetic squeeze as he turned toward his wife.

Brooke said, 'Let's go inside, okay?'

Chick nodded and joined her.

Brooke shaded her eyes with her right hand. 'Myron?'

He glanced around and spotted a Costa coffee shop across the street. 'I'll wait there. Text if you need me.'

Chick and Brooke entered the hospital. Myron crossed the street and headed to the right for the Costa coffee shop. Costa was a chain coffee shop and resembled, more than anything else, a chain coffee shop. Swap the dark red décor for green and you could be in a Starbucks. Myron was sure that passionate defenders of either company would be offended by this observation, but Myron decided that he wouldn't lose sleep over it.

He ordered a coffee from the barista, and then, realizing his stomach was growling, he checked out the food options. On that front – food variety – Costa seemed to have a leg up on its American competitor. He ordered a British Ham and Cheese Toastie. Toastie. 'Toastie' was a cute word. Myron hadn't heard it before, but he deduced, correctly as it turned out, that a 'toastie' was probably a toasted sandwich.

Some stand in awe of Myron Bolitar's power of deduction.

A text came in from Brooke: **Not letting us see him. Told to wait.**

Myron replied: Want me to come over?

Brooke: Not yet. Will keep you posted.

Myron sat at a table and ate the toastie. Not bad. He downed it too quickly and debated getting another. When had he last eaten? He sat back, drank his coffee, read articles that he'd saved on his smartphone. Time passed. The place was a little too quiet. Myron looked around at the drawn faces. Perhaps it was his imagination, but he could almost feel the misery hanging in the air. He was, of course, across the street from a hospital, so maybe that was why he was seeing suffering or anxiety, faces waiting for news, faces dreading news, faces that had come here to try to escape into the comforting sameness and normalcy of a chain coffee shop.

His phone vibrated. Another text message, this time from Terese: Got a job interview in Jackson Hole. For prime time anchor slot.

This was great news. Myron wrote back: Wow, that's terrific.

Terese: Heading to owner's ranch on his private plane tomorrow.

Myron: Great. I'm thrilled for you.

Terese: I don't have the job.

Myron: You'll kill the interview.

Terese: He can be a little handsy.

Myron: And I can kill him.

Terese: Love you, you know.

Myron: Love you too. But I mean it about killing him if he gets handsy.

120

Terese: **You always know just what to say.**

Myron was smiling. He was about to text a comeback when something caught his eye.

Or someone.

Nancy Moore, Patrick's mother, had just entered the coffee shop. He typed a quick 'Have to run' and hit send.

Where Brooke Baldwin was all strength and resolve, Nancy Moore looked small and drained. Her blond hair was pulled back into a rushed ponytail, the grays poking free. She wore a baggy sweatshirt with the word LONDON across the front, the *L* being formed by an old phone box and a double-decker bus. She had probably rush-packed and bought it at some tourist shop when she arrived.

Nancy Moore said something low to the barista, who gestured that he couldn't hear her by putting his hand to his ear. She repeated her order and then started fumbling in her purse for some money.

Myron stood. 'Mrs Moore?'

His voice startled her. The coins fell from her hand and landed on the floor. Myron bent down to pick them up. Nancy started to follow, but it was as though the effort was too much for her. Myron stood up and dropped the coins into her hand.

'Thank you.'

Nancy Moore stared at him for a moment. An odd look crossed her face. Was it recognition? Surprise? Both?

'You're Myron Bolitar,' she said.

'Yes.'

'We've met before, haven't we?'

'Once,' Myron said.

'At . . .' She stopped. It had been at the Baldwin home, the site of the awful event, maybe a month after the kidnapping. Win and Myron had been called in too late. 'You're Win's friend.'

'Yes.'

'And you . . . you're the one who . . .' She blinked, looked down. 'How do I even begin to thank you for saving my boy?'

Myron blew past that. 'How's Patrick doing?'

'Physically, he'll be fine.'

The barista came back over with two coffees in to-go cups. He placed them down in front of her.

'You saved his life,' she said. There was awe in her voice. 'You saved my son's life.'

'I'm glad he'll be okay,' Myron replied. 'I hear he's awake?'

Nancy Moore didn't reply right away. When she did, she said, 'Can I ask you something?'

'Sure.'

'How much do you remember of your life before you turned six?'

He knew where this was going, but he went there anyway. 'Not much.'

'And how about between the ages of six and sixteen?'

This time Myron stayed silent.

'It was everything, right? Elementary school,

middle school, most of high school. That's what shapes us. That's what makes us everything we are.'

The barista gave her the total. Nancy Moore handed him the coins. He handed some back to her, along with a to-go bag.

'I don't mean to push you,' Myron said. 'But has Patrick said anything about what happened to him or where Rhys might be?'

Nancy Moore put the money back into her purse with a little too much care. 'Nothing that would help,' she said.

'What does that mean?'

She just shook her head.

'What has he said?' Myron asked. 'Patrick, I mean. Who took them? Where have they been all this time?'

'You want answers,' she said. 'I just want my son.'

'I want answers,' Myron said, 'because there is still a boy missing.'

Her gaze had steel behind it now. 'You don't think I care about Rhys?'

'No, not at all. I'm sure you care a lot.'

'You don't think I know what Brooke and Chick are going through?'

'To the contrary,' Myron said, 'I don't think anyone knows as well as you do.'

She closed her eyes. 'I'm sorry. It's just . . .'

Myron waited.

'Patrick can barely talk right now. He's . . . not well. Mentally I mean. He hasn't really spoken yet.'

'I don't mean to sound insensitive,' Myron said, 'but are you sure it's Patrick?'

'Yes.'

No hesitation. No doubt.

'Have you done a DNA test?'

'No, but we will, if that's required. He recognizes us, I think. Me anyway. But it's Patrick. It's my son. I know it sounds like an awful cliché, but a mother knows.'

Might be a cliché. Might not. Then again, to coin another cliché, we see what we want to see, especially when we are a desperate mother hoping to end a decade of pain.

Tears started flooding her eyes. 'Some maniac stabbed him. My boy. You found him. You saved him. Do you get that? He would have bled out. That's what the doctors said. You . . .'

'Nancy?'

The voice came from behind him. Myron turned and spotted Hunter Moore, Nancy's ex-husband and Patrick's father.

'Come on,' the man said. 'We have to go.'

He let go of the door and disappeared to the left.

If Hunter Moore had recognized Myron, he didn't show it. Then again, there was little reason he would have. They had never met before – he hadn't been at the Baldwin house that day – and he seemed in a rush to hurry along his ex-wife.

Nancy scooped up the bag and coffee. She turned to Myron.

'It feels so inept to say thank you again. The idea that after all these years, that after finding Patrick alive, he would have been killed if it wasn't for you . . .'

'It's okay.'

'I'll always be in your debt.'

She hurried away then, out the door and turning left to follow her ex's path. For a moment Myron didn't move. The barista said, 'Would you like a refill?'

'No, thanks.'

Myron still didn't move.

'You okay, mate?' the barista asked.

'Fine.'

He stared at the door some more. And then a curious thought hit him. The hospital was to the right. But both Hunter and Nancy Moore had turned left.

Did that mean anything?

Nope. At least, not on its own. They could be picking up something at a pharmacy or getting some fresh air or . . .

Myron moved to the door. He stepped outside onto the street and looked to his left. Nancy Moore was stepping into a black van.

'Wait,' Myron said.

But she was too far away and the street was noisy. The van door slid closed as Myron started to run.

'Hold up a second,' he shouted.

But the van was already on its way. Myron

watched it head down the street and disappear around a corner. He stopped and took out his smartphone. It was probably nothing. Maybe the police were taking them someplace for questioning. Maybe after round-the-clock sitting beside their son they needed a few hours of rest.

Both of them?

Uh-uh, no way. Did Nancy Moore strike him as the type who would need a break from the child who had been missing for ten years? No chance. More likely that she would never leave his side, that she would be afraid to take her eyes off him for more than a moment.

Myron took out his phone and hit what was still speed dial 1 on his phone. He didn't worry about a trace. The number would bounce to and fro and end up on some untraceable burner.

'Articulate,' Win said.

'I think there's a problem.'

'Do tell.'

He told him about Nancy and Hunter Moore and the black van. He crossed the street and headed toward the hospital entrance. He finished telling Win what he knew and hung up. Then he called Brooke's phone. No answer.

A hospital sign – several signs, now that Myron looked around – read NO MOBILE PHONE USE. People were staring. Myron put his away with an apologetic shrug and headed for the check-in desk.

'I'm here to see a patient.'

'Name of the patient?'

'Patrick Moore.'

'And your name?'

'Myron Bolitar.'

'Please wait one moment.'

Myron's eyes scanned the room. He spotted Brooke and Chick sitting by a window in the corner of the waiting area. Brooke lifted her eyes, met his, and stood. He hurried toward her.

'What's wrong?' Brooke asked.

'What did the police tell you?'

'Nothing. We haven't been allowed up to see him.'

'Do you know his room number?'

'Yes, Nancy told me yesterday. It's 322.'

Myron turned. 'Let's go.'

'What happened?'

He hurried around the corner. There was a security guard. 'Pass, please.'

'No,' Myron said.

That confused the guard. 'What?'

His name tag read LAMY.

Myron was big, six four, 225. He knew when to make himself even bigger. Like now. 'I need to go up to the third floor and check on a patient.'

'Then get a pass.'

'There are two ways this can go, uh, Lamy. I can knock you on your ass and embarrass you, and who knows the repercussions. You may be tougher than you look, in which case I will be forced to hurt you. Maybe more than I want to. Or you can go with me up the stairs and see that I'm just

127

going to look in on a patient, making sure that the patient is okay, and then come right back down again.'

'Sir, I must insist—'

'Your call.'

Myron didn't give the guard time. He rushed past him and started sprinting up the stairs. The security guard hurried after him, but there wasn't much jump in his step.

'Stop! Desk Two calling for assistance! Intruder in the stairwell.'

Myron didn't bother to slow down. He ran up the stairs. His knee, the one that had ended his career so long ago, ached a bit, but that didn't slow him. He didn't know if Brooke or Chick were behind him. He didn't much care. The guard would call for backup. They would get there or they wouldn't. They'd arrest him or they wouldn't. But either way, they wouldn't be able to stop him in time.

He pushed open the door at the third floor. Room 302 was in front of him. He turned to the right and sprinted past room 304. Behind him he heard someone yell, 'Stop! Stop now!'

He didn't listen.

He ran until he reached room 322. He opened the door and stepped inside as he heard more footsteps approach him. He didn't move. He stood and waited, but it was just as he had suspected.

The bed – and indeed the room – was empty.

CHAPTER 11

There were some hassles with the guards, but not many.

Myron backed out of the room and started back toward the exit, hands raised. The guards weren't sure what to do about this intrusion. The man had run into an empty room. Was that reason to try to hold him? Myron explained that he wasn't going anywhere anyway, and that seemed to satisfy them.

Chick went crazy, especially when the cops' reaction was one of utter calm: They couldn't hold Patrick; he was a victim, not a criminal, and he wanted to go home with his parents.

'Did you ask him about my son?' Chick screamed.

Of course they had, the cops told him in measured voices. Patrick and his parents claimed he didn't know anything relevant and was too traumatized to talk about it.

Chick: 'And you let that slide?'

The cops gave a polite sigh and a small shrug. They did not let it slide. But at the end of the day, they couldn't force a traumatized and injured teenager to talk to them. The boy indicated that he wanted to return to the United States with his parents. The doctors agreed that might be best. There was no legal reason to hold him against his will.

It went on for some time, but it was pointless.

So now, two hours after discovering that the Moore family was on a private plane back to the United States, Brooke and Chick Baldwin held the press conference in the ballroom at the Grosvenor House on Park Lane.

Myron and Win stood in the back and watched.

'She doesn't look like a grieving mother, does she?' Win said.

He was talking about Brooke.

'That doesn't mean she's not.'

'No, but I told her to cry a little for the camera.'

Myron nodded. 'That would be good.'

'I don't know if she can. I told her the public wants to see the pain. If they don't, they assume you cannot possibly be suffering.'

'I remember when the boys first disappeared,' Myron said. 'All those news sources about your cousin's' – Myron made the quote marks in the air – ' "demeanor." '

'Even then she didn't show enough anguish for the cameras,' Win said.

'Right. So some columnist started to theorize that maybe she was involved. It was her house, her nanny – and worst of all, she showed little outward sign of distress.'

'Pathetic,' Win said.

'Exactly. If Brooke had sobbed and collapsed, the world would have sobbed along with her. Instead they used her.'

'I remember. It started up the whole stay-at-home-mom debate. Brooke was neglectful. She was spoiled, just another rich woman who hired an au pair because she didn't want to take care of her own children.'

'No one wants to think it can happen to them,' Myron said.

'So they look for blame,' Win said. 'It's part of the human condition.'

Up on the podium, the police did most of the talking. Brooke stared out at seemingly nothing. She did not, despite Win's instructions, cry. Chick, in that natty suit, hardly cut a sympathetic image either, but at least you could see the devastation on his face.

Myron leaned toward his friend. 'It's good to have you back, Win.'

'Yes,' Win said. 'Yes, it is.'

The police told the story in the vaguest terms possible. One of the American boys missing for ten years, Patrick Moore, had been rescued in London. No details on how. They didn't take credit for it. They didn't give Myron credit either.

Which was more than fine with him.

The police believed that the other missing teen, Rhys Baldwin, the son of these two long-suffering parents, might be close by too. A reporter shouted out, 'How do you know?' The police ignored him.

When they flashed up an old picture of Rhys, age six, along with several age-progression illustrations, Myron saw the first crack in Brooke's facade.

But she didn't cry.

'They're flying back when this is done,' Win said.

'They're not staying?'

Win shook his head. 'They want to go home. They know there is nothing they can do in London. You need to go with them. You need to figure out a way to get Patrick to talk. You need to start at the beginning and move toward me.'

'You mean the original scene of the crime?'

'Yes.'

'You think we need to go back that far?'

'The story may have ended up here – but it started in that house.'

'What do you make of the Moores sneaking back home with Patrick?'

'Nothing good,' Win said.

'It could be that he's just too traumatized to talk.'

'Could be.'

'What else could it be really?'

'What you said before,' Win said.

'What's that?'

'We're missing something.'

Then the police flashed up a photograph of Fat Gandhi, giving his name as Chris Alan Weeks, and saying he wasn't a suspect but a person of interest. The man in the photograph had hair and looked fifty pounds thinner than the man Myron had encountered.

'Do we want the police to find him,' Win asked, 'or me?'

'Does it matter?'

Win looked at him. 'How will it go if the police capture him?'

'If he's with Rhys, well, then we are done. Case solved.'

'Unlikely that will happen,' Win said. 'He's a cautious man. He'll either kill Rhys – which there is no point in entertaining since it will lead us nowhere – or your rotund friend will store him someplace safe, someplace with no connection to him.'

'Okay.'

'So I ask again: How will it go if the police capture him?'

'First, they bring him in.'

'Right.'

Myron saw where Win was headed. 'He lawyers up. They have nothing on him. He kept everything in some locked cloud. The kids won't testify against him. He was careful. They'll have my testimony about the stabbing, but they'll say it was dark and there is no way I could have seen him do it for certain, which is true.'

Win nodded. 'Do you think he'll talk?'

'To quote you, "Unlikely that will happen."'

'Yet if I find him . . .,' Win said.

Myron turned back to the press conference.

'You don't approve,' Win said.

'You know I don't.'

'Yet you know what I am and what I do.'

'Which might have been, I don't know, okay in the past. In certain circumstances.'

'But not in this brave new world of ours?'

'Are you really in favor of the government torturing people for information?'

'Good God, no,' Win said.

'Just you personally?'

'Yes, exactly. I trust my judgment and motives. I don't trust the government's.'

'Different rules for you?'

'Yes, of course.' Win tilted his head. 'Is this confusing to you?'

Myron shook his head. 'One other thing.'

'What's that?'

'You've been away for a long time.'

Win did not reply.

'If I head back,' Myron said, 'I don't want to lose you again.'

'You heard what Brooke said.'

'I did.'

'I messed up. Whatever the price, I have to find her son.'

An hour later, just as they were boarding Win's plane, Brooke got a text. She read it and stopped. Myron and Chick stopped a step later.

'What is it?' Chick said.

'It's from Nancy.'

134

She handed Chick the phone. He read it out loud: 'I'm doing what's best for my son. And yours. Trust me. Will be in touch soon.' Chick still had the scowl going. 'What the hell does that mean?'

Brooke took back the phone. She tried to call Nancy again, but there was no answer. She sent a text asking her for some clarification or details. Again there was no reply.

'She never liked us,' Chick said. 'She blamed us for what happened, even though our kid went missing too.'

He ducked inside the plane. Mee was there in her formfitting flight attendant uniform. She gave them a small smile, as befitted the situation, and took their coats.

'She acts like it's our fault,' Chick said to his wife. 'I've told you that before, you know.'

'Yes, I know, Chick. Many times.'

'Even before all this. I mean, Hunter, he's a drunk now, but he was always a ne'er-do-well. Everything handed to him. Boring as hell. It's like talking to a rock. But Nancy, I mean, what the hell is she trying to pull here?'

They had no answer for him.

Chick turned to Mee. 'Anyone using the bedroom?'

'It's at your disposal, sir.'

'Great. Can you get me some water?'

'Immediately, sir.'

Chick grabbed a bottle of pills from his pocket. He shook out two tablets and then, thinking better of it, shook out a third. Mee handed him the water. He swallowed all three and gestured toward the room in the back of the plane. 'Do you mind if I . . .?'

'Go ahead,' Brooke said.

Three minutes later, they could hear him snoring. Mee closed the bedroom door, and the sound was gone. The plane rushed down the runway and climbed into the air. Myron and Brooke sat side by side.

'So what's Win's plan?' she asked.

'He wants to catch Fat Gandhi before the police do.'

Brooke nodded. 'That would be good. Do you think he can do it?'

'If Win were here, I think he'd say, "I'll pretend you didn't ask that."'

That made her smile. 'He loves us.'

'I know.'

'There aren't many he loves,' she said. 'But when he does love you, it's both ferocious and comforting.'

'He has saved my life more times than I can count.'

'And you, his,' she said. 'He's told me. You met at Duke, right?'

'Yes.'

'When?'

'Freshman year.'

'Tell me: What was your first impression of him?'

Myron looked off and tried not to smile. 'My dad drove me down to Duke. I was nervous, first year of college and all that. He kept it light, distracted me. I remember he helped me move in. We lugged all this stuff up four flights of stairs. I kept telling him I could do it. I was worried because my dad was so out of shape . . .'

Myron shook his head, got back to it.

'Anyway, there was the freshman face book in my dorm. Do you remember those?'

'Oh yes,' Brooke said, and a sad smile came to her lips. 'We went through ours and rated the boys on a scale of one to ten.'

'God, you're so shallow, Brooke.'

'I am, yeah.'

'So anyway, my dad and I take a break and start going through it. And I can still remember seeing Win's photo – all blond hair and blue eyes and looking like he was modeling for the cover of *Preppy Ass Waffle* magazine. He had that haughty expression on his face. You know the one.'

Brooke imitated it to perfection.

'Yes, exactly.'

'Like he's the most superior creature on God's green earth.'

'Right, and it listed his snooty prep school, and his full name was there. So I'm reading this – Windsor Horne Lockwood III – and I'm laughing about it, and I show my dad and he laughs, and I say, "I won't even see this guy in my four years, never mind be friends with him."'

Brooke smiled. 'Oh, I know what you mean.'

'We met that night. He's been my best friend ever since.'

'So you get what I'm saying.'

'Sure. People see him and they hate him. They see him and think arrogant, Waspy wimp who couldn't bruise a peach.'

'Easy pickings,' Brooke said.

'Yes. And Win mostly kept it under wraps at first. I mean, I could sense the darkness right away. Even when we met at the first orientation social.'

'Maybe that's what drew you to him.'

'What, the darkness?'

'Yep. His yin to your yang.'

'Maybe,' Myron agreed.

'So when did you know for sure?' she asked. 'I mean, about his, uh, talents. Do you remember?'

He did. Too well. 'Freshman year, maybe a month into the school year, a bunch of football players decided to shave Win's head. You know how it is. They thought his hair looked too perfect, what with the straight part and the yellow blond and all that.'

'Right.'

'So one night, these big football players break into the room when Win's sleeping. Five of them, I think. Four to hold his arms and legs down, one to shave his head clean.'

'Oh boy,' Brooke said.

'Yes.'

'So how did that go for them?'

'Put it this way,' Myron said. 'The football team had a terrible season. Too many guys on the injured list.'

Brooke shook her head. 'Good to have him on our side,' she said.

'Yes, it is.'

'So what's our plan here, Myron?'

'It's like Win said. Whatever horrible thing happened to those two boys, it went to London but it started in your home. He's on one end of that. We take the other. We go back to the beginning. We figure out what might have happened.'

Brooke considered that. 'I'm not sure I see the point. We've been over the crime scene a million times.'

'Yes, but we go back at it now with fresh eyes. We can see ahead of us a bit. It's like a car trip where you don't know where you're going. Last week, you only knew the starting point. Now we know where the car was three days ago. So we can try again.'

'It can't hurt to try,' Brooke agreed.

'But more than that, we have to get Patrick to open up.'

'Yes.'

'Nancy's text before we boarded – what did you make of it?'

'I'm not sure.'

'Chick doesn't seem to trust her. How about you?'

Brooke thought about that. 'She's a mother.'

'Meaning?'

'Meaning, in the end, she'll do what's best for her kid. Not mine.'

Mee brought over waters and warmed nuts. She set them down and turned away.

'You don't think she wants to help?' Myron asked.

'No, Nancy gets the pain. She gets it more than anyone, I suppose. But self-interest is a powerful motive. So is a mother concerned for her child. She said in her text, "I'm doing what's best for my son. And yours." She didn't type, "I'm doing what's best for our sons." Do you see?'

'I do.'

'So what do we do about it?'

'We do what's best for your son,' Myron said. 'And hers.'

CHAPTER 12

When they landed, there was another message from Nancy to Brooke: We'll come by your house tomorrow at 9 AM, okay?

Brooke read the message to Myron and Chick.

'Who the hell is "we"?' Chick asked.

'I don't know.'

'Ask her.'

'I think we should wait,' Brooke said. 'I feel like maybe it'll spook her.'

'Spook her how?' Chick asked.

'I don't know. Myron?'

'I think you wait,' Myron said.

Brooke typed the reply: Ok, see you tomorrow.

There were two limos waiting, one for the Baldwins and one for Myron. Brooke stopped before she got in and turned to Myron.

'You should be there tomorrow. You saved their son. They're in your debt.'

Myron wasn't so sure about that, but he said, 'Okay.'

He waited until Brooke and Chick and the limousine were out of sight before heading toward his. When he slid into the back, the driver said, 'It's all been arranged. I'm to stay with you all night.'

'Great.'

'So to the high school?'

Myron checked his watch. 'Yeah, that should work.'

He sat back. The world would probably fall apart tomorrow, but tonight would be, if not life affirming, somewhat normal. It was six thirty P.M. when they hit the town oval in front of the high school. The oval, a half-mile perimeter where the townsfolk liked to jog or take brisk walks or share some gossip, had been cleverly dubbed 'the Circle' because, hey, close enough. The town police station was across the street. The town library was on the bottom right as you entered the Circle. The town recreation center was on the top right. The town church took up a lot of the left, and there on the top of the oval, front and center, if you will, was the expansive town high school.

Key word: 'town.'

The driver pulled up to the gym. Myron opened the heavy metal door and stepped inside. The gym was empty, dark. That surprised him, but then he remembered that they had built a new facility back behind the football field. This one, the one that had meant so much to Myron, was now the 'old gym.' It looked it. It looked a hundred years old. It looked like something that should have peach baskets instead of basketball hoops.

Myron took a few steps, his shoes echoing against the old parquet wood floor. He stopped and stood at center court for a moment. The familiar smell of sweat still hung in the air. They probably still held gym classes in here, or was that a smell, mixed with some sort of heavy-duty janitorial cleaner, that would always be embedded in the woodwork? To some the smell was probably horrid. For Myron it was something closer to celestial.

Smells brought you back. 'Déjà vu' was too weak a term for what Myron was experiencing now. He slowly spun, taking it all in. He looked up at the concrete-and-brick wall above the door. The sign was still there.

TOP BASKETBALL SCORERS OF ALL TIME
1. MYRON BOLITAR

The memories rushed at him so hard and fast he nearly fell back. The old rickety stands were pushed into the wall, but in Myron's eyes they were accordion-pulled-out and full. His mind's eye saw his old teammates and coaches, and for a moment he tried to calculate how many hours he had spent in this gymnasium, how it had all gone so well here, on this floor, in the confines of the basketball court. Sports were supposed to be a reflection of life, a life lesson, a test of endurance and strength, a great preparation for the real world. That was what they always told you. But that wasn't the case for Myron.

143

Everything came easy to Myron on the court. In real life, not so much.

He walked back outside and into the sunlight. He got back into the limo. 'Wrong gym,' Myron said. 'I think the new one is around the other side of the football field.'

The driver took him toward the new facility. When he opened the door, he heard the comforting echo from a dribbling basketball and the familiar squeak of sneakers on the playing surface. Mood music. The new gymnasium was state-of-the-art, whatever that meant. It had bright lights and cool scoreboards and comfortable seats with backs. Everything glistened. But the smell – the combo of sweat and chemical cleaners – was still there. That made Myron smile.

The high school boys' team was scrimmaging, half the team wearing white, the other half green. Myron sat in the front row and watched and tried not to smile too broadly. They were good players, in better shape and more physical than in his day. The Lancers were undefeated so far this season, and rumor had it that they had a chance of breaking the winning streak set more than twenty-five years ago when the last basketball All-American graced this court.

Yep, you guessed it.

There were good players running up and down this court, some even great, but one stood out among the rest.

A sophomore named Mickey Bolitar. Myron's nephew.

Mickey circled to the corner, juked, got the pass, faked the three, drove hard to the hoop on the baseline. The kid was poetry in motion. It was damn near impossible to take your eyes off him. You could see it right away. The greatness. Myron studied his nephew's face and saw that look of what they called 'being in the zone,' focused yet relaxed, on edge yet laid back, whatever terminology you wanted to use, but really it could all be summed up in one word.

Home.

When Mickey was on the court, like his uncle before him, he was home. The court made sense. You could control life on the court. You had friends; you had enemies; you had the ball and those two hoops. You had rules. You had consistency. You were yourself. You were safe.

You were home.

Coach Grady spotted Myron and came over. Some things might change. Others didn't. The coach still wore a polo shirt with an embroidered logo on the pocket and shorts that were a hair too tight. He gave Myron a handshake and followed it with a hug.

'Been too long,' Myron said to him.

'Yeah.' Coach Grady spread his hands. 'What do you think of the new gym?'

Myron looked around for a moment. 'I kinda miss the old one, you know?'

'I do.'

'Then again, maybe we are just being old and grumpy.'

'Could be that too.'

'Maybe I should stand on the porch and yell for the kids to get off my lawn.'

They both turned to the court and watched. Mickey faked a three-pointer, drawing the defender toward him, and then threw a pass down the middle to his teammate for an easy layup.

'He's special,' Grady said.

'Yep.'

'I think he may be better than you.'

'Hush, now.'

Coach Grady laughed and blew the whistle. The game stopped, and for the first time, Mickey let up on his focus and spotted his uncle. He didn't wave. Neither did Myron. The coach called them into the circle at center court, said a few words of encouragement, told them, 'Hands in.' They all put their hands in and shouted, 'Team!' before breaking for the showers.

Mickey jogged over to Myron. He had a towel around his neck. Myron stood. Mickey was sixteen years old, a little taller than Myron, maybe six five. He didn't smile often, at least not around his uncle, but, then again, their relationship, brief as it was, had been strained until recently.

Mickey was smiling now.

'You got the tickets?' Mickey asked.

'They're at will call.'

'Let me just quickly shower. I'll be right back.'

He jogged off. The gym emptied. Myron picked up a stray basketball and headed out onto the court.

He stood at the foul line. He bounced the ball three times. His fingers found the grooves without conscious thought. He released the ball with perfect backspin. Swish. He did again. And again.

Time passed. Impossible to say how much.

'Myron?'

It was Mickey.

They headed outside toward the parking lot. Mickey stopped when he saw the limousine.

'We're taking that?'

'Yep. Problem?'

'It's a little showy.'

'Yeah, it is.'

Mickey looked around to make sure none of his friends was in sight. When he was sure the coast was clear, they both slipped into the back. Mickey leaned forward and stuck his hand out to the driver. 'I'm Mickey.'

'I'm Stan,' the driver said. 'Nice to meet you, Mickey.'

'Same here.'

Mickey sat back and fastened his seat belt. The car started up. 'So I thought you were traveling and we weren't going tonight,' Mickey said.

'I just got back.'

'Where were you?'

'London,' Myron said. 'How's Grandma and Grandpa?'

Grandma and Grandpa were Ellen and Alan Bolitar, Myron's parents. They were staying with Mickey for the next few days.

'They're good.'

'When will your parents be back?'

Mickey shrugged and looked out the window. 'It's supposed to be a three-day retreat.'

'And then?'

'Then if it goes well, Mom can be an outpatient.'

Mickey's tone told Myron to leave it alone. For once, Myron did.

The ride into the heart of Newark took half an hour. The Prudential Center arena is known as the Rock, a reference to the Rock of Gibraltar on Prudential's logo. The New Jersey Devils hockey team played here, and that was about it for the pro teams. The Nets ended up moving to Brooklyn, abandoning their roots, but Myron had seen a lot of college basketball games here, and Springsteen twice.

Myron picked up the tickets at will call. They also got laminated backstage passes.

'Good seats?' Mickey asked.

'Ringside.'

'Sweet.'

'Your aunts take care of us. You know that.'

Tonight's entertainment: professional wrestling.

In the old days, before the Internet made images of scantily clad women readily available, adolescent boys watched titillation in the guise of women's professional wrestling on Sunday morning local television. The undercard for tonight's main events featured a return to those days, to the days of FLOW, the Fabulous Ladies of Wrestling (originally they wanted to call themselves the Beautiful Ladies of Wrestling but the local networks had issues with the ensuing acronym), and some of the organization's all-time favorites.

FLOW had gone out of business many years ago, but somebody, mainly Myron's friend and former business partner, Esperanza Diaz, had resurrected the organization. Nostalgia was in, and Esperanza, known back in her FLOW days as 'Little Pocahontas, the Indian Princess,' hoped to cash in on it. She didn't hire hot young female wrestlers to dazzle the adolescents. That market was already satiated.

Welcome instead to the 'cougar tour' of pro wrestling.

It was the 'senior tour' of professional wrestling. And why not? Golf's senior tour was a big draw. Tennis had one. Those autograph conventions with old actors from seventies TV shows were hotter than ever. Just take a quick gander at the schedule of rock performers at your favorite venues – the Rolling Stones, the Who, Steely Dan, U2, Springsteen – and you realized that either youth was out or maybe they just had no disposable income.

So why not capitalize?

Tonight's Tag Team Championship in the Cougar Division featured the team of Little Pocahontas and Big Chief Mama.

Aka Esperanza Diaz and Big Cyndi.

When they entered the ring – Esperanza still

149

teeth-meltingly rocking a skimpy leopard-print suede bikini with a hair lasso; Big Cyndi, all six six, three hundred pounds of her, squeezed into some kind of leather merry widow and a full feather headdress – the crowd erupted.

Mickey turned to his right to see the opponents coming out of the tunnel. 'What the . . .?'

The crowd began to boo.

Here was where FLOW really tested the boundaries. If Esperanza's and Big Cyndi's ages might qualify them as 'MILFs,' their evil opponents – 'Ladies and gentlemen, give it up for the Axis of Evil, Commie Connie and Iron Curtain Irene!' – would fit more into the 'GILF' category.

For those who might be a little slow in the area of acronyms, the *G* would stand for 'grandmother.'

Still, Commie Connie proudly (or defiantly) wore the same supertight, revealing red costume with Chinese stars and pictures of Mao that had made her famous, while Irene sported a two-piece that formed an old Soviet sickle across her cleavage.

Mickey started playing with his phone.

'What are you doing?' Myron asked.

'I'm looking something up.'

'What?'

'Hold on.' Then: 'According to this, Commie Connie is seventy-four years old.'

Myron smiled. 'Looks great, doesn't she?'

'Uh, yeah, I guess.'

Mickey didn't get it. Then again, he was sixteen. Myron had been ten when he watched Connie, so maybe he was still seeing her through his child-hood goggles the same way we hear our favorite bands through childhood earphones. Whatever. As they sat back and watched the match unfold, Myron downed popcorn.

'So Aunt Esperanza is supposed to be Native American?' Mickey asked.

'Yes.'

'But she's Hispanic, right?'

'Yes.'

'And Big Cyndi is?'

'Anyone's guess.'

'But she's not Native American.'

'No, she's not.' Myron glanced at him. 'There isn't much about pro wrestling that's politically correct.'

'More like downright insensitive.'

'Yeah, I guess. It's a role. We can be outraged about it tomorrow.'

Mickey grabbed some of the popcorn. 'I told a couple of my teammates I knew Little Pocahontas.'

'I bet they were impressed.'

'Oh yeah. One says his dad still has her poster in his weight room.'

'And that's probably politically incorrect too.'

In the ring, Big Cyndi wore enough makeup to put a Kiss concert out of business. Then again, she wore the same in real life too. Big Cyndi made a quick move near the turnbuckle, grabbed Commie Connie in a headlock, and then, with her free hand, she blew Myron a kiss.

'I love you, Mr Bolitar,' she shouted.

Mickey loved that. So did the crowd. So, well, did Myron.

Again, the 'senior tour' for the 'cougar division' title was all about memories, which was tantamount to wanting your favorite band to play its old hits. So that was what the four wrestlers gave the crowd.

Little Pocahontas had always been a fan favorite. She would always be winning on skill, all lithe and tiny and beautiful, dancing around the ring, darting to and fro, earning high marks and cheers from the crowd, when suddenly her evil opponents would cheat to turn the tide. This cheating usually took the form of either jamming sand in Little Pocahontas's eyes (Esperanza was great at acting out 'burning eyes') or using the dreaded 'foreign object' to render her helpless.

Tonight Commie Connie and Iron Curtain Irene did both.

With Big Chief Mama being distracted by the crooked referee, who had been seduced by Commie Connie's promise of sexual favors, Iron Curtain Irene used the sand in the eye while Commie Connie jabbed Esperanza in the kidney with the foreign object. Little Pocahontas was in trouble! The two evil wrestlers now teamed up on Little Pocahontas – something else that was illegal! – pounding her mercilessly, the crowd begging someone to help the poor beauty, when finally Big Chief Mama saw what was happening, pushed the referee out of the ring, and rescued the hot heroine, and together Little Pocahontas and Big Chief Mama faced down the Axis of Evil.

Massively entertaining.

The crowd, including Myron and Mickey, stood and roared.

'So why were you in London?' Mickey asked.

'I was helping an old friend.'

'Do what?'

'We were trying to locate two missing kids.'

Mickey turned to him, his face suddenly serious. 'Wasn't one found?'

'You saw that?'

'It was on some news alert. Patrick something.'

'Patrick Moore.'

'He's my age, right? Disappeared when he was six?'

'That's right.'

'What about the other kid?'

'Rhys Baldwin.' Myron shook his head. 'We're still looking for him.'

Mickey swallowed, turned back to the match. In the ring, Little Pocahontas had just swept the leg of Iron Curtain Irene, knocking her to the mat. Commie Connie was already on the ground and – gasp – Big Chief Mama was standing on the top rope.

'The big finale,' Myron said with a grin.

Seemingly defying gravity, Big Chief Mama bent at the knees and leapt off the top rope and high into the air. The crowd held its collective breath as, almost in slow motion, she began to hurtle back toward earth, landing on both of her opponents with a clearly audible splat.

Neither opponent moved.

When Big Chief Mama rose, you half expected her two adversaries to be pancake flat on the canvas, like Silly Putty or something out of a cartoon. Big Chief Mama rolled over Connie. Pocahontas rolled over Irene. Together they pinned their opponents and the bell rang and the ring announcer shouted, 'The winner and still Cougar Tag Team Champions, from the reservation straight to your heart, let's hear it for Little Pocahontas and Big Chief Mama!'

With the entire arena up on its feet, Big Cyndi lifted Esperanza onto her shoulders. They waved and blew kisses as the applause rained down on them.

And then the next match began.

CHAPTER 13

An hour later, Myron and Mickey flashed their passes and headed backstage. Big Cyndi, still in the leather merry widow and headdress, ran over to Myron and shouted, 'Oh, Mr Bolitar!'

Big Cyndi's makeup had started to run, so that her face resembled a box of crayons left too close to the fireplace.

'Hey, Big Cyndi.'

She wrapped her tree-trunk arms around Myron and pulled him close, lifting him ever so slightly off his feet. Big Cyndi was still covered with sweat, and when she hugged you, it was all consuming, like being wrapped up in damp attic insulation.

Myron smiled and enjoyed the ride. When she finally put him back down, he said, 'You remember my nephew.'

'Oh, Mr Mickey!'

Big Cyndi bear-hugged him the same way. Mickey looked a little confused – it was a wild ride for the inexperienced – but he hung in there. 'Hey, Cyndi, you were great out there.'

She gave Mickey a funny look. 'Cyndi?'

'Sorry. Big Cyndi.'

That pleased her. Big Cyndi had been Myron's receptionist when he and Esperanza had their sports agency. She preferred formalities, so Myron was always Mr Bolitar and she had always insisted others call her Big Cyndi, not just Cyndi. She had even legally changed her name so that official documents now read, last name: Cyndi, first name: Big.

'Where's Esperanza?' Myron asked.

'Doing a VIP meet-n-greet,' Big Cyndi said. 'She's very popular, you know.'

'Yeah, I know.'

'Most of the VIPs are men, Mr Bolitar.'

'Right.'

'They pay five hundred dollars per ticket. The perk is they get a photograph with Little Pocahontas. Not that I don't have my own fan base, you know.'

'Oh, I know.'

'I charge a thousand, Mr Bolitar. I'm more discriminating.'

'Good to know.'

'Care for a green smoothie? You don't look good, Mr Bolitar.'

'No, thanks.'

'Mr Mickey?'

Mickey held up a hand. 'I'm good.'

Two minutes later, Esperanza entered the room wrapping a bathrobe around the suede bikini costume. Mickey quickly stood when she entered. There were no two ways about it. Esperanza had the kind of looks that made all men and boys react. She had the kind of beauty that reminded you of sunsets on the Caribbean or moonlit strolls on the beach.

'Oh, that's sweet of you to stand, Mickey.'

Esperanza frowned at Myron, who remained seated just to prove his point. She gave Mickey a quick kiss on the cheek. Mickey congratulated her on a great show. Myron sat and waited. He and Esperanza had been close friends for a long time. She'd worked with him at the sports agency, going to law school at night, and ended up being his partner. He knew her. She knew him.

So he waited.

After a few minutes of chatter, Esperanza took Mickey's hand. 'Do you mind if I talk to your uncle alone for a few minutes?'

'Oh, sure thing.'

'Come on, Mr Mickey,' Big Cyndi said, beckoning him to follow her. 'Commie Connie spotted you in the first row and said she wanted to meet you.'

'Uh, okay.'

'She said that you looked – and I quote her directly – "delicious."'

Mickey blanched, but he followed her out of the room.

'He's a good kid,' Esperanza said.

'He is.'

'He stop hating you yet?'

'Yeah, I think so.'

'And how are his parents?'

Myron lifted his hand, tipped it left, then right. 'We'll see.'

Esperanza closed the door. 'So you were in London.'

'Yep.'

'You didn't tell me you were going.'

'It was last-minute.'

'And I saw on the news that a missing boy was found in London.'

'Yep.'

'But not Win's cousin.'

'No,' Myron said. 'It was the other kid. Patrick Moore.'

'I also read about some big explosion where the kid was found. It took out an entire wall.'

'You know Win,' Myron said. 'He isn't much for subtlety.'

Esperanza met his eye. 'So it's true? You really saw Win?'

'Yes. He called me for help.'

'Is he okay?'

'Was he ever?'

'You know what I mean.'

'He seems fine.'

'So all those rumors about Win losing his mind and being a recluse . . .?'

'He started them.'

Myron filled her in on everything that had happened. Esperanza sat across from him and listened. It brought him back to better days, when they were younger and starting out and they would discuss contracts and endorsement deals for hours on end. For so many years, Esperanza had been a part of Myron's everyday life. He missed that.

When he finished, Esperanza shook her head. 'Something isn't right here.'

'I know, right?'

'And tomorrow you meet with the boy you rescued?'

'We hope.'

'Big Cyndi and I can help with this, you know.'

'I can handle it. You two are busy.'

'Don't do that, Myron.'

'Don't do what? You have a business to run.'

'A business I run. Big Chief Mama and Little Pocahontas get rotated in and out of the lineup. We can be free anytime you need us.' Esperanza leaned forward. 'This is Win's cousin. I want to be a part of it. So will Big Cyndi. Don't shut us out.'

Myron nodded. 'Okay.' Then: 'Where's Hector, by the way?'

Her face darkened. When she spoke again, the words came out in an angry spit. 'He's with his father.'

'Oh. I take it from your tone that the custody battle is not going well.'

'Tom has an in with the judge. A golfing buddy, believe it or not.'

'You can't get a venue change?'

'My attorney says no. Guess what Tom's claiming.'

'What?'

'I lead a' – Esperanza made quote marks with her fingers – ' "prurient" lifestyle.'

'Because you're a wrestler?'

'Because I'm bisexual.'

Myron frowned. 'For real?'

'Yep.'

'But bisexuality is so mainstream now.'

'I know,' Esperanza said.

'Practically a cliché.'

'Tell me about it. I feel so passé.'

She turned away.

'So it's bad?'

'I may lose him, Myron. You know Tom. He is one of those master-of-the-universe, take-no-prisoner types. It isn't about what's right or wrong or the truth. It's all about winning. It's all about beating me no matter what the cost.'

'Anything I can do?'

'Answer one question.'

'What?'

'You knew he was a twat waffle, didn't you?'

Myron didn't reply.

'So how did you let me marry him?'

'I didn't think it was my business to interfere,' Myron said.

'Whose business was it, then?'

Boom. Drop the mic. Esperanza just stared at him for a second. She had no family. She had only Myron and Win and Big Cyndi.

'Would you have listened to me?' Myron asked.

'No more than you listened to me when I told you how awful Jessica was.'

'I eventually saw the light.'

'Oh yes, you saw the light. Right after she dumped you and married another man.' Esperanza held up her hand. 'Sorry, that was stupid. I'm just pissed off.'

'Don't worry about it.'

'Besides, now you have Terese.'

'And you approve of her.'

'I love her. If I could get her to switch sides, I'd steal her from you.'

'Flattering,' Myron said.

'Wait.'

'What?'

'If Win is back, does this mean I'm not your best man anymore?'

'You never were,' Myron said. 'It's the "man" part that gives him the edge.'

'Sexist.'

'But Terese and I wanted to ask you something.'

'What?'

'We want you to officiate the ceremony.'

Esperanza didn't often look stunned. She did now. 'Really?'

'Yeah. You have to get ordained online or something, but we really want you to be the one who marries us.'

Esperanza said, 'Bastard.'

'What?'

'I have to do another meet-n-greet and now I'm going to start crying.'

'No, you won't. You're too tough.'

'True.' She rose and started for the door. 'Myron?'

'Yeah.'

'How many times has Win asked for help?'

'I think this is the first.'

'We need to find Rhys,' Esperanza said.

Mickey was quiet on the ride home.

Uncle and nephew didn't always see eye to eye. Mickey blamed Myron for a lot of what had happened to his father and mother. In a way, that was fair. Esperanza had wondered why Myron had never butted in to warn her about Tom. The reason involved Mickey. Way back when, Myron had butted in when his brother (and Mickey's father) Brad had wanted to run away with troubled tennis wunderkind (and Mickey's mother) Kitty Hammer.

That decision, made with the best of intentions, had led to disaster.

'The missing boy,' Myron said. 'He's your age.'

Mickey was looking out the window. He had been through a lot for someone so young – his unstable upbringing, his mother's drug addiction, his father's bizarre return from the grave. Mickey had also, it seemed, inherited the Bolitar 'hero complex' gene. He had done a lot of good in a very short time. That made Myron equal parts proud and worried.

'I was thinking maybe you could give me some insight into what he's thinking,' Myron said to his nephew.

'For real?'

'Yes.'

Mickey made a face. 'So when I'm dealing with a guy in his forties, should I get insight into everything about him by asking you?'

'Fair point,' Myron said.

'He was kidnapped, what, ten years ago?'

'Right.'

'Do you know anything about where he was all this time?' Mickey asked.

Myron shook his head. 'Just that we found him working as a street hustler.'

Silence.

'Myron?'

'Yeah.'

'Tell me everything, okay?'

Myron told him the story. Mickey listened without interrupting.

'So Patrick is home now,' Mickey said.

'Yes.'

'And you're supposed to see him tomorrow.'

'That's the plan.'

Mickey rubbed his chin. 'If that doesn't go well, let me know.'

'What makes you think it won't go well?'

'Nothing.'

'And what will you do if it doesn't go well?'

Mickey didn't reply.

'I don't want you involved in this, Mickey.'

'It's a missing teen, Myron. Like you said, I might have some insight.'

CHAPTER 14

Myron's car climbed up past the nouveau riche mansions, so expansive they appeared to have been taking some sort of growth hormone. The lawns were overly manicured, the hedges cropped with too much precision. The sun shone down as though someone had pressed a button and cued it up to do so. The brick was perfectly faded, too perfectly, adding to the faux–Las Vegas–Disney effect of the surroundings. No one had a tar driveway. They were made of some kind of fancy limestone that you didn't want to ruin by driving over it. Everything reeked of money. Myron rolled down the window expecting to hear a fitting soundtrack to this ideal setting, maybe Bach or Mozart, but there was only the sound of silence, which, come to think of it, was the ideal soundtrack.

The homes were beautiful and picturesque and had all the warmth of a chain motel.

There were several news trucks on the street, though not as many as you might think. The gate was open, so Myron pulled into the Baldwins', yep, limestone driveway. It was eight thirty, half an hour until the meeting with the Moores. Myron stepped out of the car. The grass was so green he almost bent down to see if it'd been freshly painted.

A chocolate Labrador sprinted toward him. Her tail was wagging so excitedly that her butt could barely keep up. She half slid the last few yards to him. Myron got down on one knee and gave the dog a good scratch behind the ears.

A young man – Myron guesstimated his age at twenty – came up behind her. He had the dog's lead in his hand. His hair was long and wavy, the kind of long and wavy where you keep throwing back your head to keep it out of your eyes. He wore a black Lycra jogging ensemble with navy blue sleeves that exactly matched the navy blue in his sneakers. Myron thought that maybe he could see a little of both parents in his features.

'What's your dog's name?' Myron asked.

'Chloe.'

Myron stood. 'You must be Clark.'

'And you must be Myron Bolitar.' He took a step and extended his hand. Myron shook it. 'Nice to meet you.'

'Same,' Myron said.

Myron did the math quickly in his head. Clark was Rhys's older brother. He'd been eleven when the kidnapping occurred, making him twenty-one now.

For a moment they both just stood there awkwardly. Clark looked to his right, then his left, then forced up a smile.

'You in school?' Myron asked, just to ask something.

'Yeah, I'm a junior.'

'Where do you go?'

'Columbia.'

'Great school,' Myron said, just to say something. 'Do you know your major, or is that an annoying question only adults ask?'

'Political science.'

'Ah,' Myron said. 'That was my major.'

'Great.'

More awkwardness.

'Any idea what you want to do when you graduate?' Myron asked because he couldn't think of something more hackneyed and inane to ask a twenty-one-year-old.

'None whatsoever,' Clark said.

'No rush.'

'Thanks.'

Was that sarcasm? Either way, more awkwardness ensued.

'I should probably go inside,' Myron said, pointing toward the front door, in case Clark didn't know what he meant by 'inside.'

Clark nodded. Then he said, 'You're the one who saved Patrick.'

'I had help.' Which again was a stupid thing to say. The kid wasn't looking for humility right now. Then: 'Yeah, I was there.'

'Mom says you almost saved Rhys.'

Myron had no idea how to reply to that, so

he started to glance around, and then it dawned on him.

This was the crime scene.

The path he was now standing on had been the one Nancy Moore took when she first rang the bell to retrieve Patrick from his playdate. It was the one Brooke would take a little while later when they couldn't reach Vada Linna, the au pair.

'You were eleven,' Myron said.

Clark nodded. 'Yeah, that's right.'

'Do you remember anything?'

'Like what?'

'Like anything. Where were you when it happened?'

'Why does that matter?'

'I'm just taking another look at the whole thing, that's all.'

'So what do I have to do with it?'

'Nothing,' Myron said. 'But that's how I do it. Investigate, I mean. I stumble in the dark. I ask a lot of dumb questions. Most go nowhere. But sometimes even a dumb question creates a spark.'

'I was in school,' Clark said. 'Mr Dixon's class. Fifth grade.'

Myron considered that. 'Why weren't Rhys and Patrick in school?'

'They were in kindergarten.'

'So?'

'So in this town, kindergarteners only go for a half day.'

Myron mulled that over for a moment. 'What do you remember?'

'Nothing really. I came home from school. The police were here.' He shrugged.

'See?' Myron said.

'See what?'

'You helped.'

'How?'

The front door opened. Brooke stepped out. 'Myron?'

'Yeah, sorry, I was just talking to Clark.'

Without another word, Clark put the lead on the dog and started jogging toward the road. Myron headed toward Brooke, not sure if he should kiss her cheek or shake her hand or what. Brooke pulled him in for a hug, so he went with it. She smelled nice. She wore blue jeans and a white blouse. They looked good on her.

'You're early,' Brooke said.

'Do you mind showing me the kitchen?' Myron asked.

'Getting right to it, eh?'

'I didn't think you'd want me to ease into it.'

'You thought right. This way.'

The floor was marble, so their footsteps echoed in the three-story foyer. There was a grand staircase, a look you didn't often see in real life. The walls were light mauve and covered in tapestries. There were steps to move from the living room into a rectangular kitchen the approximate size and dimensions of a tennis court. Everything was either white or chrome, and Myron wondered at the effort it must take to keep a room like this clean. There were floor-to-ceiling windows offering a rather breathtaking view of the backyard, a swimming pool, and a gazebo. Farther out, Myron could see the start of the woods.

'So if I remember the police report right,' Myron said, 'your nanny was by the sink.'

'That's right.'

Myron spun to his left. 'And the two boys were sitting at the kitchen table.'

'Right. They'd been out playing in the yard.'

Myron pointed out the windows. 'The backyard?'

'Yes.'

'So they're playing outside. Then your nanny brings them in here for a snack.'

Myron walked over to the sliding glass door and tried it. It was locked. 'They would have come in this door?'

'Yes.'

'And then she left the door unlocked.'

'We used to always leave it unlocked,' Brooke said. 'We felt safe back here.'

That quieted the room.

Myron broke it: 'According to your nanny, the kidnappers were wearing black and ski masks and all that.'

'Right.'

'And you don't have any surveillance cameras or anything like that?'

'We do now. But then, no. We had a camera by the front door so we could see who rang the bell.'

'I assume the police checked it out.'

'Nothing to check. It didn't record. We only used it for live viewing.'

There was a round kitchen table with four chairs. Rhys had only the one sibling – Clark – so Myron wondered whether it had always been like that, the four chairs, and after what happened to Rhys, no one had the heart to move it. Did they sit there at dinner every night for ten years, at that table, the one chair empty?

He looked at Brooke. She knew what he was thinking. It was all over her face.

'We sometimes eat on the island too,' she said.

There was a large rectangular marble island in the middle of the kitchen. A variety of upscale brass pans hung from the ceiling above it. One side had storage. The other had six barstools.

'One thing,' Myron said.

'What?'

'Everything faces the windows. I mean, except for one of the chairs at the kitchen table. The sink has a view. The stove has a view. The barstools and even the table.'

'Yes.'

Myron walked over to the sliding glass door. He looked to his left, then to his right. 'So three men in ski masks get all this way – all the way to this door – and no one sees them?'

'Vada was busy,' Brooke said. 'She was preparing

171

the snack. The boys, well, they wouldn't be looking out the window. They were probably playing some kind of video game or messing around.'

Myron looked at how wide open the yard was, how big the windows were. 'I guess that's possible.'

'What else would it be?'

No reason to answer that quite yet. 'Clark told me he was in school when the boys were taken.'

'Right. So?'

'Most kids finish school around three in the afternoon. The kindergarteners in this town only go half a day, right?'

'Right. They were let out at eleven thirty.'

'And the kidnappers knew that too.'

'So?'

'So nothing. It suggests some planning on their part; that's all.'

'The police figured that. They figured that they probably followed Vada or Rhys and knew their schedule.'

Myron thought about that. 'But Rhys didn't come home after school every day, did he? I mean, I assume sometimes his playdates took him to other kids' homes. I assume he went to Patrick's sometimes, for example.'

'Right.'

'So on the one hand, this looks carefully planned out. Three men. Knowing the schedule. And then on the other, they rely on your au pair leaving this sliding door unlocked and no one seeing them as they approached.'

'They could have known she never locked it.'

'By spying on how she entered the kitchen from the yard? Unlikely.'

'They also could have smashed the window,' Brooke said.

'I'm not following.'

'Let's say Vada had spotted them. Do you think she could have gotten to the door and locked it in time? And then what? They could have smashed the glass and grabbed the boys.'

It was all possible, Myron thought. But why wait? Why not grab the boys when they were out in the yard? Were they afraid someone would see?

It was too early to theorize. He needed to gather more facts.

'So here they are, the kidnappers, stepping inside right where we are now,' Myron said.

Brooke stiffened for a moment. 'Yes.'

'That was kind of abrupt, I'm sorry.'

'Don't patronize me.'

'I'm not. But it doesn't mean I have to be insensitive either.'

'Let's get this out of the way,' Brooke said.

'Get what out of the way?'

'You're probably wondering how I do it,' Brooke said. 'How I come into this kitchen every day and walk right past where Rhys was taken. Do I block? Do I cry sometimes? I do a little of both, I guess. But mostly I remember. Mostly I come in this kitchen and what happened is my companion. And I need that. Everyone wondered why we didn't move away. Why we invite this pain. I'll tell you why. Because this pain is better. This pain is better than the pain of giving up on him. A mother doesn't give up on her child. So I can live with the pain. I can't live with giving up.'

Myron thought about what Win had told him, about how the lack of closure was eating at Brooke, making it all the more unbearable. There comes a time when you have to know the answers. Maybe you can live with the pain, but the not knowing, the purgatory, the limbo, had to eat away at your bones.

'Do you understand now?' Brooke said.

'I do, yeah.'

'Then ask your next question,' she said.

Myron dove right in. 'Why the basement?' He pointed to the sliding glass door. 'You break in here. You've grabbed the boys. You have the nanny. You decide to leave her alive. You decide to tie her up. So why not do it here? Why bring her down to the basement?'

'For the reason you just stated.'

'That being?'

'If they tied her up here, you'd be able to see from the backyard.'

'But if the backyard is that exposed, why go that way in the first place?'

Myron heard heavy footsteps coming down the steps. He checked his watch. Eight forty-five A.M.

'Brooke?'

It was Chick. He hurried into the room and

174

pulled up when he saw Myron. Chick wore a business suit and tie and sported a fancy leather tote, the modern-day equivalent of a briefcase. Was Chick planning on talking to Patrick, and then, what, catching a few hours at the office?

Chick didn't bother with hello. He held up his mobile phone.

'Don't you check your texts?' he asked his wife.

'I left my phone in the foyer. Why?'

'Group text from Nancy to both of us,' Chick said. 'She wants us to meet at their house, not here.'

CHAPTER 15

They took Myron's car. Myron drove. Chick and Brooke sat in the back. They held hands, which somehow seemed out of character for them.

'Turn left at the end of the road,' Chick said.

Left started them back down the mountain. The area was slightly less affluent, but you were just talking about varying degrees of high rent. Chick told him where to make the right and the next left. The journey was a short one. The two houses were less than a mile apart.

When they made the final turn onto the Moores' street, Chick looked up ahead and muttered, 'Crap.'

News vans, lots of them, lined both sides of the road. That made sense, of course. After a ten-year absence, Patrick Moore was home. The press wanted pictures and video of the missing boy and the happy parents and the big reunion. So far, only one image of the recently rescued Patrick had surfaced in the media. An orderly at the hospital in London had taken a somewhat blurry picture of the sleeping teen from a distance and sold it to a British tabloid.

There was an obvious hunger for more.

The media began to swarm the car, but Myron kept moving so that no one could get in front of them. There was a town cop at the foot of the driveway. He waved Myron in and stopped anyone from following. The media obeyed, choosing instead to rely on their zoom lenses. Myron noticed a FOR SALE sign in the yard. In front of him, the garage door slid open. He pulled inside, the electric door beginning to close behind him. Myron turned off the engine. They waited for the door to close completely, cutting off those probing lenses, before all three of them opened their car doors and stepped out.

The garage fit two cars. The car parked next to them was a Lexus sedan. There was no clutter in the garage, not so much because the owners appeared to be orderly but because there simply wasn't anything here. Nothing about this place felt 'suburban family,' but then again why would it? Patrick too had an older sibling, a sister, Francesca, who'd be about Clark's age if Myron recalled correctly, and no younger siblings. Hunter and Nancy were divorced, so up until a few days ago, that was it – single mom, one college-age daughter. Nancy had probably been ready to move out and start the next chapter of her life.

The door between the house and garage opened. Hunter Moore leaned his head out. He seemed surprised to see Myron with them, but he shook it off. 'Hey, guys, come this way.'

They took the two steps off the concrete and

onto the tile. The kitchen was quasi-homey, done up to look rustic with stone veneers and wood-paneled cabinetry. Nancy stood by the kitchen table with a man Myron didn't recognize.

The man smiled at them. The smile made Myron cringe a bit. He was balding, wiry, probably in his early fifties, with the kind of glasses you call spectacles. He wore a denim shirt tucked into faded jeans. His whole persona had an emcee-at-an-outdoor-folk-festival vibe.

The six of them all stood there for a moment, as though both couples had brought surrogates who would duel it out. Myron tried to get a bead on Nancy and Hunter. He came up only with nervous. Mr Folk Festival, on the other hand, seemed in his element. He spoke first.

'Why don't we all have a seat?' he said.

'Who the hell are you?' Chick asked.

He turned his cringingly gentle smile toward Chick. 'I'm Lionel.'

Chick looked at Myron, then at his wife, then at the Moores. 'Where's Patrick?'

'He's upstairs,' Lionel said.

'So when can we see him?'

'In a bit,' Lionel said. 'Why don't we all just sit down in the living room, where we can be more comfortable?'

'Hey, Lionel?' Chick said.

'Yes?'

'Do we look like we're in the mood to be comfortable?'

Lionel nodded in the most understanding, compassionate, phony way possible. 'Point taken, Chick. Is it okay if I call you Chick?'

Chick looked at Myron and Brooke as though to say, *What the eff?*

Brooke stepped toward Nancy. 'What's going on here, Nancy? Who is this guy?'

Nancy looked helpless, but Lionel stepped between them.

'My name is Lionel Stanton,' he said. 'I'm a doctor looking after Patrick.'

'What kind of doctor?' Chick asked.

'I'm a psychiatrist.'

Uh-oh. Myron didn't like where this was headed.

Nancy Moore took Brooke's hand. 'We want to help.'

'Of course we do,' Hunter added. He swayed a little bit, and Myron wondered whether he was sober.

Chick said, 'Why do I think I hear a "but" coming?'

'No "but,"' Lionel said. And then: 'I just need you to understand. Patrick has been through a tremendous ordeal.'

'Really?' Chick said, his voice thick with sarcasm. 'We wouldn't know anything about that, would we?'

'Chick.' It was Brooke. She shook her head for him to stop. 'Go on, Doctor.'

'I could dance around this for a bit,' Lionel said, 'but let me just tell you this right from the get-go.

179

No stalling. No fancy words. No excuses. Just the flat-out truth.'

Oh boy, Myron thought.

'At this juncture, Patrick can't help you.'

Chick opened his mouth, but Brooke silenced him with a wave. 'What do you mean, he can't help us?'

'I understand that last night Mrs Moore suggested you meet at your house.'

'Yes, that's right.'

'I overruled that decision. That's why you're here. To bring Patrick back to the place where it all began, the scene of the crime, if you will – it could be devastating to his already fragile psyche. Patrick is nearly catatonic. When he does speak, it is to say he's hungry or thirsty, and even that only occurs when he's prompted.'

Myron spoke for the first time. 'Have you asked him about Rhys?'

'Of course,' Lionel said.

Brooke: 'And?'

Lionel again gave her the most understanding, compassionate, phony expression possible. 'He can't tell us anything about your son. I'm sorry.'

'That's BS,' Chick said.

Nancy stepped toward Brooke. 'We're trying our best,' she said.

'You have your son back,' Brooke said. 'We don't. Don't you get it? We are no closer to finding Rhys than we were before all this.'

'I don't think there is much he can tell you anyway,' Lionel said.

Chick was having none of that. 'Excuse me?'

'Don't get me wrong. I am with him constantly. We are doing all we can so that Patrick opens up. But right now he remembers very little. It's as though he remembers being a child here, and that's it. Even if he could tell you about the actual kidnapping, I don't think that would help very much. All we know for now is that your son was being held by the same man who held Patrick.'

Myron said, 'Patrick confirmed that?'

'Not in so many words. The key is to get him acclimated. Patrick is spending a great deal of time with his sister, Francesca. I think he finds Francesca to be a comfort. We want to let him start hanging out with people his own age, start to socialize a bit, but we need to take baby steps.'

Chick: 'What the hell is going on here?'

Hunter said, 'Calm down, Chick.'

'Like hell, I'll calm down. Your kid knows what happened to mine. He has to talk to us.'

'I'm afraid that's impossible,' Lionel said.

'Are you for real? This is a kidnapping investigation. I'm calling the cops.'

'That won't do any good,' Lionel said.

'Why the hell not?'

'The police have been here, of course. But as Patrick's doctor, I've advised the family against allowing him to be questioned at this time. My job is to worry about my patient and my patient only, but in truth, I think it's best for all. Again, I want to assure you that we are doing all we can to put Patrick in a space where he feels comfortable opening up.'

'And when might that be?' Chick asked.

'Chick,' Nancy said, 'we are all trying our best here.'

'So what do you expect us to do?' Brooke asked, the edge in her voice now. 'Should we, what, go home and wait for you to call us?'

'I know how difficult this must be,' Nancy said.

'Yeah, Nancy, I'd think you would.'

'But I have to worry about my son too.'

'Your son' – Brooke's hands formed two fists – 'is home. Do you not get that? He's home. You can hold him. You can feed him and make sure he's warm at night. My son . . .'

And for the first time, Myron saw the chink in Brooke's armor. So did Chick.

'The hell with this,' Chick said. He stormed out of the room and toward the front of the house.

'Where do you think you're going?' Lionel asked.

Chick didn't answer. He headed for the stairs. 'Patrick?'

'Wait,' Hunter said, 'you can't just go up there.'

'Stop,' Lionel said. 'You'll traumatize him.'

Chick didn't even bother glancing behind him. He started up the stairs. Hunter hurried after him. Not sure exactly what to do, Myron moved his body a little, just enough to throw Hunter off the straight path.

Chick called out, 'Patrick?'

Myron heard a door open, then close. Hunter

and Lionel rushed up the stairs. Myron stayed right behind them, ready to intervene further if he needed to. Brooke and Nancy were behind him. Everyone, except Myron, was shouting. When they got to the top of the stairs, Chick was in front of the final door.

'No!' Hunter shouted. He dove toward Chick, but he was too late.

Chick opened the door. When he looked inside, he froze.

Myron was a lot bigger and stronger than Lionel. It didn't take much to block him out so Myron could get to the door first. When he got there, he followed Chick's gaze to the far corner of the bedroom.

There, huddled into the corner as though he was trying to burrow into the wood, was Patrick Moore.

The room had clearly not been changed in the past decade. It was the room of a six-year-old. The bed was shaped like a race car. There was a poster for an old superhero movie on one wall. Three modest-sized sports trophies sat on one shelf. His name was spelled out in big wooden letters above his closet. The wallpaper was a lively blue. The carpet was designed to look like a basketball key.

Patrick wore flannel pajamas. There were head-phones on the floor in front of him, but right now, he had his hands covering his ears. His eyes were shut. His knees were up against his chest, and he rocked back and forth.

He started muttering, 'Please don't hurt me, please don't hurt me,' as though it were a mantra.

Nancy Moore pushed past Myron and ran across the room. She dropped to her knees and took her son into her arms. He buried his face in her shoulder. Nancy turned toward the door with a baleful look. Hunter stepped into the room behind her. Lionel did the same. The three of them were lined up now, almost in a formation, to protect the crying teen.

'We tried to explain it to you nicely,' Hunter said. 'Now I want you to get out of our house.'

CHAPTER 16

I love Rome.

I always stay in the Excelsior hotel's Villa La Cupola, a suite that takes up the top two stories of this former palace. I like the outdoor sundeck overlooking the Via Veneto. I like the frescoes on the dome, painted in such a way as to match the horizon out the window. I like the private theater, the sauna, the steam bath, the Jacuzzi.

Who wouldn't?

Back in the day, Vincenzo the concierge knew and handled my, shall we say, entertainment likings. It would be his task to have what they politely referred to as a 'lady of the evening' or 'courtesan' awaiting my arrival. Sometimes two. On rare occasions, three. The Villa La Cupola suite had six bedrooms. This made it easy for whatever company was hired to spend the night, if she so desired, but not with me. This was my way. This was how I preferred it.

Yes, I have hired prostitutes on many occasions. I will pause while you gasp out loud in indignation and then tsk-tsk your moral superiority.

Done? Terrific.

I would point out that these escorts were 'high-end' or 'upscale,' but in truth that makes it no better or worse and it would make me even more of a hypocrite to pretend otherwise. For me it was a business transaction that worked both ways. I like sex. Alert the media. I like sex – and by sex, I mean strictly the pleasures of the flesh – a great deal. I like sex in its purest form, meaning I do not like strings or attachment or other common distractions. Myron believes that what he labels 'love' or 'feelings' enhances sex. I do not. I believe that those things dilute it.

Do not look into that too deeply. I do not fear commitment. I just have no interest in it.

I have never pretended otherwise. I do not lie to the women I have been with, those hired or those I've met and with whom I engage in what might commonly be called a one-night (often two or even three nights) stand. They understand the situation. I explain the limitations and, I hope, the joy. Many have, of course, thought that they could win me over, that once I experienced their skills in the bedroom, once I got close to them and saw how fantastic they were, I would be smitten and it would lead to more than what one might refer to as bedroom romps.

Fair enough. Give it your best shot, my sweet. I will not discourage you.

My dearest friend, Myron Bolitar, though 'friend' seems an inadequate word to describe our relationship, worries about this aspect of my personality.

186

He feels there is something 'missing' inside of me. He traces it back to what my own mother did to my father. But does the origin matter? This is what I am. I am quite content this way. He claims that I don't get it. He is wrong. I do understand the need for companionship. My favorite times are when he and I sit around together and simply discuss life or watch television or dissect a sporting event – and then, when we are done, I go to bed with a gorgeous body and, uh, gorge.

Does that sound like 'something is missing' to you?

I have no interest in defending myself to the judgmental, but for the record: I am for equal rights, equal pay, equal opportunity. Feminism, by dictionary definition, is the 'theory of political, economic, and social equality of the sexes.' By that definition, and almost every definition I encounter, I am a feminist.

I don't lie to women. I don't cheat on them. I treat every guest or employee well and with respect. They, in turn, reciprocate. Except, of course, during those inflamed moments when neither one of us wants to be treated well or with respect, if you get my obvious drift.

You may be wondering, then, why I have stopped the practice of engaging in said professional services that has worked so well for so long. The simple truth is, I worked off an illusion of consent, of a fair business practice, of a contract without duress. I have been educated to the fact that this is not always the case. Recent history, especially when you consider the plights of Patrick and Rhys, has just reiterated this point for me. There are those who feel I should have realized this many years ago, that I should have seen the abuses earlier, that I turned a blind eye due to self-interest.

Again my reply: Fair enough.

I leave my room and take the elevator to the Excelsior's overly baroque lobby. Vincenzo spots me and meets my eye. I gently shake him off. He worries that he will miss my gratuity, but why should he suffer because of my somewhat hypocritical moral code?

I know Rome fairly well. I'm far from a native, but I have traveled here extensively. I head down the Via Veneto toward the American embassy. I make the right at the Via Liguria and wind my way to the top of the Spanish Steps. The walk is nothing short of delightful. I take the 135 steps down to the bottom and make my way to the famed Trevi Fountain. It is overrun with tourists. That is okay. I join them. I take out a coin and, using my right hand, I throw it over my left shoulder.

Too touristy a move for such a sophisticate as *moi*? Of course. But there is a reason certain activities become touristy, no?

My mobile phone rings. I hit the answer button and say, 'Articulate.'

A voice on the other end says, 'They are there now.'

I thank him and hang up. The walk to the shop on the Piazza Colonna takes me five minutes. This is Rome. Everything is old. Nothing has been redone. There is no pretense of updating, and I, for one, am thankful. The marble column in the center of the piazza, named for Marcus Aurelius, has stood where it is now since AD 193. In the sixteenth century, almost fourteen hundred years later, the then pope ordered a bronze statue of St Paul to be placed atop the column.

History in a nutshell: Bye-bye, your god. Hello, mine.

A palace sits on the north end of the piazza. There is a fancy 'galleria' on the east. 'Galleria,' by the way, is just a snooty way of saying 'mall.' The sporting goods shop I am looking for, with its small, tacky window display, is located right next to the tiny white church from the eighteenth century. There is a child mannequin wearing an AS Roma soccer jersey in the window. There are a variety of soccer balls and soccer cleats and soccer socks and soccer scarves and soccer caps and soccer sweatshirts.

In a word: soccer.

I enter. The man behind the counter is ringing up a customer. He pretends not to see me. I head toward the back of the store and up the stairs. I have never been here before, but I've been given pretty specific instructions. The door is in the back. I knock. The door opens.

'Come in,' the man says.

I step in the room and he closes the door behind me. He puts out his hand for me to shake. 'I'm Giuseppe.'

Giuseppe is wearing a soccer referee uniform. He is going all in with this look. Not only does he sport the shirt, but he rocks the regulation black shorts, the matching socks pulled high, and a whistle around his neck. His watch is big and thick and probably doubles as a game clock.

I look past him. The room is set up like a mini soccer pitch. The carpet is grass green with white lines delineating midfield, out of bounds, the box. There are desks on the opposite walls where the goals would be. The desks face the wall, so that the two men sitting at them have their backs to each other. They are both furiously typing on computers.

'That's Carlo,' Giuseppe says, pointing to the man on the right. Carlo is decked out in a Roma home uniform of imperial purple with gold trim. His wall is decorated with all things Roma, including the team logo, a wolf feeding human boys Romulus and Remus from her teat, which is historically interesting and visually confusing. Head shots of current Roma players line where the wall meets the ceiling.

Carlo keeps typing. He does not so much as nod in my direction.

'And this is Renato.'

Renato at least nods. He too wears a soccer uniform, his of sky blue with white. His desk/goal is all for a team called Lazio. Everything is in sky blue. The head shots here also line where the wall meets the ceiling. The Lazio logo is far simpler than Roma's: an eagle carrying a shield in its talons.

'Gentlemen,' Giuseppe says in his accented English, 'this is our new sponsor.'

In a sense, Myron has sent me here. He has a remarkable memory. I asked for as much specific detail as he could give me on his brief time with Fat Gandhi. He told me about the gamer situation going on when he entered – I don't know much about video or computer games or what have you – but he noted how Fat Gandhi wanted to beat his chief rivals – the 'damned Italians' with the team name ROMAVSLAZIO.

Roma vs. Lazio.

For those not so educated in the ways of European football, Roma and Lazio are hated soccer rivals. They are both teams from Rome and even share a stadium. Without going into much detail, every year the two teams face off in the Derby della Capitale – the translation, I think, is obvious enough – which could be perhaps the fiercest inner-city match in sports.

Giuseppe leans close to me and whispers, 'They don't like each other much.'

'More like hate,' Carlo mutters, still typing.

'He's a terrible man,' counters Renato, throwing what the kids call 'shade' at Carlo.

'Both of you stop it,' Giuseppe says. Then to me:

191

'Carlo and Renato met at a brawl outside the Stadio Olimpico.'

'Roma won,' Carlo says.

'By cheating,' counters Renato.

'You're just a bad loser.'

'The referee. He was paid off.'

'No, he wasn't.'

'Your man was three meters offside!'

'Stop,' Giuseppe says. 'So you see there was a brawl.'

'Crazy bastard tried to kill me,' Carlo says.

'Ah, you so exaggerate!'

'He stabbed me with a knife.'

'It was a pen!'

'It broke skin.'

'No, it didn't.'

'It scratched for sure. I had a blue mark down my arm!'

'Roma is afraid of the dark.'

'Lazio players wear skirts.'

'You take that back.'

Carlo puts his hand to his ear. 'Which team has won more derbies again?'

'Oh, that's it.' Renato's face is scarlet. 'Let's go!'

Renato stands and throws a paperclip across the room. It hits the back of Carlo's chair, going nowhere near Carlo's face, but Carlo falls to the floor as though he's been shot.

'My eye! My eye!'

Carlo cups his eye with one hand and rolls back and forth as though in great pain. Giuseppe blows his whistle. He races over to Renato, reaches into his pocket, and pulls out a yellow card.

'Sit back down!'

'He's faking!' Renato shouts.

Carlo is smiling now. He moves his hand away and winks at Renato. When Giuseppe turns toward him, Carlo cups his eye and starts grimacing in pain again.

'He's faking!' Renato insists.

'I said, sit down. Don't make me bring out the red card.'

Renato, still fuming, sits back down. Carlo gingerly gets back into his chair.

Giuseppe comes back toward me. 'They're insane, both of them. But they are great at what they do.'

'Which is gaming.'

'Yes. But pretty much anything involving computers.'

'They lost to Fat Gandhi, though.'

Both Carlo and Renato turn in unison: 'He cheats.'

'How do you know?'

'No one can beat us fairly,' Carlo says.

'Fat Gandhi has to use more than two players,' adds Renato.

I think back to Myron's description of the room. 'He does.'

Both men stop typing now. 'You know for sure?'

'I do.'

'How do you know?'

193

'It's not important.'

'It is to us,' Carlo says.

'He took away our title,' adds Renato.

'You'll have your chance at revenge,' I tell them. 'Have you started implementing my plan?'

'One hundred thousand euros?'

'Yes.'

Carlo types with a smile on his face. So does Renato.

Giuseppe says, 'We're ready.'

CHAPTER 17

Esperanza met Myron in the back corner of
Baumgart's.

Baumgart's restaurant was an old Jewish
soda fountain/deli that had been purchased by
Chinese immigrant Peter Chin. Wanting to do
something both different and wise, Peter had kept
all the old touches and added an Asian fusion
(whatever that meant) menu and some neon lights
and hip décor. Now you could order Kung Bao
Chicken or a Pastrami Reuben, the Chinese
Eggplant Combo or a Turkey Club.

Peter came over and bowed toward Esperanza.
'You do my restaurant a great honor with your
presence, Ms Diaz.'

Myron said, 'Ahem.'

'And you don't completely kick its reputation to
the curb.'

'Good one,' Myron said.

'Did you see it?' Peter asked.

'See what?'

Beaming now, Peter pointed behind him. 'Look
at my wall of honor!'

Like many restaurants, Baumgart's hung up

framed autographed photographs of the celebrities who had dined there. It was an eclectic mix of New Jersey celebrity. Brooke Shields was up there. So was Dizzy Gillespie. Grandpa 'Al Lewis' Munster was on the same wall, along with several stars from *The Sopranos,* a few New York Giants players, local news anchors, a *Sports Illustrated* swimsuit model, and an author Myron had once read.

There, hung dead center between a rapper and a villain from the old *Batman* TV show, was a photograph of Esperanza 'Little Pocahontas' Diaz dressed in her suede bikini. The bikini top was starting to slide down her shoulder. Esperanza posed in the ring, sweaty and proud and looking up.

Myron turned to her. 'You stole that pose from Raquel Welch in *One Million Years B.C.*'

'I did.'

'I had that poster on my wall when I was a kid.'

'So did I,' Esperanza said.

Peter was still beaming. 'Great, right?'

'You know,' Myron said, 'I was a professional basketball player.'

'For about three minutes.'

'You're so nice to your customers.'

'Part of my charm. Your food will be out soon.'

Peter left them alone. Esperanza was killer in an aqua blouse. She wore gold hoop earrings and a thick bracelet. Her cell phone buzzed. She took a look and closed her eyes.

'What?' Myron asked.

'Tom.'

'He's texting you?'

'No, it's my attorney. Tom canceled all settlement talks.'

'So he's going full frontal.'

'Yep.'

'I'd like to help.'

She shook him off. 'We're not here to discuss Tom.'

'Doesn't mean we can't.'

Nicole the waitress came over with appetizer-sized Cold Sesame Noodles and a Sizzling Duck Crepe. Serious yum. They both went quiet for a moment and ate. Way back when, Myron Bolitar had founded a sports agency cleverly dubbed MB SportsReps. The *M* stood for Myron, the *B* for Bolitar, the SportsReps because he repped athletes. Marketing – it's a gift, really.

Esperanza came on as his receptionist/assistant/ confidante/assorted other hats. She went to school at night to get her law degree. Eventually she moved up to full partner, though she didn't insist on changing the name to MBED because, really, that would be confusing. They did drop 'Sports' from the name when they started representing actors and musicians and the like, so that in the end, the company had been called MB Reps.

Big Cyndi took over as receptionist and, well, agency bouncer. Things went along pretty swimmingly until they all fell apart. When Tom started this slash-n-burn custody hearing a year ago – back then he'd claimed Esperanza was an unfit mother because she worked too hard – Esperanza had been so freaked-out by the threat that she asked Myron to buy her out. Myron hesitated, but then when Win disappeared, the thought of continuing without both of them was too disheartening. They ended up selling MB Reps to a mega-agency that took their clients and got rid of the name altogether.

'So I went to the Alpine police station,' Esperanza said, 'to see what they were doing with the Moore-Baldwin case.'

'And?'

'They wouldn't talk.'

Myron stopped eating. 'Wait, they wouldn't talk to you?'

'That's right.'

He thought about that. 'Did you flash cleavage?'

'Two buttons' worth.'

'And that didn't work?'

'The new police chief is female,' Esperanza said. 'And straight.'

'Still,' Myron said.

'I know, right? I was a little insulted.'

'Maybe I should try,' Myron said. 'I'm told I have a terrific ass.'

Esperanza frowned.

'I could meet her. Turn the charm on full blast.'

'And have her disrobe right in the station?'

'You may have a point.'

Esperanza rolled her eyes without actually rolling

her eyes. 'I don't think she can help us anyway. The local force has had a lot of turnover since Rhys and Patrick were kidnapped.'

'I doubt they'll handle the case this time anyway.'

'I'm sure it'll get kicked up to state or federal, but Big Cyndi did a little digging. The guy who ran the case ten years ago is retired. His name is Neil Huber.'

'Wait, I know that name.'

'He's a state senator in Trenton now.'

'No. Something else . . .'

'He used to be a high school basketball coach.'

Myron snapped. 'That's it. We played Alpine when I was in high school.'

'So maybe you should be the one who talks to him,' Esperanza said. 'Do your male sports bro-connect thing.'

'Sounds like a plan,' Myron said.

'Or wiggle your once-terrific ass.'

'I'll do what it takes,' Myron said. Then: 'Wait, "once-terrific"?'

Myron waited outside the nightclub.

New York City's Meatpacking District tradition-ally runs from West Fourteenth Street down to Gansevoort Street on the far west side of the island. In the 1900s it was known for, what else, slaughterhouses, but with the rise of supermarkets and refrigerated trucks, the area began to fall into disrepair. In the 1980s and 1990s, drugs and street prostitution were the main industry down there.

It was a place where transsexuals and BDSM practitioners could thrive side by side with the Mafia and NYPD corruption. Nightclubs catering to what was then considered 'subculture' began to open.

But like most of Manhattan, the Meatpacking District underwent another transformation. It started in part because people are drawn to the illicit – to the sleaze, if you will – but then, of course, the rich who crave danger want to go out on that edge with the most comfortable safety harness possible. So gentrification took hold. High-end boutiques offered commerce with trendy exposed brick. The grungy nightclubs became overrun with hipsters. The restaurants started to cater to whatever they started calling yuppies. The old rusted elevated railroad tracks became a tree-lined promenade called the High Line.

The Meatpacking District was now clean and safe and you could bring your kids, and yet when something like that happens, where does the sleaze go?

Myron checked his watch. It was midnight when the man finally lurched out of the trendy Subrosa nightclub. He was drunk. He'd grown a beard and wore flannel and, oh man, was that really a man bun? He had his arm draped like a strap around a young – too young – woman. The words 'midlife crisis' weren't tattooed on his forehead, but they should have been.

They started stumbling down the road. The man

took out his car keys and pressed the remote button. His BMW beeped its location. Myron crossed the street and made his approach.

'Hello, Tom.'

The man, Esperanza's ex, spun toward him. 'Myron? Is that you?'

Myron stood and waited. Tom seemed to sober up a bit. He stood up a little straighter. 'Get in the car, Jenny,' he said.

'It's Geri.'

'Right, sorry. Get in the car. I'll be with you in a second.'

The girl teetered on her heels. It took three tries but she managed to open the passenger door and fall inside.

'What do you want?' Tom asked.

Myron pointed at his head. 'Is that really a man bun?'

'So you're here to make jokes?'

'Nope.'

'Did Esperanza send you?'

'Nope,' Myron said. 'She has no idea I'm here. I'd be grateful if you didn't tell her.'

The passenger door opened. Geri said, 'I don't feel so good.'

'Don't you dare throw up in my car.' Tom turned to Myron. 'So what do you want?'

'I want to encourage you to make peace with Esperanza. For her sake. And for your son's.'

'You know she left me, right?'

'I know your marriage didn't work.'

'And you think it was my fault?'

'Don't know. Don't care.' More young people spilled out of the nightclub, laughing and cursing in the obnoxious way of the greatly intoxicated. Myron shook his head. 'Don't you think you're too old for this, Tom?'

'Yeah, well, I was married and settled, you know.'

'Let it go,' Myron said. 'Stop lying about her.'

'Or what?'

Myron said nothing.

'What, you think I'm afraid of you?'

Geri said, 'I think I'm going to be sick.'

'Not in the car, honey, okay?' Tom turned back to Myron. 'I'm working on something here.'

'Yeah, I can see that.'

'She's hot, right?'

'Hot,' Myron agreed. 'And about to vomit. Yeah, I'm all turned on.'

'Listen, Myron, no offense. You're a good guy. You're not much of an intimidator. Just piss off, okay?'

'Esperanza is a good mother, Tom. We both know that.'

'It isn't about that, Myron.'

'Yeah, well, it should be.'

'I don't want to sound immodest,' Tom said, 'but do you know why I'm a big success?'

'Because your daddy is rich and gave you lots of money?'

'No. It's because I go for the jugular. It's because I win.'

Never fails. Scratch a guy who always talks about what a winner he is or how he's 'self-made' or how he's pulled himself up by the bootstraps, and underneath you'll always find a little boy who had everything handed to him. It was like they needed a blind spot to justify their tremendous luck. Something like: *I can't have all of this because of fate or chance – I must be special.*

'I'm asking you to be reasonable, Tom.'

'That's your message to me?'

'It is.'

'I'll pass, thanks. I'm on the verge of victory. You' – he pointed at Myron – 'are proof of that. She's getting desperate. Tell her I said to kiss my ass.'

'I told you already: Esperanza doesn't know I'm here. I just think you should do the right thing.'

'For her sake?'

'For her sake. For Hector's sake. And for your sake.'

'For mine?'

'I think it would be best.'

'Well, I don't give a shit what you think. Go home, Myron.'

Myron nodded. 'Will do.'

Tom waited. Myron started to cross the street, but he stopped and did his best Columbo turn. 'Oh, one thing.'

'What's that?'

Myron tried not to smile. 'I saw Win.'

The street went silent. Even the music spilling out of the nightclub seemed to hush.

'You're lying.'

'No, Tom, I'm not. He's coming home. And when he does, I'm sure he'll want to pay you a visit.'

Tom stood there, frozen. Geri, still inside the car, finally lost it and threw up in the loudest way possible. Windows rattled. Tom still didn't move.

Myron let the smile come to his face as he waved good-bye. 'Have a great night.'

CHAPTER 18

It was a bright, clear New Jersey morning.

Huge neon lettering on the southern side of the Lower Trenton Toll Supported Bridge spelled out the following slogan: TRENTON MAKES, THE WORLD TAKES. The letters were installed in 1935, and maybe back then, with linoleum, ceramics, and other manufacturing plants in full swing, there was a modicum of truth in the wording. Not now. Trenton was the capital of New Jersey, home to the state government and thus filled with politicians and their ensuing scandals, which made the entire city, when you thought about it, as honest as the message on the bridge you crossed to enter it.

Still, Myron loved this state, and anyone with even an inkling of knowledge knew that New Jersey hardly held a patent on governmental corruption. The political scandals might be more colorful here, but then again, everything was. New Jersey was hard to define because it was a hodgepodge. Up north, it was the suburbs of New York City. To the southwest, it was the suburbs of Philadelphia. Those two major cities drained resources and attention from New Jersey's own urban centers, leaving Newark and Camden and the like sucking for life like a retiree with an oxygen tank at an Atlantic City casino. The suburbs were lush and green. The cities were destitute and concrete. And so it goes.

Still, it was odd. Anyone who lived within a forty-minute drive of Chicago or Los Angeles or Houston said they were from that city. But you could live two miles from New York City and you would say you were from New Jersey. Myron grew up half an hour away from New York City and maybe five miles from Newark. He never said he was from either. Well, one time he said he was from Newark, but that was because he wanted to apply for financial aid.

You put all that together – the beauty, the blight, the sophisticated cities, the inferiority complex, the tacky, the classy – and you got the indefinable color and texture of the great state of New Jersey. Better to find the definition of New Jersey in Sinatra's voice, in Tony Soprano's ride, in a Springsteen song. Listen closely. You'll get it.

Myron was a little disappointed to see that Neil Huber looked the part of a New Jersey politician. His fingers were sausage thick, a gold pinkie ring on his right hand. His suit was striped; his tie shimmered as though someone had sprayed it with tanning oil. The collar of his shirt was too tight, and when he smiled, Neil Huber resembled a barracuda.

'Myron Bolitar,' he said, greeting him with a firm handshake and showing him to a seat. The office had a plainness you might associate with your high school vice principal's.

'I coached against you when you were in high school,' Huber said.

'I remember.'

'No, you don't.'

'Pardon?'

'What, did you look it up when you knew we were meeting?'

Myron held out his hands, wrists together. 'Caught.'

Neil gave him a good-natured wave. 'No worries. So you know you beat us.'

'Yes.'

'And that you scored forty-two points.'

Myron said, 'It was a long time ago.'

'I coached high school basketball for eighteen years.' He pointed a stubby finger at Myron. 'You, my friend, are the best I've ever seen.'

'Thank you.'

'I hear you got a nephew playing.'

'I do.'

'He as special as they say?'

'I think so.'

'Good, great.' Neil Huber leaned back. 'So, Myron, have we done enough of the break-the-ice, chitchat thing?'

'I think we have.'

Neil spread his hands. 'What can I do for you?'

He had the prerequisite family photographs on the desk – a blond wife with big hair, grown married children, a sprinkling of young grandkids. On the wall behind him, the New Jersey State flag featured a shield with three plows and a horse's head above it. Yep, a horse's head. You can fill in your own *Godfather* joke, but it will be obvious and beneath you. Two female goddesses, the goddess of liberty (okay) and the goddess of agriculture (again too easy), stood on either side of the shield. The flag was bizarre and dense, but then again, bizarre and dense described New Jersey pretty accurately.

'It's about a case you worked when you were a cop in Alpine,' Myron said.

'The Moore and Baldwin kidnappings,' he said.

'How did you know?'

'I was a detective. So I deduced.'

'I see.'

'Clue one' – he raised his index finger – 'I worked on very few major cases. Clue two' – he was making a peace sign now – 'I worked on exactly one major case that remains unsolved. Clue three' – you get the drift with the fingers – 'one of the abducted boys was just found after ten years.' He lowered his hand. 'Yes, sir, really took all my powers of deduction to come up with that one. Myron?'

'What?'

'Did you know the Moores are going on CNN in a few hours?'

'No, I didn't.'

'Instead of a big press conference, they're doing a sit-down with Anderson Cooper at noon.' He leaned forward. 'Please tell me you're not press.'

'I'm not press.'

'So what's your interest in this?'

Myron debated how to play it. 'Could I just say it's a long story?'

'You could. It won't get you anywhere. But you could.'

Nothing ventured, nothing gained. Plus, politico though he might appear, Myron was taking a shine to Neil Huber. Why not be honest if you can?

'I'm the one who rescued Patrick.'

'Come again?'

'In London. Like I said, it's a long story. My friend is Rhys Baldwin's cousin. He got a tip on his whereabouts. We tracked him down.'

'Whoa.'

'Yes.'

'You said it was a long story.'

'Right.'

'Maybe you should tell it to me.'

Myron gave him as much as he could without incriminating or even mentioning Win by name. Still, Neil Huber wasn't an idiot. It wouldn't be difficult to find out who Rhys's cousin was. But so what?

When he finished, Neil said, 'Holy crap.'

'Yeah.'

'So I still don't get why you're here.'

'I'm looking into the case again.'

'I thought you became a sports agent or something.'

'It's complicated.'

'I suppose it is,' Neil said.

'I just want to take a fresh look at it.'

Neil nodded. 'You figure I made a mistake and maybe you can look at it and see what I was missing?'

'It's been ten years,' Myron said. 'We know new things now.' He thought about how Win had put it. 'It's like a car trip where you don't know where you're going. Last week, we only knew the start. Now we know where the car was a few days ago.'

Neil frowned. 'What?'

'It sounded better when my friend said it.'

'I'm just busting your balls. Look, I only had the case a short time. The FBI took it away from me pretty fast.' He tilted back in his chair and rested his hands on his belly. 'Ask away.'

'So yesterday I was at the crime scene.'

'The Baldwins' house.'

'Yes. And I was trying to piece together how it all happened. That backyard is wide open, and the kitchen has those big windows.'

'Plus,' Neil added, 'there's a gate by the driveway entrance. And fencing around the property.'

'Exactly. And there's the timing.'

'The timing?'

'They were kidnapped around noon. Most kids are still in school at the time. How did the kidnappers know they'd be home?'

'Ah,' Neil said.

'Ah?'

'You see holes.'

'I do.'

'You think the official scenario doesn't add up.'

'Something like that.'

'And you think, what, we didn't notice all this stuff ten years ago? We raised all the issues you're raising now. And more of them. But you know what? Lots of crimes don't make sense. You can poke holes in almost anything. Take the gate, for example. The Baldwins never closed it. It was useless. The backyard? The Baldwins had lawn furniture. You could sneak up that way. Or you could press your body against the back of the house and no one would see you until you were by the windows.'

'I see,' Myron said. 'So you satisfied your doubts?'

'Whoa, I never said that.'

Neil Huber loosened his tie and undid the top button of his shirt. The red in his face seemed to drain away. Now Myron did have a sense of déjà vu. He could see the younger man, the coach for the other team, or maybe it was just a fake memory he was concocting for the occasion.

'I had doubts,' he said, his voice a little quieter now. 'We all did, I guess. But at the end of the day, the two boys were gone. We followed every angle we could find. Stranger abductions like this – breaking into a house, asking for a ransom – are extremely rare. So we looked hard at the parents.

We looked hard at the families, the neighbors, the teachers.'

'How about the nanny?'

'Au pair,' he said.

'Pardon?'

'She wasn't a nanny. She was an au pair. Big difference.'

'In what way?'

'An au pair is like an exchange program. They're always from a foreign country. In this case, Vada Linna – yep, I remember the name – was from Finland. They are usually young. Vada was eighteen. Her English was fair at best. They are supposedly there in part on something of a cultural education, but most people go with them because they're cheap labor.'

'You think that was the case here?'

He thought about it. 'Nah, I don't. Not really. The Baldwins have a lot of money. I think they bought into the whole international experience stuff and loved the idea of having their kids in the company of a foreigner. From what I understood, Brooke and Chick treated Vada well. That whole angle – it's one of the reasons I hate the press so much.'

'What is?'

'When the crap hit the fan, the media had a field day with all of that slave labor–au pair talk. You know – privileged rich girl Brooke Baldwin hires poor, cheap worker so she can get her hair done or lunch with the ladies or whatever. Like she wasn't already victimized enough. Like losing her son was somehow her fault.'

Myron remembered reading a bit about the controversy at the time. 'Vada's story about the break-in,' he said. 'Did you believe it?'

Huber took his time on this one. His hand rubbed his face. 'I don't know. I mean, the girl was clearly traumatized. She may have been fudging some of the details, trying to make herself look better or something. Like we've both noted, there were parts that didn't add up. But that could have been the language barrier too. Or the cultural barrier, whatever. I wish we'd had more time with her.'

'Why didn't you?'

'Vada's father showed up within twenty-four hours. Flew in from Helsinki and hired a shark lawyer. The father demanded to take her home. The ordeal was too much for her, he said. He wanted her to get care in Finland. We tried to stall, but we had no reason to hold her. So he flew her home.' Neil looked up. 'Truth? I would have liked another crack at Vada.'

'Do you think she was involved?'

Again he took his time. Myron liked that Neil Huber was trying to give him thoughtful answers. 'We looked at her hard. We went through her computer history. There was nothing. We checked her text messages. There was nothing there that stood out. Vada was just a teen alone in a foreign country. She had one friend, another au pair, and that was about it. We tried to work out various theories where she'd been in on the kidnapping in some way. You know. Maybe she gave the kids to an accomplice. Then the accomplice tied her up. They make up a story about a kitchen break-in. That kind of thing. But nothing added up. We even explored the possibility that maybe Vada was a psycho. Maybe she snapped and killed them and hid the bodies. But nothing came of that either.'

Their eyes met.

'So what do you think happened, Neil?'

There was a pen on his desk. He picked it up and started twirling it between his fingers. 'Well, that's why recent developments are interesting.'

'How so?'

'They blow away my theory.'

'Which was?'

He shrugged. 'I always figured that Patrick and Rhys were dead. I figured that whatever happened – abduction, break-in, whatever – that the two boys were killed right away. The killers then pretended to be kidnappers and did that whole ransom-drop thing to distract us. Or maybe they hoped that it would be easy money but they realized that they'd get caught. I don't know.'

'But why would someone kill two boys?'

'Yeah, motive. That's a tougher nut to crack. But I think the crime scene is the key.'

'Meaning?'

'The Baldwin home.'

'You think Rhys was the target?'

'Had to be. It was his house. The playdate was planned two days before, so you couldn't know Patrick Moore would be there. So maybe these guys are told to grab a six-year-old boy. But when they break in, there are two of them. So they don't know which is which or their instructions aren't so clear, so they figure, let's grab both. Just to be sure.'

'And again: Motive?'

'Nothing concrete. Hell, not even wet cement. Just wild conjecture on my part.'

'Like?'

'The only parent who we had anything on was Chick Baldwin. The guy's a crook, plain and simple, and right about then, when his Ponzi scheme collapsed, he pissed off a lot of people. Some of his money came from questionable Russians, if you know what I mean. Chick skated too. No jail time, small fine. Good lawyers. That upset a lot of folks. All his assets were in his kids' names, so no one could touch him. Do you know the guy at all?'

'Chick? Just a little.'

'He's not a good guy, Myron.'

Almost word for word what Win had said.

'Anyway,' Neil said, 'that's what I thought. They were dead. But now that Patrick is alive . . .'

He just let it hang there. The two men looked at each other for a long moment.

Myron said, 'Why do I have a feeling you're holding back on me, Senator?'

'Because I am.'

'And why would you do that?'

'Because I'm not sure if the next part is any of your goddamn business.'

'You can trust me,' Myron said.

'If I didn't trust you, I would have thrown you out of my office a long time ago.'

Myron spread his arms. 'So?'

'So this is ugly. We kind of buried this ten years ago because it was ugly.'

'When you say "kind of buried—"'

'We looked into it. It came to nothing. I was told to back off. I did so but with some reluctance. In the end, I still don't think it's relevant. So I'm going to need a second or two to ponder the repercussions of telling you.'

'If it helps,' Myron said, 'I promise to be discreet.'

'It doesn't.'

Neil stood and walked over to the window. He turned the wand controlling the blinds, closing them for a moment, then opening them again. He stared down at a construction site.

'There were text messages,' Neil said, 'between Chick Baldwin and Nancy Moore.'

Myron waited for him to say more. When he didn't, Myron asked, 'What kind of text messages?'

'Lots of them.'

'Do you know what they said?'

'No. They were deleted off both their phones. The phone company doesn't keep a record of the content.'

'I assume you asked Chick and Nancy about them?'

'We did.'

'And?'

'They both claimed it was just normal stuff. Some of it was about their boys. Some of it was about the Moores maybe investing with Chick.'

'Did the Moores invest with Chick?'

'They did not. And the texts were at all hours of the day. And night.'

'I see,' Myron said. 'Did you talk to their spouses about it?'

'We did not. The FBI was involved by now. You have to remember what it was like. The pressure, the fear, the not knowing. The families were already hanging on by a thread. We investigated this angle hard and came up with nothing. We didn't see a reason to cause anyone any more pain.'

'And now?'

Neil turned away and looked down at Myron in the chair. 'And now I still don't see a reason to cause anyone any more pain. That's why I didn't want to tell you.'

There was a knock on the door. Neil told the knocker to come in. A young man stuck his head in the doorway. 'You have that meeting with the governor in ten minutes.'

'Thank you. I'll meet you in the lobby.'

The young man closed the door. Neil Huber moved back to his desk. He scooped up his mobile phone and wallet and jammed them into his pockets. 'It's an old saw, but a case like this never leaves you. I blame myself in part. I know, I know, but I do. I wonder maybe, just maybe, if I were a better cop . . .'

He didn't finish the sentence. Myron rose.

'Do what you have to,' Neil said, starting for the door. 'But keep me in the loop.'

CHAPTER 19

'Is it noon yet?' Chick asked.

Myron checked his watch. 'Five minutes away.'

'I better set up the laptop, then.'

They were sitting at the enormous marble bar at La Sirena, an Italian restaurant in Chelsea's famed Maritime Hotel. The place was somehow sleek and warm, modern yet with a definitive sixties vibe. The border between dining inside and dining alfresco was almost nonexistent. Myron made a mental note to take Terese here pronto.

There was no television on the wall – it wasn't that kind of place – so Chick brought a laptop so they could live-stream the CNN interview.

'I couldn't stay home today,' Chick said. His skin always glistened, so that he looked as though he'd undergone some kind of hot-wax treatment. Maybe he had. 'Brooke and I just stare at each other and wait. It brings it all back, you know?'

Myron nodded.

'It's hard on so many levels, but it's like we've been living in purgatory for ten years. You have to keep yourself busy or you lose your mind. So I

219

came into my office this morning. Then I met with my lawyers to see what we could do.'

'Do about what?' Myron asked.

'About Patrick not talking. I was looking for some legal recourse. You know, to make him cooperate.' Chick looked up from the laptop. 'What did you want to see me about anyway?'

Myron wasn't sure how to raise the subject of the texts with Nancy Moore yet. Should he go the direct route or ease into it?

'Hold up,' Chick said. 'It's about to air.'

The modern era. La Sirena had a good blend of the art world, Village hipsters, and Wall Street masters of the universe. The place was lively with the arriving lunch crowd, and here, at the bar, two men were huddled over a laptop watching a news program. No one looked twice.

'Wait, where are they?' Chick asked.

Myron recognized the room. 'That's the Moores' living room.'

'They're not doing it in a studio?'

'Guess not.'

On the screen, Anderson Cooper sat in a plush leather chair. Nancy and Hunter sat on a couch across from him. Hunter wore a dark suit and dark tie. Nancy wore a light-blue dress that was stylish yet conservative.

'Where's Patrick?' Chick asked. 'Myron?'

'I don't know. Let's watch, okay?'

The interview began without Patrick. Anderson started with some background – the kidnapping, the ransom drop, the strain of no answers, the long wait for this day. He raised the fact that Nancy and Hunter were now divorced, clearly implying that the breakup was a direct result of what had happened. Neither Nancy nor Hunter bit, though.

'We share custody of our beautiful daughter,' Nancy said by way of explanation.

'We raised her together,' Hunter added.

After a few more minutes, Chick shook his head and said, 'Unbelievable. They're giving him nothing.'

It was somewhat true. Anderson wasn't pushing them, which was understandable under the circumstances. These weren't politicians running for office. These were parents who had suffered greatly and were now trying to comprehend their sudden . . . Would you call it luck?

Nancy did most of the talking. She explained to Anderson how grateful they were to have Patrick home again. 'Our son has been through a terrible ordeal,' she said, biting her lower lip. When Anderson tried to get some details, they deflected by talking about Patrick's need for privacy and 'space for recovery and transition.'

This was the message, repeated in various forms: Please give Patrick and the Moore family privacy to recover from this terrible ordeal. They used the phrase 'terrible ordeal' to the point that Myron wondered whether they'd been coached to say it.

Anderson pressed on. He asked about the kidnapping, if they were any closer to catching the perpetrators. The Moores offered no real answer, deferring questions 'about possible apprehensions' to the 'authorities.'

When Anderson raised that 'horrible day,' Nancy said, 'It was a long time ago. You need to remember he was only six years old.'

'How much does he remember?'

'Very little. Patrick was moved around a lot over the years.'

'What do you mean, "moved around"?'

Tears flooded her eyes. Myron waited for Hunter to take her hand. He didn't. 'Our son nearly died from a stabbing.'

'That was during his rescue in London, correct?'

'Yes.'

'How long had he been in London?'

'We don't know. But he went through' – Myron mouthed the words with her this time – 'a terrible ordeal.'

Myron watched Nancy and Hunter on the screen, looking for any clues or body language that might suggest . . . What exactly? Deception? Did he think that they might be lying here? Why? What would they be hiding, if anything? He also sneaked glances at Chick, as though that might tell him something too. How was Chick reacting to Nancy? Did Myron sense a wisp of – again, what? – longing, regret, guilt?

Conclusion: Studying body language was tremendously overrated.

Myron had so often heard of people wrongly

convicted (or wrongly exonerated) because jurors felt that they could 'read' the perpetrators, that they didn't show enough (or showed too much) remorse, that their reactions were not in what the jurors considered the range of normal. As though humans came in one size and shape. As though we all react the same way to a horrible or stressful situation.

We all think we can spot the tell in everyone else, but ironically, no one can spot it in us.

Finally, Anderson got to it: 'What about the other boy who was taken that day?'

Chick sat up.

'What has your son been able to tell you about Rhys Baldwin, who is still missing?'

'Finding Rhys is our number one priority right now,' Nancy said.

Chick muttered something under his breath.

'This will never be over,' she continued, 'until we know the truth about Rhys.'

Hunter nodded his vigorous agreement. 'We are cooperating as much as possible with law enforcement . . .'

Chick sat back. 'Do you believe this crap?'

'. . . but unfortunately there is little that Patrick knows that can help.'

'They're cooperating? That's what they're claiming?' Chick was nearly apoplectic. 'I should hold my own press conference.'

Like that would do any good.

Toward the end of the segment, Nancy and Hunter rose from their seats and turned to the right. Chick quieted down as the camera pulled out. A woman of about twenty years old appeared.

'This is our daughter, Francesca,' Nancy said.

Francesca gave the viewers an awkward nod. Then she looked off camera and mouthed the words 'It's okay.' Three seconds passed.

When Patrick stepped into view, he was holding his sister's hand.

'And our son, Patrick,' Nancy said.

It was the same boy Myron had rescued, the same boy he had seen huddled in the corner of his bedroom. He wore a Yankees baseball cap, a blue hoodie, jeans. The camera zoomed in tight on his face. He kept his eyes down. Nancy and Hunter moved to either side of their children. For a moment it looked as though they were posing, albeit clumsily, for a holiday photo. Hunter and Nancy tried to look strong and defiant. Francesca looked overcome with emotion, her eyes brimming with tears. Patrick kept his eyes down toward the ground.

Then Anderson thanked them for 'opening up their home' before going to commercial.

Chick stared at the blank screen for a few seconds.

'What the hell was that?'

Myron didn't reply.

'What's going on, Myron? Why won't they help us?'

'I don't know that they can.'

'You too? You're buying this?'

'I don't even know what they're selling, Chick.'

'I told you I went to my lawyers today, right?'

'Right.'

'So I asked them what we could do. You know. To make the kid talk.'

'What did they suggest?'

'Nothing! They say there's nothing to be done. Can you believe that? Patrick doesn't have to say a damn thing. You can't compel him to tell you. Even if he knows something crucial. Hell, even if he knows where Rhys is right now. It's nuts.'

Chick signaled to the bartender, who poured him some Johnnie Walker Black. The bartender looked over at Myron. Myron shook his head. Too early in the day.

When Chick got his drink, he huddled around it as though it were a fire providing warmth. 'I appreciate your help here,' he said, a little calmer now. 'Win, well, I know Win doesn't like me. No surprise really. We are from two different worlds. Plus he thinks Brooke walks on water. No one would be good enough for her, you know?'

Myron nodded, just because he wanted him to keep talking.

'But Brooke and me, we have a solid marriage. It's had its problems, sure. Like any other. But we love each other.'

'Those problems,' Myron said, spotting the opening. There was no reason to wait any longer. 'Was Nancy Moore one of them?'

Chick had been bringing the whiskey to his lips.

He hesitated, debating whether he should reply first or take a sip. He chose the sip. He placed the drink back on the bar and turned to Myron.

'What's that supposed to mean?'

Myron just stared at him. He tried to wait it out.

'Well?' Chick said.

'I know about the texts.'

'Ah.' Chick rose, took off his suit jacket, hung it neatly over the back of the barstool. He sat back down and fiddled with the gold cuff link on his left wrist. 'And how do you know about the texts?'

'Does it matter?'

'Not really,' Chick said, shrugging it away too casually. 'They're nothing.'

Myron tried to stare him down again.

Chick was trying to sound nonchalant, but it wasn't holding. 'Does Win know?'

'Not yet.'

'But you'll tell him?'

'Yes,' Myron said.

'Even if I ask you not to?'

'Even if.'

Chick shook his head. 'You don't get my life.'

Myron said nothing.

'The rest of them, they got everything handed to them. I worked. I scraped. I got nothing easy. News flash, Myron' – he leaned and cupped his hand around his mouth – 'the game is rigged for the rich. It ain't a level playing field. I started with nothing. My father owned a barbershop in the

Bronx. You want to get up there with them? You need to cheat a little.'

'Wait, let me write this down.' Myron mimed a pen and paper. 'Cheat. A. Little.' He looked up. 'Great tip. Are you also going to tell me that behind every great fortune there's a great crime?'

'You mocking me?'

'Maybe a little, Chick.'

'You think, what, this country is a meritocracy? That we all start in the same place, all have the same chances? That's crap. I played college foot-ball. I was a running back. Was pretty good too. One day I realize that every guy who is trying to tackle me is on steroids. And every guy who is trying to take my position? Steroids. So I have a choice. I can take steroids too. Or I can stop competing.'

'Chick?'

'What?'

'This is an odd argument for cheating on your wife,' Myron said.

'I didn't cheat.' He leaned in close. 'But my point is, either way, you're leaving this alone.'

'Is that a threat, Chick?'

'Those texts have nothing to do with my kid. And I get your motive here.'

'My motive is finding your kid.'

'Right, sure. You want to hear something that still haunts me? Brooke wanted to call Win as soon as Rhys was taken. Day one. But I talked her out of it. I thought the cops could handle it. I wanted to – and this is funny after what I just told you – I wanted to play by the rules. Do things by the book. Funny, right? So I live with that.'

'You're not making any sense, Chick.'

He leaned in close. Myron could smell the whiskey. 'Whatever happened between me and Nancy,' he said through gritted teeth, 'it has nothing to do with my son. You hear me? You need to step off before someone gets badly hurt.'

Myron's cell phone sounded. He looked at the caller ID and saw that it was Brooke Baldwin calling. He showed it to Chick before bringing the phone to his ear.

'Hello?'

'Chick told me you two were meeting,' Brooke said. 'Is he with you now?'

Myron looked at Chick. Chick nodded and leaned into the phone. 'I'm right here, hon.'

'Did you both see CNN?'

'Yes,' Myron said.

'I taped it,' Brooke said. 'I've been watching it freeze-frame.'

Chick said, 'So?'

'So I'm not convinced that boy is Patrick Moore.'

CHAPTER 20

Just seeing Terese's name on his caller ID made Myron's bunched shoulder muscles unknot. He hit the answer button as he headed to his car and without preamble said, 'I love you so much.'

'No knock on Win,' Terese replied, 'but that's a much cooler way of answering the phone than "Articulate."'

'I may not use it for everyone,' Myron said.

'Oh, why not? Make someone's day.'

'Where are you?'

'In my hotel room,' Terese said. 'Hey, remember the last time we were in a hotel room together?'

Myron couldn't help but grin. 'How many calls did we get complaining about the noise?'

'Well, Myron, you were awfully loud.'

Myron switched the phone to his other ear. 'My toes were numb for a week.'

'I don't get that reference.'

'Me neither, but somehow it sounded right.'

'It did,' she agreed. 'I miss you.'

'Me too.'

'This job.'

'Yes?'

'If I get it – and that's a big if – but if I get it, they may want me to relocate to Atlanta or DC.'

'Okay,' Myron said.

'You'd move?'

'Sure.'

'Just like that?'

'Just like that.'

'I mean, I could commute at first,' she said.

'No commute. We move.'

'God, you're sexy when you're bossy.'

'And even when I'm not.'

'Don't push it.' Then Terese said, 'Are you sure? I can back out. There will be other job opportunities.'

Myron had lived his whole life in this area. He had been born here, raised here, spent four years in college in North Carolina, returned here. He was so attached to this area that he had even bought his childhood home rather than let go of the past.

'I'm sure,' Myron said. 'I want you to have the career you want.'

'Ugh, don't sound so PC.'

'I also want to be a kept man.'

'That might require performing sexual favors on demand,' Terese said.

Myron sighed. 'I give and I give.'

She laughed. Terese didn't laugh often. He loved the sound. 'I better get ready,' she said. 'The second interview is in an hour.'

'Good luck.'

'Where are you headed?' Terese asked.

'After this call? To a cold shower. Then I'm going to see my parents and Mickey.'

'I saw that press interview on TV.'

'Any thoughts?'

'What you said.'

'What's that?'

'You're missing something.'

They got off the phone then with a minimum of mushiness. Myron started driving toward his hometown. Could he really do it? Could he move out of the area he had always called home?

The answer, for the first time in his life, was a resounding yes.

Win called him during the drive.

'Hello?'

'Tell all,' Win said.

'Did you see the Moore family interview?' Myron asked.

'I did.'

In the background, Myron could hear men shouting in a foreign language. 'Where are you exactly?'

'Rome.'

'Italy?'

'No. Rome, Wyoming.'

'No reason for sarcasm.'

'Who needs a reason?'

'Brooke is not positive the boy is Patrick,' Myron said.

'Yes, she texted me that.'

'I called PT down in Quantico. He has a friend who might be able to help us. She does stuff with forensic facial reconstruction or something.'

'I did my own cursory check,' Win said. 'Comparing a still shot of what we saw today with Patrick at age six and via age progression.'

'Any conclusions?'

'No,' Win said. 'But I ask myself two questions. If it isn't Patrick, then who is it? If it isn't Patrick, what possible motive would Nancy and Hunter have to lie about it?'

Myron thought about it. 'I don't know.'

'A DNA test would help.'

'It would,' Myron agreed. 'But again, suppose we find out it isn't Patrick. What would that mean? You got a second?'

'I do.'

'So let's look at all the possible angles, even the most outrageous.'

'Such as?' Win said.

'Such as, suppose Nancy and Hunter killed both boys and hid their bodies. I know, I know, outrageous, but just for the sake of this thought experiment, let's suppose it's possible.'

'Okay.'

'So maybe to throw suspicion off themselves, they set out to bring a fake Patrick back. They find a teenager who's the right age and right look. They send you those emails leading you in that direction. You find the teen at King's Cross or whatever. You with me?'

'Not fully,' Win said.

'Right, because even the most outrageous scenario makes no sense. That's my point. There was no heat on any suspects – not after all these years. No one was starting to suspect them. If they had killed the boys – again I'm just talking here; I don't think that's the case – they'd gain nothing by pretending Patrick was found.'

'True,' Win said. Then: 'Of course, it could be another sort of con.'

'That being?'

'Let's say the boy isn't Patrick.'

'Okay.'

'Let's say, though,' Win continued, 'that someone is setting up Nancy and Hunter. They arrange to have this fake Patrick found. They know that Nancy and Hunter want it so much to be their son that they'd be easily fooled.'

'The desire for resolution,' Myron said.

'Precisely. It can be blinding.'

'But again: What's the motive? Is this fake Patrick going to steal money or something?'

Win considered that. 'No, I don't think that would be it.'

'And the boy's injuries were real. He was stabbed. We're lucky he didn't die.'

'At the hands of Fat Gandhi,' Win said. 'Myron?'

'Yes?'

'We are doing it again.'

'Doing what?'

'Ignoring Sherlock's axiom. We need more data.'

Win was right. They often quoted Sir Arthur Conan Doyle's beloved Sherlock Holmes: 'It is a capital mistake to theorize before one has data. Insensibly one begins to twist facts to suit theories, instead of theories to suit facts.'

'Myron?'

'Yes.'

'What else is wrong?'

Myron let loose a deep breath. 'You're not going to like this.'

'Oh, then please stall and sugarcoat it for me.'

'More sarcasm?'

'More stalling?'

Myron dove straight in, telling Win about his visit to Neil Huber and the texts between Chick Baldwin and Nancy Moore. When he finished, Win went quiet for a moment. Myron could still hear the men shouting in a foreign – he assumed Italian – tongue.

'Why are you in Rome?' Myron asked.

'I'm getting close to Fat Gandhi.'

'He's in Italy?'

'Doubtful.' Then: 'Do you believe Chick when he says those text exchanges were innocent?'

'No,' Myron said. 'But that doesn't mean they have anything to do with the kidnapping.'

'True,' Win said.

'You want me to take a run at Nancy? Confront her about the texts?'

'I do, yes.'

'And what about Brooke?'

'What about her?'

'Do we tell her about the text exchanges?' Myron asked.

'Not yet.'

Myron remembered her reaction in London to not being told about the emails Win had received. 'She'll be angry you're holding out on her again.'

'I can live with that,' Win said. There was a pause. 'Are we done, Myron?'

'I think so.'

'Good, I need to go.'

CHAPTER 21

The team name popped up just as Myron was noting that Cousin Brooke would be angry that I was holding out on her again. SHARK CRYPT I.

'I can live with that,' I tell him, completely distracted now. It is time to get off the phone. 'Are we done, Myron?'

'I think so,' Myron says.

'Good, I need to go.'

I end the call before Myron replies. I am in that same back room with Carlo, Renato, and Giuseppe. They are all still geared up, but their mood is more serious today, more somber, as the Muzzles of Rage challenge has begun. My plan is a simple one: Draw out Fat Gandhi.

From everything I know about him, Fat Gandhi is a competitive bastard in this techno-video-whatever world. His biggest rival is ROMAVSLAZIO, which is, thanks to my anonymous largesse, hosting this brand-new prestigious event. The question we need to answer: Even if Fat Gandhi is somewhat underground, even if he is at least temporarily in hiding, will he come out if challenged to a high-stakes, heavily sponsored quasi-military first-person-shooter tournament?

The answer, I now know, is yes.

I point to the new name, SHARK CRYPT I, on the leaderboard. 'That's Fat Gandhi,' I say.

'You can't tell,' Carlo shouts at me, still clicking the keyboard. 'He hasn't started to play yet.'

'But once he plays for a few minutes, we'll know,' Renato adds. 'Half hour tops. He's got a distinct style of play. He never uses machine guns or automatic weapons – only a sniper rifle, and he never misses.'

'There's always a distinct system,' Carlo says.

'Like any sport, you don't have to see the face to know the players,' Renato agrees.

'Don't wait,' I say. 'That's our target.'

'How can you be so sure?'

It is simple, really. 'Shark Crypt I' is an anagram of 'Patrick Rhys.'

My plan here is obvious. The challenge for ROMAVSLAZIO has nothing to do with winning the Muzzles of Rage championship. The challenge for them is to pretend that there is a match so that they can figure out via some hacking method I have no interest in understanding exactly where Fat Gandhi is currently residing.

Referee Giuseppe says, 'Let's go, boys. Find him.'

My car and private plane are at the ready. I have the pilots and a key associate waiting. The moment they find Fat Gandhi's location, whilst the Muzzles of Rage contest continues, we will speed to the location and take Fat Gandhi down.

At least, that is the plan.

'I still don't know if we should do this,' Carlo says.
Again he is facing one wall, Renato the other.

'Me neither,' Renato agrees.

'We aren't cops.'

'You heard Mr Lockwood,' Giuseppe says. 'The man pimps out underage boys.'

'How do we know he's telling the truth?' Carlo asks.

'Yeah,' Renato adds, turning to Win, 'how do we know you're not the pervert?'

'You know,' I say, 'because you already researched it.'

Silence.

Then Carlo says, 'We researched you too.'

'I'm sure you did,' I say.

'You're rich.'

'I am.'

'They also say you've gone crazy. They say you're a weird recluse now.'

I spread my arms. 'Do I look like a recluse?'

'So why do they say that?'

'I made it up.'

'Why would you do that?'

'Because,' I say, 'some bad people have been trying to kill me.'

'So you've been, what, hiding?'

'Something like that.'

'So why are you here now?'

'We've rescued one boy,' I say. 'I need your help to rescue the other.'

That seemed to satisfy them.

'It shouldn't be hard,' Carlo says. 'To join the game you have to log in to our server.'

'This will give us his IP address.'

'Damn,' Carlo says, 'he's using a VPN.'

'Of course he would,' Renato replies, 'but we can get around it with . . .'

They slip back into Italian, which is fine with me. I don't speak tech-ese anyway. Their voices are loud and angry. They start cursing at each other. I hear the names of players on Roma and Lazio and I'm certain now that they are starting with the team-rival insults. That, Giuseppe warned me, was how they worked.

'The angrier they get,' he assures me, 'the closer they are to getting you an answer.'

So I wait. They are trying, it seems, to keep up with both the game on their screens and finding the location of SHARK CRYPT I.

'You're right,' Carlo says to me, still typing furiously. 'It's Fat Gandhi.'

'He's trying to cover up,' Renato adds.

'Hide his identity now that we know his moves,' Carlo says.

They start screaming again in Italian. Ten minutes later, I hear a cheer. Giuseppe nods at me as a printer starts whirring. He heads over and picks up a sheet of paper. 'The address,' Giuseppe says, handing it to me.

I look at it. The location is in the Netherlands.

'How much time do I have?'

Carlo takes that one. 'If we try our best, we will be done in about two hours.'

I start for the door. 'Then don't try your best,' I tell him.

Myron pulled up to the aging split-level home.

He had been raised in this dwelling. Well, more than raised. He had lived here with his parents up until, well, recently. In fact, when his parents, Ellen and Al ('People call us El Al,' Mom would explain, 'you know, like the Israeli airline?'), finally decided to sell the house and retire to Florida, Myron had purchased it from them.

In the old days, whenever Myron would be dropped off or pull into the driveway, his mother would run out the door and throw her arms around him as though he were a just-released hostage she hadn't seen in five years. That was her way.

It had, of course, embarrassed him. And then – equally, of course – it pleased him to no end. When you're young you don't get how great it is to be loved unconditionally.

Now, as the front door opened, Mom's steps were a slow shuffle. Dad helped her, holding her by the elbow. Mom, the still-fiery feminist, shook from the cruelty of Parkinson's. Myron waited a moment in his seat, letting her get closer to the car. She finally shrugged away Dad's hand, not wanting, he knew, for her son to see that she was older and frailer.

Myron slid out of the car as Mom reached him. She still threw her arms around him as though he were a just-released hostage. He hugged her back. Dad came up behind her. Myron kissed his cheek. That was how he greeted his father. With a kiss. Always.

'You look tired,' Mom said.

'I'm fine.'

'Doesn't he look tired, Al?'

'Leave him alone, El. He looks fine. He looks healthy.'

'Healthy.' She turned to her husband. 'What, you're a doctor now?'

'I'm just saying.'

'He needs to eat more. Come inside. I'll order more food.'

Ellen Bolitar didn't cook. Not ever. There had been an attempt at a meat loaf involving Ragú sauce sometime during Myron's high school years. They'd had to repaint the kitchen to get rid of the smell.

Myron offered her his hand. His mom gave him the stink eye.

'You too? I'm fine.'

She started back toward the house with a discernible limp. Myron looked over to his father, who just gave him a small shake of the head. They followed behind her.

'I'll tell Nero's to throw in another veal Parmesan. He needs to eat. And your nephew, he eats like he's a building with a tapeworm.' She made a shooing

241

gesture with her hand. 'You two boys go in the den and do whatever manly bonding stuff you guys do.'

She grabbed the handrail and made her way into the kitchen. Dad nodded for Myron to follow him. Myron just stood there for one moment and let the feeling rush over him.

He loved his parents.

Yes, we all do, but rarely is it so uncomplicated. There was no confusion, no remorse, no resentment, no hidden rage, no blame. He loved them. He loved with no buts or stipulations. They could do no wrong in his eyes. There were some who claimed that he just looked at them through rose-tinted glasses, that Myron was prone to both fits of nostalgia and familial historical revisionism.

Those people were wrong.

Myron and Dad sat in the same spots in the den or TV room, whatever you want to call it, that they had sat in for more years than Myron cared to remember. When Myron was young, experts warned about the dangers of too much television watching, which might or might not be true, but this particular father and son had bonded in this room sharing mutually loved programs. Prime time was eight to eleven P.M., and back then, before everyone watched on demand or via streaming, a father and son would sit and laugh at a stupid sitcom or discuss the clichés in a detective series. You'd watch and you'd be together, in the same room, and that meant, whatever else you want to say about it, some concept of bonding. Now parents went to their rooms and kids went to theirs. They all stared at smaller screens – laptops, smartphones, tablets – and watched exactly what they wanted to watch. The experience now was entirely solitary, and Myron couldn't help but think that was a terrible thing.

Dad grabbed the remote, but he didn't turn on the TV.

'Is Mickey here yet?' Myron asked.

His parents had come up to stay with Mickey while Mickey's parents went on their retreat.

'He should be here any minute,' Dad said. 'He's bringing Ema to dinner. You know her?'

'Ema? Yeah.'

'She always wears black,' Dad said.

Mom from the other room: 'Lots of women do, Al.'

'Not like that.'

Mom: 'Black is slimming.'

'I'm not judging.'

Mom: 'Yes, you are.'

'I am not!'

'You think she's a big girl.'

'You're the one talking about wearing black because it's slimming, not me.' Dad turned to Myron. 'Ema wears black nail polish. Black lipstick. Black mascara. Black hair. Not naturally black. I mean, like ink black. I don't get it.'

Mom: 'And who are you to get it?'

'I'm just saying.'

'Look at Mr Haute Couture over there. What,

you're suddenly Yves Saint Laurent with the fashion tips?'

'I thought you were on the phone changing the order!'

'The number was busy.'

'So call back.'

'Yes, master. Right away.'

Dad sighed and shrugged. This was their way. Myron just sat back and enjoyed the show.

Dad leaned toward Myron and spoke in a low voice. 'So where is Terese?'

'In Jackson Hole. On a job interview.'

'As an anchorwoman?'

'Something like that.'

'I remember when she was on the air. Before you two . . .' He brought his hands together and separated them and then brought them back together. 'Your mother and I would really like to get to know her better.'

'You will.'

He leaned a little closer. 'Your mother worries,' he said.

'What about?'

Dad was not one to hold back, and he didn't now. 'She worries that there is a sadness there.'

'With Terese.' Myron nodded. 'And what about you? Do you worry?'

'I don't interfere.'

'But if you did?'

'I see the sadness too,' Dad said. 'But I also see strength. She's been through a lot, hasn't she?'

'Yes.'

'She lost a child?'

'A long time ago, when she lived overseas, yeah.'
Dad shook his head. 'I'm sorry to raise this.'

'It's okay.'

'And you still don't want to tell me why she was in Africa for so long?'

'I can't,' Myron said. 'It's not my place to tell.'

'I respect that,' Dad said. He smiled now. 'Terese was probably on a secret mission.'

'Something like that.'

'A secret mission,' Dad repeated, 'like you in London?'

Myron said nothing.

'What, you think we didn't know? You going to tell me what that was all about?'

Mom from the other room: 'It was about that Moore kid who was rescued.'

Dad turned toward the kitchen. 'How long have you been listening in?'

'I just started,' Mom said. 'I totally missed the part where you threw me under the bus with that whole sad-fiancée thing.'

The front door burst open in a way that signaled a teenager was entering. Mickey stomped through the door with Ema close behind him. He looked at Myron. 'Hey, what are you doing here?'

Mickey was a terrible actor.

'Nice to see you too,' Myron said. 'Hi, Ema.'

'Hey, Myron,' Ema said.

Ema, the girl Dad described using the color

black, was what they used to call goth and then they called emo (ergo the nickname), and Myron wasn't hip enough to know what they called it now. Everything was indeed in black against the palest white skin achievable. Mickey and Ema had started out as friends, best friends even, but somewhere through their bonding, Myron now wondered whether the friendship line had been crossed.

Mickey gave his grandfather a kiss on the cheek. He turned to his grandmother and said, 'You look beautiful, Grandma.'

'Don't call me that.'

'Call you what?'

'Grandma. I told you. I'm too young to be your grandmother. Call me Ellen. And if anyone asks, tell them I'm your grandfather's second, much-younger trophy wife.'

'Got it,' Mickey said.

'Now give your Ellen a kiss.'

He hopped up the step into the kitchen. Whenever Mickey moved, the house shook. He gave her a kiss and a hug. Myron watched, swallowing hard. Then Mickey turned toward Myron.

'Are you crying?' Mickey asked.

'No,' Myron said.

'Why is he crying?' Mickey turned to his grand-mother. 'Why is he always crying?'

'He's always been an emotional boy; pay no attention.'

'I'm not crying,' Myron said. He looked around

the room and found no solace. 'I got something in my eye.'

'I need someone to help me set the table,' Mom said.

Mickey said, 'I got it.'

'No,' Mom said. 'I want Ema to help me.'

'I'd love to, Mrs Bolitar,' Ema said.

'Ellen,' Mom said, correcting her. 'So are you and Mickey a thing now? What do the kids say? Dating? Hooking up?'

Mickey was mortified. 'Grandma!'

'Oh, never mind, Ema, his reaction tells me all. Isn't it cute when they turn red?'

Ema, who looked equally mortified, shuffled her way into the kitchen. Dad said, 'I better stay with them. Just in case.'

He left Myron and Mickey alone in the den.

'I got your text,' Mickey said.

'I figured. Do you think you can help?'

'I do. I think Ema can help too.'

'How?'

'We have a plan,' Mickey said.

CHAPTER 22

The press was gone from Nancy Moore's house.

Myron didn't know if that came from a media decision to respect the family's request for privacy or from news cycles being so short or from the fact that there was no new kindling for the coverage fire. Probably a combination of all three, but either way, Myron was grateful. It was eight P.M. when he pulled into the driveway and knocked on the door.

Nancy Moore opened the door with a glass of white wine in her hand. 'It's late,' she said.

'Sorry,' Myron said. 'I would have called.'

'It's been a long day.'

'I know.'

'I wouldn't have even opened the door except . . .'

He knew. She still felt obligated. 'Look, I need to talk to you for just a few moments.' Myron looked past her into the house. 'Is Hunter here?'

'No. He drove back to Pennsylvania tonight.'

'That's where he lives?'

She nodded. 'He's been there since the divorce.'

Myron looked at the FOR SALE sign. 'You're moving too?'

'Yes.'

'Where?'

'Same.'

'Pennsylvania?'

'I don't want to be rude here, Myron.'

He held up a hand. 'Can I just come in for a moment?'

She grudgingly moved out of the way. Myron stepped inside and pulled up when he saw the young woman standing by the foot of the steps.

'This is my daughter, Francesca,' Nancy said.

Myron almost made the standard 'you mean sister' line, but he bit back the flattery. He hadn't really noticed the strong resemblance during the TV interview, but he had been otherwise distracted. If a potential spouse wanted to know what Francesca would look like in twenty-five years, Nancy left very little to the imagination.

'Francesca, this is Mr Bolitar.'

'Call me Myron,' Myron said. 'Hi, Francesca.'

She blinked away tears. Had the tears been there before?

'Thank you,' she said with sincerity that almost made him turn away. Francesca hurried over to Myron. She gave him a brief albeit fierce hug. 'Thank you,' she said again.

'You're welcome,' Myron said.

Nancy rubbed her daughter's shoulder and gave her a gentle smile. 'Do you mind going upstairs and checking on your brother? Mr Bolitar and I need to talk.'

'Sure,' Francesca said. She took Myron's hand in both of hers. 'It was really nice to meet you.'

'You too.'

Nancy watched her head up the stairs. She waited until she was out of sight before she said, 'She's a good kid.'

'She seems it.'

'Very sensitive. Cries at the smallest thing.'

'I think that's a good quality,' Myron said.

'I guess. But when her brother disappeared . . .' Nancy didn't finish the thought. She shook her head and closed her eyes. 'If Patrick had died in that tunnel, if you hadn't gotten to him in time . . .' Again there was no need to finish the thought.

'Can I ask you something straight out?' Myron asked.

'I guess.'

'Are you positive that the boy upstairs is Patrick?'

She made a face. 'You asked me that before.'

'I know.'

'So why do you keep asking me that? I already told you. I'm certain.'

'How can you be?'

'Pardon?'

'It's been ten years. He was a little boy when he was taken.'

She put her hands on her hips. There was a hint of impatience in her tone now. 'This is why you're here?'

'No.'

'Then you better get to it. It's getting late.'

'Tell me about your texts with Chick Baldwin.'

Myron said it just like that. Boom. No warning, no clearing of his throat, nothing. He wanted to see her reaction, but if he expected something dramatic or revealing, that wasn't happening. Nancy put down the wineglass and folded her arms.

'Are you serious?'

'I am.'

'Why on earth . . .?' She stopped herself. 'I think you should leave.'

'I spoke to Chick about it.'

'Then you know already.'

'Know what?'

'It was nothing.'

Interesting. The same argument. Myron decided to do a little bluffing. 'That's not what he said.'

'Pardon?'

'Chick admitted you two were having an affair.'

A small smile came to her lips. 'You're full of shit, Myron.'

And so he was.

'We were friends,' Nancy said. 'We talked. We talked a lot.'

'Yeah, Nancy, no offense, but I'm not buying that.'

'You don't believe me?'

'I don't, no.'

'Why not?'

'For one thing, Chick doesn't hit me as a great talker.'

'But he does hit you as being a great lay?'

Touché, Myron thought.

Nancy moved close to him. She looked up at him with the eyes of a doe. It was, he imagined, a move she'd made before to get a point across to a man. It was, he imagined, a move that had served her well in the past.

'Will you trust me that it has nothing to do with what happened to the boys?'

'No,' Myron said.

'Just like that?'

'Just like that.'

'You think I'm lying?'

'Maybe,' Myron said. 'Or maybe you don't know.'

'What's that supposed to mean?'

'Things ripple. Things wiggle beneath the surface. You can't always see them, especially when you're as close to it as you are. You know about the butterfly effect, the concept that a butterfly flapping its wings may seem inconsequential—'

'But can change everything,' Nancy finished for him. 'I know it. It's nonsense. And anyway—'

She stopped when she heard the clumping footsteps. They both turned toward the stairs. There, stopping on the third step from the bottom, was Patrick Moore. Or maybe–Patrick Moore. Either way, it was the boy Fat Gandhi had stabbed in the tunnel.

Myron surreptitiously hit a button on his mobile phone.

For a moment, no one spoke. Nancy broke the silence.

'Is everything okay, Patrick? Can I get you something?'

Patrick had his eyes on Myron.

'Hi, Patrick,' Myron said.

'You're the guy who saved me,' he said.

'Yeah, I guess I am.'

'Francesca said you were here.' He swallowed hard. 'That fat guy. He tried to kill me.'

Myron glanced at Nancy.

'It's okay,' Nancy said in the soothing, unmistakable tone of a worried mother. 'You're home now. You're safe.'

Patrick still had his eyes on Myron. 'Why?' he asked. 'Why did he stab me?'

It was a common enough question after a violent crime. Myron had seen it before – this need to know. It was an unselfish 'Why me?' Rape victims often wonder why they were chosen. So do victims of any crime.

'I think,' Myron said, 'he was trying to save himself.'

'How?'

'He figured that if he stabbed you, I'd stop chasing him. I'd have to choose between going after him and saving you.'

Patrick nodded, seeing it now. 'Right. I guess that makes sense.'

Myron took a tentative step toward the boy. 'Patrick,' he said, trying to keep his voice even and as nonthreatening as possible, 'where have you been?'

Patrick's eyes widened. He looked toward his mother with panic on his face.

That was when the doorbell rang.

Nancy turned toward it. 'Who could that—'

'I got it,' Myron said. 'Hold on a second, Patrick. I have someone I want you to meet.'

Myron moved to the front door and opened it. Mickey and Ema, who had been waiting in a separate car for Myron's phone signal, came in with no hesitation. Mickey had a big smile on his face. Ema was carrying a pizza. The aroma filled the room.

It was a long shot, Myron knew, this plan of Mickey's, but Ema had been more optimistic.

'He's a lonely teen locked in his house,' Ema explained, 'and more than that, pizza in London is pretty basic.'

So this was really Mickey and Ema's play. Myron let him take over.

Mickey started toward the steps. 'Hey, I'm Mickey. This is Ema. We figured you might want to hang out or something.'

Patrick looked at him. 'Umm.'

Ema said, 'Have you tried pizza with buffalo chicken as a topping?'

Patrick's voice was tentative. 'No.'

Ema nodded. 'And bacon bits.'

'Seriously?'

'I would never kid about bacon.'

'Whoa.'

'We were going to save the cheese-filled crust as a surprise,' Mickey said, 'but some things are too good to keep secret.'

Patrick smiled.

'I don't want to build it up,' Ema said, opening the box, 'but this may be the greatest thing ever.'

Nancy said, 'Oh, I don't think this is a good idea.'

Myron stepped between her and her son. 'You said he needed to get acclimated to people his own age,' he reminded her.

'Yes, but we've had a long day—'

Patrick interrupted her. 'Mom,' he said, 'it's okay.'

'I think it might be gluten-free,' Ema tried. Her face broke out in the brightest, goofiest, most endearing grin Myron had ever seen.

Then Patrick laughed – genuinely laughed – and from the look on Nancy's face, Myron guessed that it was the first time she'd seen her child laugh since he was six years old. Ema had been right. Whether it was overgarnished pizza or the normal human need for companionship – most likely a combo of both – Patrick needed this. He'd been deprived too long.

Francesca appeared at the top of the steps. 'We were just about to start a movie,' she said. 'Mom, is it okay if we rent something on demand?'

All eyes turned to Nancy Moore.

'Of course,' Nancy Moore managed, her voice choking up. 'Go have fun.'

Myron didn't stay.

Those had been the explicit instructions handed down from Mickey and Ema. Leave it to them. Don't hang out downstairs. Don't cloud the atmosphere with your adult presence. Don't make anyone wary. If you have questions for Patrick's mom, ask them before they get inside. Then leave.

So he did.

The phone rang as he got into his car. Myron didn't recognize the number.

'Hello?'

'This is Alyse Mervosh,' a woman said with no preamble. 'I'm PT's contact.'

'The forensic doctor?'

'Forensic anthropologist specializing in forensic facial reconstruction, yes.' Her tone was as neutral as you could get without electronic altering. 'You want to know if the Patrick Moore who appeared today on CNN is the same Patrick Moore who vanished ten years ago. Is that correct?'

'Yes.'

'I just obtained the video of today's interview. I then Googled the kidnapping to secure photographs of Patrick, age six. Finally, I located an age progression of Patrick that was performed by this agency. Where are you?'

'Right now?'

'Yes.'

'Alpine, New Jersey.'

'Do you know where our office in Manhattan is located?' she asked.

'Yes.'

'The drive should take you approximately an hour. I should have my results by then.'

Alyse Mervosh hung up without waiting for his reply. Myron checked the clock. Eight thirty P.M. If Dr Mervosh didn't mind working late, neither did Myron. He knew the FBI's main laboratory was down in Virginia, but he suspected that this kind of work mostly required computers and perhaps software. In Manhattan, the FBI's main office was on the twenty-third floor at 26 Federal Plaza.

Myron found a parking lot on Reade Street and started walking north toward FBI headquarters. He passed Duane Street and recalled a fun factoid. Duane Reade pharmacies, which dominated New York, had derived its name from its first warehouse being located between Duane Street and Reade Street.

Odd thoughts go through your head at random times.

Alyse Mervosh greeted him with a firm handshake. 'Can I just get this out of the way?' she said.

'Get what out of the way?'

'My fangirling? I loved, loved, loved the documentary on your injury. Loved it.'

'Uh, thanks.'

'Seriously, to be that high, that close to the pinnacle, and then to be destroyed like that, to be left in a heap with nothing . . .'

Her voice trailed off.

Myron opened his arms and smiled. 'Yet here I am.'

'But are you really okay?' she asked.

'I can do ten one-handed push-ups if you'd like.'

'Really?'

'No. I can maybe do one.'

She shook her head. 'Sorry, I'm being unprofessional. It's just . . . that documentary really made me pity you, you know?'

'Just the feeling I was hoping for.'

She turned a little red. 'Pardon the way I'm dressed. I was in the middle of a tennis lesson when PT called.'

Dr Mervosh wore a sweat suit so old-school that Myron almost looked for the Fila label. Her hair was blond and she wore a headband. The whole look was Early Eighties Björn Borg.

'No worries,' Myron said. 'Thanks for doing this so late.'

'Do you want a long explanation or do you want my conclusion?'

'Conclusion, please.'

'Inconclusive,' she said.

'Oh,' Myron said. 'So your conclusion is, what, you just don't know?'

'In terms of answering the question, "Is the

teenager interviewed today on CNN the same Patrick Moore who was abducted ten years ago?" sorry, I can't be firm. Can I explain?'

'Please do.'

'What I mostly do – forensic facial reconstruction – is about identifying remains. You know that, right?'

'Yes.'

'This isn't an exact science. Our hope is that our work may lead to a tip or a thought, but a lot of things can skew our results.' Alyse Mervosh made a face. 'Is it hot in here?'

'A little.'

'Do you mind if I take off the jacket?'

'Of course not.'

'I don't want you to think I'm flirting with you or anything.'

'Don't worry about it.'

'I have a serious boyfriend.'

'And I'm engaged.'

'Really?' Her face brightened. 'Oh, I'm so happy for you. I mean, after what you went through.'

'Dr Mervosh?'

'Please call me Alyse.'

'Alyse,' Myron said. 'It was just a hurt knee. I appreciate your' – he wasn't sure of the word – 'concern, but I'm fine.'

'And you want to know more about Patrick Moore.'

'I do, yes.'

'I'm not great socially,' she said. 'It's why I'm

best in the lab. I have a tendency to be a nervous talker. I'm really sorry.'

'It's fine,' Myron said. Then: 'You were saying something about the results being skewed sometimes.'

'Yes, that's right. We are trying to imagine, if you will, what a six-year-old boy would look like as a sixteen-year-old. Those are, as you can imagine, difficult years to deduce. If Patrick Moore went missing when he was, say, twenty-six, and we found him now when he's thirty-six, well, you get the idea, right?'

'Right.'

'Aging is about genetics mostly, but there are other factors. Diet, lifestyle, personal habits, trauma – any of that can alter the aging process and even, in some cases, your appearance. And again: You are also talking about perhaps the most difficult years to analyze. The alteration in appearance from child to adolescent can be an extreme one. As a child ages, the bones and cartilages develop and determine the proportions and shape of your face. So then, as forensic anthropologists, we have to fill in what might be there. The hairline might have receded, for example. Bone tissue is being formed, removed, elongated, and replaced. In short, it's all hard to predict.'

'I see,' Myron said. 'Can you make a guess?'

'About if this teenager is Patrick Moore?'

'Yes.'

She frowned and looked confused by the question. 'Guess?'

'Yes.'

'I'm a scientist. I don't make guesses.'

'I just meant—'

'I can only give you the facts as they are.'

'That's fine.'

Alyse Mervosh slowly picked up a notepad and checked her notes. 'The teenager's features, with one notable exception, are well within the norm of the six-year-old's. His eye color has altered slightly, but that's not noteworthy. It is also very difficult to tell the exact color from a television interview. I was able to get a solid estimation of the height of his parents and sibling and compare it to Patrick's height at age six. From those calculations, this teenager is two inches shorter than the median, but again that's certainly within the margin of error. In short, this teenager could indeed be Patrick Moore, but one thing does concern me and leads to my inconclusiveness.'

'And that is?'

'His nose.'

'What about it?'

'The nose of the teenager, in my opinion, does not match what I see on the six-year-old. That's not to say it couldn't have aged this way, but it would be unlikely.'

Myron considered that for a moment. 'Would a nose job explain it?'

'A classic nose job? No. Nose jobs by and large

261

make noses smaller. In this case, the new Patrick Moore has a larger nose than expected.'

Myron thought about that. 'How about, I don't know, if his nose was broken repeatedly?'

'Hmm.' Alyse Mervosh picked up a pencil and tapped the eraser against her cheek. 'I would doubt it, but it's not impossible. There are also surgeries to build up a nose, due to trauma or congenital deformities or, mostly, cocaine abuse. Perhaps that would explain it. But I can't say with anything approaching certainty. That's why I am ruling as I am.'

'In other words,' Myron said, 'we miss a conclusive identification by a nose?'

Alyse Mervosh looked at him for a second. 'Wait, was that a joke?'

'Sort of.'

'Ugh.'

'Yeah, sorry.'

'Humor aside,' she said, 'you need a DNA test.'

CHAPTER 23

I stare at the Dutch farmhouse through binoculars.

The flight from Rome to Groningen Airport Eelde in the Netherlands took two and a half hours. The ride from the airport to this farm in Assen took twenty minutes.

'Only four people in the house, dreamboat,' a heavily accented voice says to me.

I turn to Zorra. Zorra's real name is Shlomo Avrahaim. He is former Mossad and a cross-dresser, or whatever the appropriate term is for a man who likes to dress as a woman. I have known many cross-dressers in my time. Many are quite attractive and feminine in appearance. Zorra is neither. His beard is as heavy as his accent. He does not manscape in the brow area, so both appear to be hairy caterpillars with no interest in turning into butterflies. His knuckles could best be described as midtransition werewolf. His curly red wig looks like something he stole from Bette Midler's show trunk in 1978. He wears stiletto heels, literally, as in an actual blade is sheathed in the heel.

Way back when, Zorra nearly killed Myron with that blade.

'We know that from the thermal imaging?' I ask.

'The same Zorra used in London, dreamboat.' His voice was a deep baritone. 'This will be too easy. How you say? Fish in barrel. You waste talents of legendary professional like Zorra.'

I turn to him and look him up and down.

'Problem, dreamboat?' Zorra asks.

'Peach skirt with orange pumps?' I say.

'Zorra can pull it off.'

'Glad Zorra thinks so.'

Zorra's head swivels back to the house. The wig doesn't move with it. 'Why are we waiting, dreamboat?'

I do not believe in intuition or sensing something is not quite right. But then again, I don't simply dismiss what I'm feeling either. 'This seems too easy.'

'Ah,' Zorra says. 'You sniff a trap.'

'Sniff a trap?'

'English is Zorra's second language.'

We turn back to the house.

'We have one goal,' I say.

'Your cousin, yes?'

'Yes.' I think about the various possibilities. 'If you were Fat Gandhi, would you keep Rhys here?'

'Maybe,' he says. 'Or maybe Zorra would hide him so if bad man like Win come after me I have leverage.'

'Precisely,' I say.

We met years ago, when Zorra was on the other side, a sworn enemy. In the end, I had chosen to spare Zorra's life. I'm not sure why. Intuition perhaps? Now Zorra feels that he must be forever in my debt. Esperanza compares this particular outcome to one of her pro-wrestling scripts where the bad wrestler is shown kindness by the good wrestler and thus turns good and becomes a fan favorite.

I am debating my various options when the door of the farmhouse opens. I do not move. I do not pull out my gun. I stand and wait for someone to appear at the door. Five seconds pass. Then ten.

Then Fat Gandhi steps outside.

Zorra and I are standing behind shrubbery. Fat Gandhi turns that way, smiles, and waves.

'He knows we are here,' Zorra says.

Zorra, Master of the Obvious Observation.

Fat Gandhi begins to stroll casually toward us. Zorra looks at me. I shake my head. As has been pointed out, Fat Gandhi knows exactly where we are. I consider that for a moment. We had been careful in our approach, but this is a quiet road. If Fat Gandhi had men posted – and clearly he had – they would have seen us turn down the road.

Fat Gandhi waves again when he sees me. 'Hello, Mr Lockwood. Welcome!'

Zorra leans close to me. 'He knows your name.'

'Your Mossad training. It's really impressive.'

'Zorra misses nothing.'

Fat Gandhi could have figured out who I am via a hundred different avenues. He could have employed some complicated hacking scheme, but I doubt that would have been necessary. He knew Myron's name. Myron and I are business partners and best friends. He also knew about Rhys and Patrick and the kidnapping. He could have done a modicum of research and learned of my personal connection.

Or, more to the point, Rhys could have told him.

Either way, here we are.

Zorra slowly slides off the sheath on his heel. 'What's our play, dreamboat?'

I check my mobile to see if our other two men are still in place on the perimeter. They are. No one has taken them out. Fat Gandhi continues to stroll toward us. He tilts his face toward the sun and grins.

'We wait and see,' I say.

I take out my weapon – a Desert Eagle .50 AE. Fat Gandhi stops when he sees this. He looks disappointed.

'There is no need for that, Mr Lockwood.'

I had 'sniffed' a trap, hadn't I? Had he known that the Italians would try to track him down via that contest? Had he let them? Apparently. Many believe that I am infallible in such matters, that I am so professional and dangerous that death itself gives me a wide berth. I confess that I do all I can to encourage, amplify, and intensify this reputation. I want you to fear me. I want you to cringe every time I enter a room because you do not know what I might do next. But I am not naïve enough to buy my own press, if you will. No matter how good you are, a sniper can take you out.

As one of my enemies once put it, 'You're good, Win, but you ain't bulletproof.'

I had tried to be careful, but missions such as this require a degree of rush. No one had followed us from the airport. I know that. But still Fat Gandhi knew that we were here.

'We need to talk,' Fat Gandhi says.

'Okay,' I say.

He spreads his arms. 'Do you mind if I call you Win?'

'Yes.'

He still holds the grin. I still hold the gun. He glances at Zorra. 'Does she have to be here for this conversation?'

'Who you calling she?' Zorra snaps.

'What?'

'Does Zorra look like girl to you, dreamboat?'

'Uh . . .' There is no good answer to this.

I hold up my hand. Zorra steps down, if you will.

'Both of you can relax,' Fat Gandhi says. 'If I wanted you dead, you'd be dead.'

'Wrong,' I say.

'Pardon?'

'You're bluffing,' I say.

Fat Gandhi continues to smile, but I can see the light flickering.

'You know who I am,' I say. 'That would take very little research on your part. You probably had a man watching the airport and another man watching the road. My guess is, it was the bearded guy in the Peugeot.'

'Zorra knew it!' Zorra says. 'You should have let me—'

Again I stop him with my hand.

'You have eyes on us,' I continue, 'but that doesn't mean you have a sniper who would be good enough to hit us at this distance. I have two men out there. If you had someone, they would know. You have other men inside. Three to be exact. None have a long-range weapon pointed at us. We'd have spotted it.'

More flickers in that smile. 'You seem very sure of yourself, Mr Lockwood.'

I shrug. 'I could be wrong. But the odds you have enough firepower hidden to take out all four of us before you die seems beyond remote.'

Fat Gandhi does a slow clap. 'You live up to your reputation, Mr Lockwood.'

Reputation. See what I mean by encourage, amplify, and intensify?

'I would go into an entire bit about this being a stalemate,' Fat Gandhi says, 'but we are both men of the world. I came out here to talk. I came out here so we can make an arrangement and put this matter behind us.'

'I don't care about you,' I say. 'I don't care about your enterprise.'

268

His enterprise, of course, involves teenagers being raped and abused. Zorra makes a face at me to indicate that maybe he cares.

'I'm here for Rhys,' I tell him.

The smile slips off Fat Gandhi's face. 'You were the one who killed my three men.'

Now it's my turn to grin. I am buying time, drawing his eye. I want Zorra to keep checking the house and perimeter, just in case.

'You were also the one who blew that hole in my wall.'

'Are you looking for a confession?' I ask.

'No,' he says.

'How about vengeance?'

'Not that either,' Fat Gandhi says too quickly. 'You want Rhys Baldwin. I understand that. He's your cousin. But there are things I want too.'

There is no reason to ask him what. He will tell me.

'I want my life back,' Fat Gandhi says. 'The police have nothing on me. Patrick Moore is back in the United States. He won't come back to testify. Myron Bolitar may claim to have seen me stab him, but in the end, it was dark. I could also claim self-defense. Someone had obviously attacked us. The hole in the wall proves that. None of my people will talk. All the files and evidence remain locked away in a cloud.'

'The police have nothing,' I agree. 'But I don't think your big worry is the police, is it?'

'My big worry,' Fat Gandhi says, 'is you.'

I grin again.

'I don't want to spend the rest of my life waiting for you to knock on my door, Mr Lockwood. May I be honest for a moment?'

'You can try,' I say.

'I didn't know for certain, but when "Romavslazio" put up that challenge, well, after what we had uncovered about you, we realized that it would be a risk. That was when I knew. I knew that I would have to face you directly, so we can put an end to this once and for all. We debated – and I'm just being honest – getting a bunch of men and trying to kill you.'

'But you changed your mind.'

'Yes.'

'Because I would have spotted the men. And I would have brought more men. And I would have killed your men and killed you. And even if you and your group somehow got the upper hand on us—'

Zorra makes a choking noise and laughs out loud. 'On Zorra?'

'We are talking hypotheticals,' I assure him. I turn back to Fat Gandhi. 'Even if you somehow could kill us, you knew that it wouldn't end there. Myron would go after you.'

Fat Gandhi nods. 'It would never end. I would have to spend the rest of my life looking over my shoulder.'

'You're wiser than I thought,' I say. 'So let's make it simple. Give me Rhys. I take him home. The end. I never think of you again. I forget you exist. You forget I exist.'

It is a good deal, I think, but I wonder whether I can keep it. Fat Gandhi had tried to eliminate Myron. That was no small matter. I wouldn't kill him out of revenge for that act – it was, in its own way, quite understandable – but I have to worry about both his mental stability and self-interest. He wanted to show strength to his workers. He wanted to show power. That motive was still present.

His 'looking over my shoulder' concern works both ways.

'It's not that simple,' Fat Gandhi says.

I put a little steel in my voice. 'It's just that simple. Give me Rhys.'

He lowers his eyes and shakes his head. 'I can't.'

There is a moment's hesitation, no more. I know that it is coming, but I do nothing to stop it. With grace that never fails to surprise me, Zorra spins and sweeps Fat Gandhi's legs. Fat Gandhi drops like a sack of peat moss onto his back. He makes an oof noise as the air leaves his lungs.

Zorra stands over his prone form. He raises his razor-sharp (literally) heel, perfectly poised to stomp down on Fat Gandhi's face. Instead Zorra lowers the point of the heel so that the blade is scant millimeters (again literally) from Fat Gandhi's cornea.

'Bad answer, dreamboat,' Zorra tells him. 'Try again.'

271

CHAPTER 24

Myron sat in his dad's chair in the TV room.

Dad asked, 'Are you going to wait up for Mickey?'

When Myron was a teenager, his father would sit in this chair at night and wait for his children to come home. He never gave Myron a curfew – 'I trust you' – and he never told Myron that he waited up for him. When Myron would come through the door, Dad would either pretend to be asleep or have already sneaked upstairs.

'I will.' Then with a smile on his face, Myron said, 'You think I didn't know.'

'Didn't know what?'

'That you stayed awake until I came home.'

'I couldn't sleep until I knew you were safe.' Dad shrugged. 'But I knew you knew.'

'How?'

'I never gave you a curfew, remember? I said I trusted you.'

'Right.'

'But when you realized I stayed awake, you started coming home earlier. So I wouldn't have to stay up and worry.' Dad arched an eyebrow at him. 'Ergo, you actually came home earlier than if I gave you a curfew.'

'Diabolical,' Myron said.

'I just took advantage of what I knew.'

'Which was?'

'You were a good boy,' Dad said.

Silence. Silence that was broken when Mom shouted from the kitchen: 'This is a very touching father-and-son moment. Can we go to bed now?'

Dad chuckled. 'On my way. Are we going to Mickey's game tomorrow? It's home.'

'I'll pick you up in the morning,' Myron said.

His mother leaned her head in from the kitchen. 'Good night, Myron.'

'How come you never stayed awake until I came home?' Myron asked her.

'A woman needs her beauty sleep. What, you think I stay this hot by accident?'

'It's a good lesson on marriage,' Dad said.

'What is?'

'Balance. I stayed awake at night. Mom slept like a baby. It doesn't mean she didn't care. But our strengths and weaknesses complement each other. We're a couple. See? That was my contribution. I took night watch.'

'But you were also first up in the morning,' Myron said.

'Well, yes, that's true.'

'So what was Mom good at?'

Mom from the kitchen: 'You don't want to know.'

'Ellen!' Dad shouted.

'Oh, relax, Al. You're such a prude.'

Myron already had his fingers in his ears. He started saying, 'La, la, la, I can't hear you,' as his father trudged toward the kitchen. He took his fingers out when they had both gone upstairs. He sat back and looked out the window. Funny. The chair was perfectly set up so you could watch both the television and any car approaching from the street.

Diabolical indeed.

It was almost one A.M. when Myron spotted Mickey's car. He wondered whether he too should feign being asleep, but Mickey wouldn't buy it. Myron had waited up for three reasons. One: General concern. Two: So his father wouldn't have to. And three – most obvious: To find out what had happened after Myron left Mickey and Ema at the Moore house.

Myron sat in the dark and waited. Five minutes passed. Myron looked out. The car was still there. No lights. No movement. Myron frowned. He picked up his mobile and sent Mickey a text: All ok?

No reply. Another minute went by. Nothing. Myron checked his phone for a reply. *Nada.* A feeling of unease began to descend upon him. He called Mickey's phone. It went straight to voicemail.

What the hell?

He got out of Dad's chair and started for the

front door. No, that would be too direct. He headed into the kitchen and out the back. The yard was pitch dark, so Myron used the flashlight on his mobile phone. He circled toward the driveway where the streetlights provided enough illumination.

Still nothing.

Myron ducked low and crept toward the back of the car. Dad had watered the lawn recently. Myron's slippers were quickly waterlogged. Terrific. He was twenty yards from the trunk of the vehicle. Then ten. Then he was ducking behind the back bumper.

He did a mental check, sifting through his brain in search of probable explanations for why no one would have come out of the car yet. Then just as Myron made the leap and grabbed the door handle and pulled open the driver's door, the answer came to him . . .

. . . a second too late.

Ema screamed.

Mickey shouted, 'What the hell, Myron?'

Two teenagers. In a car. Late at night.

Myron flashed back to a time when his own father had walked in on him and Jessica, his old love, during a most indelicate moment. His father had just stood there, unmoving, frozen, and at the time, Myron didn't get it, why his father didn't quickly apologize and close the door.

He got it now.

'Oh,' Myron said. Then: 'Oh.'

'What's wrong with you?' Mickey snapped.

'Oh,' Myron said again.

They were both, Myron was glad to see, dressed. Clothes, hair, makeup, showed some degree of distress. But they were dressed.

Myron pointed with his thumb behind him. 'Maybe I should wait in the house.'

'Ya think?'

'Right. Okay, then.'

'Go!' Mickey shouted.

Myron turned and slouched his way back toward the house. Before he got to the door, Mickey and Ema were out of the car, doing slight wardrobe adjustments and following him. When Myron opened the door and they all stepped inside, Dad was standing there in the Homer Simpson pajamas Myron had bought him last Father's Day.

Dad looked at Myron. Then he looked at Mickey and Ema.

'You went outside?' he asked Myron.

'Yes.'

'Weren't you a teenager once?' Dad shook his head, trying to hold in the smile. 'I knew I shouldn't have left the night watch to you. Good night, all.'

Dad left. Myron and Mickey stood and looked at the floor. Ema sighed and said, 'Grow up. Both of you.'

The three of them grabbed cold drinks and took their seats around the kitchen table.

'So,' Myron asked, 'what's your impression of Patrick? I mean, if it is Patrick.'

'He's a normal kid,' Mickey said.

'Too normal,' Ema added.

'What do you mean?'

Ema put her hands on the table. Besides dressing in black and wearing black makeup, Ema had numerous tattoos up and down her arms. She had silver jewelry including two skull rings on her hand. 'He knew recent movies,' she said.

'He was up-to-date on the latest video games,' Mickey said.

'He knew about the newest apps.'

'Same with social media sites.'

Myron considered that. 'I don't think he's been kept in a cage all this time. Especially in recent, I don't know, years. I mean, he was out on the streets. He lived under an arcade. The guy who was holding him in London is a major gamer. Couldn't that explain all that?'

'It could,' Mickey said.

'But you don't buy it?'

Mickey shrugged.

'What?'

'I don't think he's who he says he is,' Mickey said.

Myron looked at Ema. Ema nodded.

'His hands,' she said.

'What about them?'

'They're soft.'

'It wasn't like he was doing hard labor,' Myron said.

'I know,' Ema said, 'but they don't look like the hands of someone who's been out on the streets either. And more than that, his teeth. They're straight; they're white. He may have incredible genes, but a safer bet would be that he's had proper dental care and braces.'

'It's hard to put a finger on it,' Mickey added, 'but Patrick doesn't look or sound, well, street. He doesn't look abused, except, you know, for the recent stuff. I mean, ugh, he might have been "kept" or taken care of by some . . . whatever . . . but . . .'

'Did you talk about the kidnapping at all?' Myron asked.

'We tried,' Ema said. 'But we always got shot down.'

'Francesca was running interference,' Mickey said.

'Interference how?'

'She was protecting him,' Ema said. 'Which is understandable, I guess.'

'So whenever we raised what happened—'

'Or even mentioned Rhys's name.'

'She would interrupt and get all emotional, crying and hugging him,' Mickey said. 'I mean, Patrick seemed kind of normal, but the sister was off.'

'I'm not sure I'd use the word "off,"' Ema said. 'Her brother comes home after ten years. I think it would be weird if Francesca wasn't all emotional.'

'Yeah, maybe,' Mickey said. But he didn't say it with much enthusiasm.

'We tried to raise the kidnapping again after she left with Clark.'

'Wait,' Myron said. 'Clark Baldwin? Rhys's brother?'

'Yes.'

'He was there?'

'He came in to pick up Francesca,' Mickey said.

'They go to Columbia together,' Ema said. 'He was giving her a ride back to campus.'

Myron said nothing.

'Is that a big deal?' Ema asked.

'I don't know.' Myron thought about it some more. 'It's odd; that's all. Maybe, I don't know, do you think they're romantically involved?'

Mickey rolled his eyes as only a teenager could. 'No.'

'What makes you so sure?'

'Old dudes,' Ema said to Mickey with a shake of the head. 'No gaydar.'

'Clark is gay?'

'Yes. And what difference would it make if they were romantically involved? Weren't they, like, ten, when this all went down?'

Something was niggling at the back of Myron's brain, but he couldn't figure out what yet. He moved back to the topic at hand.

'So after Francesca left, you tried to broach the subject of the kidnapping again?'

'Yes, but Patrick got real quiet.'

'Completely clammed up.'

'We left not long after that.'

Myron sat back for a moment. 'How did he sound?'

'Sound?'

'We found him in London,' Myron said. 'We have no idea how long he's been there. Did you detect anything in his accent?'

'That's a good question,' Ema said. 'His accent was American overall, but . . .' She turned to Mickey. He nodded.

'It did have something else in it,' Mickey said. 'I can't put my finger on it exactly. He didn't sound like he'd grown up here. But he didn't sound like he'd grown up in England either.'

Myron tried to process that but came up with nothing. He tried something else. 'So what did you do the whole time?'

'We ate pizza,' Ema said.

'We watched a movie,' Mickey added.

'We played video games.'

'We talked.'

'Oh, Patrick said he had a girlfriend,' Ema said. 'But not from around here.'

'A girlfriend?' Myron said.

'Yeah, but he backed right off. He said it, I don't know, like a kid bragging a little.'

'You know,' Mickey said. 'Like when the new kid comes to town and says he has a girlfriend in Canada or something.'

'Don't get us wrong,' Ema said. 'He was nice

enough. All kids talk about those kinds of things. It was just . . . I don't know. It felt so normal.'

Mickey nodded.

'Thanks, guys. This was really helpful.'

'Oh, we're not done,' Ema said.

Myron looked at them.

'I put a keylogger on his computer,' Mickey said.

'As in . . .?'

'As in we can see whatever he types on it. Emails, social media, whatever.'

'Whoa,' Myron said. 'Who's monitoring him?'

'Spoon.'

Spoon was Mickey's other close friend – if you still counted Ema as only a 'friend' – and what they used to call (or heck, maybe still do) a lovable nerd or geek or dork. Spoon was also ridiculously brave.

'How is he doing?'

Mickey smiled. 'He's walking again.'

'And annoying everyone again,' Ema added. 'Anyway, he'll let us know if anything important comes up.'

Myron wasn't sure what to say here. He didn't like these teenagers crossing this particular ethical line, but he wasn't in the mood to lecture them about privacy or, more important, give up a chance of possibly finding out the truth. It was a close call. Patrick might not be Patrick. Patrick might hold the key to finding another missing boy. Then again, was spying on a teenager justified? Was it even legal?

If you were the type of person who knew for sure what to do here, if you could make the call to spy or not spy without qualms or caveats, you'd be the kind of person Myron would find somewhat suspect.

Life ain't that black-and-white.

'There's one more thing,' Ema said.

'What?'

Ema glanced uneasily at Mickey.

'What?' Myron said again.

Mickey gestured for Ema to go ahead. Ema sighed and reached into her purse. She pulled out a small clear plastic bag, the kind you used to get your toiletries past TSA. 'Here.'

Ema handed the bag to Myron. He held it up in the air. There was a toothbrush and strands of long hair. He put it down and waited a moment. 'Are these . . .?'

Ema nodded. 'I got the toothbrush from Patrick's bathroom,' she said. 'Then I sneaked down the hall and grabbed the hair from Francesca's hairbrush.'

Myron said nothing. He just stared at the contents in the plastic bag.

Mickey stood. Ema followed suit.

'We figured maybe you could run a DNA test on them or something,' Mickey said.

CHAPTER 25

We are inside the farmhouse now.

It is just the two of us, Fat Gandhi and *moi*. Zorra now stands guard by the front door. Fat Gandhi's traveling companions – two of the men Myron had described as the 'gamers' from his visit and one male who could possibly be underage – are in the front yard with him.

'Your friend Zorro,' Fat Gandhi begins.

'Zorra.'

'Pardon?'

'His name is Zorra, not Zorro.'

'I mean no offense.'

I just stare at him.

'I've made us tea,' Fat Gandhi says.

I don't touch it. I think instead about the young male, the one who may be underage. In movies, one often hears the bad guys talk about how 'this is only business.' I for one rarely believe it. Be you good or bad, you tend to gravitate toward what interests you. Most drug dealers, for example, partake of their wares. The people I've encountered who work in the porn industry have a predilection

283

for the same. Those who run protection rackets enforced by violence rarely have an aversion to injuring others or the sight of blood. In fact, for the most part, they relish it.

I look at my own role in this without irony, by the way.

My point? Fat Gandhi may talk about how this is all business and profit to him, but I am not sure that I believe it. I wonder whether there is a personal and unsavory explanation for his chosen line of work.

And I wonder whether I should do something about it.

'I can't give you your cousin,' Fat Gandhi says, 'because I don't have him.'

'That's very unfortunate,' I say.

He does not meet my eye. This is good. He fears Zorra. He fears me. As he said before, he does not want to spend the rest of his life looking over his shoulder. This is why I believe in massive and disproportional retaliation. It makes your next enemy think twice.

'Where is he?' I ask.

'I don't know. I never had him.'

'Yet you had Patrick Moore.'

'I did, yes. But not like you think.'

He leans forward and grabs his cup of tea.

I ask, 'How long was Patrick Moore in your employ?'

'That's just it,' he says, taking a sip from the cup. 'He never was.'

I cross my legs. 'Please explain.'

'You killed my men,' he says. 'Three of them.'

'Are you still looking for a confession?'

'No, I'm telling the story. I'm starting at the beginning.'

I sit back and beckon him to continue. Fat Gandhi doesn't use the delicate handle of the teacup. He embraces it gently using both hands, as though protecting an injured bird. 'You never asked my men why they approached Patrick Moore, did you?'

'There was no time,' I say.

'Perhaps. Or perhaps you overreacted.'

'Or perhaps they did.'

'Fair enough, mate. Fair enough. But we're getting off track. I'm going to tell you what happened. You then decide where we go from there, okay?'

I nod.

'So this kid, this Patrick Moore, he shows up on our turf. You understand about that sort of thing, don't you, Mr Lockwood? Territorial disputes?'

'Go on.'

'So my men heard about it. You could be right. They may have been too heavy-handed; I don't know. I wasn't there. But that was their job. I've learned that on the streets, it's sometimes better to be heavy-handed. To overreact.'

I hear the echo of my own self-justification. It does not faze me in the least.

'So they braced Patrick Moore. I assume they

decided to make an example of him. Then you appeared. You acted in such a way as to protect him. But tell me, Mr Lockwood, what did Patrick Moore do?'

'He ran away,' I say.

'Exactly, my friend. He ran. Everyone ran. Including Garth.'

'Garth?'

'The young man with the dog collar.'

'Ah,' I say.

'Garth naturally reported what happened. It got back to me. I called him. He told me about this new kid showing up on our turf and then how some effete gentleman disposed of them.'

I arch an eyebrow. 'Effete?'

'His word, not mine.'

I smile. I know that's untrue, but I let it go. 'Continue.'

'Well, you can imagine, Mr Lockwood, what I thought. Three of my men slaughtered over what seemed a small territorial dispute. I don't know about America, but here that kind of thing doesn't just happen. I concluded that someone – you, sir – were declaring war on me. I concluded that the boy, Patrick Moore as it turned out, was part of a setup – that he was working with you to test my strength and resolve. Do you understand?'

'I do.'

'And to be candid, I didn't quite understand it. Those streets aren't all that profitable. So I put feelers out for the boy who ran away. Patrick. Garth said that he heard him utter a few words and that he sounded American. That confused me even more. Why would Americans be out to get me? But from there, I put out the word.' He puts down the tea. 'May I be immodest for a moment?'

'Please.'

'I more or less rule the streets of London. At least, when it comes to this particular market. I know the hotels. I know the brothels. I know the shelters and rail stations and public transport where youngsters hide. I know the parks and alleys and dark corners. There is no one better at finding a missing teen than yours truly. My employees can scour the city better than any branch of law enforcement.'

He takes another sip of his tea, smacks his lips, sits the cup back down. 'So I put out a code red, Mr Lockwood. It didn't take long for one of my contacts to find the boy. He was trying to check into a small hotel paying cash. So I sent a few of my more mature employees – you probably noticed them in camouflage pants – to apprehend him. They did so. They brought him back to the arcade.'

He takes another sip of tea.

'Patrick was alone when you found him?' I ask.

'Yes.'

I mull this over. 'Did any of your people know him?'

'No.'

'Proceed,' I say.

'Please understand, Mr Lockwood, that at this time, I believed that this American was working to disrupt and even destroy my business.'

I nod. 'So you treated him as a hostile.'

Fat Gandhi's smile is one of relief. 'Yes. You understand, then?'

I give him nothing.

'I, shall we say, interrogated him.'

'He tells you who he is,' I say, putting it together. 'That he was kidnapped.'

'Yes.'

'What did you do?'

'What I always do. I conduct research.'

I remember what Myron told me about Fat Gandhi's Hindu aphorism. 'Knowledge is bigger than debate,' I say.

He is unnerved by my knowledge of his quote. 'Uh, yes.'

'What did you find?'

'I was able to confirm his story, which put me in something of a quandary. On the one hand, I could turn him over to the authorities. I could even end up a hero for rescuing him.'

I shake my head. 'But that would put too much heat on you.'

'Precisely. Heroes put targets on their backs, even with the police.'

'So you decided to look for a payoff.'

'Honestly, I didn't know what to do. I am not a kidnapper. I also still needed to understand the threat. Three of my men were dead, after all. So

I confess to you, Mr Lockwood, that I wasn't quite sure what to do.'

I see it now. 'And then Myron shows up.'

'Yes. He found Garth in the park. I have Garth bring him to the arcade. I figure that this is my chance. I can make money. I can get rid of Patrick. I can avenge my dead men.'

'The other boy that Myron saw in the cell,' I say. 'I assume he was just a plant.'

'Yes, he was just one of the boys around that age.'

'You figured you could collect more money for two than for one.'

Fat Gandhi nods and spreads his hands. 'You know the rest.'

I do, but I need to clarify. 'You never saw Rhys Baldwin?'

'No.'

'And you have no idea where he is?'

'None. But this is my proposal, if you want to hear it.'

I sit back and cross my legs. I gesture for him to proceed.

'You forget me. I forget you. I go back to my life. Except for one thing. I have the sources on the street. I have the contacts. I use them now. In the same way I was able to find Patrick Moore, I use them to find Rhys Baldwin, if he can be found.'

I consider this. It sounds like a fair deal. I tell him this. Relief washes over him. We have a deal. For now.

'One more question,' I say.

He waits.

'You said, "if he can be found."'

His face falls a little.

'I assume,' I continue, 'that you asked Patrick Moore about Rhys Baldwin's whereabouts.'

He squirms just enough. 'It didn't really interest me,' he replies.

'But you asked.'

'I did, yes.'

'What did he say?'

Fat Gandhi looks me square in the eye. 'He said that Rhys was dead.'

CHAPTER 26

The Morningside campus of Columbia University features a startlingly picturesque quad nestled between Broadway and Amsterdam Avenue on the west and east and 114th Street and 120th Street south and north. You enter by College Walk on 116th Street, and suddenly, like something out of a wardrobe portal to Narnia, you are transported from the aging city, from the purely urban, from Manhattan at its most citified, to an idyllic campus of green and brick and domes and ivy. You feel protected in here, isolated, and maybe, for the four years you spend here as an undergraduate, that's how it should be.

Esperanza had found a campus directory that told her Francesca Moore lived in a six-person suite in Ruggles Hall. It was seven A.M. The quad was near silent. You needed a student ID to enter the building, so Myron waited by the door. To blend in, he donned a baseball cap and carried an empty pizza box.

Myron Bolitar, Master of Disguise.

When one kid finally emerged, Myron grabbed the door before it closed. The kid, probably used to deliverymen coming at all hours, didn't say a word.

Myron Bolitar, Master of Disguise, was inside.

The corridors were eerily quiet. Myron headed to the second floor and found the door to room 217. He'd come this early figuring that Francesca, like any college student, would still be asleep and thus he was sure to find her here and maybe even a little groggy. That might be a good thing. Catch her off guard and all that. Sure, he might disturb her roommates too, but he chalked that up to acceptable collateral damage.

Myron didn't know what he hoped to find here, but stumbling around blind was a big part of his so-called investigations. You don't so much painstakingly search for the needle in the haystack as haphazardly leap into various haystacks, barefoot and naked, and then flail wildly and hope that hey, ouch, there's a needle.

Myron knocked on the door. Nothing. He knocked a little harder. More nothing. He put his hand on the knob and gave it a small turn. The door was unlocked. He debated just going in, but no, a strange adult entering the room of a college co-ed? Not a smart move. When he knocked again, the door finally opened.

'Mr Bolitar?'

It wasn't Francesca Moore. It was Clark Baldwin.

'Hey, Clark.'

Clark wore a T-shirt several sizes too large and checkered boxer shorts that even Myron's dad would consider retro. His face was pale, his eyes bloodshot. 'What are you doing here?' he asked Myron.

'I could ask you the same question.'

'Uh, I go to school here. I live here.'

'Oh,' Myron said. 'You and Francesca are roommates?'

'Suitemates, yeah.'

'I didn't know.'

'No reason you should,' Clark said.

True that.

'There are six of us,' Clark continued, feeling the need to explain or perhaps get his bearings. 'Three guys, three girls. It's the twenty-first century. Co-ed dorms, co-ed rooms, transgender bathrooms, we got it all.'

'Can I come in?' Myron asked.

From behind him, a male voice said, 'What's going on, Clark?'

'Go back to sleep, Matt,' Clark said. 'It's nothing.'

Clark slipped outside into the corridor and closed the door behind him. 'Why are you here?'

'I came to talk to Francesca,' Myron said.

Something crossed his face. 'What about?'

'About the econ final,' Myron said. 'I hear it's going to be a bitch.'

Clark made a face. 'That supposed to be funny?'

'Well, I admit it's not one of my better lines but—'

'Mom said you and Cousin Win are trying to find Rhys.'

Myron nodded. 'We are.'

'But Francesca doesn't know anything about that.'

Myron spared him the flailing-in-a-haystack metaphor. 'She may know more than she thinks she knows.'

Clark shook his head. 'She would have told me,' he said.

Patience, Myron thought. If you're standing in front of a haystack, flail in that one before you move on. Or something like that. In short, stay patient for now with Clark.

'You two must be pretty tight,' Myron said.

'Francesca is my best friend.'

'You grew up together?'

'Yes. But there's a lot more to it than that.'

A door opened down the corridor. A boy stumbled out as only a college student waking up early can.

'She's the only one who got it,' Clark continued. 'You know what I mean?'

Myron did, but he said, 'Pretend I don't.'

'We were just kids. We were only in fifth grade.'

'I remember. Mr Hixon's class.'

'Dixon.'

'Right, sorry. Dixon. Go on.'

Clark swallowed and rubbed his chin. 'So we're just little kids. Francesca and I were friends, I guess, but we didn't hang out or anything. You know what that age is like, right?'

Myron nodded. 'Boys hung out with boys, girls with girls.'

'Right. But then everything . . . I mean, both our little brothers just' – Clark snapped his fingers – 'vanished. Like that. Do you not get what that did to us?'

Myron wasn't sure if the question was rhetorical or not. The corridor had the stale stench of spilled beer and academic worry. There was a bulletin board overloaded with flyers, meetings for all kinds of groups and clubs, everything from badminton to belly dancing, from feminist thought to flute choir. There were clubs with names Myron didn't understand, like Orchesis or Gayaa or Taal, and what was the Venom Step Team?

'For a while, after your brother disappears, you stay home from school,' Clark said, his voice faraway. 'I don't remember how long anymore. Was it a week, a month? I can't remember. But eventually you have to go back, and when you do, everyone looks at you like you're some kind of alien. Your friends. Your teachers. Everyone. Then you go home from school, and it's even worse. Your parents are falling apart. They're extra clingy because now they're scared of losing you too. So you come home and you try to escape to your room, but when you do, you walk right past his room. Every day. You move on – and yet you never move on. You try to forget, but that makes it worse. You try to get out from the shadow, but then you see your mother's sad face and it knocks you back down again.'

Clark lowered his head.

And meanwhile, Myron thought, you're just a kid.

Myron wasn't sure it was the right move, but in the end, he put a hand on the boy's shoulder.

'Thank you,' Myron said.

'For what?'

'For sharing that. It must have been a nightmare.'

'It was,' Clark said, 'but that's my point. She made it better.'

'Francesca?'

Clark nodded. 'I had someone who didn't just *say* they got it. I had someone who understood completely.'

'Because she was going through the same thing.'

'Right.'

'And,' Myron said, 'vice versa. She had someone too.'

'Yeah, I guess. You get it, right?'

A friendship bonded in tragedy – maybe the strongest kind of all. 'Of course.'

'I came out to Francesca before anyone, even my parents, but of course, she already knew. We could talk about anything.'

'You were lucky to have her.'

'You have no idea, Mr Bolitar.'

Myron took his time with the next question. 'And now that her brother is back?'

Clark said nothing.

'Now that her brother is back and yours isn't,' Myron continued. 'Has your relationship changed?'

His voice was soft. 'Francesca is not here.'

'Where is she?'

'Back home, I guess.'

'I thought you drove her in last night.'

'Who told you that?' he half snapped. Then: 'Oh, right. Your nephew. He was at the house.'

Myron waited.

'See, there was a party at the DKA house. I know it sounds stupid, what with finding her brother and all. She's been really confused lately. On edge. I mean, don't get me wrong, she's ecstatic. She couldn't even let Patrick out of her sight. At first anyway. But now maybe it's getting claustrophobic, you know what I mean?'

'Sure,' Myron said. 'That's natural.'

'So she texted me to come get her.'

'And you drove her there?'

'Yeah. We went to the party. It was a little out of control, but nothing we hadn't seen before. We drank. Maybe too much, I don't know. Anyway, at some point, she started freaking out.'

'Freaking out how?'

'She started crying. I asked her what's wrong. She just shook her head. I tried to comfort her. I took her outside, you know, to get a little fresh air. She just cried harder.'

'Did she say anything?'

'She just kept sobbing it wasn't right, it wasn't fair.'

'What wasn't fair?'

Clark shrugged. 'That she got her brother back and I didn't.'

297

Silence. Then: 'What did you say?'

'I told her I was happy for her. I told her that Patrick coming home was good news, that we can still find my brother too. But she just kept sobbing. Then she said she needed to see her brother. She just wanted to make sure it was real or something. Like maybe she dreamt Patrick was back. I get that, don't you?'

'Sure.'

'I used to have dreams like that all the time. Rhys would be home and it was like he was never gone or whatever. So I said I would drive her, but next thing I know an Uber pulled up. She got in and said she would call me soon.'

'Has she?'

'No. But it was only a few hours ago. I'm telling you, Mr Bolitar. She doesn't know anything.'

There was no point in heading to the Moore house to question Francesca. Nancy or Hunter would just call a halt to it. Besides, Myron had other plans.

His dad was waiting in the yard when Myron pulled up. The two men headed out for breakfast at Eppes Essen, a 'Jewish-style' (according to the brochure) deli and restaurant on the other side of town. Myron and Dad both ordered the same thing – Eppes's famed Sloppy Joe sandwich. Many of you associate Sloppy Joes with that ground possible-meat thingie in school cafeterias. This was not that. Eppes Essen makes the authentic Sloppy

298

Joes, momentous triple-decker sandwiches with rye bread, Russian dressing, coleslaw, and at least three meats – in this case, turkey, pastrami, corned beef.

Dad stared down at his plate and then nodded his appreciation. 'If God made a sandwich.'

'That should be Eppes's slogan,' Myron agreed.

They finished, paid the check, and drove to the high school just as the boys' basketball team ran out for warm-ups. Mickey was in the middle of the pack. The home team was playing its archrival, Millburn High.

'Remember the game you had against them junior year?' Dad asked.

Myron smiled. 'Oh yeah.' With Myron's team up by only one point, Millburn had an easy fast-break layup to win it with two seconds remaining. The Millburn player cruised in, ready to score the game winner, when Myron, trailing the play, somehow leapt over the guy and pinned the ball onto the backboard as time ran out. The Millburn players screamed for goaltending – hard to tell if it was or wasn't – but the ref didn't make the call. To this day, if Myron ran across one of the Millburn guys who'd played in that game, they would still good-naturedly complain about that no-call.

Ah, basketball.

The gym had a healthy crowd for the rivalry. Some people pointed and whispered as Myron walked by. Welcome to Minor-League Local Celebrity. A few came over and said hello – old teachers, old neighbors, those guys in every town who hang out at games even when their kids aren't playing anymore.

From near the foul line, Mickey spotted them and gave a quick wave. Dad – or in Mickey's case, Grandpa – waved back. Dad started to make his way up the stands. He always took the back row. He didn't want to be the center of attention. Dad never yelled, never called out, never 'coached,' never rode referees, never moaned, never complained. He might clap. When he got really excited during a big game, when Myron would hit a big shot, he might say, 'Nice pass, Bob,' or something like that, deflecting the praise. Dad never cheered for his own son. It simply wasn't done.

'If I have to cheer for you to know I'm proud,' Dad once told Myron, 'then I'm doing something wrong.'

Never one to miss a moment of nostalgia, Myron flashed back to those long-ago days when he would warm up on a court like this and look across the gym and watch his dad take the steps of the bleachers two at a time. Not today, of course. Today Dad's movements were more hesitant and shuffle-like. He took frequent breaks. He grimaced and got out of breath. Myron put his hand out to help him, but his dad shook it off.

'I feel great,' he said. 'It's just the knee.'

But he didn't look great. 'Okay, Dad.'

They sat in the top row, just the two of them.

'I like it up here,' Dad said.

Myron nodded.

'Myron?'

'Yeah?'

'I'm fine.'

'I know.'

'Your mother and I are getting older; that's all.'

And that's the problem, Myron wanted to say. He got it – to everything there is a season, turn, turn, turn, the earth revolves, life cycles – but that didn't mean he had to like it.

The horn buzzed. The players stopped warming up and headed to their benches. The guy on the microphone began, as every New Jersey high school basketball game must, by reading the state's sportsmanship policy:

' "There will be no tolerance for negative statements or actions between opposing players and coaches. This includes taunting, baiting, berating opponents, 'trash-talking,' or actions which ridicule or cause embarrassment to them. Any verbal, written, or physical conduct related to race, gender, ethnicity, disability, sexual orientation or religion shall not be tolerated, could subject the violator to ejection, and may result in penalties being assessed against your team. If such comments are heard, a penalty will be assessed immediately. We have been instructed not to issue warnings. It is your responsibility to remind your team of this policy." '

'A necessary evil,' Dad said. Then, motioning to the spot where the fathers sat, he added, 'It doesn't stop those jackasses.'

Mickey's short tenure at the high school had not been without controversy. He was back on the team, however unlikely that had seemed a few weeks back, but there were some residual bad feelings. Myron saw among those vocal dads his old nemesis and former high school teammate Eddie Taylor, now the chief of police in town. Taylor hadn't seen Myron yet, but he glared hard at Mickey.

Myron didn't like that.

Myron stared at the chief until finally Taylor felt his eyes, turned, and looked Myron's way. The two men glared at each other another second or two.

If you got a problem, you glare at me, Myron tried to say with his eyes, *not my nephew.*

Dad said, 'Ignore him. Eddie has always been what the kids today call an "ass waffle."'

Myron laughed out loud. 'Ass waffle?'

'Yep.'

'Who taught you that?'

'Ema,' Dad said. 'I like her, don't you?'

'Very much,' Myron agreed.

'Is it true?' Dad asked.

'What?'

'That Ema's mother is Angelica Wyatt?'

It was supposed to be a secret. Angelica Wyatt was one of the most popular actresses in the world. To protect her only child and her own privacy, they had moved to a large estate on a hill here in New Jersey.

'It's true.'

'And you know her?'

Myron nodded. 'A bit.'

'Who's her father?'

'I don't know.'

Dad started craning his neck. 'I'm surprised Ema's not here.'

They settled back as the game began. Myron loved every second of it. Sitting with his dad in a gym, watching his nephew dominate the game Myron so loved – it was simple and primitive and blissful. There were no pangs anymore. He missed it, sure, but it was way past his time, and man oh man, did he love watching his young nephew reveling in the experience.

It made Myron a little teary.

At one point, after Mickey made a turnaround jumper, Dad shook his head and said, 'He's really good.'

'He is.'

'He plays like you.'

'He's better.'

Dad considered that. 'Different eras. He may not go as far as you.'

'Hmm,' Myron said. 'What makes you say that?'

'How to put this . . .?' Dad began. 'For you, basketball was everything.'

'Mickey is pretty dedicated too.'

'No question. But it's not everything. There's a difference. Let me ask you a question.'

'Okay.'

'When you look back at how competitive you were, what do you think?'

Mickey made a steal. A cheer rose from the crowd. Myron couldn't help but smile. 'I guess I was a little crazy.'

'It was important to you.'

'Ridiculously important,' Myron agreed.

Dad arched an eyebrow. 'Too important?'

'Probably, yeah.'

'But that's one of the things that separated you from the other talented players. That . . . "desire" is almost too tame a word. That *need* to win. That single-minded focus. That's what made you the best.'

Win had often said something similar of Myron's playing days at Duke: *'When you're competing, you're barely sane . . .'*

'But now,' Dad continued, 'you have perspective. You've experienced tragedies and joys that have taught you that there are more important things in life than basketball. And Mickey – don't take this the wrong way – Mickey had to grow up young. He's already suffered more than his share of tragedy.'

Myron nodded. 'He already has perspective.'

'Exactly.'

The horn blew, ending the first quarter. Mickey's team was up by six.

'Who knows,' Myron said. 'Maybe his wisdom will make him a better player. Maybe perspective is as good as single-minded focus.'

Dad liked that. 'Maybe you're right.'

They watched Mickey's teammates break the huddle and take the ball out of bounds to start the second quarter.

'I loathe sports metaphors,' Dad said, 'but there is one important thing both of you learned on the court and do in real life.'

'What's that?'

Dad nodded to the court. Mickey drove through the lane, drew a defender, dished a pass to a team-mate, who scored an easy bucket.

'You make those around you better.'

Myron said nothing. His nephew had that look on his face, the one Myron knew so well. There is a Zen to being on the court, a calm in the storm, a purity, a concentration, the ability to slow down time. Then Myron saw Mickey's eyes flick to the left. He pulled up for a second. Myron followed Mickey's gaze to see what had drawn that reaction.

Ema had walked into the gym.

She narrowed her eyes and scanned the stands. Myron gave a small wave. She nodded that she saw him and started toward him. Myron rose and met her halfway.

'What's up?' he asked.

'It's about Patrick,' Ema said. 'You better come with me.'

Ema didn't take him far, just to the head custo-dian's office in the high school's main building.

She opened the door and held it for him. Myron stepped inside and recognized the kid at the desk.

'Hello, Mr Bolitar!'

They called the kid Spoon. Mickey had given him the nickname, though Myron wasn't sure of the origins. Spoon's father was the head custodian at the high school, which explained why Spoon had access to this space. The office was small and tidy and loaded with perfectly pruned plants.

'I told you to call me Myron.'

The kid swiveled his chair so that he was facing Myron. Spoon wasn't wearing a pocket protector, but he had the look of a kid who should have been. Using one finger, Spoon pushed his Harry Potter glasses up his nose.

Spoon gave Myron a crooked grin. 'You know those stickers that supermarkets put on fruit?'

Ema sighed. 'Not now, Spoon.'

'Sure I know them,' Myron said.

'Do you peel them off your fruit before you eat it?'

'I do.'

'Did you know,' Spoon continued, 'that those stickers are edible?'

'I did not.'

'You don't have to peel them off, if you don't want to. Even the glue is food grade.'

'Good info. Is that why I'm here?'

'Of course not,' Spoon said. 'You're here because I think Patrick Moore is about to leave his house.'

Myron stepped toward the desk. 'What makes you say that?'

'He just finished Skyping with someone on his laptop.' Spoon leaned back in his chair. 'Are you aware, Myron, that Skype's headquarters are located in Luxembourg?'

Ema rolled her eyes.

'Who did Patrick Skype with?' Myron asked.

'That I can't say.'

'What did they talk about?'

'That I can't say either. The keylogger planted by my lovely associate' – he gestured toward Ema, who looked like she wanted to kick him – 'does just that. It records – or logs, if you prefer – the keys struck on a keyboard. So I can see Patrick Moore signed into Skype. I can't, of course, see what they said.'

'So what makes you think he's leaving the house?' Myron asked.

'A simple deduction, my friend. Immediately after turning off Skype, Patrick Moore – or whoever is using his computer – visited the New Jersey Transit website. From what I can gather, he was searching for bus routes into New York City.'

Myron checked his watch. 'How long ago was this?'

Spoon checked the elaborate watch on his wrist. 'Fourteen minutes and eleven, twelve, thirteen seconds ago.'

CHAPTER 27

For reasons Myron could never fathom, Big
Cyndi was great at tailing people. Perhaps it
was that she was so obvious, so in your face,
so out there, that you never really saw her or
suspected a woman who wore a clingy purple
Batgirl costume to be following you. Her costume,
a somewhat larger replica of the one Yvonne Craig
wore on the old *Batman* TV show, was snug to the
point where it might be mistaken for sausage casing.

Today, however, the outfit did blend in a very
particular way. Myron spotted Big Cyndi the
moment he entered Times Square. Think of
every cliché you can about Times Square, mush
them together, stack cliché upon cliché, the ones
about the kinetic waves of humanity and the
traffic and the ginormous billboards and moving
screens and neon lights. Then take what you're
imagining and raise it to the tenth power.

Welcome to Times Square.

Times Square is an assault on every sense, and
somehow that includes not only scent but taste.
Everything is in motion and swirling and you want
to give the entire square a giant Adderall.

There, along with Spider-Man, Elmo, Mickey Mouse, Buzz Lightyear, and Olaf from *Frozen,* stood Big Cyndi in full costume. Tourists were lined up to pose for photographs with her 'Batgirl.'

'They love me, Mr Bolitar,' Big Cyndi called out. 'Who doesn't?'

Big Cyndi tee-heed and struck poses that would have made Madonna in her 'Vogue' days blush. An Asian tourist offered her some cash after taking the picture, but Big Cyndi refused. 'Oh, I couldn't, kind sir.'

'Are you sure?' the tourist asked.

'This is charity.' She bent down closer to him. 'If I wanted to be paid for wearing this outfit, I would still be hooking.'

The tourist hurried away.

Big Cyndi looked at Myron. 'I was joking, Mr Bolitar.'

'I know that.'

'I never hooked.'

'Good to know.'

'Though I made beaucoup bucks when I wore this working the pole.'

'Uh-huh,' Myron said, not wanting to go down this particular lane of memory.

'At Leather and Lace, remember?'

'I do, yes.'

'And okay, sometimes things went too far when I'd get hired for a lap dance, if you get my drift.'

'Drift gotten,' Myron said quickly. 'So, uh, where's Patrick? Can you give me an update?'

'Young Patrick sneaked out of his house two hours ago,' Big Cyndi said. 'He walked approximately one mile into town and took bus 487. I looked it up. Bus 487's final destination is Port Authority in New York City. I drove my car and arrived before the bus. I waited for him to get off and followed him here.'

'Here where?' Myron asked.

'Don't turn suddenly, because you'll be obvious.'

'Okay.'

'Patrick is standing behind you, between the Madame Tussauds wax museum and Ripley's Believe It or Not!'

Myron waited. Then he said, 'Can I look now?'

'Turn slowly.'

Myron did. Patrick stood on Forty-Second Street wearing a baseball cap pulled low. His shoulders were hunched as though he was trying to disappear.

'Has he talked to anyone?' Myron asked.

'No,' Big Cyndi replied. 'Mr Bolitar?'

'Yes?'

'Do you mind if I pose for more photographs while we wait? My public demands it.'

'Go for it.'

Myron kept his eye on Patrick, but he also couldn't help but watch Big Cyndi work the crowd. Thirty seconds after she got back into action, the queue to have a photo taken with her was so long the Naked Cowboy looked at her askance. She glanced at Myron. Myron gave her a big thumbs-up.

Here was the simple, awful truth: It was often hard to see beyond Big Cyndi's size. We as a society have many prejudices, but there are very few of our fellow citizens we stigmatize and judge less charitably than what we consider to be 'large' women. Big Cyndi was all too aware of that. She had once explained her outgoing lifestyle, if you will, thusly: 'I'd rather see shock on their faces than pity, Mr Bolitar. And I'd rather they see brazen or outrageous than shrinking or scared.'

Myron turned back toward Ripley's just as a teenage girl sidled up to Patrick.

Who the . . .?

Myron remembered what Mickey and Ema had told him about Patrick's claim of having a girlfriend. But if he'd been living in quasi-captivity in London, how would he know anyone in New York City?

Good question.

Patrick and the girl exchanged a quick, awkward hug before heading inside Ripley's. Big Cyndi was by Myron's side now. When Myron started toward the ticket window, Big Cyndi stopped him.

'He knows you,' she reminded him.

'You'll go in?'

Big Cyndi pointed to the sign with an index finger the size of a baguette. 'It's called an "odditorium." Who better?'

Hard to argue.

'You wait by the exit,' she said. 'I'll text you updates.'

Myron stayed on the street for an hour and people-watched. He liked people-watching. Great views of sunsets and water and greens are wonderful, he supposed, but after a while, they become something you barely notice. But if you're in a spot where you can watch people walk by – every race, gender, size, shape, religion, language, whatever – you are never bored. Everyone is their own universe – a life, a dream, a hope, a sorrow, a joy, a surprise, a revelation, a story with a beginning, a middle, and an end – even when they simply walk by you on the street.

The phone vibrated when Big Cyndi's text came in: **EXITING NOW.**

Big Cyndi always texted in capital letters.

Patrick kept his head low as he came out. The teenage girl stood right next to him. Big Cyndi loomed behind them.

The teenage girl gave Patrick a quick peck on the cheek. Then Patrick started heading west, away from Times Square. The girl moved east. They were splitting up. Big Cyndi looked at Myron for instructions. Myron gestured to Patrick. Big Cyndi nodded and started to follow him. Myron fell into a current of humans and tailed the girl.

She turned left on Seventh Avenue and started uptown. Myron followed. She headed all the way up to Fifty-Ninth Street and turned right on Central Park South. They passed the Plaza Hotel and turned north on Fifth Avenue. The teenager walked steadily and confidently and with no hesitation. Myron assumed from this observation that she had made this journey before and probably lived in New York City.

Myron Bolitar, Master of Deduction. Please don't shun him for his gifts.

She turned east on East Sixty-First Street. When she crossed Park Avenue, Myron saw her reach into her bag and ready her key. The town house in front of her had a wrought-iron gate. She unlocked it. Then she moved down two steps and vanished inside.

A town house near Park Avenue, Myron thought. The girl probably came from money.

Again: Myron Bolitar, Master of Deduction. If you prick him, does he not bleed?

He stood outside and debated his next move. First, he texted Big Cyndi. **Update?**

Big Cyndi: PATRICK IS ON THE BUS. ASSUME HE'S HEADING BACK HOME.

Myron: I'll be the Master of Deduction, thank you very much.

Big Cyndi: WHAT?

Myron: Never mind.

He stared at the door and hoped it would open so he could . . .

So he could what?

Was he going to approach a teenage girl on the street and ask about her relationship with the boy she just met up with at Ripley's Odditorium? Myron wasn't a cop. He wasn't licensed in any way, shape, or form. He would just be a creepy middle-aged stranger approaching a young girl. He didn't know her name. He didn't know anything about her.

No, that would be the wrong move here.

He picked up his phone and called Esperanza.

'What's up?'

'I have an address near Park Avenue.'

'Well, la-di-da. I live in a one-bedroom in Hoboken.'

'That was funny,' Myron said.

'Wasn't it, though? Give me the address.'

Myron did. 'I followed a teenage girl here.'

'Aren't you engaged?'

'Ha-ha. She met up with Patrick. I need to find out who she is.'

'On it.'

When he hung up again, his phone rang. He saw from the caller ID it was Terese.

He answered the phone saying, 'Hey, beautiful.'

'God, you're smooth.'

'You think so?'

'No,' Terese said. 'In fact, I think it's your lack of smoothness that makes you so damn sexy. Guess what?'

Myron started walking back. He had parked his car in a crowded theater lot by Times Square. 'What?'

'The network sent me home on their private jet.'

'Whoa, big-time.'

'I just landed at Teterboro.'

'Did you get the job?' he asked.

'I'll hear soon.'

Myron stopped on the corner. Should he walk back to his car or catch a taxi? 'Are you on your way to the apartment, then?'

'I am.'

'Wanna do the nasty?' he asked.

'Wow, I take it back. You are smooth.'

'Is that a yes?'

'It's most definitely a yes.'

'You can't see,' Myron said, 'but I'm sprinting to the car right now.'

'Faster,' she said, before hanging up.

Myron parked his car in the underground lot behind the Dakota. When he started up the dark ramp, three men appeared. The one in the middle he recognized. It was Rhys's dad, Chick Baldwin. The other two wore jeans and flannel shirts. They were big and trying to look bigger. One carried a baseball bat.

'I told you to let it go,' Chick said.

Myron sighed. 'Are you for real?'

'I warned you to forget those texts, didn't I?'

'You did.'

'Well?'

'And I didn't listen,' Myron said. 'Can we move this along? I kinda have plans. Big plans.'

Chick used his hand to slick back his hair. 'Did you think I was, what, playing with you?'

'I don't know, Chick, and I really don't care. So what's your next step?' Myron pointed out the two men in flannel shirts. 'Are these two monkeys supposed to rough me up?'

'Who you calling "monkey"?' asked Monkey with the Bat.

'Yeah,' Batless Monkey chimed in. 'You're the monkey, not us.'

Myron tried not to sigh. 'Do you gentlemen see that up there?' He pointed above their heads. When the two monkeys looked up, Myron kicked the one holding the bat in the balls, snatching away the bat before said monkey folded like a beach chair. Myron looked at Batless Monkey. Batless Monkey thought that this might be a good time to retreat and did so with gusto.

Myron looked at Chick.

'You didn't have to do that,' Chick said.

'Why did you bring them?'

'To make you pay attention, I guess.'

'I'm paying attention now.'

Chick moved to the former bat-carrying monkey and bent down to help him. 'You're more like Brooke's psycho cousin than I realized.'

'Chick?'

'What?'

'I'm on my way somewhere very special,' Myron said. 'I will definitely and without hesitation whack you with this bat if you don't move out of my way.'

'Just go,' Chick said.

Myron studied his face for a moment and realized

something. 'You're mad because I talked to Nancy Moore about your texts.'

'I told you not to, right? I practically begged you.'

'That's not the point, Chick.'

'What is?'

'Only one way you could know I did that. Nancy Moore told you.'

Myron Bolitar, Master of Deduction, strikes again.

Chick said nothing. Myron moved toward him and helped the former bat wielder to his feet. Myron told the man to skedaddle. He did as requested, albeit with a bit of a limp. Myron turned his attention back to Chick.

'And that means' – Myron was on a roll now – 'you two are in contact about the texts. And that means there was something really significant between the two of you.'

Chick's voice could not have been more crest-fallen without an actual crest or fall in view. 'You have to leave it alone, Myron. I'm begging you.'

'Even if it's the key to finding your son?'

'It's not. If I thought it had anything to do with Rhys, I would be shouting it every day from the rooftops. But it doesn't. Why can't you believe me?'

'Because you're too close to it. You're not objective.'

Chick closed his eyes. 'You won't let this go, will you?'

'I won't, no. And let me give you a little push

here, Chick. If you don't tell me, I'm going to ask Brooke about them.'

Chick winced as though the words had formed a fist and threatened to punch him. 'You have to understand one thing first.'

'I don't have to understand, but go ahead.'

'I love Brooke. I always have. I always will. Our life isn't perfect. I know that psycho Win—'

'Chick?'

'What?'

'Stop calling my friend names, okay?'

Chick nodded. 'Yeah, whatever. Win hates me. He thinks no one is good enough.'

Myron checked his watch. Terese would be in the apartment by now. 'You told me this already.'

'Not really,' he said. Again Chick gave him the crestfallen look. 'You need to know how much I love my wife and family. I ain't a perfect man. I've done some really questionable things in my time. The thing that gives me humanity – the only thing that really matters – is my love for my family. For Brooke. For Clark.' His chest started to hitch, and the tears started to flow. 'And for Rhys.'

Chick broke into a sob. The real thing. No faking, no trying to hide it. Oh man, Myron thought. Stay strong, stay focused, but remember: This guy is searching for his lost son.

When Chick was back in control, Myron pushed him again: 'Why were you two texting, Chick?'

'We didn't have an affair.'

'What, then?'

'We were going to. That was the thing. We didn't do it. But we were going to.'

'I thought you loved your wife.'

'You're not married, are you, Myron?'

'Engaged.'

Chick wiped the tears. He managed a smile, but there was no joy there. 'We don't have time to get into it. But you're old enough to know that life isn't black-and-white. It's lived in the gray. We get older, we think we're going to die, we reach for something, even if it's stupid. So that's what we did. Me and Nancy. We started flirting. It went too far. We started to make plans because that's how these things are. Like everything else in this horrible world, it gets worse, not better. You reach a stage where you either go through with it or it dies.'

'So what happened, Chick?'

'It died.'

'You didn't go through with it?'

'We stopped in time.'

Myron thought about that. 'Who stopped it?'

'Mutual.'

'It's never mutual, Chick.'

'We both eased into it,' he said. 'And then we both eased out of it.'

'When?'

'What?'

'When did you both ease out of it?'

'I don't know.'

'How long before your son disappeared?'

'I told you. It had nothing to do with that.'

'How long?'

'I told you. I don't know.'

'And why were you so afraid to tell anyone?'

'I didn't want Brooke to find out.'

'Really? Even back then? Your kid is missing and you're worried about that? I mean, you lied to the police over a flirtation.'

'There wasn't just me and my family to consider.'

'There was Nancy Moore's too?'

'See it from our perspective, okay? Suppose we told the police. Okay? Suppose we told the police all about it. What would have happened?'

Myron did not bother replying.

'You get why we didn't say anything. Who'd believe us? They find these texts and we say, "Oh yeah, we almost hooked up," you think the cops are going to look at this right? We were already getting hard questions. We admit to almost having an affair, and that's all they'd look at. And now, if Brooke finds out . . .' Chick started tearing up again. 'It would kill us, okay? Please. It's all I got left.'

Myron tried to ignore the pain on his face. 'So Brooke never found out?'

'No.'

'And Hunter?'

'Same. Don't you see? If we copped to this thing back then, when everyone was so weak, when all the relationships were already so strained, it would have destroyed us all. We'd have never made it.'

320

'But Hunter and Nancy didn't make it anyway, did they?'

He shook his head. 'That had nothing to do with this.'

'How do you know, Chick? How do you know for sure?'

CHAPTER 28

Myron opened the apartment door, trying to nudge himself back in the mood, though he wasn't really worried. At the end of the day, sexist or not, he was a guy. Guys are remarkably consistent about this part of their lives. Ladies, here's a little seduction tip: It doesn't take a lot to get your man in the mood. You know this already. You see all those articles in women's magazines about how to seduce your man, how to use massage oils or candles or music to get him in the mood. Men, for better or worse, aren't that complicated. Here are two short articles on how to seduce your man: 'Ask him if he wants to have sex.' And: 'Say, "Yes, that would be nice."'

He smiled at the thought, already returning to form, when he entered the apartment and saw that they had company.

Esperanza was there.

'Sorry for the cock block,' she said.

Myron ignored her for the moment and swept Terese into his arms. They just held each other in a tight embrace. That was all. A simple, deep hug. Myron closed his eyes. Terese pulled him even closer.

Esperanza said, 'We, uh, have ten minutes, if you want me to wait outside.'

They let each other go and still held hands.

Myron arched an eyebrow. 'A full ten minutes?'

'Oooh,' Terese said, 'time for extended foreplay.'

'You two are cute,' Esperanza said in a voice that indicated that they were anything but. 'You know how it's never annoying to be around people madly in love? That.'

'Want to tell us why you're here?' Myron asked her.

'I got the information on that residence faster than you might have liked. The town house is owned by a Jesse and Mindy Rogers. Big bucks. Dad is a hedge fund guy. Mom is a career diplomat. They have a sixteen-year-old daughter named Tamryn.'

'So why do we only have ten minutes?'

'She's doing a summer internship at Fox News on Avenue of the Americas and Forty-Eighth Street. The News Corp building, like pretty much every high-rise in Manhattan, has security and requires ID to enter. Her ten-hour shift starts at two P.M., so if we get over there now—'

'We can maybe talk to her before she gets inside.'

'Right.'

Myron looked at Terese. 'Will you wait for me?'

'Better than starting without you.'

'Not sure about that,' Esperanza added.

Both women laughed. Myron did not.

'Let's go,' he said.

★   ★   ★

323

Myron and Esperanza were standing on the Avenue of the Americas in front of the high-rise when Myron finally asked, 'What's wrong?'

'Tom wants to negotiate custody of Hector now.'

'Hey, that's great news.'

Esperanza just stared at him. 'Don't do that.'

'What?'

'You're going to lie to me now?'

'I didn't touch him, I swear.'

'What did you do?'

'I just paid Tom a little visit.'

'You mean like Win does?'

'No, I didn't go near his apartment.'

'Where, then?'

'It was outside a nightclub,' Myron said. Then: 'Do you know your ex-husband is sporting a man bun now? He's over forty, isn't he?'

'Don't deflect attention from the matter at hand. What did you do?'

'I nicely suggested he make peace with you.'

'That wouldn't sway Tom.'

'I may have mentioned that Win was back.'

Esperanza tried not to smile at the thought of Tom's face when he heard that. 'You shouldn't have done that without telling me.'

'Sorry.'

'It's so patronizing, you know that, right?'

'It wasn't meant to be.'

'It may also be vaguely sexist,' Esperanza said. 'If Tom were a woman, would you have made the same threat?'

Myron opened his mouth, closed it, spread his hands. 'Did I mention he was sporting a man bun?'

She sighed. 'Okay, I can't argue with that.'

They stood and waited.

'Remember when you asked me why I didn't say anything before you married Tom?'

'It was a few days ago. I can sometimes remember back a whole week.'

'I told you I didn't think it was my business to interfere. Do you remember what you replied?'

Esperanza nodded and quoted herself: ' "Whose business was it, then?" '

'Right,' Myron said. 'I won't make that mistake again.'

That was when he spotted the teenage girl who had gone to Ripley's with Patrick Moore. Myron gestured to Esperanza. She nodded back. They'd already agreed to approach her together, figuring that as a couple, they might come across as less threatening and yet more authoritative.

Esperanza took the lead. 'Tamryn Rogers?'

She stopped, looked at Myron, then back at Esperanza. 'Yes.'

'My name is Esperanza Diaz.'

'I'm Myron Bolitar.'

'Do you mind if we ask you a few questions?'

She took half a step back. 'Are you cops?'

'No, nothing like that,' Esperanza said.

'I'm sixteen,' Tamryn Rogers replied. 'Talking to strangers isn't really my thing. So, uh, bye, now.'

Esperanza glanced at Myron. They both got it.

Nice wasn't going to work here. Myron went straight at it.

'I saw you today,' he said.

'Excuse me?'

'At Ripley's. A few hours ago. I saw you.'

Tamryn Rogers's mouth formed a small O. 'You're following me?'

'No. I was following Patrick.'

'Who?'

Esperanza took that one. 'The boy you met up with today.'

'That's not . . .' She stopped herself and took another step away from them. 'I didn't meet up with anybody.'

'I saw you,' Myron said.

'Saw what exactly?'

'You met up with Patrick Moore.'

'I went to a museum,' she said. 'Some boy started talking to me. That's all.'

Myron frowned at Esperanza. Esperanza frowned at Tamryn. 'So you didn't know the boy before today?'

'No.'

'Never saw him before?'

'Never.'

'You always hug boys you've never met?' Myron asked. 'Give them a little kiss on the cheek before you leave?'

'Look, no one is trying to get anyone in trouble here,' Esperanza said. 'We are just looking for the truth.'

'By spying on me?' She turned to Myron. 'I'm sixteen years old. What kind of man spies on a sixteen-year-old?'

'A man who is trying to find another sixteen-year-old,' Myron said. 'A man who is trying to find a boy who has been missing for ten years.'

'I don't know what you're talking about.'

'Yeah, you do,' Myron said. 'How do you know Patrick?'

'I told you. I don't know him. He just started talking to me.'

'That's not true,' Myron said.

'You' – Tamryn pointed at Myron – 'stay away from me.' Then she turned to Esperanza. 'You too. Leave me the hell alone or I'm going to scream for help.'

She started toward the door.

'We could talk to your parents,' Myron said.

'Go ahead,' she shouted, drawing a few glances. 'Just leave me alone!'

She hurried toward the glass door and entered. Myron and Esperanza watched her take out her ID, swipe it, and head toward the elevators. When she was out of sight, Myron said, 'I think that went well, don't you?'

'So,' Myron said to Esperanza, 'how does a wealthy girl from Manhattan know a boy who has been missing ten years?'

'Most obvious answer is that he hasn't been missing for ten years,' Esperanza said.

'Then where has he been?'

'Or more to the point, who is he? If he's really Patrick Moore—'

'Did you catch how she balked when I first said his name?'

'Like she didn't know him by it,' Esperanza said. 'In a way, it's the only thing that makes sense. If he's Patrick Moore who was kidnapped ten years ago, I don't know that Tamryn Rogers would know him. But if he's an imposter . . .'

'Then maybe,' Myron said. 'Of course, we would still need to figure out how a rich New York teen would know our imposter.'

'Oh, that one's easier,' Esperanza said.

'Do tell.'

'We women love a bad boy. You think, what, rich Tamryn only knows wealthy socialites?'

Myron thought about that. 'You think she's slumming?'

'I don't know. But it's certainly possible. First, we need to figure out if the boy you rescued is Patrick Moore or not. What's the story with the DNA test?'

'We got it over to Joe Corless at the lab,' Myron said. 'He said it might take a few days. Some problem with the collection. He's having trouble finding a hair with a decent root on it. The DNA off the toothbrush might be contaminated. I don't know all the details. In the meantime, we need to get all we can on Tamryn Rogers.'

'I'll do all the traditional sleuthing,' Esperanza

said. 'But as she repeatedly just told us, she's a sixteen-year-old girl.'

'Meaning?'

'How about we get that Spoon kid on it too? He can figure out the social media angles.'

'Good idea.'

'Mickey wants to meet with me anyway,' Esperanza said. 'I'll get him the info for Spoon.'

Myron made a face. 'Wait, why does Mickey want to meet with you?'

Esperanza shrugged. 'He didn't say; I didn't ask. Now, get back to your apartment and defile your honey.'

'I don't "defile."'

'Then you're not doing it right,' Esperanza said with a wink. She gave Myron a kiss on the cheek. 'Stay safe, okay?'

'You too.'

They split up. Myron hopped in a taxi. He texted Terese: On my way. You ready?

Myron's heart sank when he saw the answer: Uh, no.

When Myron got back to the apartment, Win was there.

'Sorry for the cock block,' he said.

CHAPTER 29

'So,' Win began, swirling his snifter of cognac, 'let's review, shall we?'

'Okay.'

'I'll go first,' Win said. 'Patrick Moore told Fat Gandhi that Rhys is dead.'

Win's living room at the Dakota resembled something you might see on a tour of Versailles. The two old friends sat in their usual spots – spots they hadn't sat in together for more than a year. Win took a sip of the cognac and took in the surroundings. Feeling nostalgic, Myron chugged Yoo-hoo from an ice-cold can.

'Do you believe him?' Myron asked.

'Who? Fat Gandhi or Patrick?'

Myron nodded. 'Either. Both. Neither.'

'Precisely.'

Terese had excused herself as soon as Myron returned. She had suggested, now that Win was back, that she and Myron pack and depart to give Win his privacy. Win had replied that he'd had a year of privacy, thank you very much, and that he'd be insulted if they left.

'Self-interest,' Win said. 'At the end of the day, it comes down to that always.'

'Meaning?'

'Meaning I see no motive for Fat Gandhi to lie here. I'm not saying he wouldn't lie, is not a compulsive liar, is not a horrible human being who may not only be selling underage sex but participating in said rape and abuse. But I don't see how this lie works in his self-interest.'

'Maybe he killed Rhys and is covering that.'

Win lifted his free hand and tilted it one way, then the other. 'It is certainly a possibility, but I see no motive. It is also a possibility that he stored Rhys somewhere and hopes to use him as a pawn at a later time. But I don't think so. Fat Gandhi was frightened.'

'You can do that to a person.'

Win tried not to smile. 'I can, can't I? Oh, and I had an old friend of ours with me.'

'Who?'

'Zorra.'

Myron's eyes widened. 'For real?'

'No,' Win said in a tone so dry it could have caught fire, 'I'm making it up.'

'You and Zorra.' Myron took another chug. 'Heck, I'm scared just thinking about it.'

'I offered Fat Gandhi an opportunity to rid himself of his issues with us by handing over Rhys. I believe that he would have snapped up that chance, if he could.'

They sat in silence for a few moments.

'We always knew this was a possibility,' Myron said.

'That Rhys was dead?'

'Yes.'

Win nodded. 'Of course.'

'But we still have a long way to go. We don't even know for sure that Patrick is Patrick.'

'We look at the beginning,' Win said. 'And we look at the end.'

'Yeah, you've said that. You should probably put that in a fortune cookie.'

'Zorra,' Win said.

'What about him?'

'I sent him to Finland.'

Myron thought about that. 'To find the nanny.'

'Au pair,' Win corrected.

'I'm going to skip the eye roll.'

'Her name, if you recall, is Vada Linna.'

'I recall.'

'She doesn't exist anymore.'

'Pardon?'

'She would be twenty-eight. There is no Vada Linna in Finland – or anywhere else, for that matter – anywhere near that age range.'

Myron thought about that. 'She changed her name.'

'God, you're good.'

'With all the press attention during the kidnapping, that's not much of a surprise.'

'Perhaps,' Win said. 'Except her father doesn't exist anymore either.'

'He could have passed away.'

'No record of it. They both, it seems, vanished.'

Myron considered that. 'So what's your theory?'

'I don't have a good one yet. It's why I put Zorra on it.'

'Sure that's wise?'

'Why wouldn't it be?'

'Might be a case of using a blowtorch when all you need is a match.'

Win smiled. 'I always use the blowtorch.'

Hard to argue.

Win sat back and crossed his legs. 'Now let's go through the rest of this point by point, shall we?'

Myron filled him in on everything – the visits to the Moore house, Mickey and Ema's opinion, Ema stealing the toothbrush and the hairs for DNA (Win smiled broadly at that one), the texts, Chick's reaction, Tamryn Rogers, all of it. They discussed, analyzed, drove down various dark roads that all led to dead ends.

They ended as they began: 'Do we tell Brooke what Fat Gandhi said?'

Win pondered that. 'It's your call.'

That surprised Myron. 'Mine.'

'Yes.'

'I don't get it. Why?'

'Simple.' Win put down the snifter and steepled his hands. 'You're better at this than I am.'

'No, I'm not.'

'Don't feign modesty. You are more objective. Your judgment is sounder. You and I have been

333

doing this a long time – helping those in trouble, finding missing people, rescuing those in need – have we not?'

'We have.'

'And in every situation, you have been the leader. I'm the support staff. I'm your muscle, if you will. We are partners, a team, but to keep within this quick metaphor, you are the captain of the team. I've made mistakes.'

'So have I.'

Win shook his head. 'I didn't have to kill all three of those men that first day. I could have kept one alive. I could have offered them money to back off. The fact is, I'm objective enough to know I cannot be objective. Did you see Brooke's face?'

Myron nodded.

'You know,' Win said, 'that I care about very few people.'

Myron did not reply.

'You know that when I care, I care with a ferocity that doesn't always make me rational. We have had success in the past with you taking the lead.'

'We've also messed up,' Myron said. 'We've lost a lot of people.'

'We have,' Win agreed, 'but we win more than we lose.'

Win waited for Myron to continue.

'Brooke would want to know,' Myron said. 'We should tell her.'

'Okay, then.'

'But first,' Myron said, 'let's confront Patrick with what we know.'

You don't get anywhere on the phone, so Myron and Win took the drive out to the Moore home in New Jersey. There was no answer at the door. Myron took a peek in the window of the garage. No car. Win spotted the FOR SALE sign in the yard.

'You saw this?' Win asked.

Myron nodded. 'They're all moving to Pennsylvania to be closer to Hunter.'

'Do you have Hunter's address?'

'I do.'

Myron took out his mobile phone and brought up a map. 'According to this, we can make it in an hour and fifteen minutes.'

'Perhaps,' Win said, 'I should drive.'

Less than an hour later, they reached a dirt road deep in the woods. There was a chain blocking access. A rusted sign read:

LAKE CHARMAINE − PRIVATE

Myron got out of the car. There was a padlock on one end of the chain. Using his heel, Myron kicked down on it. The lock broke. The chain fell to the ground with a heavy clunk.

'We're trespassing,' Myron said.

'Let's live on the edge, old friend. That's where all the goodies reside.'

As they drove up the dirt road, Lake Charmaine in all its splendor rose before them. The sun glistened off the water. Myron checked the GPS. It instructed them to circle to the other side of the lake. They veered to the left and drove past the kind of log cabin you thought existed only in old movies. A car with an MD license plate was parked in front of it. On the dock, a man about Myron's age cast out his fishing line slowly, gracefully, like poetry in motion. He then handed the rod to a small boy and put his arm around a woman's waist. They stood there, this idyllic family of three, and Myron thought about Terese. The man on the dock turned at the sound of the car. The woman kept her eyes on the little boy with the fishing rod. The man's eyes narrowed as Myron and Win cruised past. Myron waved to show him that they meant him no harm. The man hesitated and then waved back.

They drove past ruins of what might have once been camp cabins or cabins used on a retreat or something. A construction crew was now building a house on the site.

'Nancy Moore's new residence?' Win asked.

'Maybe.'

A pickup truck was parked at the top of Hunter Moore's long driveway, blocking access.

'Seems he doesn't welcome visitors,' Win said.

They parked on the road. Myron and Win got out of the car. Everything echoed in the stillness – the car doors closing, their feet hitting the dirt road. Myron had read once that a sound never fully dies, that if you scream in woods like these, the echo will just keep reverberating, traveling, growing fainter and fainter but never disappearing in total. Myron didn't know whether that was true or not, but if it was, he could imagine a scream here staying vibrant for too long.

'What are you thinking about?' Win asked him.

'How screams echo.'

'You're fun.'

'Remind me never to buy a lake house.'

They walked past the pickup truck and up the drive. Up ahead, in a front yard overlooking all of Lake Charmaine, Hunter Moore sat on an Adirondack chair. He didn't get up when he spotted them. He didn't wave or nod or show any signs he saw them coming. He just kept his gaze on the horizon, on his perfect view of Lake Charmaine. A whiskey bottle sat on his right.

There was a rifle on his lap.

'Hey, Hunter,' Myron said.

Win moved to the side a bit, putting distance between him and Myron. Myron got it. Don't give anyone two targets so close together.

Hunter smiled up at him. It was the smile of the heavily inebriated. 'Hey, Myron.' The sun was in his eyes, so Hunter used his hand to block it. 'Is that you, Win?'

'Yes,' Win said.

'You're back?'

'No.'

'Huh?'

'I'm kidding,' Win said.

'Oh.' Hunter's cackle-laugh ripped through the

stillness. The sound almost made Myron jump. 'Good one, Win.'

Win looked at Myron. The look said that they had nothing to fear. There was no way Hunter would be able to reach for his rifle and aim it before Win, who was always armed, took him out. They moved closer.

'Look at that,' Hunter said with awe, gesturing at the vista behind them.

Myron looked. Win didn't.

'Unbelievable, right?' Hunter said. 'This spot' – he shook his head in wonderment – 'it's like God painted this giant canvas himself.'

'If you think about it,' Win said, 'he did.'

'Whoa,' Hunter said, like a stoner. Myron wondered whether he had consumed substances other than alcohol. 'That's so true.'

'Where's Patrick?' Myron asked.

'I don't know.'

Myron pointed to the house behind him. 'Is he inside?'

'Nope.'

'How about Nancy?'

Hunter shook his head. 'Also nope.'

'Can we all go inside?'

Hunter kept shaking his head. 'No reason to; no one in there. A beautiful day like this is to be cherished. We got a couple of chairs, if you want to sit and enjoy the view with me.'

Myron took him up on the offer. This chair too was turned to the lake, so that Myron and Hunter sat side by side, both facing the view rather than each other. Win stayed standing.

'We really need to find Patrick,' Myron said.

'Did you call Nancy?'

'She's not answering. Where are they?'

Hunter still had the rifle on his lap. His hand had been slowly sliding toward the trigger, almost indiscernibly. 'He needs time, Myron. Can you imagine what his last ten years have been like?'

'Can you imagine,' Win said, 'what Rhys's current year is still like?'

Hunter winced when he heard that and closed his eyes. Myron was tempted to grab the rifle, but Win shook him off. He was right. The rifle was not a threat. Not with Win nearby. If they snatched it away, Hunter would clam up, get defensive. Let him keep his security blanket.

'You met Lionel,' Hunter said. 'Dr Stanton, I mean. He says that if you want Patrick to open up, he needs time. We want a quiet, simple life for him.'

'Is that why Nancy is moving him out here?'

A slow smile came to his lips. 'This place has always been my solace. I'm third generation here. My grandfather taught my father how to fly-fish on that lake. My father taught me. When Patrick was little, I taught him. We'd catch sunnies and trout and . . .'

His voice faded away.

Win looked at Myron with flat eyes and played the air violin.

'I realize how hard this must have been on you,' Myron tried.

'I'm not looking for pity.'

'Of course not.'

'It's like . . .' Hunter never took his eyes off the lake, never so much as glanced at Myron or Win. 'It's like I've lived two lives. I was one person – a normal, ordinary person, really – up until that day. And then, poof, I was someone else entirely after. Like we all walked through some science fiction portal and entered a different world.'

'Everything changed,' Myron said, trying to keep him going.

'Yes.'

'You got divorced.'

'Right.' His hand found the bottle, his eyes still glued to the vista. 'I don't know. That might have happened anyway. But yeah, Nancy and I broke up. The constant reminder of what happened, the horror, and this person, your life partner, she's just there every day, in your face, poking your memory, you know what I mean?'

'I do.'

'The pressure becomes so great. I mean, maybe if there are no cracks to start with, you can get past it. But I couldn't handle it. So I ran away. I lived overseas for a while. But I couldn't move on. The horror, the images . . . I started drinking. A lot. Then I would do AA, get better for a little while, start drinking again, sober up. I kept cycling like that. Lather, rinse, repeat.'

Hunter held up the bottle. 'Guess where I am in the cycle now?'

Silence. Myron crushed it.

'Did you know about the texts between your wife and Chick Baldwin?'

The muscles in his face stiffened. 'When?'

Interesting response, Myron thought. He looked at Win. Win found it interesting too. 'Does that matter?'

'No,' Hunter said. 'I don't know, don't care. And she isn't my wife.'

Myron turned toward him. 'I'm talking about back then. Before your son disappeared. Nancy and Chick were close to having an affair. Maybe they went through with it; I don't know.'

Hunter's grip on the gun tightened. He still stared out, but if the view was offering even an iota of comfort, you wouldn't know it from his face. 'Who cares?'

'Did you know?'

'No.'

He said it too quickly. Myron looked toward Win. Win said, 'I found Fat Gandhi.'

That got Hunter's attention. 'Is he in jail?'

'No.'

'I don't understand.'

'He told me that Rhys is dead.'

'Oh my God,' Hunter said, but the surprise in his voice sounded forced. 'He killed him?'

'No. He never met Rhys. He said that Patrick told him that Rhys is dead.'

'He said what?'

Win bit back a sigh. 'Please don't make me repeat myself.'

Hunter shook his head. 'So let me get this straight. This psycho criminal who stabbed and almost killed my son' – Hunter looked at Win, then at Myron, then back at Win – 'you believe him?'

'We do,' Win said.

'Hunter,' Myron tried, 'don't you think Patrick owes the Baldwins the truth?'

'Of course. Of course they're owed the truth.' Hunter looked stunned now. 'I'll try to talk to Patrick about this as soon as I can. See what he says.'

'Hunter?'

It was Win.

'Yeah?'

'I'd like to use your washroom before we leave.'

Hunter smiled up at him. 'You think they're inside?'

'I wouldn't know,' Win said. 'Either way, I need to urinate.'

Only Win could use the word 'urinate' in a completely natural way in a nonmedical setting.

'Use a tree.'

'I don't use trees, Hunter.'

'Fine.'

As he started to his feet, Win easily grabbed the rifle from him, which was the closest thing to the old saw about stealing candy from a baby Myron had ever witnessed.

'I got a license,' Hunter said. 'I can shoot deer on my property. It's perfectly legal.'

Win looked at Myron. 'Would it be beneath me to note that Hunter is a hunter?'

'Way beneath,' Myron said.

'Har-har.' Hunter stumbled toward the house. 'Come on,' he said. 'Let's get you, uh, urinating and out of here.'

CHAPTER 30

Back in the car, Myron asked, 'How was your urination?'

'Hilarious. They aren't there. He's alone. For now.'

Myron knew that had been Win's play with the 'urination' request. 'So why was he holding the rifle?'

'Perhaps he was hunting. It's his property. He has the right. Perhaps that's his thing.'

'Hunting?'

'Yes. He sits out there on a lovely day, enjoys his view, imbibes his whiskey – then a deer strolls by and he blasts it.'

'Sounds like an awesome time.'

'Don't judge,' Win said.

'You don't hunt.'

'I also don't judge. You eat meat. You wear leather. Even vegans kill animals, albeit very few of them, when they plow out fields. None of us have completely clean hands.'

Myron couldn't help but smile. 'I've missed you, Win.'

'Yes. Yes, you have.'

'Have you been back in the States at all?'

'Who says I ever left?' Win pointed to the sound system. 'I even saw this.'

Myron had his smartphone hooked up to the car's sound system. They were listening to the soundtrack from *Hamilton*. Lin-Manuel Miranda was singing with raw, naked pain in his voice, '*You knock me out, I fall apart.*'

'Wait,' Myron said, 'you saw *Hamilton*?'

Win did not reply.

'But you hate musicals. I was always trying to get you to go.'

Win put his finger to his lips and pointed again. 'Shh, here it comes.'

'What?'

'The last line. Listen . . . now.'

The song dealt with Hamilton's grief after losing his son in a duel. Win put his hand to his ear as the company sang, '*They are going through the unimaginable.*'

'That's Brooke,' Win said. 'That's Chick. Going through the unimaginable.'

Myron nodded. This song broke his heart every time. 'We need to tell Brooke what Fat Gandhi said.'

'Yes.'

'We need to tell her now.'

'In person,' Win said.

Myron was back in the driver's seat. He didn't drive like Win, but he could hit the accelerator when needed. They crossed the Delaware River over the Dingmans Ferry Bridge, putting them back in New Jersey.

'Something else is bothering me,' Myron said.

'I'm listening.'

'Fat Gandhi said he didn't know Patrick, that Patrick didn't work for him.'

'That's correct.'

'Patrick showed up on his turf, got into trouble with some of Fat Gandhi's thugs, and ran away when you intervened.'

'Correct again.'

Myron shook his head. 'Then this whole thing has to be a setup.'

'How so?'

'Someone emails you anonymously. He tells you where Patrick is and when he'll be there. You go. Patrick is there, probably for the first time. Because if he had been there before, Fat Gandhi's thugs would have roughed him up back then, right?'

Win considered that. 'Makes sense.'

'So someone wanted you to find him. Someone sent Patrick – if it is Patrick – to that spot so you would' – Myron used his fingers to make quote marks – ' "rescue" him.'

'Makes sense,' Win said again.

'Any thoughts on who?'

'No thoughts. But there is something else we need to consider.'

'What's that?'

'According to what you told me, Mickey and

Ema seem to feel that the boy might not be Patrick.'

Myron nodded. 'That's right.'

'When will we have the DNA results?'

'Joe Corless said he was working on it, priority one. Should be soon.'

'Suppose this boy isn't Patrick,' Win said. 'What's the play then?'

'I don't know,' Myron said. 'Suppose this boy is Patrick. What's the play then?'

On the soundtrack, Leslie Odom Jr.'s Aaron Burr is furious that Alexander Hamilton has endorsed Thomas Jefferson.

'A setup makes no sense,' Win said, 'and yet it has to be a setup of some kind, doesn't it?'

'It does,' Myron said. 'Or it doesn't.'

'Deep.'

'In short,' Myron said, 'we still don't know what the hell is going on.'

Win smiled. 'You'd think we'd be used to that by now.'

They were ten minutes away from Brooke's when Win said, 'Take a right.'

'Where?'

'Union Avenue.'

'Where are we going?'

'Bear with me. Park here.'

The name of the shop selling 'Organic Coffee & Crêpes' was CU Latte. Myron frowned at the pun. Win loved it.

'What are we doing here?'

'A little surprise for you,' Win said. 'Come on.'

The barista wore a hipster beanie and fungus-like facial hair. His poncho had to be made from hemp.

CU Latte was all in.

They ordered two Turkish coffees and sat down.

'What's going on?'

Win checked his phone and pointed to the door. 'Now.'

Myron looked at the door as Zorra entered in all his sartorial splendor. He wore his Veronica Lake–on–meth wig, a green monogrammed sweater, and a skirt in a hue Zorra would undoubtedly call 'sea foam.'

When Zorra spotted Myron, he spread his arms and shouted, 'Dreamboat!'

Zorra's wig was half on, half off. His facial hair would make the barista even greener, though this time with envy. Myron remembered an old clip his father had shown him of Milton Berle in drag. Like that, only less attractive.

'I thought he was in Finland,' Myron muttered to Win as Zorra approached.

'He just landed at Newark,' Win said.

'Long flight,' Zorra said. 'Zorra had no time to freshen up. I must look a fright.'

Myron wasn't about to touch that one. He rose and gave Zorra a hug. He smelled like a male flight attendant's cologne.

'How long has it been?' Zorra asked.

'Too long,' Myron said. Or maybe not long enough.

'Zorra is happy to see you.'

'Same,' Myron said. Then, getting back on track, he asked, 'So what's the deal with Vada Linna?'

'Her new name is Sofia Lampo.'

'Did you find her?'

'She works at a fast-food restaurant, dreamboat. In a small town outside Helsinki. How you say – the middle of nowhere. So I went there. But her boss said she hasn't shown up for work for three days. This concerned Zorra. So I do some research. She's not home either. I make some calls. You know. Old contacts. They can find anything.'

'So did you find her?' Myron asked.

Zorra smiled. It was not a pretty smile. 'Very soon, dreamboat.'

'I'm not following.'

'Yesterday Sofia Lampo took a plane from Helsinki to Newark. She's here, dreamboat. Vada Linna – or Sofia Lampo – is back.'

'Let's start with the obvious question,' Myron said when he and Win were back in the car. 'Why would the au pair come back to the United States?'

'What have we told ourselves since this all began?'

'That something isn't right,' Myron said. 'That we're missing something.'

'Whatever that "something" is,' Win said, 'it's

349

been missing for ten years. It's been missing since the boys vanished.'

'So what now?' Myron asked.

'Your call.'

Myron made the final turn onto the Baldwins' street. 'We need to tell Brooke what Fat Gandhi told you. We don't have the right to keep it from her. She also needs to know about the au pair coming back.'

'That's a lot,' Win said.

'Too much?'

'No,' Win said. 'Brooke can handle more than you can imagine.'

As they pulled into the driveway, the front door opened. Brooke stepped out. She came to the passenger side of the car and gave her cousin Win a long hug. Win wasn't normally much for long hugs, but he held on. Brooke put her head on Win's shoulder. Neither cried. Neither collapsed or anything like that. They didn't move or readjust their arms or pull each other closer. They just stayed there for several beats.

'I'm glad you're back,' Brooke said.

'Me too.'

When they let each other go, Brooke turned and studied Myron's face. 'This isn't good news, is it?'

'Nothing definitive,' Win said.

'But not good.'

'No,' Win said, 'not good.'

They were about to head inside when another car started down the driveway. Myron recognized the Lexus sedan from Nancy Moore's garage. They all stood and waited as the car came to a stop. The driver's door opened. Nancy Moore stepped out. The front passenger door opened.

Patrick Moore stepped out.

Brooke stiffened when she saw their faces. Under her breath, she said, 'This isn't good news either.'

CHAPTER 31

They were back in the kitchen, the place where it all began.

Patrick, Nancy, and Brooke all sat at the kitchen table. Myron and Win stood off to the side, close enough to hear but not be involved. Patrick sat with his back to the big glass doors, intentionally, Myron supposed. His mother sat next to him and held his hand. Brooke sat across from him and waited.

Patrick looked at his mother. She nodded for him to go ahead. Patrick stared down at the table in front of him. His hair was close cropped, almost shaved. He rubbed his head for a moment before letting his hands drop.

'Rhys is dead, Mrs Baldwin.'

Myron glanced at Brooke. She had steeled herself for this. There was barely a tell. Myron turned to Win. His expression was blank, the same as his cousin's.

'He died a long time ago,' Patrick said.

Brooke's voice did not crack. 'How?'

Patrick kept his head lowered. His hands were folded on the table in front of him. His mother kept her hand on his forearm.

'We were taken from this kitchen,' Patrick began. 'I don't remember a lot of things. But I remember that.'

His voice was stilted now, a chilling monotone. 'The men, they stuck us in the back of a van.'

'How many men?' Brooke asked.

'Brooke, please.' It was Nancy Moore. 'It's the first time he's been able to speak. Just let him get through this, okay?'

Brooke said nothing. She turned her focus back to Patrick. Patrick had his head down. 'I apologize,' she said with too much formality. 'Please go ahead.'

'They stuck us in the back of a van,' he repeated, almost, Myron thought, as though someone had backed up the teleprompter. 'We drove for a long time. I don't know how long. When we stopped, we were on a big farm someplace. There were animals. Cows, pigs, chickens. Rhys and I, we shared a bedroom in the farmhouse.'

Patrick stopped, keeping his head down. The silence was suffocating. Brooke wanted to ask something, maybe a million things, but the moment felt bubble fragile. No one moved. No one spoke. No one dared disrupt the moment.

Nancy gave her son's arm a squeeze. Patrick gathered himself and continued.

'It was a long time ago,' he continued. 'Sometimes it feels like a dream. It was nice there. On the farm. They . . . they were nice to us. We got to play a lot. We could run around. We got to feed the animals. I don't know for how long. It might have been like that for a few weeks. It might have been like that for a few months. Sometimes I even think it might have been like that for years. I just don't know. It's not like me and Rhys kept track or anything.'

Again Patrick stopped. Myron looked past Patrick, out that back window into the spacious yard, all the way to the trees in the back. He tried to see it as Patrick spoke, the men breaking in here, grabbing the two boys, vanishing into that yard.

'Then one day,' Patrick said, 'it changed.'

His tone was more hesitant, the words coming out in a strange, uneven flow.

'They brought men around,' Patrick said. 'I . . . I was abused.'

Brooke still hadn't moved, still hadn't changed her expression, but it was as though Patrick's words sped up the aging process. Nothing about Brooke changed, and yet Myron could see that she was hanging on by the most brittle of threads.

'Rhys . . . he was stronger than I was. Braver. He tried to save me. He tried . . . he wouldn't let them do that to him. He stood up to them, Mrs Baldwin. He fought them. He poked one guy in the eye with a pencil. Really got him good. So . . .' Patrick still couldn't lift his eyes from the table, but he managed something like a shrug. 'They killed him. They shot him in the head. They made me . . .'

Patrick's shoulder started hitching. Myron saw a tear hit the table.

'They made me go with them to this ravine.' The monotone was gone now. Patrick's voice was raw, struggling. 'They made me watch . . .'

His mother put her hand on his shoulder. 'It's okay,' she whispered. 'I'm right here.'

'I saw it . . . I was there . . . They just . . . just dumped his body into this ravine. Like it was nothing. Like Rhys was nothing . . .'

Brooke let out a low moan, a sound unlike anything Myron had ever heard.

'I'm so sorry, Mrs Baldwin.'

And then the tears came from both of them.

When Nancy hurried her son toward the door, Win stepped in her way.

'We need to know more,' Win said.

Patrick was sobbing uncontrollably.

'Not today,' Nancy said, pushing past Win. 'Dr Stanton warned me this might be too much for him. You know the truth now. I'm so, so sorry.'

She hurried outside. Win gestured to Myron, then moved toward Brooke. Myron quickly followed Nancy and Patrick. When the three of them were outside, Myron shouted, 'How long have you known, Nancy?'

She spun toward him. 'What?'

'How long have you known Rhys was dead?'

'What are you . . . Patrick just told us this morning.'

Myron rubbed his chin. 'Odd timing.' Patrick was still crying. The tears seemed real, and yet once again, something wasn't adding up.

'What is that supposed to mean?' Nancy asked.

'Patrick,' Myron said, turning his attention to the distraught teen, 'why were you in New York City yesterday with Tamryn Rogers?'

Nancy took that one. 'What business is that of yours?'

'You knew?'

'He needed to get out,' Nancy said.

'Really? So you knew?'

'Of course.'

'How come he took a bus? How come you didn't drive him?'

'That's not your business.'

'He met up with Tamryn Rogers. I saw them together.'

'You were following my son?'

'Yep.'

Nancy put her hands on her hips, trying to look angry, but somehow it came across as more for show. 'What gave you the right?' she snapped. 'He went out by himself, he started talking to a girl his own age. Don't make it more than what it is.'

'Hmm,' Myron said. He started walking toward them. 'Your story matches hers.'

'So?'

'Even the outrage over me following them. Tamryn Rogers expressed it nearly the same way.'

'You were following my son. I have a right to be angry.'

'Is he your son?'

Patrick stopped crying, almost all at once.

'What are you talking about?'

Myron tried staring into the boy's eyes, but again he kept his head down. 'You both seem to be one step ahead of us, don't you think, Patrick?'

He didn't reply, didn't look.

'I confront Tamryn Rogers. Suddenly your story matches hers. Win and I tell your dad you told Fat Gandhi that Rhys was dead. Suddenly you've recovered enough to tell Mrs Moore about it.'

Nancy used her remote to unlock the car door. 'Are you out of your mind?'

Myron bent at the waist, trying to force Patrick to look at him. 'Are you really Patrick Moore?'

Without a warning, the boy reeled back his fist and threw it at Myron's head. Myron was off-balance from leaning forward, but this was, after all, an inexperienced teenage fighter throwing a wild punch. All Myron had to do was duck down a bit, not much, not enough to stumble, and let the blow sail harmlessly over his head.

The survival instinct, paired with his training, took over, giving him various options for how to counter the attack. The most obvious was to wait another millisecond. With the punch at full extension, the teenager would be completely exposed. Myron's knees were bent. He could pop a shot to the throat, the nose, the groin.

But he wouldn't do that.

Instead, he stayed in a standing tuck and waited to see how the boy would respond. Using the momentum from his missed punch, Patrick broke into a full run. Myron stood, about to give chase, when Nancy started pounding on his back with her fists.

'Leave my son alone! What the hell is wrong with you? Are you crazy?'

Myron weathered the blows for a moment. He stood upright as Patrick disappeared up the driveway and down the street. Nancy ran to her car and opened the door.

'Please,' she pleaded, sliding in the car and putting it in reverse. 'Please leave my boy alone.'

Myron was about to head back into the house when his cell phone rang. It was his nephew, Mickey.

'We got something on Tamryn Rogers,' Mickey said. 'You're going to want to see this.'

'Where are you?'

'Ema's house.'

'I'm on my way.'

Win stayed with Brooke. He had been filling her in on all the recent developments, the most puzzling for her being the return of her former au pair, Vada Linna, now known as Sofia Lampo.

'Why would Vada be back?' Brooke had asked. 'I don't get it.'

Neither did they.

Two stone lions guarded the driveway to the mansion where Ema resided with her mother and grandparents. The gate was closed. Myron leaned out. The security guard recognized him and hit the button. The gate creaked open.

When Myron was a kid, the estate had been owned by a famed Mafia don, or boss or capo or whatever you called the head mobster. Rumor had it that there was a furnace on the property where the don cremated the bodies of his victims. When the house was later sold, a furnace was indeed found back behind the pool area. To this day, no one knew whether it had been used for his weekend barbecues or whether those rumors were true.

The mansion was enormous and baronial and dark. It looked like someone had combined a medieval fortress with a Disney castle. The estate was sprawling and probably – and this had been the appeal for the current occupants – the most private in the area. There was a helicopter pad so they could come and go without being seen. The home was in a corporation's name, so as to protect the identity of the real owner. Up until a few months ago, even Ema's closest friends had no idea she lived here or why she kept it secret.

There was a lion-head knocker on the door, but before Myron could reach for it, Angelica Wyatt opened the door. She gave him a warm smile and said, 'Hey, Myron.'

'Hey, Angelica.'

Even though he had known her for years, even

acting as her bodyguard at one point, it took a few seconds to see Angelica Wyatt as a person and not a poster or distant celluloid image up on a big screen. What, Myron often thought, must that be like – to be that kind of beautiful and famous that people, maybe even those close to you, always see you through the haze of movie stardom?

The famous face leaned in and gave him a kiss on the cheek.

'I hear you're getting married,' Ema's mom said to him.

'Yep.'

Fifteen years ago, when Angelica Wyatt had given birth to her daughter, the tabloids had been horrible, following them nonstop, snapping photos with high-powered lenses whenever they'd leave her Los Angeles home, demanding answers about the baby's paternity. Headlines screamed stuff like ANGELICA WYATT SECRET BABY SHOCKER or WE KNOW THE DAD and then speculated on some recent costar or Arabian sultan or even, in one case, a former British prime minister.

The attention grew to be too much for the little girl. She started having nightmares. Angelica Wyatt even quit the business for two years, disappearing with the child to France, but that just led to more rumors and other issues, the most salient being that Angelica Wyatt missed making motion pictures. It was her calling.

So what to do?

Angelica Wyatt secretly moved back to the United

States and found this private home in New Jersey. She enrolled her daughter in the public school under the pseudonym Emma Beaumont, though eventually the nickname Ema stuck. Ema's grandparents took care of her when Angelica was on set.

No one knew the identity of her daughter's father except, of course, Angelica.

Not even Ema.

'I'm really happy for you,' Angelica Wyatt said to him.

'Thanks. How are you?'

'Good. I'm off tomorrow to a shoot in Atlanta. I had hoped Ema might come with me, but, uh, she seems distracted right now.'

'You mean with Mickey?'

'I do, yes.'

'They're good kids.'

'This is her first boyfriend,' Angelica said.

'He'll be good to her.'

'I know, but my little girl . . . Is it too cliché to note that she's grown up too fast?'

'Things become clichés because they are apropos.'

'Breaks my heart.' Angelica smiled through it. 'They're all in the basement. You know the way?'

He nodded. 'Thanks.'

Movie posters featuring Angelica Wyatt lined the stairwell down to the basement. Ema had put them up against her mother's wishes. The basement, Ema had explained, was the one place she didn't want to hide anything about her true self. It made sense, Myron guessed.

361

The three teens – Mickey, Ema, and Spoon – were sprawled out on three oversized and upscale beanbag chairs. All three were typing on laptops at a furious pace.

'Hey,' Myron said to them.

All three said 'Hey' without looking up.

Ema was the first to close her laptop and rise. She wore short sleeves today, and Myron could see the extensive tattoo work. The tattoos had troubled Myron at first. As common as tattoos were nowadays, Ema was only a sophomore in high school. Mickey had explained to him that the tattoos were temporary, that a tattoo artist named Agent used her to experiment with different designs and that they all would fade away after a few weeks.

Mickey said, 'Hey, Spoon?'

'Give me a second to organize our findings,' Spoon said. 'Talk amongst yourselves.'

Ema and Mickey came over to Myron. He had debated getting them involved in something like this – they had already experienced too much of this kind of stuff for ones so young – but as Mickey had pointed out, this was what they did.

Myron remembered something. 'Esperanza said you wanted to see her.'

'That was more me,' Ema said.

'It was both of us,' Mickey said. 'We talked to Big Cyndi too.'

'What about?'

Mickey and Ema exchanged a glance. Ema said, 'Little Pocahontas and Big Chief Mama.'

'What about them?'

'They might have been funny in the day,' Ema said. 'They aren't funny now.'

'It's just kitsch,' Myron said. 'They don't mean any harm. It's all just a nostalgic throwback.'

'Esperanza made the same argument,' Ema said.

'Times change, Myron,' Mickey added.

'We just suggested she get in touch with a friend of mine who is Navajo.'

'How did that go?' Myron asked.

'Don't know. They haven't talked yet.'

Spoon said, 'I got it.' He started waving at Myron. 'Come here, take a look.'

Spoon stayed on the enormous beanbag chair. Myron bent down, his bad knee creaking a bit, and collapsed next to him. Spoon pushed up his glasses and pointed to the screen.

'Tamryn Rogers,' he began, 'has almost no social media presence. She does possess a Facebook and a Snapchat account, but she rarely uses either. Everything she does do is set on private. We assume that this is because her father is a wealthy hedge fund manager. The family keeps a low profile. With me so far?'

Myron adjusted his body in the beanbag chair. It was hard to get comfortable. 'With you.'

'We know about her summer internship at the television station. We know that she is sixteen years old. We know she goes to an elite boarding school called St Jacques in Switzerland.' Spoon looked at

Myron. 'Did you know that in Switzerland it's illegal to keep just one guinea pig?'

Ema said, 'Spoon.'

'I did not,' Myron said.

'You have to have them in pairs,' Spoon explained. 'See, guinea pigs are sociable animals, so it's cruel to have only one. Or that's what the Swiss think.'

Ema again said, 'Spoon.'

'Right, sorry. Anyway, the only photo of Tamryn Rogers I could find is her profile pic on Facebook. So I took that image and I put it through an image search. Nothing came back. That's not surprising, of course. Image searches find identical photographs only. Why would someone else have her profile photograph? Still with me?'

'Still with you,' Myron said.

'So I decided to take it to the next level. I located a beta program that uses facial verification software across several social media sites. You may have seen the technology on Facebook.'

'I don't use Facebook.'

'You what?'

Myron shrugged.

'But all old people use Facebook,' Spoon protested.

Ema said, 'Spoon.'

'Right, okay, so let me explain. Let's say you post a group photograph of your friends on Facebook. Facebook has a new AI software called DeepFace that automatically performs a facial verification search on the photo.'

'Which means?' Myron said.

'Which means it will recognize your friends. So you post the picture and suddenly, Facebook will circle a face and say, "Do you want to tag John Smith?"'

'For real?'

'Yes.'

'They do that now?'

'They do, yes.'

Myron shook his head, happy for his naïveté.

'Notice,' Spoon continued, 'that I said "facial verification," a technology that recognizes that two images show the same face, versus the more common facial recognition, an attempt to put a name to a face. Big difference. So I put the profile photograph of Tamryn Rogers through the beta program – "beta" meaning that it's still being tested – to see what it came up with. Oh!'

Spoon slapped his own forehead.

'I almost forgot. I first tried it on Patrick Moore. I was able to get a still frame from his appearance on that television interview. I thought, wow, maybe someone has taken a photograph of him. Maybe I can find something about him and thus Rhys somehow.'

'And?'

'Nothing. Not a single hit. Except . . . well, let me show you.'

He clicked the mouse pad on his laptop. A group photograph came up, maybe twenty, twenty-five teenagers. The caption underneath read SOPHO-MORE CLASS, with names below it.

'This photograph popped up on an alumni site for students who attended St Jacques. If you look over here' – he let the cursor do the pointing for him – 'well, do you recognize that young lady?'

Myron did. 'It's Tamryn Rogers.'

'Precisely, Myron. Excellent work.'

Myron glanced at Ema to see if Spoon was goofing on him. Ema shrugged a 'what can you do?'

'And if you look down here at the caption' – again Spoon used the cursor – 'you'll see a list of first names only. I assume that has something to do with a privacy program at the school, but I can't say for sure. Tamryn is the fourth person in on the second row . . . See?'

Myron saw it. It read simply: Tamryn.

'So?'

'That's what we thought,' Spoon said, 'at first. In fact, well, I confess I'm not that great with details. I'm more of a big-picture guy, you know what I mean?'

'Assume I do.'

'Ha, good one! It was Ema here who . . . Ema, you want to show him?'

Ema used her finger and pointed at the boy standing right behind Tamryn Rogers. Myron frowned and bent down for a closer look.

'No need to strain your eyes, Myron,' Spoon said. 'Not at your age. I can zoom in.'

Spoon started clicking the image until it got bigger and bigger. It was a good shot, taken recently and with a decent enough camera, but onscreen the pixels were starting to blur as he clicked. Spoon stopped. Myron stared again.

'So you think . . . ?' Myron began.

'We don't know,' Spoon said.

'I know,' Ema said.

Myron looked for the boy's name and read it out loud: 'Paul.'

The boy in the photograph had long, wavy blond hair – the prep boy trying to assert his independence. Patrick Moore's hair was stubble short and dark. 'Paul' in the photograph seemed to have blue eyes. Patrick Moore's eyes were brown. Their noses were different too. Paul's appeared to be smaller maybe, differently shaped.

And yet . . .

Myron wouldn't have spotted it, not on his own, but now when he looked closely . . .

'I know what you're thinking,' Ema said. 'And I'd probably agree with you. Teenagers look alike. We all get that. I probably wouldn't have thought twice about it except that this school is small. This sophomore class has twenty-three students. Patrick Moore goes out and meets with Tamryn Rogers. Why? He was lonely. We saw that when we visited him.'

Mickey nodded in agreement. 'It's too much of a coincidence, Myron. I mean, cut the hair. Do something with contact lenses to change eye color. Maybe some kind of surgery on the face, I don't know. But Ema shows this to me and I'm looking at him and at first I don't see it and then . . .'

Mickey pointed at the face on the screen. 'I think Tamryn's classmate Paul is now calling himself Patrick Moore.'

Myron sprinted back to the car. He got on the phone and called Esperanza.

'We need all we can on this Paul kid attending St Jacques near Geneva in Switzerland. Last name is most important. Parents, whatever.'

'This won't be quick,' Esperanza said. 'The school is closed, it's overseas, we have no contacts in Switzerland, plus, I imagine, this kind of place is pretty damned secretive.'

Esperanza was, of course, right.

'Just do the best you can. Spoon is going to email you the picture.'

'I already got his email before you called,' Esperanza said. 'Did you know that the most common password for email accounts is 123456?'

'Yep, that would be Spoon.'

'I'm looking at the two pics – one of this Paul kid, one of Patrick at that TV interview. If I look closely, yeah, I can see the resemblance, but would you ever guess Paul and Patrick are the same kid?'

'No,' Myron said. 'But that's probably the point.'

'Oh, I found that fifth grade teacher. The one who taught Clark and Francesca.'

'Mr Dixon?'

'Rob Dixon, yeah.'

'Where is he?'

'He still teaches fifth grade at Collins Elementary.

I made an appointment for you to see him today at seven thirty.'

'How did you pull that off?'

'I told him you'd heard he was a great teacher and that you were writing a book about your experiences.'

'What experiences?'

'I didn't say. Luckily, Mr Dixon saw your documentary on ESPN. D-lister fame, baby. It opens doors.'

After they hung up, Myron called Win and told him what he had learned.

'So the boy is an imposter,' Win said.

'I don't know. There's still a chance it's just two teenage boys who look alike.'

'And happen to know Tamryn Rogers?'

'Seems a stretch,' Myron said. 'Just for the record, both Tamryn and Patrick – let's just call him Patrick to make this easier – claim that they just happened to meet at Ripley's.'

'Happened to meet?'

'Yep.'

'Today's youth,' Win lamented. 'You'd think they could come up with more credible lies.'

'To be fair, we did catch Tamryn unaware. How's Brooke?'

'Blocking,' Win said. 'Which is probably good. Right now, she is very focused on why her former au pair has returned to the United States.'

'Does she have any theories?'

'Not a one. So what's your next step?'

'We keep gathering information,' Myron said.

'Whoa, slow down with the specifics.'

'Nancy Moore keeps insisting that the boy we rescued is her missing son, Patrick.'

'Correct.'

'So I'm wondering if these photographs of Paul will change her mind at all.'

'Is that where you're headed?'

On the left, Myron spotted the Moores' house. When he pulled into the driveway, he saw the Lexus sitting in the garage.

She was home.

'I've just arrived.'

Myron didn't bother with the front door. The garage was open so he headed toward the Lexus. When he saw the door between the house and garage had been left open, he grew concerned.

He leaned his head in and shouted, 'Hello?'

Nothing.

He stepped inside and crossed the kitchen. From upstairs he could hear a rustling sound. He wasn't armed, which was stupid, but so far there hadn't been much need for weaponry. He took the steps slowly.

Whoever was upstairs was not trying to hide their movements.

Myron reached the top step. The rustling was coming from Patrick's room. He approached the door slowly, sliding his back against the wall, which might or might not be effective in cases like this.

It was hard to say. He reached the door, waited a second, took a quick peek inside.

Nancy Moore was tearing the room apart.

'Hello,' Myron said.

She jumped at the sound of his voice and spun toward him. Her eyes were wide, almost maniacal. 'What are you doing here?'

'Everything okay?'

'Does everything look okay?'

It did not. 'What's wrong?'

'You don't get it, do you? You think . . . I don't know what you think. I was trying to protect my son. He's fragile. He's been through so much. How do you not get that?'

Myron said nothing.

'Do you know what it took for him to do what he did today? To relive the horror of what happened to him? To Rhys?'

'It had to be done, Nancy,' Myron said. 'If it had been the other way, if Rhys had come home—'

'Brooke Baldwin would have done what was best for her child, not mine.' Nancy stood upright. 'Make no mistake about it. A mother protects her child.'

Whoa.

'Even at the expense of another?'

'Patrick wasn't ready to talk. We knew that. We just wanted to give him enough time to get his strength. What's a few more days after ten years? Dr Stanton was right. It was too much for him. And then, as if it wasn't hard enough to get through that, as if it wasn't hard enough to tell Brooke that Rhys was dead, you' – she pointed an accusing finger at him – 'go after him. Patrick ran away because of you.'

'It's not Patrick.'

'What?'

'The boy we brought home. It's not Patrick.'

'It *is* Patrick!'

'His name is Paul.'

'Get out,' she said.

'Why don't you get a DNA test, Nancy?'

'Fine, if that will get all of you to leave us alone, we will, okay? Now, get out, please.'

Myron shook his head. 'I need you to look at these photographs.'

She looked confused. 'What photographs?'

He reached out a hand holding the two printouts Spoon had given him. For a moment Nancy didn't take them. She just stood there. Myron moved his hand toward hers a bit more, holding it there until she reluctantly let him pass the pictures to her.

'I don't understand.'

'The group shot was taken at a boarding school in Switzerland,' Myron said.

She stared at it. 'So?'

'There is a boy in that picture. His name is Paul. We don't have the last name yet. But we will get it. The second photograph is a close-up.'

'I still don't understand.' Nancy Moore's hands were shaking. She slid the top photograph under the bottom picture. 'You can't think . . .?'

'Paul and your Patrick are one and the same.'

She shook her head. 'You're wrong.'

'I don't think I am.'

'There's barely a resemblance.'

'Do you remember me asking you about Tamryn Rogers?' Myron took the photographs back and put the group one on the top. 'That's Tamryn. The same girl Patrick met with yesterday.'

'We told you—'

'Right, they just happened to meet outside Ripley's for the first time ever. I was there, Nancy. I saw them. There was no accidental meet. They knew each other before.'

'You can't know that from just watching them,' she said, but her voice was weak now, defeated.

'I just emailed these photos over to a forensic anthropologist named Alyse Mervosh. She is going to compare the image of Paul to the tape of Patrick during that interview yesterday. She'll be able to confirm that they are one and the same.'

She shook her head, but again there was nothing behind it.

'Nancy, let me help you.'

'You, what, think he's an imposter? You're wrong. A mother knows.'

'You said a mother protects her child,' Myron said, trying to keep his voice as even and gentle as possible. 'Maybe that want, that need, can also warp perception.'

'It's Patrick,' Nancy insisted. 'It's my son. He's finally come home. After all these years, I finally have him back.' Her eyes lifted. She met him with a glare. 'And then you scared him away.'

'Let me help you find him.'

'I think you've done enough. It's my son. I know. I *know*. He's not an imposter. His name isn't Paul.'

She pushed past him and headed down the stairs. Myron followed.

'When he gets home, we can do a DNA test to shut all of you up. But right now, I have someplace to be.'

Nancy didn't stop. She moved through the garage and out the door. She slid into her car and started it up.

'Don't come back, Myron. Don't ever come back.'

Win and Brooke sat in the Baldwin kitchen. The photographs from the boarding school in Switzerland were spread out on the table in front of them.

Myron was finishing up the call with Alyse Mervosh, the forensic anthropologist. When he finished, Brooke and Win looked at him and waited.

'In her opinion,' Myron said, 'it's the same kid.'

Brooke looked at the photograph again. Myron leaned over her and pointed as he spoke.

'This Paul kid cut and dyed his hair,' Myron said. 'The eye color change is easy with contact lenses. The nose could have been plastic surgery.'

Brooke just sat there with the photograph in her hand. 'And Nancy doesn't see it?'

'That's what she said. She insisted it's Patrick.'

'Do you believe her?'

'I believe she believes it.'

'So she's deluding herself?'

Myron gave a half shrug. 'I don't know.'

Win spoke for the first time. 'So we need to figure out who this Paul is. We need to find out where he lives, who his parents are—'

'Esperanza is on that. But it's going to take some time.'

'I'll make some calls overseas. See if we can speed things up.'

'I don't understand,' Brooke said. 'Is he an imposter? Is he trying to con the family?'

'It's possible.'

'I read about a case like this,' Brooke said. 'When you have a missing son, you . . . Anyway, this was in the late nineties maybe. A family in Texas had their son go missing when he was twelve or thirteen. Three years later, some imposter from France said he was the missing kid. He fooled a lot of people.'

Myron vaguely recalled the story. 'What was his motive?'

'I don't remember. Money in part, but I think he got off on fooling people this way. It wasn't his first time posing as someone else. He was warped. The family fell for it in part, I guess, because they wanted it to be true.' She looked up. 'What's going on here, Myron?'

'I don't know.'

'None of this makes any sense.'

'We need to know more.'

As if on cue, Myron's mobile phone rang. He looked at Win. 'It's Joe Corless at the DNA lab.'

'Put him on speaker.'

Myron did just that, laying the phone on the table. 'Joe?'

'Myron?'

'Joe, I'm sitting here with Win.'

'Whoa. Win's back?'

Win spoke. 'Please tell us the results.'

'Let me cut right to it,' Joe Corless said. And then he said something that surprised Myron: 'The boy is indeed Patrick Moore.'

Myron looked at Win. Brooke's face lost color. 'You're sure?'

'The hair samples you provided are from a female. The DNA off the toothbrush belongs to a male. These two people are full siblings.'

'A hundred percent?'

'As close as you can get.'

The doorbell rang. Win started for the door.

'Thanks, Joe,' Myron said.

He hung up.

'He's Patrick,' Brooke said. She kept her face steady, but there was a quake working the corner of her mouth. 'He's not an imposter. He's Patrick.'

Myron just sat there.

'So why is Vada back? Why is Patrick meeting with this Tamryn girl?'

'It's the other way around,' Myron said.

'What do you mean?'

'Paul isn't someone posing as Patrick. Paul is Patrick.'

Before he could explain further, Win returned to the kitchen with Zorra. If Brooke was surprised to see the manly looking transvestite in her kitchen, she didn't show it.

'Zorra has update on the au pair,' Zorra said.

Brooke rose. 'Vada?'

'She calls herself Sofia Lampo now,' he said. 'She flew into the country yesterday. She rented a Ford Focus at Newark Airport.'

Brooke said, 'So how do we find her?'

'It's already done, dreamboat,' Zorra said. 'All rent-a-cars are equipped with GPS systems – in case the car is stolen. Or you cross state lines so they can charge you more. Reasons like that.'

'And they allow you to track it?'

Zorra adjusted his Veronica Lake wig with both hands and smiled. His lipstick was all over his teeth. ' "Allow" would not be the word Zorra would use. But your cousin's money. It is very persuasive.'

'So where is Vada?' Brooke asked.

Zorra took out his mobile phone. 'Zorra is tracking her on this.'

He showed them the screen. A blue dot blinked the car's location.

'Where is this exactly?'

Zorra pressed an icon. The map was replaced by a satellite image. Myron almost gasped out loud. The blue dot was surrounded by green. There was a lake that even from above looked familiar.

'Lake Charmaine,' Myron said. 'Vada is at Hunter Moore's house.'

CHAPTER 32

The fifth grade classroom looked out over an expansive and complicated playground with slides and swings and forts and pirate ships and tunnels and pipes and ladders. Rob Dixon greeted Myron with a firm handshake and ready smile. He wore a suit of high-school-vice-principal brown and a bright tie Myron usually associated with pediatricians who were trying too hard. He sported a ponytail and a fresh shave.

'Hi, I'm Rob Dixon,' he said.

'Myron Bolitar.'

Back at the Baldwin house, they'd decided that Win would drive up to Hunter's place on Lake Charmaine while Myron would keep his appointment with the fifth grade teacher and stay in the area.

'I'm going too,' Brooke had said. 'I know Vada. I can help.'

There was no room for debate in her voice.

'Please,' Rob Dixon said, 'have a seat.'

The desks were those school kind with the chair attached. It took some effort for Myron to squeeze into one. The classroom itself was timeless. Sure, curriculums change and Myron assumed that somewhere there were hidden signs of modernity, but this could have been his own fifth grade classroom. Running across the top of the chalkboard was the alphabet written in capital and lowercase script. A potpourri of student artwork and projects took up the wall on the left. Newspaper clippings were tacked up beneath a handwritten sign reading CURRENT EVENTS.

'Oh, I'm sorry,' Rob Dixon said.

'Pardon?'

'I watched *The Collision* – and here I stick you in a chair that has to bother your knee.'

'I'm fine.'

'No, please take my chair.'

Myron winced and slid out from the desk. 'Maybe we can just stand if that's okay.'

'Sure thing. I'm excited about your research. By the way – and I don't know if this will interest you or not – I've been teaching fifth grade in this very same classroom for twenty-one years now.'

'Wow,' Myron said.

'I love this age. They're no longer little kids who can't understand deep concepts; they aren't yet adolescents with all the hardship that entails. Fifth grade is nicely on the cusp. It's an important transitional year.'

'Mr Dixon.'

'Please call me Rob.'

'Rob, I bet you're a great teacher. You look like that cool young teacher we all loved, except you're older and probably wiser, but you didn't get all jaded.'

He smiled. 'I love the way you put that. Thank you.'

'And thank you. But I may be here under false pretenses.'

He put his hand to his chin. 'Oh?'

'I'm here to talk to you about a specific, tragic event.'

Rob Dixon took a step backward. 'I don't understand.'

'I'm the one who saved Patrick Moore,' Myron said. 'But I'm still trying to figure out what happened to Rhys Baldwin.'

Rob Dixon stared out the window. A boy Myron guessed was around six hopped over to a rope and started to swing on it. The glee on his face – Myron wondered when he had last seen someone so lost in joy.

'Why come to me?' he asked. 'I had neither as a student. And I probably wouldn't have had. See, we try to make sure teachers don't get siblings. It isn't a rule or anything. The principal just thinks it's not a good idea. You come in with preconceived notions or, at the very least, a past with the parents. So even if they had stayed in school, I probably wouldn't have taught either boy.'

'But you did teach Clark Baldwin and Francesca Moore.'

'How do you know that?'

'Clark told me.'

'So?' Dixon shook his head. 'I really shouldn't talk about it anyway. I thought you became a sports agent. That's what the documentary said. After your injury, you went to Harvard Law School and then opened your own agency.'

'That's true.'

'So why are you involved in this?'

'It's what I do,' Myron said.

'But the documentary said—'

'The documentary didn't tell the whole story.' Myron stepped toward him. 'I need your help, Rob.'

'I don't see how.'

'Do you remember that day?'

'I can't talk to you about this.'

'Why not?'

'It's confidential.'

'Rob, a boy is still missing.'

'I don't know anything about that. You can't possibly think—'

'No, nothing like that. But I'm asking you. Do you remember the day the boys went missing?'

'Of course,' Rob Dixon said. 'You never forget something like that.'

Myron debated what to ask next and then decided to cut right to it: 'Were Clark and Francesca here?'

Rob Dixon blinked several times. 'What?'

'The day their brothers went missing,' Myron continued, 'were Clark and Francesca in your classroom? Were they both in school? Did they leave early?'

'Why would you ask that?'

382

'I'm trying to piece together what happened.'

'After ten years?'

'Please,' Myron said. 'You said you remember that day. You said you'd never forget something like that.'

'That's right.'

'So just answer me this simple question. Were both Francesca and Clark in your classroom?'

He opened his mouth, closed it, tried again. 'Of course they were. Why wouldn't they be? It was a school day. A Wednesday, as a matter of fact.' Dixon marched toward the back and stopped by a desk in the second-to-last row. 'Clark Baldwin sat right here. He wore a red basketball shirt from his town rec team. I think he wore that shirt twice a week that school year. Francesca Moore' – he moved up to the front row and to the desk on the end – 'she sat here. She wore a yellow blouse. That was Francesca's favorite color. Yellow. She drew yellow daisies on every assignment.'

Dixon stopped and looked at Myron. 'Why on earth would you ask that?'

'They were both here all day?'

'All day,' he repeated. 'I got a call from Mrs Baldwin at two thirty.'

'Brooke Baldwin?'

'Yes.'

'She called you herself?'

'Yes. Via the main office. She called the principal's office and asked to speak to me. She said it was an emergency.'

'What did she tell you?'

'She said that there had been a personal incident and that a police officer was going to pick up Francesca and Clark. She asked if I could keep the children late until they got there. I said of course.'

'Did you know about the kidnappings?'

'No, not then.' He shook his head. 'I still don't get why you're here, Mr Bolitar.'

Myron didn't know either. He could give him the same song and dance about the clumsy search for the needle in a haystack, but he didn't think there was any point.

'Did the cop pull up in a squad car?'

'No,' he said. 'It was a female officer. She was in plainclothes in an unmarked car. I don't see the point of this.'

'Tell me about Clark and Francesca.'

'What about them?'

'Do you know that they are college roommates?'

Dixon smiled. 'That's nice.'

'Were they close back in fifth grade?'

'Of course. I think their shared experience bonded them.'

'How about before the kidnappings?'

He thought about it. 'They were just classmates. I don't think they hung out together or anything. I'm really glad that they had each other, though, especially for Francesca.'

Especially for Francesca.

Needle? Meet my dear friend Haystack.

'Why do you say that about Francesca?' Myron asked.

'She was going through a bit of a rough patch.'

'What sort of rough patch?'

'This really isn't proper, Mr Bolitar.'

'Call me Myron.'

'It still isn't proper.'

'Rob, your information is ten years old. The fifth grade girl with the rough patch is now a college student.'

'The kids trusted me.'

'And I can see why. You're kind. You're caring. You want what's best for them. I had some great elementary teachers when I was a kid. I remember them all. Middle school teachers, high school teachers – not so much. But the good elementary school teachers? They stay in your heart forever.'

'What are you trying to get at?'

'I don't want you to betray confidences. But something went really wrong that day. No, not the obvious. We know that two boys went missing. But something else. Something big. Something that we need to know if we ever want to find the truth. So please, I'm asking you to trust me. Why was Francesca going through a rough patch?'

Rob Dixon took a few seconds to decide. 'Her parents,' he said at last.

'What about them?'

'They were going through a rough patch.'

He stopped.

'Can you be more specific?'

Rob Dixon looked back out the window. 'Her father found some texts on her mother's phone.'

Myron was back in the car and flooring it to the campus of Columbia University. He had gotten Clark's phone number when he'd last been there, and he dialed the number now. Clark answered on the third ring.

'Hello?'

'Where's Francesca?' Myron asked.

'We're sitting out on the quad.'

'Don't move. Don't let her move.'

'Why, what's up?'

'Just sit tight. Do not move.'

There was traffic at the George Washington Bridge. Myron tried the Jones Road shortcut. It saved him a little time. The Henry Hudson was backed up, so he took Riverside Drive down to 120th and parked close to a hydrant. He'd risk the tow. He sprinted up 120th and down Broadway and entered near Havemeyer Hall. Students stared at the seemingly old man running across campus. He didn't care.

The campus was laid out before him as he passed the domed-and-Grecian-columned Low Library, the most prominent building on campus. He headed down the steps, doing a reverse Rocky, passing the sculpture of a seated Athena and down onto the grassy South Field East.

They were both there, Francesca and Clark, sitting outside on a green Ivy League campus quad. There were, Myron knew, few places like this, few moments in life quite as pure and rich and innocent and protected as being a college student sitting in a grassy quad. Was that real or illusory? Didn't matter. Didn't matter that he was about to shatter all of that for these two young people.

He was close to the truth now.

Francesca looked up as Myron decelerated to a stop. Clark rose and said, 'What's so important?'

Myron debated asking them to go inside, to move someplace with more privacy, but they were outside now, no one really within earshot, and there was no time to play around or stall or make it more comfortable for her.

He sat across from Francesca in what they used to call 'Indian style,' but, remembering what Mickey had told him, maybe it was now 'with legs crossed.' You didn't have to be the Master of Deduction to see that Francesca was distraught. She was still crying. Her eyes were red and puffy.

'She won't tell me what's wrong,' Clark said.

Francesca squeezed her eyes shut. Myron looked back at Clark. 'Could you give us a minute?'

Clark said, 'Francesca?'

With her eyes still shut, she nodded for him to go.

'I'll be at the café in Lerner Hall,' Clark said.

Clark slung his backpack over his right shoulder and trudged away. Francesca finally opened her eyes. When he was far enough away, Myron said, 'You need to tell me the truth.'

She shook her head. 'I can't.'

'It's destroying you. It's destroying your brother. I'm going to find out anyway. So let me help. We can still make this right.'

She made a scoffing noise and started crying again. Nearby students glanced over, concerned. Myron tried to smile them off, but he imagined that this looked like either an older man breaking up with a younger girl or, he hoped, a teacher delivering bad news to a student.

'I just spoke to Mr Dixon,' Myron said.

She looked up at him, confused. 'What?'

'Your fifth grade teacher.'

'I know who he is, but why . . .?'

She stopped.

'Tell me what happened,' Myron said.

'I don't understand. What did Mr Dixon say?'

'He's a good man. He didn't want to betray any confidences.'

'What did he say?' Francesca asked again.

'Your parents were having marital difficulties,' Myron said. 'You talked to him about it.'

Francesca plucked a blade of grass from the ground. There were freckles on her face. Man, Myron thought, she looked so young. He could almost see her in that classroom, the scared fifth grader, worried about her whole world falling apart.

'Francesca?'

She looked up at him.

'Your father found texts on your mother's phone, didn't he?'

Her face lost all color.

'Francesca?'

'Please don't tell Clark.'

'I won't tell anyone.'

'I didn't know, okay? I didn't know until . . .' She shook her head. 'Clark will never forgive me.'

Myron shifted so that they were facing each other full on. Someone started blaring music from a dormitory window. The song started with the vocalist letting us know that once he was seven years old. In seconds, he was eleven years old.

Yeah, Myron thought, watching this girl, I get that.

'Tell me what happened, Francesca. Please.'

She didn't reply.

'Your father found the texts,' Myron said, trying to draw her out. 'Were you home when that happened?'

She shook her head. 'I came in a few minutes later.'

Silence.

'Was your brother home?'

'No. He was at the Little Gym. He had a class there on Mondays.'

'Okay,' Myron said. 'So you came home. Were you coming from school?'

Francesca nodded.

'Were your parents fighting?'

389

She squeezed her eyes shut again. 'I'd never seen him like that.'

'Your father, you mean?'

She nodded again. 'They were in the kitchen. Dad was holding something in his hand. I couldn't see what. He was screaming at Mom. She was covering her ears and ducking down. They didn't even notice I was home.'

Myron tried to picture the scene. Ten-year-old Francesca opens the door. She hears Hunter screaming at a cringing Nancy in the kitchen.

'What did you do?'

'I hid,' she said.

'Where?'

'Behind the couch in the living room.'

'Okay. Then what happened?'

'Dad . . . he hit Mom.'

Campus life was all around them. Students laughed and strolled the grounds. Two boys with their shirts off threw a Frisbee. A dog barked.

'My dad, he didn't drink a lot because when he did' – again Francesca closed her eyes – 'it was awful. I had maybe seen him drunk three or four times. That's all. It was always bad. But not like this.'

'So what happened next, Francesca?'

'Mom called him some horrible names. She ran out into the garage and got in her car. Dad . . .'

She stopped again.

'Dad what?'

'Dad ran after her,' she said. Her words came

slowly now, measured. 'But before he did, he put down what he was holding in his hand.'

Their eyes met.

'What did he put down?' Myron asked.

'A gun.'

Myron felt the chill tingle up toward the back of his skull.

'He ran out the door after her, so I stood up. I came out from behind the couch.'

Francesca's eyes were wide. She was back in that house now.

'I started toward the kitchen. The gun was sitting there. On the kitchen table. I was shaking just looking at it. I didn't know what to do. Dad was so angry. He was drunk. I couldn't just leave the gun there.'

'What did you do, Francesca?'

'Please,' she said. 'I didn't know until now. You have to believe me. They lied to me all these years. I didn't know until Patrick came home.'

'It's okay,' Myron said. He put his hands on her shoulders. 'Francesca, what did you do when you saw the gun?'

'I was scared Dad would use it.' Tears rolled down her cheek. 'So I took it. I hid the gun upstairs in my room.'

'And then?' Myron asked.

'And then Patrick found it.'

CHAPTER 33

I drive Brooke across the Dingmans Ferry Bridge. Zorra has stayed behind. I can handle this myself. He has matters to attend to.

I glance at my cousin. She is staring straight ahead. I remember a family holiday when we were both teenagers. We were staying on our grandfather's estate on Fishers Island. Fishers Island is nine miles long and one mile across. It's off the coast of Connecticut but is technically part of New York. You probably haven't been. It's not a place that welcomes strangers.

One night, Brooke and I got both stoned and drunk on the beach. I have rarely gotten stoned. Myron does not approve and there are very few other people I trust enough that I am willing to lose control in front of them. At one point, Brooke suggested we take a night canoe ride.

So we did.

It was late by then, probably approaching midnight. We paddled and then started drifting. Both of us lay back. We talked about life. Even now I can remember every word. I stared up at the sky. The stars were out in full force.

It was glorious to behold.

I don't know whether it was because we were high or because we were lost in the conversation or perhaps the beauty of the sky put us in a trance. But suddenly we heard a rushing noise. We bolted upright as the final ferry of the day headed directly toward us. The ferry is large – large enough to carry both passengers and vehicles from the mainland to our island.

It was bearing down on us. Nay, it was almost on top of us.

There would be no time to paddle to safety.

Brooke moved first. She jumped from her spot and tackled me, throwing us both into the water. We started to swim frantically as the ferry came closer. Even now, even as I sit in this car, I can feel that bow pass over my back. I have been close to death many times. But that, my friends, was the closest.

I didn't react in time. Brooke did.

Brooke stares out the front windshield. 'Rhys is dead, isn't he?'

'I don't know.'

She looks at me.

'I think he is,' I say, 'but I'm not giving up yet.'

'It's starting to become clear to me. My son is dead. I think I have always known. I always felt it. But I would never rely on a mother's intuition. I rely on facts, not emotion. I turned off emotion when my son vanished ten years ago.'

'You've been a good mother to Clark.'

She almost smiles. 'I have been, haven't I?'

'The best.'

'He's a good boy,' she says. 'He suffered so much over the years. Do you remember my father's funeral?'

'Of course.'

'I was eleven. You were twelve. I never saw his body. The heart attack was so sudden. My mother wanted a closed casket. There was no point in seeing him that way. That's what everybody told me. But . . . I had a friend, a soldier. She told me that the reason they made sure that they brought home the dead, even risking their own lives, was so that the families could mourn. She said that they needed something tangible in order to move on. We all need to say good-bye, Win. We need to accept it, no matter how terrible, and then move on. I knew Rhys was dead, even before Patrick told me. And yet, even though I know I'll never see my boy again, I still have hope.'

I say nothing.

'And I hate hope,' Brooke says.

We reach Lake Charmaine. Someone had put the sign back in place by wrapping the chain around a post. I simply drive through it. The chain gives way easily. Hunter's pickup truck is still blocking the driveway. I check the rental car's location on the GPS again. It hasn't moved, so the car is still at this house. I take out my revolver, a Smith & Wesson 460, and look at Brooke.

'May I request that you stay here until I suss this out?' I ask.

Her answer is to open the car door and get out. I figured that it would be a waste of time, but one must make the effort. We start up the driveway, just as I had done with Myron. Hunter is in the same Adirondack chair. The rifle is on his lap.

As we move closer, Hunter spots us. He begins to rise, pointing the rifle our way.

'Don't kill him,' Brooke says.

I shoot him in the leg. He drops to one knee. I shoot him in the shoulder. The rifle goes flying. I move toward him now. Brooke is right behind me.

Hunter looks up at me, then at Brooke. He is crying.

'I'm so sorry,' he says.

'Where is she?' I ask.

'So sorry.'

I bend down, find the bullet wound on his shoulder, and squeeze hard.

He screams.

'Where is she?'

The front door of the house suddenly opens. A young woman with long hair steps outside.

Brooke puts a hand on my arm and nods.

'That's Vada,' she says.

CHAPTER 34

Myron found Nancy Moore in her backyard.

She sat in a gazebo by her rose garden. A mug of coffee was cupped in both her hands. She didn't turn as Myron approached.

'I told you not to come back,' she said.

'Yeah, I know. Have you heard from Patrick?'

She shook her head.

'Aren't you worried?'

'Of course I am. But this is all a big adjustment for him. He needs a little space.'

'He's been gone for ten years,' Myron said. 'I would think space would be the last thing he would want.'

'Myron?'

'Yes.'

'I don't care what you think. I want you to leave.'

Myron didn't move. He just stood there until she looked at him. When she did, he just stayed right where he was, staring at her. Then he said, 'I know, Nancy.'

'You know what?'

It was a formality. He could see it in her eyes.

'Francesca told me.'

'She's confused. Her brother coming home after all these years has messed with her head.'

'He's dead, isn't he? Rhys, I mean.'

'Patrick told you that.'

'No, Patrick told us a story. You worked on it with him. It was a good story too – the best one to tell a devastated mother. Rhys was never harmed, Patrick said. Rhys was happy. He was brave. His death was quick and before all the horrors started. As I listened to it, I couldn't help but think, how convenient.'

'Get out.'

Myron moved alongside her. 'We know Vada is up at the lake.'

Nancy went for her cell phone, but Myron snatched it before she could reach it.

'Give me that back.'

'No.'

'You don't understand a thing,' Nancy said.

'Oh, I think I do,' Myron said. 'It's no wonder you convinced Chick not to talk about the texts. He thought it was because it would be a distraction. The cops would start looking at the two of you, thinking, I don't know, you were having an affair and so one of you went off the deep end or something. But that wasn't it. You knew it all started with the texts. Chick didn't.'

Nancy Moore rose and started back toward the house. Myron followed her.

'So Hunter pulls a gun on you. Did you realize

Francesca was the one who hid it? That would also explain why you kept this all a secret from her. Or maybe you realized that she was just a kid. She could never keep a secret this big. Maybe you didn't want her to blame herself. If she had just left Daddy's gun where it was. If she had just not worried about what Hunter might do with it.'

Nancy stopped by the back door. She closed her eyes.

'So she hid the gun in her room and Patrick found the gun,' Myron said. 'I'm not sure when. Francesca didn't know either. A few days later. Maybe a week. Did Hunter forget about it – or was he scared to bring it up? I don't know. It doesn't matter much. Patrick finds it. You and Hunter have been fighting a lot. Maybe Patrick knows that. Maybe he even knows why. Maybe he blames Chick Baldwin or that whole family.'

'No,' Nancy said. 'Nothing like that.'

'Doesn't really matter. He's a six-year-old boy. He has his father's loaded gun. He keeps it in his backpack. He takes it to school with him. One day – maybe even the day he first finds the gun, I don't know – he has a playdate with Rhys Baldwin. They're playing in that wooded area in the back. That's what you told Francesca anyway. The au pair, Vada Linna, she isn't watching too closely. Or maybe she is. I don't know. She's a scared kid in a foreign country. What does she know?'

Nancy Moore stood perfectly still. Myron didn't even think she was breathing.

'I don't know if they were playing a game. I don't know if the gun just went off by accident. I don't know if Patrick was angry about his father. I don't know any of that. But I know that one six-year-old boy shot and killed another.'

'It was an accident,' Nancy said.

'Maybe.'

'It was.'

'How about what happened next?'

'You don't understand,' Nancy said.

'Oh, I think I do. You showed up at the Baldwin house to pick up your son. My guess would be that Patrick shot Rhys right before you got there. Within seconds. Because if he had shot him, say, ten minutes before, Vada would have dialed nine-one-one.'

'I heard the gun go off,' Nancy said. 'I parked my car and . . .'

Myron nodded. That made sense. 'You rushed around back.'

'Vada and I . . . We both started running for him. But it was too late. The bullet . . . Rhys was shot in the head. There was nothing we could do.'

Silence.

'Why didn't you just call the police?' Myron asked.

'You know why. It was our gun. Mine really. I bought it. Hunter and I – we'd be charged. There are cases. I read about a father who kept his loaded gun under his bed. His six-year-old found it. He started playing cowboys and Indians with his four-year-old sister. Shot her dead. The father got convicted of manslaughter and spent eight years in prison. I thought about that. And I thought about Patrick. Yes, he knew we were fighting. He had overheard that. So even though he was six, suppose someone made something of that? Suppose someone said he didn't do it accidentally, that he killed him on purpose. Patrick would be tainted for life – the kid who murdered another kid. And then you have Chick and Brooke. Do either of them hit you as the forgiving type?'

'So you made it look like a kidnapping.' Myron tried to keep his voice steady.

She didn't bother to answer.

'How did you get Vada to cooperate?'

'I told her that the police would say she was responsible. She was supposed to watch the kids. I told her that they'd blame her and put her in jail. I said it was best for her to do what I said. To protect herself. Vada was scared, too confused to argue. By the time she had second thoughts, she was already in too deep.'

'So you clean up the scene. I assume there was blood.'

'Not a lot. And it was in the woods. I cleaned it up.'

'You go over your story with Vada. You tie her up in the basement. You leave and call Brooke. You tell her that you just got to the house and no one is answering the door.'

'That's right.'

Myron swallowed. 'Where was Patrick?'

'I took him home. I told him to hide until his father got there.'

'And Rhys?'

Nancy's eyes met his. There was no waver as she said, 'I put him in a trash can in the back of our garage.'

The rest was obvious.

'When Hunter got home, did he try to talk you out of it?'

'Yes. He wanted to confess right away. But by then, it was too late. I had already faked the kidnapping. These things – they snowball. It wasn't Hunter's fault. He's a weak man. He couldn't handle what we did. He started to drink. You can probably figure out the rest. It wasn't hard to get a fake ID, though it took some time with the cops around. Hunter kept Patrick at the lake. Eventually we snuck him out of the country. His new name was Paul Simpson.'

'Why did you bring him home now?'

She shrugged. 'There were too many close calls. The background checks at the school were getting stricter. People were starting to ask questions. We couldn't keep it up forever. Francesca needed to know her brother was alive. But mostly, Patrick wanted to come home too. So Hunter and I talked about it. We were going to have him just walk into a police station and make up a story about escaping. But that would lead to even more questions.'

'So you sent that anonymous email to Win.'

'I knew Win had never given up. If he found Patrick – if he rescued him – it would all be more believable. That's what I thought anyway. So I set it up so Win would be at King's Cross at the same time as Patrick. It wasn't hard to find a spot. You can look online and find out where teenage prostitutes hang out.'

'That didn't go as planned.'

'To put it mildly, it backfired,' she said. 'When Win killed those men, Patrick ran. He called me in a panic. I told him to find a hotel and stay put. But that Fat Gandhi found him.'

'So when you tearfully thanked me for saving his life—'

'That wasn't an act.' She looked into Myron's eyes, hoping to find solace or kindness maybe. 'You did save his life. I messed up. I messed up from the start. You'll ask, why didn't you do it this way or why didn't you do it that way. I don't know. I looked at each situation and I did what I thought was best for my son. And at first, it was the right call. Patrick forgot what happened. My sister lives in France. He stayed with her a lot. He loved that school. He was happy. Sure, he missed us. And he missed his sister. And yes, that was one of the tough calls – not telling Francesca the truth. But she wouldn't be able to keep the secret – not when you're only ten years old. We tried to comfort her, tried to tell her that her brother really was okay, but of course she suffered. It was a tough choice.'

She tilted her head. 'Would you have told her?'

Myron wanted to say that he would never have started down this path, but he figured that was obvious. 'I don't know,' he said. 'But you destroyed them all, didn't you? Your husband couldn't live with it. Brooke, Chick, Clark – what you did to them, what you made them suffer through.'

'Rhys was dead,' she said. 'Don't you get that? Nothing was going to bring him back. I couldn't save him. I could only save my own boy.'

Myron felt Nancy's phone vibrate in his hand. He looked at the number and read it to her.

'It's Patrick!' Nancy grabbed it from him and put it to her ear. 'Hello? Patrick?'

Myron could hear him crying. 'Mommy?'

He sounded so much younger than sixteen.

'I'm right here, baby.'

'They know what I did. I . . . I want to die.'

Nancy gave Myron a baleful eye. 'No, no, listen to Mommy. It's all going to be okay. Just tell Mommy where you are.'

'You know where I am.'

'No, I don't.'

'Help me, Mommy.'

'Where are you, Patrick?'

'I want to kill myself. I want to kill myself so I can be with Rhys.'

'No, honey, listen to me.'

'Good-bye, Mommy.'

He hung up.

'Oh my God.'

The phone dropped from her hand.

'Be with Rhys,' Myron repeated to himself. He grabbed her by the shoulders. 'Where did you dump Rhys's body?'

She suddenly broke away from him and ran toward her car. Myron followed, overtaking her.

'I'll drive,' he said. 'Where is he?'

Nancy hesitated.

Myron flashed back to Patrick sitting at the kitchen table. His words had been stilted, monotone, because he was lying. But at the end, Patrick's voice changed, become more emotional . . .

'I saw it . . . I was there . . . they just . . . just dumped his body into this ravine. Like it was nothing. Like Rhys was nothing . . .'

Because he was telling the truth.

'Do you want your son to live or die?' Myron shouted. 'Where is that ravine, Nancy?'

CHAPTER 35

According to Myron's app, the ride to the Lake Charmaine area with current traffic would take upwards of ninety minutes. Myron first called the Pike County Sheriff's Office to inform them of the situation. They patched him directly to Sheriff Daniel Yiannikos.

'I'm in my squad car right now,' the sheriff said. 'Where is the boy?'

'Go to the top of Old Oak Road near Lake Charmaine,' Myron said. 'If you walk a quarter of a mile south, there's a ravine.'

'I know it,' Sheriff Yiannikos said.

'His name is Patrick. He's there.'

'A possible jumper? He wouldn't be the first.'

'I don't know. But he's threatened suicide.'

'Okay, I'm eight minutes from the location. How old is Patrick?'

'Sixteen.'

Nancy had been trying to reach him since they started driving. No answer.

'What's his full name?' Yiannikos asked.

'Patrick Moore.'

'Why does that name ring a bell?'

'He's been in the news.'

'The rescued kid?'

'He's under a great deal of stress,' Myron said.

'Okay, we'll be careful.'

'Let him know his mother's on the way.'

Myron hung up and called his old friend Jake Courter, another sheriff, this time of Bergen County, New Jersey. He explained the situation and asked for a police escort.

'On its way,' Jake said. 'We'll pick you up on Route 80. Just keep driving.'

Twenty minutes later, when Sheriff Yiannikos finally called back, Nancy Moore gripped Myron's arm so tight he was sure it would leave marks.

'Hello?'

'Patrick is alive,' the sheriff said, 'for now.'

Myron let himself breathe.

'But he's standing at the top of the ravine with a gun pointed at his head.'

Nancy almost collapsed. 'Oh my God.'

'It's calm right now. He's telling us to stay back. So we are.'

'Has he asked for anything?'

'He just wanted assurances his mother was on her way. We said she was. We asked if he wanted to speak to her. He said no, he just wants to see her. He said for us to stay back or he'd shoot himself, so that's what we're doing. How far out are you?'

As promised, the Bergen County squad cars joined them on Route 80 heading west. Myron pressed down on the accelerator. The police helped him past the heavy traffic.

'Half hour, maybe forty minutes.'

'Okay,' Sheriff Yiannikos said. 'I'll call you if anything changes.'

Myron hung up, made a quick call to Win, and then asked Nancy, 'Why did Vada come back?'

'Why do you think?'

'She saw the news reports,' Myron said, 'about Patrick coming home.'

'Yes.'

'She wants to come clean.'

'That's what she says. We, uh, waylaid her. Nothing harmful. We just convinced her to come to the lake to discuss it. Then we took her car keys and asked her to give us a few days. To talk her out of it.'

'And if she didn't agree?'

Nancy shrugged. 'I like to think we would have found a way.'

'Hunter was waiting for her. When we went up there.'

'Yes. She arrived half an hour after you left.'

'Hunter won't stop Win.'

'No, I don't think he will,' Nancy said. 'Can't you please drive faster?'

'And Tamryn Rogers?'

'Patrick's girlfriend at school. I thought that he could give her up when he got home. But you know teens. Your nephew was right, wasn't he? Teens get lonely. They reach out. So yes, he snuck out. It would have been no big deal, except of course you followed him.'

They crossed the Dingmans Ferry Bridge. The app said they were eight minutes away.

'It's over now,' Myron said.

'Yes, I guess it is. But I just need to save my son. That's what this is all about. Then, well, we all move on, don't we? The police will be able to bring up Rhys's body from the ravine. They can bury him properly. I checked with an attorney before I started on this journey. Guess when the statute of limitations runs out on the crime of hiding a body?'

Myron gripped the wheel tighter.

'Ten years. And think about it. In the end, I hid a body and tampered with some evidence. I told a few lies to the police. Hunter is wracked with guilt. He'll take the fall, but we will plead him out and he'll serve very little, if any, time. So yes, Myron, if we can save my boy, it will all be over.'

'Cold,' Myron said.

'Have to be.'

'None of this had to be.'

'Rhys was dead. I couldn't save him.'

'And you think you've saved Patrick? What do you think it did to a six-year-old boy, making him lie like that?'

'He was only six.'

'So you just stuffed it away. Your husband became a drunk. Your daughter had to deal with losing a brother. Vada, I don't even know what a mess you made of her life. And Brooke and Chick and Clark. Do you have any idea what you did to all of them?'

'I don't need to justify myself to you. A mother protects her child. That's just how it is. So now I get my boy back. We get him help. It's all going to be okay. I'll take him back home. Once he's home, he'll be fine again.'

Myron made the turn onto Old Oak Road. There were four police cars parked at the end of the drive. Sheriff Yiannikos introduced himself. 'We've kept back. He wants his mother.'

'That's me,' Nancy said. She started sprinting toward the woods. Myron followed. 'No,' she said to him. 'Stay back.'

She trekked into the woods. Myron turned to Sheriff Yiannikos. 'I can't go into it, but we can't leave her alone. I need to follow her.'

'I'll go with,' he said.

Myron nodded. They hurried in, following her trail up a hill. A bird cawed in the distance. They kept moving. Nancy glanced behind her, still running, but she didn't stop or yell back. She wanted to reach Patrick as soon as possible.

A mother protects her child.

At the top of the hill, Nancy stopped short. Her hands flew up to her face, as though in shock. Myron hurried his step. He veered to the right. Sheriff Yiannikos stayed with him. When they reached the clearing, they could see the same thing Nancy was seeing.

Patrick had the gun pointed at his own head. He wasn't crying. He wasn't hysterical.

He was smiling.

Nancy took a tentative step toward him. 'Patrick?'

Patrick's voice was loud and clear in the stillness of the woods. 'Don't come closer.'

'I'm here now,' Nancy said. 'I'm here to take you home.'

'I am home,' he said.

'I don't understand.'

'Did you really think I stayed in the car?'

'What, honey? I don't know—'

'You drove me up. You told me to stay in the car and close my eyes.' Patrick smiled again, the gun right up against his temple. 'Did you think I listened?'

'I saw it . . . I was there . . . they just . . . just dumped his body into this ravine. Like it was nothing. Like Rhys was nothing . . .'

'I killed him,' Patrick said, and now a single tear slipped down his cheek. 'And you dumped him here. You made me live with that.'

'It's okay,' Nancy said, her voice cracking. 'It's all going to be okay . . .'

'I see it every day. You think it ever left me? You think I ever forgave myself? Or you?'

'Please, Patrick.'

'You killed me too, Mom. You threw me down the ravine too. And now we need to pay the price.'

'We will, honey.' Nancy glanced around desperately, looking for any sort of life preserver. 'Look,

410

Patrick, the police are here. They know everything. It's going to be okay. Please, honey, put the gun down. I'm here to take you home.'

Patrick shook his head. His voice, when he spoke again, was pure ice.

'That's not why you're here, Mother.'

Nancy dropped to her knees. 'Please, Patrick, just put the gun down. Let's go home. Please.'

'My God,' Sheriff Yiannikos said under his breath, 'he's going to do it.'

Myron could see that too. He debated making a move, sprinting toward the boy, but there was no way he could get there in time.

'Home for me is here,' Patrick said. 'This is where I belong.'

He cocked back the hammer on the gun.

Nancy shouted, 'No!'

'I didn't call you here to save me,' Patrick said. His finger started to shake as it started to pull on the trigger. 'I called you here to watch me end—'

And then another voice – a female voice – yelled, 'Stop!'

For a second everything froze. Myron looked to his left. Brooke Baldwin stood on the other side of the clearing with Win.

Brooke started toward the boy. 'It's over, Patrick.'

Patrick kept the gun against his head. 'Mrs Baldwin . . .'

'I said, it's over.'

'Stay back,' Patrick said.

Brooke shook her head. 'You were only six years

411

old, Patrick. A little boy. It was an accident. I don't blame you. Do you hear me, Patrick?' She took another step toward him. 'It's over.'

'I want to die,' he cried. 'I want to be with Rhys.'

'No,' Brooke said. 'There's been enough death and destruction. Please, Patrick. Please don't add to my pain.' She reached out her hand. 'Look at me.'

Patrick did. Brooke waited until she was sure that he was looking her in the eye.

'I forgive you,' she said. 'You were just a little boy. It's not your fault. Rhys, my son, your friend . . . He wouldn't want this, Patrick. If it was the other way around, if Rhys had shot you, would you forgive him?'

The gun shook in Patrick's hand.

'Would you?'

Patrick nodded.

'Please, Patrick. Give me the gun.'

The wind seemed to stop. Nobody moved. Nobody breathed. Even the trees seemed to be holding their breath. Brooke quickly closed the gap between them. Patrick hesitated, and for a second, Myron thought that he was still going to pull the trigger.

When Brooke reached out and took hold of the gun, Patrick fell into her arms. He let out a guttural cry and started sobbing. Brooke closed her eyes and held him.

'I'm so sorry. I'm so, so sorry.'

Brooke looked out over the ravine, the place where

her son had lain for the last ten years. She gripped the boy tighter, and finally, Brooke broke down and cried with him. They stood there, the two of them – the mother of a dead boy holding firm to the boy who had killed him.

Nancy Moore approached carefully. Brooke looked at her over Patrick's shoulder. Their eyes met. Nancy mouthed the words, 'Thank you,' and Brooke nodded at her. But she didn't let go of Patrick. She didn't let go until the boy finished crying.

CHAPTER 36

The police brought up the body four hours later.

Hunter Moore was in the hospital for his bullet wounds. He would be okay. Vada Linna was fine. She had told Win and Brooke the entire truth. That was indeed why she'd come back. Hunter might be up on kidnapping charges. It was hard to know for sure.

Nancy Moore had been taken into custody, but her attorney, Hester Crimstein, got her out on her own recognizance within the hour. Nancy had been correct. No serious charges would stick to her.

Win said, 'You should go home.'

Myron shook his head. He had stayed this long. He wasn't leaving yet.

The body was just bones now, but the clothing was intact. Brooke walked over and stroked the red sweatshirt and the blue jeans.

'Rhys's,' she said.

Brooke stood without another word and started back toward her car. Win followed, but she shook her head. 'You go back with Myron. I need time alone. And I need to tell Chick myself.'

Win said, 'I don't think that's a good idea.'

'I love you,' she said, 'but I don't really care what you think.'

They watched Brooke walk away with her spine straight. She got into the car and drove away.

'Come on,' Win said. 'Let's go home.'

Win drove. A few minutes into the ride, Mickey called for an update. Ema and Spoon were with him.

'It's over,' Myron said to his nephew.

'You found Rhys?'

'He's dead.'

Myron could hear Mickey tell Ema. Then he could hear Ema cry.

Win parked the car in the garage behind the Dakota. When they entered the apartment, Terese threw her arms around both of them. They stayed like that until Win's phone buzzed. Win excused himself and said good night. Myron looked deep into Terese's eyes.

'I can't wait to marry you,' he said.

He took a long hot shower. Terese joined him. They didn't speak. Not yet. Not tonight. They made love. It was fierce and raw and perfect and maybe even healing. Myron didn't so much fall asleep in his fiancée's arms as pass out. He didn't dream. He just stayed in her arms for a long time. An hour. Maybe two.

And then the small chill started running up his spine.

'What is it?' Terese said. 'What's the matter?'

'The gun,' Myron said.

'What gun?'

'Patrick had a gun,' Myron said. 'What happened
to it?'

EPILOGUE

THREE MONTHS LATER

You are perhaps hoping for a twist and a happy ending.

You are thinking that perhaps a mistake was made, that the body did not belong to Rhys Baldwin, that somehow Brooke and Chick got their child back.

But sometimes there is no twist. And many times, there is no happy ending.

This is, however, a happy day.

Two weeks ago, I threw Myron perhaps the most legendary bachelor party of all time. How legendary? Let us say that we hit four continents. Myron, of course, was a very good boy. It is how he always is. I, you'll be happy to note, was bad enough for the both of us. So too were Esperanza and Big Cyndi.

What, you say, women at a bachelor party?

Times change, my friend.

Today I am dressed in tails as Myron's best man. It is odd. Myron has always dreamed of this day, of marrying the love of his life and settling down

417

and starting a family. The gods have, alas, had other plans for him. I, for one, have never encouraged such thinking. I don't really get the whole 'love' thing.

Or I didn't.

Myron is more than my best friend. The youngsters call what we have a 'bromance,' and perhaps that is apropos. I love Myron. I want – no, I need – him happy. I have missed him over the past year, though I was often closer than he knew. The night he saw *Hamilton*? I was three rows behind him. When he found his brother, Brad, in that horrible place, I was not that far away.

Just in case.

I love him. And I want him to be happy.

There have been other loves in his life, most significantly a woman named Jessica. But Terese is different. You notice it when you are with them. They are one thing apart from another. They are something entirely different, entirely spectacular when they are together. Simply put, if everything is a chemical reaction – and I believe it is – these two compounds combine to make an ecstatic whole.

I knock on the door. Terese says, 'Come in.'

I enter.

'Well?' she says, spinning toward me.

Have you ever seen a beautiful, happy bride in a wedding gown? Then you know.

'Wow,' I say.

'You sound like Myron.'

I pick up her hand and kiss it.

'I just wanted to wish you well,' I tell her. 'I want you to know that like it or not, I will always be there for you.'

She nods. 'I know.'

'And if you break his heart, I'll break your legs.'

'I know that too.'

I kiss her cheek and leave the room.

You are probably wondering about the repercussions after Rhys's body was discovered. Allow me to fill you in. As you saw in the news, the entire truth has come out. No one, of course, is charging Patrick with any crime. As Brooke said, standing over that ravine, he was just a child.

The Baldwins – Brooke, Chick, and Clark – are as well as one might expect. Myron likes to say that even the ugliest truth is better than the prettiest of lies. I don't know whether that is always the case, but it seems to be the case here. They know now. Brooke buried Rhys in our family cemetery outside Philadelphia. They mourn and continue to mourn.

But they also move on.

Clark remains a close friend and college suitemate of Francesca's. She didn't know the truth until Patrick returned. Nancy Moore felt that her daughter would be strong enough and mature enough to handle it then.

She was, of course, wrong.

For the most part, Hunter Moore has recovered

from his injuries. There will be charges, mostly related to his halfhearted kidnapping of Vada Linna. I don't know how that case will turn out. We will have to see.

As for Nancy Moore, law enforcement is actively searching for her, though I doubt that she is much of a priority. After her release on her own recognizance that night, Nancy Moore, it seems, took a page out of her son's playbook and disappeared into the ether. Law enforcement insists that they will not rest until she is found.

Myron asked me whether we would search for her too – if we would help bring Nancy Moore to justice.

No, I told him. We did this for Brooke. If it is over for her, then it is over for us.

But enough about that.

Myron is getting married today. I stand up on the dais with him. When his bride-to-be turns the corner, when he first gets a look at Terese in her gown, I hear Myron mutter, 'Wow.'

I smile and say, 'I concur.'

Terese's parents are deceased, so Myron's father, Al, escorts her down the aisle. I look out over the crowd. They are all in this room. Big Cyndi is the maid of honor. Esperanza comes out from behind the curtain. She will, very soon, officiate this wedding. Oh, you may be wondering about the Little Pocahontas and Big Chief Mama situation. They both decided to retire their former Native American aliases. Some may mourn that.

Not Esperanza. 'Giving a culture too much respect,' Esperanza told me, 'never killed anyone.'

Times change, my friend.

Myron takes a deep breath. I see the tears form in his eyes. I put my hand on his shoulder to give us both strength. He reaches over and acknowledges the gesture. We wait for Myron's father to bring Terese to the dais.

Much of the ceremony passes in a haze for me.

When Esperanza gives me the signal, I hand Myron the ring.

We are best friends and I love him.

But, sorry, sometimes the prettiest lie *is* better than the truth.

So I will never tell Myron. Though I wonder whether he suspects it.

The morning after Rhys's body was found, he called me on the phone. 'Where's the gun?' he asked.

'What?'

'Patrick's gun.'

'Oh,' I lied. 'The police confiscated it.'

There was a hesitation – maybe a second too long – before he said, 'Okay.'

You may think I kept the gun. I didn't.

If you remember, Brooke was the one who took the gun from Patrick.

The call I got when we arrived back at the Dakota? That was from Brooke. I went back and helped her clean up. The police were able to find enough remains to identify, even ten years later, my cousin Rhys.

That will never happen with Nancy Moore.

No one will ever find the slightest trace.

Oh, there will be sightings. An anonymous call will claim they saw her on a beach in Fiji. Someone else will say she's living in a monastery in the hills of Tuscany. Or perhaps someone will spot her in London, where Zorra is currently paying a visit to a certain rotund pedophile.

Nancy Moore will forever be in hiding, a mystery.

The ceremony ends. I watch Myron lift Terese's veil. He pauses because – I know him, you see – he wants to drink in this moment. He gets how rare this moment is and he wants to stop and appreciate it.

He just wants this moment to last.

Myron is good about that.

I don't know if I agree with what Brooke did or if I would have done the same in her place. But it is not my place to question her judgment. Nancy Moore robbed her not only of her only son but also of closure. She did immeasurable damage to Chick and Clark. She knew the truth for ten years and let her suffer. She took Brooke's life away from her. She took Brooke's child, her baby, and tossed him like so much trash down a ravine.

You tell me what the price should be.

I also confess that perhaps I'm being sexist. If Nancy Moore had been a man – if Hunter Moore had found the body that day and thrown a six-year-old away like so much refuse, ruining lives, destroying my cousin, her husband, her young child, would I think twice about making him pay?

One wonders.

Brooke and I are alike. We share a bond. Perhaps that bond is not always a good thing. Did Brooke act in a moment of understandable maternal fury? Would Brooke do it again if she had time to reconsider?

I don't know.

But I wonder about Nancy Moore's decisions too as a mother. Was Nancy Moore initially afraid to go to the police because she would be charged with a crime or because her son would be forever scarred or because Chick had some dubious business associates who might do her harm?

Or did Nancy understand that the most dangerous rage might come from a mother who lost her child?

But now I watch Myron step on the glass. The crowd stands and roars its approval. Myron Bolitar, married man, runs down the aisle with his loving bride.

I will spare you the tears and hugs and congratulations.

I will skip instead to the opening song. It is, well, gag worthy, though typical of Myron. The DJ calls Myron and his mother, Ellen, for the mother–son dance. Ellen Bolitar is shaking from Parkinson's, but Myron takes his mother's hand and leads her to the dance floor.

No one moves.

The music starts. The song Ellen chose is by

Bruce Springsteen. I listen as the Boss aptly croons:

'If I should fall behind,
Wait for me.'

We all watch them dance. I glance across the room and see the faces. Big Cyndi is crying hysterically. She does not hold back her plaintive wails. It is lovely. Myron's sister has flown in from Seattle. His brother, Brad, and Brad's wife, Kitty, are back. They stand next to Mickey and Ema. Mickey and Ema are holding hands. I try not to stare.

The DJ says, 'Will everyone please join Myron and his mother, Ellen, on the dance floor?'

Myron's dad, Al, escorts Terese to the dance floor. Young Mickey takes over for Myron and dances with his grandmother as only an awkward teenager can. Esperanza finds Myron. These two, my dearest friends, share the dance.

Others join in, filling the floor. I am content to watch.

This, my friends, is life.

Hey, I'm not above a gag-worthy sentiment now and again.

I feel her standing next to me before she speaks.

'You're Win, right?'

I turn to Ema.

'I am.'

'My mom told me to say hello.'

I manage a nod. 'Tell Angelica I say hello back.'

She looks at me a long second. Then she says, 'Do you want to dance?'

She has no idea what this means to me. Or maybe she does? I thought that her mother would never tell her. Did she? Or could it be that Ema is incredibly perceptive and intuitive?

That could be in her genes.

It is hard for me to find my voice. 'That would be lovely,' I manage to say.

We move to the dance floor. We face each other. She puts one hand on my shoulder and the other hand in mine. We start to dance. At some point Ema moves closer. She rests her head on my shoulder.

I barely move. I barely breathe.

I just want this moment to last.